Living on a Razor's Edge

ARFER APPLE

Prime Seven Media
518 Landmann St.
Tomah City, WI 54660

Printed in the United States of America

TABLE OF CONTENTS

The book is dedicated to all those people in the world who have survived cancer and just like me continue to live their lives once again with everyday bonuses.

THE SYNOPSIS

Based in Darwin a Detective Commander who is trying to raise four teenage boys on his own after his wife was killed by a drug dealer. He does now believe that all criminals in his eyes shall pay the price for their crimes. In his mind he is fixing the mole in modern society.

So, he does belong finally the judge, the jury, and the executioner, while he is <u>"Living on a Razor's Edge "</u>

CHAPTER 1

"THE TIN MAN"

It was my very first day back at work after a month of fun and enjoyment with my four boys on their school summer holiday. I was walking for a taxi when aunt candy decided to get off her backside and drive me to work. In my very own car, there was going to be a small fee Aunt Candy had decided. My first port of call was to see the new police commissioner John Knight. A man who you should never turn your back on.

After working with him over the past twenty years I have learned the hard way. In fact, if there was a pat on the head or a medal to be pinned on the chest John Knight was always first in the line holding his head high.

I went to reception and was given a visitor's badge by a Young up seat at the reception DIC. I also had to be given an escort to the lift.

When I got out of the lift, He was told to run along back downstairs, by a five-foot-tall rock wheeler who introduced herself. As being personal assistant to John Knight, who I called "The Silver Fox" not for his looks but more for his cunnilingus.

Not a hand shake instead a bear hug where he manages toto lift me off the ground. I was told just like a schoolboy to sit on that chair the silver fox had raided the hen house and only he had survived. The two female police commissioners a Glady's Marity and Judy Marzena were no longer laying any eggs in the hen house have to survive. Outside on the rest of the floor it was so quiet that you could hear a mouse fart in stereo, I was handed a coffee but dizziness on a shot of brandy to add some sparkle John Knight joked then he again rattled on about the old days I did feel like I was on the television and this is your life "Aaron Brown. "Finally, I was handed back my gun and some.

New form of identification. It read "Acting Assistant Commissioner" I looked like John Knight who looked like a fat kid in a candy store. He pointed to the open door and told me that will be your office. A long one any conversation from him of how we had worked side by side in the old days. Yes, we bent a few rules, sticking a gun in the mouth of somebody we ran to leave town or be carried out in a Pine-box. There were times that I was not energy proud of, to get to the point I was now the second highest ranking Police Officer in the Northern Territory. At this point of time, I decided to part my cheeks and led off a little wind. I was lucky with the voice of John Knight being loud, I was forgiven, pointing to the office next door, I did stick my head inside, counting. Paper clips was not my game but finally I was allowed to keep my job "Head of all Detectives" once again, but I will have to fit in the position of Assistant Police Commissioner.

It was time to head downstairs to the first floor to visit my new home. I stood off at the reception and handed back my visitor's badge. I showed the Yang recruit my actual new badge; he almost swallowed his tongue. I knew he had been set up by fat and bald Sgt Stan Ekiesa man was past his used by date now I was met at the entrance of the main office by nobody. Instead, when I renew my old office, my chair and desk with glitters of white paint all over my office, I looked at the new sign on the door that read Assistant Commissioner Aaron Brown. My faithful office manager Rachel Judd had tears in my eyes when she hugged me, if she squeezed any harder, I felt I wound passed out, standing behind her was my new right-hand Abigail Trimes, who had done well down in Alice Springs. She was sent there a first nation inspector and now she has returned with the title of Chief Inspector, she only wanted to shake my hand and tell me with those famous words of thank you for being the one who will support you in my new position, I turned to her and simply said "Don't fuck up on your first week, everybody will be watching you." I tried to smile when I noticed she took my speech like a gram of salt.

So, where's my driver Amy Fuller? I asked Rachel.

Coming down to the office, Amy looked up at me and gave me just like a kiss a father would receive from his daughter. "How are the boys boss? Amy asked if they would be happy to see their adopted sister anytime soon.

"Aunt Candy is back"!!

Well in body, but the boys love her after having two years of Asian cooking they in fact cook on the BBQ three nights a week!!

I could tell that the Chief Inspector Abigail Trimes wanted to bend my ear into a new shape. So, I told her to spit it out we are all friends here! Inspector Frank Turner from the drug unit and what you can only describe as a lone wolf had gone ahead and not even told C.I Abigail that he was going to shut down the local drug family in one fair swoop. It was up to me to light the candle on the cake and inform C.I Abigail that it was the third time lucky, the last two times that a plan was placed in action, somebody let the cat out of the bag. I did try to explain to C.I Abigail that it is better to keep everything close to your chest, not only the walls, but the office furniture does have ears I got the raised eyebrow look and a thank You for your time, Sir.

With a body found in a garden toilet at the local pub "The Royal Oak Pub ". The landlord was with ex Inspector Alf Jackson somebody that I had to put up with in the last five years of police service until he was simply booted out of the police force, with the update given to C.I Abigail who simply let it fly over her hand in my new bullet proof dream machine, I could tell that C.I Abigail was expecting a lift, but she was not invited Dr Rebecca Mitcham was already up on her eyes in the blood. I got the usual sexy wink from Dr. Rebecca. A simple update always started with the same sentence "I hope you have not eaten anytime recently Aaron?" I looked at the body. He had been shot in the head had both his eyes cut out and tongue with his eyes placed in an empty beer glass. I could see out of the corner of my eye Alf Jackson with a smile that somebody would give if they had just shit their pants, a smart "Hello Aaron it must be three years since you were last here, a drug raid which I must say that Betsy the drug dog did sniff out some drugs that my two chefs had been selling on the side, between cooking meals for my loyal patrons" I could of think that just maybe Alf Jackson was trying to dig up the past. I just asked if he knew the victim. "I know every prick who came throughout that door, was the reply before he did to tell me the name of the victim Charlie Peter's known as the Tin-man"

If you want to know anything, just ask Charlie Peters. I do remember him looking a lot different to when I saw him last, at least he could see back then and also, he was breathing. I then got the "Sorry about you Kate, did they ever catch the driver? asked Alf Turner. He knew the answer to that question of who ran over Kate outside the supermarket getting shopping not once the driver did reverse back over her. It has been three years now since heredity I still say "Goodnight Kate" every night when I turn to look at her empty pillow on the bed. We headed down to the home of Charlie Peters "The Tin Man," the front door was open and we went inside I called as to only find one uniform officer, in the back room, his need for the toilet was his excuse.

"Hey that bitch Hilda Drake from welfare some nurse, she would be the last bitch I would let touch me." The voice of Angela Sales, who went onto say she found Hilda Drake up on a chair looking for something on top of the cupboards. That nurse said Charlie who gave her keys, and I know only Charlie and I do have keys for the flat, my keys used to belong to Ida, Charlie's wife who passed away what it must be two years now"

I started to realize why Charlie was called "The Tin Man." Every cupboard was full of tinned food, fruit, vegetables, stews, curries, all in tins in a cupboard under the was a plastic bag that contained at least twenty thousand dollars "He didn't trust bloody banks" he withdraw his very first pension and put in straight into his special hiding place. If my day could note become even more interesting with another body this time the nurse Hilda Drake, she had been shot twice in the back of the head. Dr Rebecca did like to remind me that once I return to work the body can't start to go up. I just had to add the punchline of "Well think that it is not even lunch time yet."

I did turn to C.I Abigail and told her that the victim Hilda Drake Wald who knew the killer of Charlie Peters because they gave the keys from the body of Charlie Peters to enter the flat. I went on to say the killer could not justify letting Hilda Drake walk around with this evidence. I got a call from Insp. Albert Lee that the CCTV was not working in the beer garden at the time of the death of Charlie Peters, I immediately mumbled to myself "Alf Jackson", we went back to the Royal Oak pub and Alf Jackson gave me the answer that I did expect him to say "My patrons in here do not lock well on television beside with invasion of privacy" I did think what a load of Bullocks, I locked at the executive clientele in the Pool bar and nearby everybody had spent time and enjoyed the luxury of Berrimah Prison, Luxurious suites, with bars on the windows more than once.

This was not much I could contribute at this very time so I headed back to the office to catch up with Insp. Frank Turner. I had to comment to him "That he did look like the death warmed up"!!!We both laughed. A three-week operation, a lot of long hours by all members of the team had finally put Mummy Paula Hollis and her two evil son's Walter and Major behind bars sitting in the corner was Chief inspector Abigail Trimer who could not take one piece of credit for this successful operation. It did not stop Abigail unless there was a barrage of words about the chain of command. With Insp Frank Turner jumping in to remind sweet Abrigail that she was not a member of the team until three days ago. I quickly jumped in to remind Abigall that it is best to keep things close to your chest. I took Insp Frank to a journey to the toilet in the garden of the Royal Oak pub where the body of Charlie Peters was found shot and his eyes and tongue cut out and placed in an empty beer glass that he must have been drinking out of before he was shot. I gave Insp Frank my thoughts that Charlie Peters was killed because he had been passing on information about the Hollis family over many years. With Alf Jacson now landlord of the Royal Oak pub after working with me for almost seven years in the drug unit both of us over seen by John Knight of all people who had knifed many people to reach the position of top dog. The Willis brothers were owners of ''The Gully pub''. A team of twenty men mostly extra-large police officers out of condition and had been out of touch with keeping fit had in fact won the fight a few broken knuckles some restructure noses and black eyes left the police saying to each other; A GOOD JOB DONE'' had broken into the pub which resulted in one almighty punch up   A very large Drug den was found running into an extra-large financial cash find was the icing on the cake. Wally the Drug dog did think it was his birthday on that raid.

Which was a little more than what you could call "For Personal Use"?! Their cabin and tents are contained drugs this was not a party house but a party Pub and Caravan Park. I could not see much fishing being done down here., I did think to myself. The so-called topless barmaids found in total and two sleeping at in their bedrooms were going Chief Insp Abigail a few words about the only sure drinks. Two of the four were well known down in Alice Springs where Abigail was cracking the wipe down there. Doing night shift between the bed sheets and serve drinks during the day. Some would say it was good living but illegal in the eyes of Abigail. I went there to tell her "Just take it all under your wing." I looked at John and James Willis in handcuffs in the back of the police truck, we had charges are dozen tourist for drugs this will be a fishing trip that they will not forget in a long time slowly we got through the tourist, while I went down to the canteen to get some chili eggs in a roll and a thick chocolate shake. First it was Eddie Edwards the chef, we had a drug record in the city he had divided to move to the country. A better lifestyle: I told Eddie that it would be between five and ten years before he would smell the country breeze Berrimah Prison is what you could call country. Eddie Edwards was not a person you should confide in if you are Jones or James Willis because Eddie was becoming an "Open Book" and the details just rolled off of his lips about Jones ad James and the Halls Family. A mention of Alf Jackson at the Royal Oak was Edie did work for about six months before he did decide the country lifestyle. Well, I did tell him that he will now be halfway between city and country at Berri mall Prison!!

I had decided to tackle John and James Willis, in separate rooms, with the information that had been flowing about their connection to the drug world. John was the older of the two brothers but still acted like a twelve-year-old boy whenever he decided to. I mention the connection to the Mollis Family. "All Lies. I would kill them on secret., I still do believe that it was them shoot my father Fred, up came that late Ute down wide both passenger windows, out came not one but two shotguns bang bang. My old man did not stand at chance!! I decided to turn the tables on Jones. I gave him a few facts that it is were known in certain circles that in fact your father Fred took out Jake Mollis, sometimes we did call him Ted!! "Rubbish, my dad hated that family. But to shoot the head my dad only needed one gun!! I answer that was what I call an admission.

Now this did lead for me to wander, after years apart the two families joined together in the drug deal. I did tell John whatever he might say, we do have certain people have given us information "Listen and Listen Good, anybody who has pointed the finger at my family, will be spending the rest of their life, asleep with one eye open, well until somebody pays them a visit!! I did notice now that John had gone into the speech of the twelve-year-old, it was time to go and talk to the intelligent younger brother James. I knew that James was the head rooster, and any plan that was put together with the Mollis Family, must of came from him, with a deal behind closed doors with the Mollis Family. I knew that James would say no comment. He refused a solicitor because he had done nothing wrong. "Running A Drug Filled Escape in a Country pub hidden behind fishing Rods with a supply of all drugs and a brother upstairs.

I mentioned that some people had decided to come clean. It was fun to listen to James give a speech word for word about them sleeping with one eye open. I do remember that there was Father Fred had used in any interviews I had with him over the years before his death. I found that it was carrying on his legacy!! I sent James to his cell, where we demanded a solicitor, a Wilf Piper. A very old family friend who went back to the days of Fred Willis. Wilf Piper was one of those people who still used hair cream ion his hair, dyed jet black, trying to look like a young Elvis, always trying on my mind when I met him.

I decided not to interview any member of the Mollis Family, mainly because found that they sing like birds once they found out we had made the connection with them and John and James Willis.

I did decide to let Chief Insp Abigail put all the charges together and with Insp Frank Turner slowly read all the people concerned about the endless charge sheet. I headed for home. I should have gone upstairs to my assistant commissions office but it will still be there tomorrow. I found it was nice that Aunt Candy, I decided to use my car, for shopping. The four wheel drive that Kate my wife used to drive will only be driven by me when I take the boys fishing on weekends. The BBQ was on fire and with the boys cooking Aunt candy told me everything is under control, even the surprise in the garage after dinner which I did enjoy, it was time to take the boys to see their new present "A Full-Size Pool Table" I hot a huge and kiss from all fun or the boys. "Hey, homework to be done first before any game of pool!!

It was time to explain that tomorrow I have somebody who will out up a wall between the cars and pool room. They will have to paint all the walls in any way they decide. I might regrets actually making that statement I walk the boys play pool. There was pure happiness following in our home. Aunt Candy reminded me that I should start to think about sending the wardrobe of clothes to the op-shop. She was right it had been three years the next month. I had to tell Aunt Candy that the boys would decide to get to that point of eventually letting go. I did not tell Aunt Candy that every night I turned to the pillow that Kate used to rest her head and simply say "Goodnight Kate."

The next day on the way to work, I got any way driver to stop as the "Royal Oak Pub" I really wanted to rub Alf Jackson up the wrong way. Alf got the first word in and said that I should celebrate busting the Mollis Family and the Willis Brothers John and James. I had to stop Alf then and there from pouring an extra-large brandy. I had to tell him to his face. I knew that he was behind the leaking of drug information to Inse Frank turner that led to the arrest of the Mollis and Willis Family. I also looked him straight in the eye and told him that I knew that he knew who saw Charlie Peters in the very toilet and later shot Nurse Milda Drake after she was given the keys of Charlie Peter's flat and she found nothing. But she had to be silence she knew the killer of Charlie Peters!!

After drinking one large Brandy, he told me the brandy was for you, and he simply drank that one also. Aaron my old matey you will have to prove all this, even just for old to time's sake!! I just wanted to reach for my gun on my holster and point it at him and simply shoot him on the head. I left thinking that the very day is near but it will not be today, I felt that the vein on my neck had even got a life of its own. I just arrived and ready for breakfast and I had a text from John Knight the top dog he wanted me to scratch the earth on his top floor kennel with him. A pile of crispy bacon sandwiches and a large mug of that thing they call coffee on the top floor I just put down the phone once again, after listening to ex Insp Alf Jackson burn my ear about you charging at him, throwing your arms in the air, just like a bloody octopus, and behind various crimes!!

I decided to eat not one but two crispy bacon sandwiches dripping in tomato sauce before I decided to comment. "Whenever you want to please start mumbled John Knight sticking a whole bacon sandwich in his mouth. Now this meant he would have to listen to what I was saying in reply now he was multi-tasking of eating and talking. I did mention Alf Jackson and for a very brief moment John Knight actually stopped eating and mumbled still with a half-filled mouth of a bacon sandwich.

"You should have shot the mother fucker in the head and say it was self-defense, just like we used to in the old days, I looked at"

The bloated German Shepherd. "Hang-on you and that prick Alf Jackson made a few unlawful moves on certain people. I was never involved or did I ever agree that this is the best way of the reward of a problem!!

"I always knew that one day that our naughty days would come back to haunt us.

"Hang-on Johnny they were your naughty days with big fat Alf Jackson, who may I say has a finger into most people in the high ranks all except me!!

This left John Knight almost choking on his bacon sandwich. He did choke well, Infront of me drinking my coffee it was a top performance till his office manager came in to slap him on the back "He could have choked" she told me "He should of not grab the last sandwich anyway it did belong to me" I laughed.

This was time to leave now, somehow his assistant was now sitting on his lap, I thought I had better go next door to put on my assistant commissioner's hat with a pile of folders were waiting to be signed by me. This Gestapo acting female instructed me. I first divided them up. Eighteen just wanted a signature above the schoolboy scribble of the name John Knight C.P. I wondered what C.P meant then surprised it was not commissioner of the police but instead "Chief Prick." I could hear a mumble of a voice, the so-called mention of my boys and school football and her two boys also in the school team. I had to halt the conversation then and there "I do not discuss my family at work is that understood with the answer of I thought that it just might bring us closer to getter, when I heard.

I found shivers running down my back. I went to the final file and gave it to her. I did not even ask her name.

"But sir, you have not even read most of the file." I had to crack the whip again

"Nearby all of these files, I have seen and read downstairs in my active commander of detective office.

"Excuse me Sir, but why would they even send you two files on the same subject?

Now that is a good question, just maybe because I have two jobs. They or them just might think that there is two Aaron Brown in this building!! With that I bolted for the lift my team were waiting on my arrival, I could squeeze in another breakfast I forget about my waste-line today"

I had a light bulb moment to check my back account and it was then I realized that this mentally I have received two wage payments one for active commander of detectives and acting assistant police commissioner.

I then sucking on a piece of bacon I just pick up the phone and in form the pay office.

"Not on your Nellie Matey, I am doing two jobs so I should receive two wage cheque's!! Yes, I am a policeman. Now that that does depend on which side of the fence you are standing on. At this very moment in time, I am actually standing on both sides of the fence. It was then that Aunt Candy gave me a phone call to let me know that it is "Fish and Potato Pie" for dinner. I felt my stomach and quietly said "That will be just fine"!! I really had the idea to put up my feet in a matter of sense. Insp Frank Turner true to form had got another lead from the Willis Brother arrest. Much to my surprise a Toyah Brother's wife of Tony Butcher, a right nasty piece of work who always carried a small axe inside his jacket. There are many people who did not move their hands fast enough before Tony Butcher had decided that five fingers on one hand so you could afford to lose a couple on the other hand then toes and ears.

Was another one of his tricks. I stood in the entrance of the Golden Freeze Hotel. Most people would shit their pants if Tony Butcher confronted them. Myself, my heart jumps a beat once I saw him raise that meat axe at me. It was him or me and the axe was aimed at my head. It did shoot three bullets to stop Tony Butcher. One in the shoulder, just a fresh wound for Tony. Even the second shot in the leg still did not stop him in his tracks. The one on the head was the one that made his eyes meet in the middle before he slumped to the ground. Standing next to me was the future top dog, John Knight. I think he must have just shit his pants and jeans there was now twice the usual smell .

"Well done, Aaron, yes you did well, I have to pay a visit to the gent's toilet"!!

Somehow when I read the report that John Knight who was the senior police officer present. Did mention that he had everything under control and told me to use whatever means to defend us. I just do not recall John Knight saying anything at the time.

Total Butcher was not pleased to see me at the "Raven's Cottage" something that you could call a country set shop. Owned by the Willis Brothers, and they also owned "Fenders Farm." It is so called Mango Farm, but also a drug house where the brew was mixed and the pills manufactured. Toyah Butcher had nothing to do. The set was her cane. The dugs she had never touched in her life. She looked at me said "I thought you were dead" The feeling was mutual I felt Franck had been told about four worked as "Fenders Farm" working on the drugs we needed a helping hand from the new named "Active Response Unit." They did bring drones. I felt I was watching one of those American Cop sleeps on televisions. All this technology is no longer like the old days of kicking down the front anybody who moved you shot. That life was changed. The drones did give back sit images, all inside the framework cluster bonds, gas bombs, before I knew it the word action was used.

"Active Response Unit" was going to lead. I was told to put my feet up and have a nice cup of tea, by Inspector Richards, Ex Army he must of slip into the Police Force with the other rats up the drainpipe. Inspector Richards did return to give me what some word to say was an apology for his comment. All I said '' was that I do not drink tea that is for old ladies!! There was a lot of shouting and gunfire three dead and three wounded. There were enough drugs to keep the Darwin Nightclub alive for about five years, Insp Frank Turner, I did mention to him, why would the Willis Brothers John and James, go to importing drugs into Darwin, when they had this manufacturing operation at here?

Nobody had a honest had any answer for me.

I was glad to get home to a small serve of Fish Pie Ten dinner. Once again, all fun of my boys beat me at pool. I was glad to put my head on my pillow tonight. It had been an extra-long day, and at my age I do need my beauty sleep.

In the morning, a bark from the top dog John knight, had found two battle axes to become assistant Police Commission. Both female, Ivy Clinton and Elsie Jenkins. Both had been gaining extra sharp teeth at birth to bite you on the ass whenever they find the need. Both battle axes had been in uniform and that will be their place in the future. Ivy Clinton will do the administration and Elsis Jenkins will be in charge of the boots on the ground. Both being told to keep their sticky bears at of the detective units because that is my mine and mine only. I could see by the look on their faces, This Units not fully explained which they both agreed to sign up for the job. I was told that I am no longer acting as an assistant to the police commission. In fact, my job is now full time. I did remember that I am now being blessed with two units. I did not want to mention this to John Knight I felt that it just might spoil the party!!

I looked at the pile of files on my desk on the top floor and just kept walking to the lift. I sat down in my office, strong coffee and no breakfast today I told Ranes Judd my office member. My personal phone rand and it was Richard Edwards, part time Builder. Aaron came quickly, Aunt Candy was shot and I was warned. I simply jump up and shouted

"Code Red" my house, people have been shot

"Code Red"

Any Fuller was burning rubber in my car when I ran out of reception. The lights were green, but the Amy said, "Hold on Boss"!! Sirens and a police convoy of sitting cars were following us as I sat outside my house. Abigail Trims was giving orders to secure the area to search the house. I found Aunt Candy slump on the stirring wheels, listen it will have to be pizza tonight the boys can cook that and I will not be going to the Turf Club tomorrow.

I always loved Aunt Candy as how she could put a spin on everything. She had been shot twice once in the shoulder and once in the neck. She had to go to the hospital. Laying on the ground a sounding like a wounded bull elephant was Richard Green "He was in a grey UTE and drove slowly, I was going on, when I heard shots, I shouted at Aunt Candy and had screamed at for help. The driver saw me and fired at me twice. One on the shoulder and one on the window in the house next door. Tell him next door, I can fix the window at a cheap price. I did think, hang on matey you have just been shot and you are trying to drum up business for himself. My personal phone rang and it was Rachel Judd, "Your boys are safe," I sent a Protection Unit of six officers to the school they are going to a safe house. Don't worry how is your Aunt Candy? Asked.

She is off to hospital, and worried about not going to the Turf Club, the other guy Richard Edward the so-called Handy Man is also off to hospital with a shoulder wound." I replied I got off the phone, to be handed the phone of Chief Insp Abigail. Um its John Knight, "Anything I can do, just ask me the boys safe, with Aunt Candy, off to hospital and the other person is also listen anything Aaron, please do not stand alone on this area, like you did when Kate died, I am here, for you." I wished that he had not mentioned Kate just then. My past was creeping up on me. A word from traffic that no location on the Grey UTE. I decided to go to the hospital. Amy Fuller was burning rubber once again. We pulled up outside the hospital entrance and some security guard came running at to tell me "Hey matey move your car you can't park there"

I almost took a swing at the upstairs security guard. I left it to Amy, who is not a person you want to try and show how important you are. "Listen blockhead that is Assistant Police Commissioner Aaron Brown. The family have been shot at. "I don't care it is a no parking in this are!! Shouted the security guard. "If you continue this attitude, you will be needing surgery yourself, they will be trying to take your bollocks out of your mouth"!!

It was then the Security Guard went back inside and came out with back up another overweight security dog looking like a pig dog. They both looked at each other and at Amy and decided it would not be worth the trouble to take an Amy.

I had the call from Amy to say she had put the car in the car park now and was on her way up to see me. Aunt Candy was now in safe hands. I sat drinking coffee which I had to admit did not taste bad. Four bag of potato chips, three chocolate bars and two cans of coke were slowly entering the mouth of Amy while she sat talking to me. Aunt Candy had to rest. A protective detail had arrived to keep an eye on Aunt Candy and Richard Edwards. I was to be moved to a different safe house from my boys. For dinner it hit the sack. I found it hard to rest in the morning at work, the Grey Ute had been found burnt out on an industrial estate. Fifty yards away was the body of a

Billy Simpson, shot three times. We put and head together to realize that Billy Simpson was the shooter at my house. Deep down I knew that Billy Simpson was a very long-time friend of Ex Insp Alf Jackson of the Royal Oak. It was time for me to go and ruffle the feathers of Alf Jackson once again.

I had come to realize once again that all roads that contain crime led to Alf Jackson and the Royal Oak Public house. Just before I left, I had a ballistic report on the gun that was used to try and kill her and Richard Edwards. I was very surprised that the very same gun was used to kill Charlie Peters on the garden toilet in the beer garden at the Royal Oak Public House. Also, the Nurse Hilda Drake at her home. I do suspect the person to her to come to being the next victim, she knew the killer of Charlie Peters and just maybe she failed to locate the so called "Black Book" The book of the crime related people on the Royal Oak Pub already looking at death after their crimes. Aunt Candy was lucky and so was her toy boy Richard Edwards only got wounded with the very same gun. Billy Simpson, A will know associate and friend of Alf Jackson. He drives the UTE and fired at Aunt Candy and Richard Edwards, only to be shot by the same gun he used on Aunt Candy and Richard Edwards. With no sign of the gun, I did decide to take Insp Billie Mayford a very fine first nation detective, I left Chief Inspector Abigail to clean up the mass of paperwork and try and bring some order to what I would call chaos over the past few days. Alf Jackson standing behind the bar, with his usual bullshit flowing from his lips. He looked at Insp Billie and of course Amy Fuller my driver and body guard. I went straight for the tongue of Alf Jackson to stop it waging in all directions the name of Billy Simpson I mention, finally

Alf Jackson did tell me that he had not seen him today. His Grey UHT is normally parked in the rear car park next to the beer garden. I knew that Alf Jackson knew that Billie Simpson was dead, although no name had been released to the body found by the burnt at UTE There was also a small mention about the shooting of Aunt Candy and Richard Edwards the press office said it was a domestic.

I did think that Alf Jackson would be what most would call heartbroken at the death of a friend of fifteen years.

"Billy Simpson is dead"!!

"Any idea who shot him?" Asked Alf Jackson

I did not mention that Billy Simpson was shot. I just made at I was still waiting for the forensic report. His UTE we do think was stolen by some teenagers and then set it alright to cover up their fingerprints. I almost came to believe what I had told Alf Jackson. I still did not want a drink of fizzy lemon water; my two female officers also declined the offer. Alf Jackson did have a habit of trying to change the subject.

"When was the last time you saw Billy Simpson? I asked him. I knew whatever he said would not be the truth.

"Um, well let me see, um most of been after lunch, yesterday, yes, he turned to the bar maid, who said Billy left after he has lunch here. I knew at that time Billy was already dead and his UTE had what your might call a burn out!!

I left Alf Jackson to ponder, I knew that he would be wondering what was going on in my head now. Even Insp Billie Mayford made the comment that Billy Simpson was already dead lunch time yesterday and his UTE was hidden near his body and nobody had set it alright. I decided to be dropped off to the hospital to see Aunt Candy. She was sitting up watching the early morning racing from England she was fine and wanted to come home. I told her that her toy boy Richard Edwards was waiting for a lift home from his wife

"That little cheap skate was bloody married, he was too old for me, I do like my men younger and active and he did perform well on the pool table. I had to stop Aunt Candy then and there"

With a please explain I did hope that it was not what I did suspect "Yes, we had sex on the boy's pool table, twice when he was fixing up the wall and once just before I got in your bloody car and get shot. That big Sissy laying on the ground wimping like a half dead dog while I sat in the car covered in blood, I said to him, phone Aaron you bloody useless prick, in fact he was trying to locate his wife on the phone, wife I said to him, Get Aaron get the police get a bloody ambulance you dip stick!!

I did warn now that Richard Edwards would not be doing any odd fix up jobs at my house in the future. I could see that the protective officer at the door of the room of Aunt Candy had enjoyed her side of the story.

I arrived back at the office and without much shouting I told Insp Franck Turner that get did need to go get a search warrant for the Royal Oak Pub property. I did mention that all patrons will be searched and also the flat where Alf Jackson dies sleep. Daily the drug dog, and six members of the drug unit, plus everybody in this office who is not needed except of course my office manager, Rachel Judd.

Just like a dog that has just been let officer its lead in a park and charging into my office was Chief Inspector Abigail Timmes and was she on fire. I thought I smelt her knickers smoldering. I had to say

something that I do not like to say to a female and that is "Shut Up"!!
She sat down and I had to explain the ground rules of this entire
detective unit. Listen Insp Frank Turner is head of the drug unit. I
told him to go and fix up a search warrant for the "Royal Oak. Pub" I
told him to get his team together and daily the drug dog. We will need
every able body person in this office to attend the drug raid, which may
I point at will be led by you Chief Inspector Abigail, now listen good I
have enough going on in my life now, I got a relative who has been shot
mistaken for me, driving my car out of the drive way of my house, got
my four sons, in a safe house under the protection unit, on top of that
I got all these detective around thirty who need leadership from you.
My position is split between this office and my office on the top floor,
I do expect you to be my right hand to give me more support instead of
trying to score brownie points. A sought of apology from Abigail didn't
really was for me. She had in fact made herself look a right bloody idiot
and she will have to work hard to get the respect of the detectives once
again. Insp Frank arrived to settle the dust in my office.

"I have the warrant and without any hint from me, he handed the
warrant to chief Insp Abigail. Saying "More boss you are the senior
officer on this drug raid on the Royal Oak Pub. I looked at Chief Insp
Abigail and nodded with the comment "I will only be there to observe,
with that I mention the word action and at last everybody was ready
for the Royal Oak drug raid of the century. I did hope it would go well.

I sat outside in what I called the rear car park. I could see that my
driver Amy Fuller was ready to kick some ass holding her pump action
shotgun. She kissed the barrel just before I said the word's she wanted
to her "Let's go Amy!!" she was ducking and diving while we followed

the rear force in the rear of the Pub Led by chief Insp Abigial. The front of the Pub was led by Insp Frank Turner who was in his own little world today. I did hope that he was wearing extra diapers, with a lot of shouting and Alf Jackson standing at the bar looking at the search warrant. He called me and I told him to discuss any problems that he had with Chief Insp Abigial. Daisy the drug dog must have thought this was going to be a bonus day for her. Drugs under the front bar, and then when she went into the kitchen, she most of thought it was going to be Christmas for her. The two chefs, both denied any knowledge of the drugs, although both were carrying little packages of various drugs on their own uniforms. I stood back listening to Alf Jackson.

I took no notice when he called my name for some help in this mistake. One dozen patrons in the public bar and ten of them had enough drugs on them to receive a free holiday of a year or two in prison. I pulled Insp Frank over and told him that we needed them to point the finger at the supplier. The front bar was transported without their beers in hand to the Watch house. Daisy was off upstairs; I was very surprised that no drugs had been found in the living quarters of Alf Jackson instead a half-naked very young female was found by Chief Insp Abigial. I would say to Alf Jackson right now "WOOPS"!! When questioned Alf Jackson said she was eighteen and a sister of one of the bar staff. Well, the only thing Sandra Moran was now wearing was a school uniform. She was and dare I say it not yet reached sweet sixteen. Alf Jackson denied he knew this she had been drinking in the Pub now well over a year now. I just looked at Alf and shook my head.

Sex with minor, was the least of the problems for Alf Jackson. A slight technical point was to surface something that even I had not ever thought about the pub licenses had changed hands, to Hugh Motherwell a six-foot four back pole a man who once ran "Rosies Italian Café" in a back street of Darwin. He was going to bring Rosies Italian Food to the Royal Oak Pub. Bean Pole Hugh I asked to speak to me out in the garden. I did ask myself did I need want an escalator; I was getting neck acne just by talking to him. Twenty-four hours he had held the license. I did remind him that under the licenses he is responsible for all these drugs found on the promises. A reaction of his face when I told him that he will no longer have the license. From now he will be charged with various drug offences underage drinkers the list is endless and may I say "Matey you have been stitched up"

My side kick Amy Fuller had located Stan Monroe the license inspector for the hospitality industry. Stan was and will always be slightly thicker that a fence post. He arrived and it was nice to see him in living color and much to my delight he was even surprised that I had sent for him. We went to the Pub Garden. A brief explanation as why he never did attend the meeting of senior officers and a daily basis, just to let all over units know what was going on in their world and how it would have some influence on their day.

To tell the truth this slimy screw ball I felt like grabbing him by the throat and beating the shit at of him. I just mention that Alf Jackson was no longer holding the license of the Royal Oak it was now in the hands of Huw Motherwell.

I felt so pleased that he had pointed out to me that I was right in this fact. This Royal Oak is a bloody drug haven, and you should have notified me that the license had changed hands.

It was then that my phone rang it was Ramel Judd to confirm that she had traced large donations of over fifty thousand dollars had been placed in the bank account of Stan Monroe. I thought to myself he must be as thick as two bricks together if he thought we would not trace this gift to him one day.

In my arm, little way asked him if he did put on the gorses because he has a few large deposits on his bank account. I got no comment and marching in step were four members of the integrity unit. I spoke to the officer in charge and asked him if he could lead Stan Monroe away at the back gate while I talked to his second in command a Sandy Ballad. A veteran well past his used by date except to follow Stan Monroe around like "A lap dog."

A quick confession of ten thousand dollars hidden undera mattressat home, a gift to turn a blind eye to certain

I pointed to two more integrity officers who would like to talk to Sandy Ballard in more depth and maybe you could have them to your place and shoe then your early Christmas present. I went behind the bar and poured myself a lemonade.

"Busy Day boss, we only came to observe" laugh, Amy Fuller.

I had one more part of the call and that was at the launderette next door. I had a few words blown in my ear that you can buy more that laundry powder there. I decided to wander off. The back door as open so I thought I would give whoever there was in here running this joint a nice introduction. I had a big surprise when behind me was a relative of HuwMotherwell, where are all these tall being coming from, the Royal Oak could have started up a basketball team a little late for that now I thought waving was knife around I told him that I wanted to do some wasting later today and the lost.

He did not fall for that one, so I had to be upfront, I showed him my police barged he still waved the knife at me. I did remark that the last person pointed a knife at me. I simply shot him between the eyes. It was then that Amy Fuller showed up, a five-foot five stick of dynamite. One kick cut off her left leg this little giant hit the ground and then went for his knife when Amy just stamped on his hand and then hit him in the head with the butt of her punch action shotgun.

I knew Amy was happy ow. She had let off a bit of steam. Daisy the drug dog between the sweet-smelling washing powder she found enough drugs, to put this bean pole laundry duties in prisonten the next five to seven years.

The courts were going to be busy even the next few days. I was very surprised that the would-be drug dealers in the public bar had pointed the finger of their supply to Hugh Motherwell of all people who had just taken over the license of the Royal Oak Pub. I always thought it would be Alf Jackson who had the nickname of being the "King Pin," I had a bad headache that day, in fact left Alf Jackson with a smile on his face who half a million dollars bail was posted. A report each day at nine o'clock at the police reception. The old ankle bracelet was used it was like having a ribbon on the mouth of a vicious German shepherd. Four days and the ankle bracelet were left in the hotel room at the travel lodge Alf Jackson had bolted, where I had no idea. All points of call, they say, eyes everywhere. I did imagine he could hire a police officer or even helicopter to escape the Darwin area.

I sat munching on a chili bacon and egg roll. Before me stood two brain dead detectives Chief Insp Abigial and Insp Frank Turner both tried to talk at the same time it was time for me to express my opinion on both of them now.

You had one just to do and you fucked up!!"

How many times have I heard those famous words, even to myself in my younger days but I was a quick learner. Out the back window Alf Jackson fled, nobody on duty at the back only sitting together in their car at the front of the motel. I wiped the chili sauce from my lips and I told Frank to close the door. I told Frank and Abigial to sit down on the couch not exactly holding hands or even cuddling up like two teenagers. I knew now that the two detectives had moved on now, they were going to blame each other now. Abigial was really to blame, being told just sit in the car and watch roam nine no other explanations was given, like every fifteen minutes a walk around the rear of room nine.

Ex Inspector Alf Jackson does know about every trick in the book and will be hard to catch, I went on to say that I thought this was well planned and now all we have to do is to think like Alf Jackson, where would he go. Roadblocks were already in action. I commented that he would try and fly out from some remote farm over to ball on somewhere that he would already have drug connections from hi past. I step up and looked at the map on the wall,

"He could be halfway to Tennent creek now "mumbled Insp Frank acting like an over grown schoolboy.

"Listen he would not be heading in land, he would not be far from the coast, maybe a sea plane, or even a helicopter to take him at to a vessel out a sea."

I looked at Abigial and Frank and I am sorry to say they are both out of their depth now, we had to flood all media outlets, offer say one hundred thousand for any information that put a smile on the face of Frank but iced faced Abigial was still feeling upset that she could not blame Frank for this whole episode. I was starting to read her face just like a book.

It was not long before every nut job in town had seen ALF. One person said he was enjoying a quite beer with him in the front bar of the Royal Oak they were talking about the good old days another had spotted Alf now collecting trolly's in the Woolies car park while slipping on a can of _Pepsi. The calls were endless. Most of them did comment that they wanted the rewards in cash not cheque just in case the cheque bounced!!

A call from Grave Hill the old farmstead about three hours' drive, or forty-five minutes in a helicopter. I told Amy to grab her shotgun and we headed for the chopper. Two other choppers were used by Frank and Abigial and with the help of the special operation unit. If Alf was there, he would hear the three choppers and most probably have made a run for it. Now this was a chance that I would have to take. I looked at Amy and she told me she was ready for action, I told her if she did see him, take him down after a challenge. Do not trust him, he will shoot you first.

There was a lot of buildings and one did certain a camp bed and empty beer bottles. Rusty Monroe another ex-criminal tried to act innocent until I stuck my gun against his head and simply asked him where Alf Jackson was.

Simply said if you do not tell me I will shoot you here now, without question. He pointed to a barn about one hundred yards away.

"He is waiting for a Helicopter" Rusty Monroe telling me while he did his little boy act and pissed his pants.

I said to him "Still not potty trained then Rusty?"

The idiot did turn to run but young Amy wearing those steel cap boots can make a grown man cry when she simply raised her leg to show what real pain of swollen testicular can feel like she told him if you run, I will shoot you!!

I could see other members of the team running in all directions except the right direction where Alf Jackson was holding. I went ahead a lot of Amy put them all on the correct path. In the distance I could see a helicopter heading to the place where Alf Jackson I believed was hiding. I think the blue lights flashing on our helicopters made the pilot Alf Jackson get away, do a about turn. Standing in the twilight and the moon in the background, I called out to Alf Jackson and told him to drop his handgun.

Aaron you bloody pain in the ass, let me go for old time's sake, I got half a million dollars in this leather bag, take it "Just let me know the truth Alf why all those people had to die?

Charlie Peters had a black book it did contain everything he thought he knew about the Royal Oak drug business, I hated him, I shout him then I; cut out his eyes, cut off his ears and his tongue and placed them in his beer mug; now I wanted that bloody book in his flat. I held up the black book, do you mean this one? I found it stuck at the back of a cupboard in his flat there was no need to kill Milda Drake.

Listen I, she knew I killed Charlie Peters, then that Billy Simpson, he thought it was you in the car and shot you. But Charlie Peters knew too much about everything and his used by date had shown up again. I could not let the fool like a bird with a broken wing, he knew the real truth. He knew that I had to do the job on Kate, he did not have the balls.

"Running over a mother of four boys in a bloody in a bloody supermarket car park?"

So, you killed my Kate? I shouted it was that moment that I should have just pointed my gun at him and released the six bullets with all the rage inside me, now pouring out. My head was pumping of course always with the one liner, Alf told me to trace the bag money, it will not bring back Kate but the boys will be happy. What a mixed-up view on life. I found Alf Jackson once my close friend and work mate, we had been through a lot together. The big difference that Frank always stuck out his hand for the brown envelope full of money, very similar to John Knight a new Police Commissioner.

The three of us where a team, just maybe I did not want anything playing on my mind anytime in the future I did not want to feel guilty in any way. I was clean just like the top of a new born baby's head. Deep down I know this time had come to move on. There is no need for Alf Jackson to be part of my life anymore.

I told Alf to drop his gun. "If I do not do that you will simply shoot me, and if I do, I cannot trust you to shoot me."

That was a riddle not what I expected, in fact I raised my arm and being told I did not have the balls now that Alf Jackson had surprised me by dropping his gun. It was up killing Alf three bullets into his head and three in his chest.

His eyes still open looking up and the night sky. I heard the voice on Amy "Hey I got lost, I heard the shots you okay boss?"

"Yes, I am fine Amy, Alf Jackson just happen to take his eye off the ball and pointed his gun at me, I had no choice"

"Nice one boss," Shouted Amy.

It was not long before the rest of the team joined us. I felt this weight being lifted off my shoulders after all these years and I killed the man who killed my Kate the mother of my four boys.

COMING TO A HEAD

Yes, I was running late. Amy Fuller had given me two toots on the car in the morning. In front of me and standing like she was looking for a fight was my Aunt Candy.

"Got to go um got to go Candy," running late" I said the word bullocks stop me in my tracks'

"We need to talk, I want to give up this housekeeper job and move on with my life, I am going to buy one of those new flats up on the corner" Shouted Aunt Candy ate me.

Listen old girl, you could have discussed this with me last night I sat under the mango tree with a six pack of beer in an ice bucket. Why didn't you come to talk to me then "listen Aaron I am too old for this work, running around chasing your four boys, all their bloody washing and cleaning up after them.!!

Listen, tonight we will sit down and have a nice chat over the problems ok.

"I could see I was waving a red scarf to a raging bull. I opened the front door and told her do not to drive the car today after you drank three bottles of red wine on your own last night.

"I gently reduced. Listen you can be a bloody policeman at work but not at home, she screamed slamming the front down behind me. I looked at Amy who did not comment. We drove off and I wanted to take a look at these new flats that Aunt Candy is going to move into. I could see by the sign property is under control of the Catholic Church. I told Amy to drive on. I told Amy that Aunt Candy is moving on, the boys are too much for her, all the cleaning and washing and having to cook four nights a week. We arrived at work and my next flight was waiting for me upon the top floor.

There was no Hello how are you?

"Well, you shot the Mother Fucker twice in the head I read the report. That is Alf Jackson out of a lives forever now"

I sat down to sample this thing they call coffee on the top floor. John Knight was sweating. I thought that I would let him lead the conversation.

"Did you get it? Have you read it, you know that bloody black book with all the details of what Alf Jackson and I got up to years ago, slightly illegal but still within the law.

The so-called Black book. John Knight asked me again.

"There was no Black Book, he did not even mention you in his five minutes you had in private

I gave you a recording of our conversation. I replied.

Speechless is something that John Knight was never he could even talk under water if he had to in my mind. Listen he had info on ten various Senior Officers and he told me only a month ago to call you off, or he will blow the whistle!!"

I wondered why John Knight had not mentioned this before to me. I decided to change the subject. "He did admit that it was him that ran over my Kate in the car park while he did regret having to kill her, but I still could not back off. I had him in my sight and it was only a matter of time before I would have him in handcuffs. The only Black Book belonged to Charlie Peters. Who made notes of the dealings that Alf Jackson was involved in Alf Jackson was dealing drugs at the Royal Oak pub a good year before his mother won the Lotto and purchased ''The Royal Oak Pub'' A mention of a car would pull up in the car park and the boot would open at come the drugs and a brief case was handed to the passenger Alf Jackson himself would never handle the drugs or the money himself he always used somebody else.

He did control all drugs in the area you played his rules and he would make a phone call to the drug unit and set you up. Half the public bar was working for him in some way or other. His nickname was Mister Fifty Percent. What he did with all that money, he hardly ever changed his clothes, we think that he had a connection in Bali! John Knight was sitting there, speechless except to ask me once again did I had found that black book that Alf Jackson had with information on him.

"It could cost me, my job, if it fell into the wrong hands!! It was time to go, I had my job to do and playing on my mind was the episode of Aunt Candy early this morning. My office manager decided to grab me by the ankles lift me upside down and give me a good share to see what was wrong with me today. A brief explanation and the comment that I was now back to square one since Kate died trying to find somebody to be our housekeeper.

I had to admit sitting in the car coming to work I could easily give these police position up and take care of the boys myself. I wondered if I gave up my job would I receive two pensions at the moment I am banking two salaries each month. We would not be short of money. I have well over half a million _dollars by the insurance company on Kate's death. I also have just over nine hundred thousand in the bank paid by victims of crime. No matter how much money I received it could never replace Kate. I explain to Rachel and I had felt that I had been given a good sharing that Aunt Candy is only moving down the road to a new flat run by the Catholic Church. I started to laugh when I told Rachel that Aunt Candy comes home from the Turf club in a taxi, pissed as a rat, strips down to her underwear and always jump's into the pool whenever the boys and I are standing watching her or not. A few laps wet and looking like death warmed up Candy goes off to bed and is not seen till late Sunday.

Talking about the Catholic Church was an entry to being told Walter Davis has been released three years early. A well-known local priest given fifteen years for being a pedophile who abused fifteen choir boys over five years. It was a cover up by Bishop Cyrus Brent but that was not enough. The public should have hung Walter Davies on the end of a rope on time village green. The bishop survived although his flock never ever returned to normal. I phone Bill Hardy the very man who put Walter Davis behind bars. Sweet caroling tried to put me off from talking to me. I told her if he does not pick up his phone, I will be down at his office kicking down the front door!!

"One moment Aaron, O here is Bill"

"Well, no bullshit Bill who got him out three years early and why wasn't I told about this?

"Listen Aaron, hang-on, who do you think the bloody church and the fing Bishop Cyrus Brent, who is going to have Walter Davis Living at Bishops Gate, well he will be there early.

I nearly picked up the phone and threw it in rage at the window, then I remembered my office windows are bullet proof.

"Listen Aaron they went to the high court. I never ever thought he would get a bloody pass out three years early old mare!!"

"Listen if I catch him outside Bishop's gate and that nine-foot brick wall around that back garden I will shoot Walter Davis in the head and most probably reload my gun to shoot another six bullets into his chest!!

"Aaron, Aaron please calm down, take a chill pill there are restrict conditions on him living at Bishop's gate. I hate to imagine how the families of the abused choir boys, when they realize he will be back living under the so-called watchful eye of Bishop Cyrus Brent who we both know was also guilty of child abuses rub his dirty grubby hands of those naked bodies of the boys, while he filmed every minute of it.

I had to remember we did not find any of the boys, who said the bishop was taking photographs. You search that property and even the search of the church lead to "No Photographs."

"Listen we are going to have a riot squad on duty twenty-four seven to protect that slime ball Walter Davis" I told Bill.

"Listen Aaron if the drama does come to the worst and somebody does kill him, I will have the painful job of prosecution." Bill replied.

I will go there and lay down the rules, please send me the conditions of him being released three years early and under the watchful eye of Bishop Cyrus Brent. I got Chief Insp Abigial trims, and Frank Turner tried to act like Inspector after he had been promoted and I do not think anybody had broken the news to Chief Insp Abigial, I think it will be moment in the once again!!

I told Rachel Todd to request one on my behalf. I had to explain to Abigial and Frank with a brief background on Walter Davis, who was released at Five AM after the press were told Eight AM. I had found out that the church itself gave a media release saying our Brother Walter Davis will be released due to his faith and good work in the prison three years early.

Now it was show time and he had to drop the bombshell on the lap of Abigial, Yes it went down like a lead balloon. I had to inform Abigial who wanted to know why she was not consulted. I felt then here we go. I put the application in and it was given the green light for Frank to become acting Chief Inspector. I had to admit due to my lack of admin skills, I did not have any notification until I turned on my E-mail. It was another weak excuse of the team going behind her back.

The next question I am afraid Abigial had me when she asked who gave the green light or rubber stamp for this start of Frank's promotion. I told her the Assistant Police Commissioner who is actually me, upstairs in that office Abigial had me by the short and curli's Rachel Todd had saved me with something that I did not want to hear, she handed me the search warrant for Bishop's Gate and said "You do not need that now, somebody has just shot Walter Davies in the head while he sat in the rear garden drinking something that he called his "Freedom Beer".

I looked at Rachel Todd and said "It's not the first or April is it. April Fools Day!!

"No Sir" I replied to Rachel.

Amy Fuller was outside the front reception door and ready to pump some gas all the way to Bishop's Gate.

Still to this day I cannot out how uniform and forensic always beat me to the scene. I looked for Dr. Rebecca Mitcham, I was told that she was giving mouth to mouth to the Bishop Cyrus Brent who just had a heart attack. I walked past Walter Davies Body slump in a chair with two holes in his head. At last, first on the scene a uniform officer did explain what was going on when he told the ambulance crew.

"Never mind him he is dead, it's the old bloke inside, just had a bloody heart attack!!"

I stayed at of the way told acting Chief Insp Frank Turner to get the area sealed off, look for any cctv and start interviewing anybody who saw or heard anything outside Bishop's Gate. Meanwhile I got a miserable face Abigial Trims who I told was inside Bishop's Gate at last the bishop was pushed up into the ambulance and Dr. Rebecca looked at me and did quote "I normally see them dead, I do not normally have to save them, poor old Bishop, it was all a little too much he had a heart attack!!

Dr. Rebecca did point to the housekeeper Monty Bluetop who was sitting on a seat at the other end of the garden. I went over to introduce myself to her and Amy Fuller sat next to her for support.

"Listen I am going to tell you what I said to that thick bitch over there" she pointed to Chief Insp Abigial, she asked me what I was doing, I told her I was having a couple of beers I don't drink bloody red wine or I was not going to make myself a cup of tea was I!! I did agree, in fact I did Fancy a beer myself right now. My phone rang and it was the last person who I wanted to talk to John Knight, who was barking down the phone and sounding like a French Poodle on heat. We had a meeting, and also, he wished to discuss public safety now that Walter Davis is alive and tree in the community and living at Bishop's Gate.

"He was alive Johnny" I replied

"What do you mean Aaron? He is sitting near to me. Where he was drinking a cold beer before somebody shot him in the head twice!! I replied.

"So, where the F are you Aaron' asked Johnny

Simply at Bishop's Gate with my team now" "Um why wasn't I informed I am after all the fing police commissioner? I could not find anything stupid to say, so I just put down my phone. So, I started the history of Bishop's Gate with Manty Bluetop. Six am I phone up to the bishop. He looks down at me and the gate and then he does press the electronic button to release the three bolts. The other three large bolts, he does come to hand release about ten to six. Then he goes back upstairs and why he cannot make himself a cup of tea then has always left me puzzled. Anyway, it's my first job I put the paper next to his bed and a tea pot and milk with a mug that does say bishop on the side a normal good morning and if he has declined to have cereal and fruit or a cooked breakfast at six thirty AM. Today it was cereal, banana and corn flakes.

He called me back to say breakfast will be set for three today, we have a special guest who that was I had no idea. Everything with the bishop is very secretive and I have to say after eight years he still does not trust me. One person who will be there is Berni Macky, a right nasty man and what he is doing, sitting at the right hand of the bishop still I fail to understand he showed up six years ago straight from Berriman prison. Straight away Amy Fuller had sent a message to Rachel my office manager for more details on Berny Mackay.

"Berni was not at breakfast, but sitting like a fly on a pile of dog shit was the one and only Walter Davis. He still smells like an ex-prisoner. He had a full breakfast he did not speak, nor did the bishop speak while I was in the room. I went back inside and Walter Davis was gone still no sign of Berni Macky. The bishop sat reading the paper.

I could see that the departure of Walter Davis from prison was leaked far paces all about the ex-priest and choir master. The surname of Monty, I did ask and she told me she had married Stephen Bluetop one of the victims by Walter Davis and his sexual pleasure and also, I did remember that Stephen was one of the victims who pointed the finger at the bishop who sat and watched everything he even took photographs and film on his cameras. We did go over the Bishop's Gate and the church and did not find one picture of the sixteen boys. I did ask how the bishop feel about you coming to work with him as a housekeeper and being married to Stephen "he had no fing choices nobody else wanted the jobs a young priest did the homework and looked after fat and bald" I did mention "fat and bald" name and it was her name for the bishop. He was not only fat and bald but naked under his rub. No bloody undies" Laugh Monty!!

I did learn that Monty found Walter Davis in a slump in that chair, he must of help himself to a beer or two from the main fringe. He did not ask, he dropped the can on the payment, I told him to pick it up and put it in the bin, he just sat there with a smirk on his face. I heard the voice of Alice Morgan my assistant called out, she almost fainted when she saw Walter Davis sitting there in the garden. I told her to say nothing. A black stork dropped a package overnight and he was here when I arrived, he has had a breakfast, now I think he has the idea to sit in the garden and get pissed. I told Alice, we got to polish the church furniture we will use spray not real wax polish. The bishop is expecting people to come and rejoice at the return of Walter Davis in a special service at midday. The local catering company is going to make sandwiches and fancy cakes. I looked at Monty and tried not to laugh at her facial expression.

Our conversation switched to Berni Macky who Monty had not seen today. Taking more rubbish cut to the bin at the end or the garden was when Monty was slump in a head and will not be able to finish his beer, she did comment that the gate was unlocked. Somebody had gone out or somebody had come in. She rushed to tell the bishop that Walter Davis was dead.

The fat pig asked me "How do you know he is dead?"

"He may just be sleeping" She replied because he has got two great bloody holes in his head

Monty phoned the police the ambulance and she pushed back to see the bishop who told her to phone for help "He did ask where Berni Macky was" Monty rushed at to see the police and ambulance arrive.

It was then she went to inform the bishop who was laying on the floor, she found Dr. Rebecca from Forensic who started mouth to mouth with a plastic guard on the mouth. Seen the ambulance finally came in and took over Monty walked out into the kitchen and headed for the beer supply and it was then he mentioned that she caught the tail end of Berni Macky going upstairs. She went out to the garden found a quiet spot and phoned her husband Stephen and all he said was

"Good!!"

I have to think now, was somebody leave through the back gate Alice Morgan the cleaner had been in the church, until she heard the emergency services arrive. By the time she arrived at the bishop's breakfast room, Dr Rebecca was giving the bishop mouth to mouth. She did admit she turned to see Berni Macky coming down the stairs and asking what was going to. he just stood there speechless according to Alice Morgan, which as unusual for him and had a big mouth!!

At a meeting under a willow tree across the from the church. Chief Insp Abigial began to give us her update. I had to put my foot in and say that Monty did see Berni Macky go up the stairs when she was running between the bishop on the floor and the rear door gate. He did not arrive downstairs until the ambulance arrived acting chief Inspector did remind me that there was no CCTC around the church or of Bishop's gate due to the public pointing out fifteen years ago school children used the path what went past Bishop gate on their way to school. I had rewind everybody that only the Bishop and Berni Macky knew of the arrival of Walter Davis at a much earlier time that was expected.

"He was tired and went upstairs to bed Berni Macky told me, he even missed breakfast"

Chief Insp Abigial had to throw back at me. I had to remind her that he was seen creeping up the stairs by Monty while she waited for the emergency services. I asked my team did our Berni Macky shoot Walter Dais, then hide somewhere?

There was another door into the breakfast room on the far right that did leave out to the garden. I also mention that Walter Davis had heard words with the bishop during breakfast. In fact, Monty was asked to close the Kitchen door so she could not hear what being said at the time. Monty said Walter Davis eat his cooked breakfast and left the bishop still sitting and reading the newspaper. It was not until after seven thirty AM that Walter Davis was seen drinking a couple of beers in the rear garden. It was the last time he was seen alive. I had only one question to ask my team.

"So what time was he really shot?"

Dr. Rebecca did put an early forecast to the death of Walter Davis.

"In the time around seven thirty to eight o'clock"

Now I would say around seven forty-five, but I am no doctor because the team did arrive around eight AM. It was time to head back to the office now, we were only going around in circles nobody more than Chief Insp Abigial. I took a walk downstairs to see Dr. Rebecca to see if she had anymore insights into the death or Walter Davis.

I was surprised to learn that the Ex Priest had some cocaine, still stuck up his nose.

"So, he was as high as bloody Kite when like died" Dr. Rebecca told me with a cheeky smile. She next informs me about her various thoughts of the actual shooting.

"Of course, a thirty-eight with a silencer and first shot into the left eye, so he must have been looking at the shooter, and then the second shot was into the top of his head with somebody standing behind him. Now take a deep breath and think that there were even two killers. One shot him in the eye and the second killer in the head. After being handed the handgun."

I looked at Dr. Rebecca and asked her why she always had to make it so complicated. To me two shooters did make sense, the second shooter keeping an eye at for anybody else around we had gone over that garden with a toothpick and also inside Bishop's gate and found no weapon so far!!

I went upstairs to find Chief Inspector Abigial trims jumping around like a kangaroo waiting to see me. It was not the news I really wanted to hear.

"I call it spitting the dummy" sweet Abigial had been upstairs and I did imagine sitting on the knee of John Knight upstairs in the top dog Kennel. I did know that they had history between the bed sheets of the past years. She had gone over my head and got herself a job on the top floor. Where was that phone on my table I wanted to have another go to see if I could crack the glass on that window. Straight away I thought after fifteen to twenty years that John Knight himself could of mention this to me about sweet cock sucking Abigial was not exactly happy. That team had bent over backwards to make her welcome. Many had to bite their own tongues after listening to her opinion.

I told her to leave the file to this case of Walter Davis on her desk and simply F off quickly out of my sight. It only tool a minute for my office manager Rachel stood there in the office door and shouted out the word "Bitch" so everybody could hear her acting was not the word for acting Chief Insp Frank Turner, he was now my number two so my next move was to somebody to take up the little of acting Inspector of the drug unit to replace Frank Turner roll Sgt Gilbert Picking was the right hand to Frank and was really the only one qualified to take control after five years under the watchful eye of Frank Turner.

The day dragged on before I had to go home to confront Aunt Candy and her departure as an out of touch with reality of being the housekeeper and some kind of mother to my four boys. I have to ask myself was I thirsty or was its Aunt Candy making me drink almost all of my dozen beers during a lengthy conversation. In the end Aunt Candy was not going to move into the Catholic units and slowly became a nun. She still wanted her freedom. It was decided that Friday was going to be her last day. On Saturday it would be the Turf Club and on Sunday on a plane back down to her farm. Now the farm accounts were sky high and her brother was a new assistant one nineteen years old female, who is sleeping in Aunty Candy's bedroom well that is until she does arrive home on Sunday. So, I really had only three days to find a new housekeeper. I had better start looking when I walked upstairs to my bedroom and away from that plate of dried-up pasta sitting on the table in the kitchen being told to "Warm it up" in the old microwave was not on my agenda.

In the morning Aunt Candy had slept in and two of the boys had eaten my pasta for breakfast and gone to school before I declined to kick the other two boys out of the bed. I ran outside but their transport was already down the road' but the car turned around and came to pick them up.

I arrived at work and I asked if she knew anybody who could take over from Aunt Candy she had a cousin, two daughters, and a husband who left three years ago. Would not be able to live with my family, two teenage girls and my four teenage boys would be too much to cope with.

"Meals housework Monday to Friday name my price" I said

"One thousand a week" to Rebecca

"Um make it only eight hundred. I will secure the deal and I do imagine that she will start tomorrow, after meeting the boys tonight" replied Rebecca.

The other good news was that Bishop Cyrus Brent had sent a request to speak to me. He was sitting up in his bed all the old bloody crap flowed from his lips of how Walter Davis had been taken from us only hours of freedom after being locked away in solitude ten fifteen years. I was not going to get into a discussion about the solitude of Walter Davis because so many inmates had wanted to kill him in jail. I had the same thought that a large part of the community around Bishops gate had also wanted to kill him. I thought to myself "John the Que' did the bishop in what I would call "Waffle on about nothing" nothing really of interest. Although he did ask if I had actually caught the killer, if not what had I been doing. I told him that I had thought somebody may have let the killer into the garden of Bishop's gate. Once again if my memory of fifteen years ago the bishop did try and lead the conversation. I soon put a stop to that and mention that Walter Davis was found dead with some cocaine up his nose being told that Walter Davis had become an adult in tail, in fact to my surprise, Walter Davis did sniff a line of cocaine up his nose after he finished his breakfast on that fatal morning, of his death.

The bishop did not see worried about the Walter Davis drug habit, and I was surprised to hear from the very lips of the Bishop that "If I had not put Walter Davis for those trump up charges of sex abuse, he would not have gone to prison and he would still be alive today." He then pointed the finger at me.

My reply was given that Walter Davis would still be leading the choir and still be A. in world of abuse wit young chair boys and you would still be sitting in the dark corner taking home movies while masturbating under your robe!!

Now just maybe I should have not given that reply but at least I knew now that both the Bishop and I do understand that nothing in the past fifteen years has changed between us. On the way back to the office John Knight form his kennel had made a request to see me straight away I thought this must be showtime!!

First of all, and not what I had expected John Knight was pleased that I had stood up to the Bishop Cyrus Brent and protected the police values. Second on the agenda was my right-hand Abigial Trims.

"She did not fit in, you work in a fast-paced world" John Knight told me, that we should work much closer together and not change the rules behind each other's back.

Being told then that John Knight was himself sitting on the throne and h did have the final world of words that I will have to comply with. He then pointed to the door, now was this a hint about I you do not like it, there is the door, or was it simply it was time for John Knight be given another blow job by a female member of his staff. I would have put my money on a blow job. A man of his age was still a sex addict in my eyes, and just one day it may cost him his very own position. I had a call from Dr. Rebecca she had a ballistic report on the two bullets that were used to kill Walter Davis.

The gun was not found six years ago but was used to scare the living daylights out of people when none other than Berni Mackay had used it. He denied

That he used in a robbery "it was the other bloke!!" was the answer that Berni Mackay had given and eventually the witness did agree. Now just over six years later the same gun was used to kill Walter Davis.

Dr. Rebecca looked at me and simply said "Now who was living at Bishop's gate at the time of the death of Walter Davis?

She asked me and I had to reply

"Berni Mackay"

"Well go and get him Aaron, go and get him" Shouted three times at me when I left her forensic office.

It was then that after the issue of a warrant for Berni Mackay I had to learn that he had bolted from the pub that he had taken a room just let a wet rat up a drainpipe. Full alert and traffic control was given the job of finding him. He had driven off in the car that the pub owner would take. I sent Frank Turner to the pub "The good Angel" talking in riddles will take had to admit that he gave Berni Mackay the keys to his car for a country drive and the break from all the drama. I got

Rachel to run a check on this connection between Will Tate and Berni Mackay.

They are closer after he came out and moved into Bishop's gate. The job of personal Assistant to Bishop Cyrus Brent still left me wandering what was called a connection did Berni Mackay have with both men burning down the Stuart highway and heading south it was not long before the traffic patrol was on his tail after he refused to stop at a vehicle check that was nothing to do with him, just a normal check of vehicles heading south. With the lights blazing sirens Berni Mackay was caught and I did not believe that he was dressed up as priest. I was afraid this did not fool traffic control and within two hours he was sitting in an interview room at the watch house. When I walked into the room, I could tell that Berrni Mackay was not very pleased to see me. If I was a dog, you would sit it was having a snarl at me.

Berni was going to act in the world of silence bit I had just too many questions to ask him, he tried to tell me once he heard the police sirens arrive at Bishops gate, he knew that he had to get out of there on the finger would be pointed at him about the death of Walter Davis. I did want to know how he knew that Walter Davis was even dead since the report he first gave that he was_ by the ambulance and then the police sirens. I had to mention that I had witness to say that he was seen going back upstairs to his room when she was waiting for an ambulance for the bishop who had a suspect heart attack. He must have seen the bishop laying on the floor and so why didn't he stop to help in the situation.

"She was screaming out of control a mad woman, I just bolted for cover"

I only had one reply for Berni "How did you know that Walter Davis was dead?

A wimp answer was that he had no idea. It was time to blast the big guns at him.

'Now believe it or not and even myself find it hard to believe that Walter Davis was shot with the very same gun that was used in the robbery six years ago at "Blackstone hardware stone" which you paid the prize of six years in the jail and you so called friend in the crime of the century actually drove off into the sunset on a motor bike, you remember him, the one who fired two shots into the mall of the hardware store and left you standing to be overcome by the local shop keeper and two costumers".

You give me the name of your friend in crime and it may look like what I call "Good for you" at this stage.

"Listen I will not drop him in it now"!! He will end up in prison and six years'"

"A little more than six more like at least twelve years I replied to this very silly man who think he is going to just get a slap on the wrist for his joy ride today.

"Listen I did earn when I came down Frank my room, a female police officer did interview me, well she did believe me the bishop rushed to hospital, Walter Davis dead it was time to take control of the Bishop's Gate but instead you slowly took a step back and headed for the back door of the pub to see your old friend will take the landlord. I heard alarm bells ringing that will take only a local odd job man around the arena could be another missing person who was the partner in what I am now calling "The crime of the country."

I had to open the flood gates even more now to Berni Mackay and confess that I knew he nuts and bolts, he was in the store ten the so called drugs being sold from the rear of the shop twelve months later the wells family wo ran the hardware store were in facts busted for drugs worth over a million dollar worth of drugs were seized well you would of heard about that in jail Berni Mackay!!

I had left the room to venture back into the past to find the life and times or will take at the time hit alibi was at the Royal Oak pub and given by the ghost from my past ex Insp Alf Jackson my old work mate. The actual missing link to this batch robbery could have been Alf Jackson he would have known about the drug dealing at the Blackstone hard-ware shop. I went back into the interview room and mentioned the name of Alf Jackson to Berni Mackay and I could tell by the look on his face that I had hit the nail on the head. I also knew that will would also take a motorbike at the time. I also do remember that will take only drove his work van around his excuse was that somebody had stolen his motorbike, yet he did not report it even stolen according to our records.

I had to scare Berni Mackay a little now, I told him I had enough to connect him to the murder of Walter Davis, with that being in the same place at the same time he was active.

Now I was back in the world of Berni Mackay after a short break. Frank Turner had gone to ask if he would take to join us for afternoon tea, while I did ask Berni about the drug habit that Walter Davis had taken up in prison.

"He was asking where his fix was looking at me just after he got into the car" where is my fix my bloody cocaine? I told him I do not do drugs and would be bloody stupid in picking you up from prison with drugs in my car. All he got was that he could have a fix to code with him coming out of prison the bishop had promised him. I had to explain that there was a gift up in his desk in his room on arrival. He never even went to speak to the bishop till after he had his fix, Berni told me he had to admit now Berni did know the drugs were there this in my mind had open another can of worms. I had a call from Frank Turner about his search of the Walton's Pub. A certain Jane Kandle, the so-called Arena Manager for the brewery had decided to stick her nose in while sitting at the bar. Det Billie Mayford a fine-looking Lady from the first nation, does not know the color of her skin but being called a black bitch did elevate Det Billie to slap the handcuffs on Jane Kandle and have two Burly uniform officers place sweet mouth Jane in the back of a paddy police wagon. Will take did try and look innocent. It was not his beer brewery on site set the alarm bells ringing it was his own drug manufacturing plant in the room next door. The Walton's Pub was owned by the Walton Family now it was called the "Bishop's gate pub" until Walter Davis got caught. A public outcry and the pub changed hands and the Walton family took over. Years later will take ended up getting a job behind the bar in his spare time he got into Kate Walton knickers they married and after a yet they are living in different properties Kate back with her parents and walt at the pub.

Where he has been involved with Jane Kandle. Now the Walton Family had shown up ll in a flap trying to close their eyes to what walt had been up to, was a little hard to swallow for Frank Turner showing his police authority had the pub shut down. No matter what the upper-class Walton family said it was not enough to say "they had no idea or the on the side drug manufacturing business"

In the eyes of Frank Turner, they had simply taken over from the Blackstone hardware store that had now been turned into a Yuppie Kate and was doing great business. I really thought that I would never get home tonight. I want to clear things up with Aunt Candy, I gave a call to my name, Aunt Candy was shut up in her room and the boys had a voted and decided that Aunt Candy stick her past where the sun does not shine anymore and a BBQ was in order.

Detective Billie Mayford was still working. I have to admit that there was going to be some sought of promotion in the wind unknown to Frank Turner who did seem to be cracking the whip. A trip to the garden of Bishop gate and with two uniform officers. Det Billie decided to go in for a bit of gardening. With a long metal rod, she went around the garden, poking into the garden and the two uniform officers did the same.

"Give that lady a promotion" I screamed at when Det Billie phoned me on my private phone.

"I found it" she said

'Found what?" I replied

"That bloody gun it was buried two feet down in a flower bed that is used for flowers in the church, boss it is an its way to Dr. Rebecca in forensic I will catch you tomorrow, I have had a busy day replied Det Billie.

I called Frank Turner who himself looked like a sleeping dormouse I told to go home, then I told him and put an extra step in his bounce that Det Billie had found the gun that was used to shoot Walter

Davis. I had to go home myself. I missed my meeting with the future housekeepers. Aunt Candy refused to show her around the house. I agree with that decision. On the way to work I got a mouthful from this woman who told me that she was a supporter of Bishop Cyrus Brent so she will not be taking up the position. A bad start to the day and the next problem was Andrew Walter owner of the Pub.

A rattle of words with John Knight the police commissioner they even went to school together.

"Sorry Andy old mate but when my second in commons Aaron Brown has a bee in his bonnet about something it's like trying to take a cone away from a mad dog!!"

I was pleased that John Knight was still on my side. I had to take a sidestep then and head downstairs to see Dr. Rebecca who had worse news for me.

"Not one fingerprint on the gun and also there was only two bullets in the gun no fingerprints on the shells!!"

It was now time to start my long day of interviews. I passed detective Billi Mayford who told me she had been offered ten thousand dollars to drop the case against Jane Kandle. The area manager for the brewery racist rewards and personal threats could not stop detective Billi at any cost. She told the solicitor for Jane Kandle to stick it up her ass!! I did expect that action from Billi. Time to break the news to Berni Mackay about the gun being found I would not mention the part about no fingerprints. If Berni thought he was having a bad day by being locked up in a cell he had only just started.

"You found the gun where?" Berni asked

"Sorry cannot stay, at this time it is being examined for fingerprints" I replied

I took a deep breath before I continued.

"Oh, by the way your old mate will take got busted for having a meth lab at in the shed where they brew that selective house beer"

"So, I will be going to prison for a long time was that wife Kate Walton involved? Asked Berni.

Can I say Berni I am waiting to see who will throw who under the bus first? I had left the room for a phone call Inspector Ray Coore drug unit down in Adelaide had busted a drug ring that has a connection to the church in Darwin. I was asked if I was sitting down because Ray was about to open up and give names of the people of interest up in Darwin.

"Spit it out Ray" I said Well a Berni Mackay and Will Take and wait for it Bishop Cyrus Brent who has been fiddling his church form drug money through the hands of Berni Mackay his so-called financial adviser. If you let were not selling them, they were having them, and the transportation was done in boxes of bibles I have a priest down here who is driving the bus that he has also thrown about a dozen people in Darwin "underneath."

I do have a will take busted for drug manufacturing in the local pub in a cell and Berni Mackay I am at this very moment got him in an interview.

Stay in touch and I will update you with the outcome.

"O the Bishop is in a hospital bed under armed guard, handcuff to the bed at present;

I went back inside the interview room to speak to Berni Mackay.

"Now that was interesting, a connection to a drug ring down in Adelaide a priest in fact, well he has rolled over and thrown a few people under the bus, and guest what? He has named you and Will Take and God forbid the bishop himself Cyrus Brent who has been living off the proceeds of drug selling to take care of the daily expenses of the so-called upkeep or the church.

I could feel that I had in fact "broken the camel's back" now with that speech.

There was silence and still, much to my surprise Berni Mackay did not want a solicitor.

"It does not matter much now; I will expect to get the fifteen to twenty years in prison"

Bet I am not going down alone, can I say the missing link to that robbery six years or so ago will take. I would also like to confess to the term of money laundering drug money through the church perks with the full knowledge of Bishop Cyrus Brent who even suggested. He was into it a long time before I arrived on the scene. I did not expect Berni Mackay to roll over so easily. All I wanted to know was he the one who shot Walter Davis. I did not expect a yes but a long explanation about how he had no idea that gun was still around he did think that will take had dump the gun years ago, after their botch robbery, I asked Berni will he sign a statement to what he had confessed to? He agreed so I got detective Angus Cantine to do the paperwork.

I knew I had his confession on tape but I did want everything tied down. My next part of the call was to see Kate Walton wife of Will Take. I knew that lived separate lines now although still married. Kate went back home with mommy and daddy while Will Take lived a bachelor life at the pub. The name of Jane Kandle area manager of the brewery was three months pregnant. Will Take was the proud father it was funny the timeline Andrew Walton was going to sack Will Take at the pub in two days and take on the brewery himself. I did not ask about the "Meth Lab." We had no idea he had a fing meth lab in that back shed. I had to remind Kate that her name her father's name is above the door on entry to the pub. It was their license, plus just a small bonus "that they are responsible for everything that does go on under that roof. I do hope for not only her sake but her father's sake that Will Take does agree to say that the Waltons had no knowledge of the meth lab. I went on to say that Kate and her father might have to prove that they had no knowledge to a judge on they will also face jail time.

Yes, there was tears now and Kate Walton was in a meltdown. I had to send for the nurse who is active in the police complex. She did look at me like I was a bully boy. In some ways I have to say she was right but, in the end, I was only doing my job. Bail was granted for Andrew and Kate Walton and deep down I did not think they were mixed up in this "meth lab" business. Mind you, I was still in shock about bishop Cyrus Brent and his use of drug money to prop up his church.

Will Take was my next victim but first a double egg and bacon roll, loss of church and a treble shot of a coffee thick shake. I thought that was stomach would be at war with itself for the rest of the day until I went and sat on the toilet. Will Take had an answer for everything but he did shoot down once I mention the gun that was used in the robbery and now was used to shoot Walter Davis. I was given the old reminder that I had to let him go because of lack of evidence in the so-called robbery of the Blackstone. store. I had to admit but once I said that 'times change" Berni Mackay has thrown you under the bus for the robbery, so add those years to the so-called meth lab it could be around thirty years, just think when you come at you will be eligible ten-year-old age pension!!

Then being told that his best pal Berni Mackay was mixed up in the "meth lab" Berni was head of sales belong with Jane Kandle who is going to have my baby and I had a plan in two months to move on from the Waltons pub with Jane and start a new life over in Queensland. I did think that sometimes your plans do not exactly work out. I wanted to know if the Walton family had any idea about the "meth lab." No bloody idea and on top of that I was milking the tiles Kate Walton though she knew everything but she had no idea how to handle money. She herself started to fiddle with the till to steal money from her parents. I caught her but agreed not to say anything if she married me, she had no choice. This was how I kept my silence and I also took the cream off of the top of the bottle of money. She could not even open up to her father.

A few months ago, she came to work early and found me in bed with Jane Kandle. It was then she moved out. I did expect Andrew Walton to sack me, instead everything just went on as it was. Jane sold drug to other landlords and everybody was happy. Berni Mackay was involved in the church and I knew he would not answer any question I did want to know will take was open with his answers so I changed the subjects. I wanted to know about guns. I was surprised that he had in fact given it to bishop Cyrus Brent and when I told will about the gun being found he immediately told me he thought that the bishop himself had shot Walter Davis. This was also train of thought that was going on in my mind ever since Walter Davis had been shot.

Much to all the shooting by bishop Cyrus Brent I had him taken to the underground garage of the watch house.

"I am being treated by an animal keeper I am not an animal I am a bishop of the catholic church of Darwin" I just told the bishop to sit down and shut up.

I wanted to let him know just in case he had not heard we had found the gun that was used to shoot Walter Davis. His face had a color change. I had to remind him that it was the same gun that will take had given him six years ago for safe keeping. I knew he was going to say I do not know any Will Take. He worked at the pub. I had to hold myself back now and slowly reveal all that I had on the bishop.

Next up on my mind was my conversation with the so-called drug unit down south led by Insp Ray Cooke. A local priest had thrown himself under the bus after driving the bus himself and had named people like Berni Mackay, will take and even bishop Cyrus Brent. All the bishop did was laugh at me until I did mention that Berni Mackay and Will Take had made a confession. Both had pointed the finger at the bishop himself. I could see that I was jumping up and down in a raw nerve now inside the bishop. So, I put more pressure on him about the gun. I was surprised that he had the gun behind a wooden panel in a bookcase. When Walter Davis arrived back at bishop's gate, he was a different man he was now a bloody drug addict

Berni Mackay came to tell me even before I had seen him.

"He will bring us all down, he will ruin everything, he must be stop. Berni told me, while eating his breakfast he told me of his plans now he is free.

I simply told him "Bishop's gate was his home now, and he will not be wondering about outside these four walls. Walter complained that it was just a much larger prison cell, expect he had a few more dreams of a garden. This was the state of play and the watcher said he would set us his own ground rules and would not abide by mine. Walter was a little high on cocaine and was already drinking beer in the garden. I went outside to reason with him and he simply told me to F off!!

I told him he cannot tell the bishop to simply F off. Then he did again. I pulled at the gun and shot him in the eyes, I then shot him in the top of his head. I found a garden spade dug a huge hole and buried the gun. I made my way back to the breakfast room and simple reached out for the table and ended up on the floor. The next thing same woman was going me mouth to mouth and then I was in an ambulance. I wanted to confess about shooting Walter just in case I died on the way to hospital but I did not have the courage.

I read the bishop his rights and charged him with murder. Living off the profits of illegal drugs. That was enough to put him away for life. It was only twelve days later the bishop had another heart attack and this time there was nobody to save him.

CHAPTER 3

PRIDE

At last, it was time to go home, dare I say I had bolded my head and be humble to my neighbor when she bought the boys home from swimming. I looked in the front seat to see identical twins even dressed the same. Slow in my words and with a look of desperation, I mention the word "Need" in a housekeeper, meals four days a week for dinner. A bit of housework Monday and Friday and some care at weekends if I have to work. I still had their attention and the words of "Five hundred a week cash."

I was thinking more like seven hundred "we will take it, do you won't us to start tonight?" said Tilda.

"No, but a walk around and a start tomorrow morning. I explain the boys make their own breakfast, make their own sandwiches except Friday when fish and chips in on the menu at school lunch. Very tidy house trained, I pointed to the dirty washing. A spring clean twice a week is normally enough I said. I was then told that tomorrow they will give the house a deep clean. They pointed to a garden cottage "not included" I told them. They did seem happy. I had to mention that the boys do like to eat alone so their three girls are a not included at mealtimes at our home. I was told that my four boys will be a no no at their request I did hope that we understood each other. Ok it was quarter to eight pick up in the morning then the twins will enter my house. "Clean and ship shape fit for humans. I have to say it was a weight off of one shoulder and to be placed on the other. The boys did seem happy they knew Aunt Candy had not been happy since she got shot a couple of months ago after the twins left, the boys had a seafood pasta that Aunt Candy had made for them.

Followed by bowls of ice cream each boy had a different topping. Homework and the a few games of pool. I sat alone eating my seafood pasta, when like a dark shadow at step Aunt Candy "had to beg had to bow to their demands Aaron. You all will miss me when I go back down south to the farm. Some lame excuse about going to the races at the Turf Club and staying with a friend overnight, I was afraid to ask if it was a toy boy, plane on Sunday morning. In some ways I will miss her but now it is a new start for the family, if the boys are happy then so will I be. Aunt Candy went to bed and I was not far behind her. First part of call at work was to see John Knight who was going away for a few days Aaron you will be running this bloody circus stand your ground matey, no bloody nonsense

"Not a word of where he was going or even if he was going with somebody else. If he was, I did imagine it would be a married woman.

"Don't worry about my paperwork I will fix that um when I return," with that he just pushed past me and headed for the lift. I had no time to explain anything about "Bishop's gate and who we had placed under arrest. So, I went to my assistant police commissioner office and sat down. Signed a few files. When I met by Carol my new office manager up here. The last one thought the pressure was a little too much for her working with me. I just sat there and drank a lukewarm coffee eat six chocolate biscuits which I did treat as my breakfast and then went downstairs to my office "active commander of detectives"

A double bacon and egg sandwich with lots of chilly and a treble coffee thick shake could fit in, yes I could. A quick staff meeting a pat on the head to all my team.

Everything did seem to go so well until this cat walk model did a parade down the office and simply said "I am Belinda janes an Inspector and I am going to be the assistant to the police commissioner, after I have had a good work at down here in the detective unit John Knight knew of this and did not mention one word to me about this female. Who then let loose that the police minister Carol Kelly was Auntie and she is actually staying with her you can imagine that this did send a chill right across my team. Rachel Todd my office manager to point to a desk where Belinda can take up her position.

"Shall we have it into this office" I mean I will be the assistant to Aaron" I had to stop her in her tracks. I am either sir or boss to you, young lady I replied.

Rachel told her that I do not share my office with anybody. Being told that John Knight told me it will be just fine and I will be working very closely with active commissioner Aaron brown. I can imagine old John Knight giving her that bullshit.

I just finished my cold bacon and egg sandwich and I was told in a flat in Parap there are four bodies. When I arrived, I spoke to Dr. Rebecca who told me that

"Four dead queens are not a royal flush!! Four young men all dressed up with somewhere to go, where all shot several times while still in their drag outfits Insp Belinda Jones, most probably some straight person who had a hate for drag queens!! Dr Rebecca asked who this big mouth on my team was giving her opinion. I had to do the introduction to Dr. Rebecca who just continued with what she thought had happened Insp. Insp Belinda did feel that her presence was not needed now so she stormed off in a tantrum. I had forgot about police officers throwing tantrums. I had to admit it did make her look like a complete idiot, Chief Inspector Frank Turner, had found at that the four dead drug queens had been to the Turf Club races. It was dragging queen race day. Something that did trigger my memory that Aunt Candy had found a new person in her life a drag queen to stay overnight with. I had a report that a Fitz Gaff a taxi driven he had brought the four young men home around ten o'clock last night from the "Sparkling room" a local gay club in town. It was time to take a trip into town to see if anybody was still active at the "Sparkling Room." During my drive there Amy my driver, did inform me. While I was talking to my team and Dr. Rebecca Insp Belinda did ask her about her sexuality to quote Amy "I am a raving lesbian one woman is not enough for me I live with two in "manage a trio" situation. I love it!!

I was taken back; I really have no interest in the sexuality of any members of my team I have promoted a free and easy attitude between all of them members. I do say I was taken back when Rachel Todd did tell me seven years ago that she was living with a woman and she just had our baby and now Rachel is a proud mother of two. I have been asked by Rachel if I would father a third child but I have put that on hold for now. Poor Amy, but I did have to laugh and say, "nice one Amy tell her to simply F off if she does mention it again, please" two limp handshakes from a Dexter Riley and Lionel Milo owners of "The sparkling Room." Hold them the sad news a Leroy Cadone, Will Oslo, a Jay Milton and John sherry. Poor Dexter Riley broke down I tears and all of his makeup did decide to take a water fall down his face all for longtime friends, all lived together but all led straight lives at work.

They all had jobs working for Tello they were not call girls but call boys Lionel Milo told me.

It was time to move back into my real world I took a visit to Dr. Rebecca to see if she could give me an update of the death of four victims.

"Shot with a twenty-two bullet in the mouth and a thirty-eight in the chest. At point blank range and I would say only two guns but could be two killers. The thirty-eight first which would f killed them then the twenty-two bullet into the back of their throat, she did say it was a 'Mate killing' why kill them twice was like a message I thought to the drag queens of Darwin on was it simply a falling at of the drag queen.

Moe forensic would follow later I was told. It was two hours later that I got a call from Dr. Rebecca that they had found the fingerprints of Lionel Milo. In a quiet room with o lad background dance music, it was a different atmosphere for Lionel Milo to talk to me. Sitting beside him was somebody I once knew as solicitor Charlie look now and I found this hard to swallow that it was solicitor Charmaine Looke. I knew Charlie when he was bald, he was now wearing a lady's wig that was sitting exactly right on his head. It took Insp Belinda to inform him that he must have been in a wind tunnel on his way to this meeting at the a flat where Linal Milo lived with Dexter Riley of the top floor of the building that did house the 'Sparkling Room." There was jewelry and other items and even a wallet that belong to a Jay Milton. I did remind Lionel Milo that we already had his finger prints from his teenage years on he was a "tea leaf" a bloody thief. I could tell that even a poor Charmine had no idea of his post. Giving lots of excuses and trying to tell me the bag was dumped in the club sometime last night. I did try to find out why he did not try and contact the owners and get them together with their property. It was like talking to a flushing toilet it would not stop Dexter Riley who did own "The Sparkling Room' and the license had shown up. He gave the same story of how they found it under a table in their club.

Later that day they were going around to return this stolen bag of cheap drag queen jewelry. I had to toss a coin and heads it was trying to get an explanation about the fingerprints, I found out that Lionel Milo had been there to the flat looking through the clothes of the four dead victims and trying to find something to wear in their space of a few minutes I almost believed him, our four dead victims, had a side line after work they would make outfits for drag queens and one of them Will Oslo used to make oversized jewelry for drag queens Will Oslo did train in a jewelry shop until he met Leroy Cadon and became a call boy for Telco. I just wish that Lionel Milo would at least come clean. Within the hour Charmine Cooke the transsexual solicitor had arrived with some CCTV from within The Sparkling Room" we had at last footage of our four victims. They only stayed for one drink and caught a cab with the same driver Fits Gaff and went home. Two hours later I spotted the bag with the jewelry and personal items of the four victims. It was strange that the bag was placed under the table by two more people of interest.

We were told that it was henry the first and henry the second. They ran a weekend retreat on a farm at Humpty Doo. A place where all your dreams can come true. I heard enough details that made my mind boggle. I was glad that I still live in what I call a normal world the Henry's came here looking for costumers. They tend to be jealous of the business at the "Sparkling Room." Within half an hour with two young drag queens the Henry's headed off without their little bag under the table. At closure you can see Lionel Milo pick up the bag and take it upstairs. A comment about him moving deep inside he discovered that the bag did belong to the four friends who had arrived earlier. Nothing else was done about the bag, I did ask Lionel Milo didn't he find it funny that the bag that was not brought in by the four victims should be brought in by Henry the first. I did notice that both Henry's wear white gloves it was their trademark. At the back of him mind the two Henry's had stop off in park. Did the Robbery shot the four victims and in a not shell ended up in the "Sparkling Room." This so-called sex escape was at "Marris Creek Farm a turn off near Humpty Doo. I got a team together, plus some tactical support in case there is a shootout in the mean while I left Lionel Milo in a cell until he had made some progress with the two Henry's.

It was exactly what I thought it would be in my wildest sexual dreams. Talk about being buck naked, everybody was except the police on duty. Caught out in some sexual positions with a lot of shouting going on, demands to see a warrant. I told Henry the first "Go with this officer and put some clothes on and I will show you the warrant. I few minutes later Henry the first and the second were placed in handcuffs and the other eight men were told to go home we will not be laying any charges that involved their sexual activity. Chippy the drug dog was kept busy. I did say I did not care about their sexual activities but drugs that was what I call another matter. All eight men had some illegal drug on them. I always try not to laugh when the owner of a property does try to tell me that they had no idea their so-called costumers were all holding illegal drugs on their person.

Poor old henry the first tried to tell me that my Police Officers had planted the drugs in their private sex nest. I would hate to think when Henry's sex nest smelt fresh air. Two large bongs one each at the side of the bed, plus a nice little pink box with some assorted pills that you could make you go up or down whatever took your fancy at the time.

I was sure the forensic team will have fun trying to work at what colored pill did what the two Henry's were transported in separate cars back to the watch house, while the eight all over sex men were transported in a prisoner wagon and none were allowed to even "Fart" without permission.

After a while almost two hours I sat down with henry the first, his solicitor, Mary Wilton and acting SGT Billy Mayford as my side kick. Chief inspector Frank Turner with Insp Belinda Jones took on the spaced out eigh when each of them finally came down to earth to discuss their so-called drug habit in relation to free for all sex.

I had the usual banter Mary Wilton who I do remember used to a pleasant woman. Slowly and now, she had become a right pain in the ass in fact a real battle axe. I had to break the ice and simply mention the four victims in Parap shot dead and the bag of jewelry. Even after watching the film show, I had of inside the "Sparkling Room good old Henry 1st, did comment that they found it on the stairs to the night club on their way in. we had no proof that they had stolen it because they were wearing gloves. I had to remind henry the first in his first line of defense that "I never mention that the jewelry had been stolen. It was time to throw in another gem at Henry the first. I had some CCTV from Mitchell Street where he had parked his car that night with him, holding the same grey bag when he left the car. This must have been around one hour after the four victims had died. Henry the first had little to say to this footage in fact he did ask for a break to speak to his solicitor alone leave him a wish and told him I will see him at a later time.

I walked back to my office; I noticed that chief Insp Frank Turner had already gone home and so had Insp Belinda Jones. I have been on duty for twenty-three hours now. So had acting SGT Billi Mayford. I found Amy Fuller sleeping at her desk. I need to come back to walk just for a short while to make sure everything is "Ship Shape" I arrived home to sit to catch the four boys about to head off to school. I did give them an update on a new house keeper, not one but two ladies it was the twins. I could tell that this somewhere had not gone down well Aunt Candy was still getting packed and ready to leave a day earlier than we agreed in her words "No need to hang around for anything"

A hug to each of the boys and they were off to school one twin sofa drove the kids to school while the other twin tilde did a kitchen tidy up. I made myself a drink and turned to talk to Aunt Candy when she had already closed the front door and was sitting in her taxi. I did feel sad in some ways, but I must adapt to change.

I closed my bedroom door and turned off my work phone and personal phone and enjoyed six hours of deep sleep. I came downstairs to find the twins had prepared the boys dinner that curry and rice with salad. I had a sample myself I had to admit it was tasty. I switched on my phone to find six messages from the Police Minister herself, asking where I was. I would say that Carol Kelly was not early what I would say an understanding person.

"Who was running the show' she asked. Then 17 verbal attacks because like the staff on the top floor had no idea where John Knight the part time Police Commissioner was at this very moment of time that I did laugh at when Carol Kelly Laid down that reference about six times. It was no way to run modern police in this world today. When I mention that I had worked twenty tree hours shift Suddenly the tide had turned, but still I had no idea where John Knight I had to bite my tongue when I wanted to say Johnny Boy had been like it all his life since I had known him.

I was going to come into work, to make sure the "Circus" is running alright not too many police doing their own thing and taking advantage of this situation. I did say there was a commander in charge twenty-four hours a day who was overseeing each department. She had no idea what reality went on in the mechanics of the Police Force. A mention that her niece looks exhausted after working a fifteen-hour shift on her first day at work. I had to mention that we do not pay overtime, which did not go down very well, been told that no police officer should be working more than ten hours a day, I had to admit did put a smile on my face when I heard those words. The reason that we work extra hours is because we do not have the staff numbers to cover sniffs. I think I made my point when she slammed the phone down on me. I went back to finish my now cold curry and rice and Amy my driver had shown up. I gave her a quick homelife update only because she is a big sister to the boys.

Back at work and being asked by the solicitor Mary Wilton and also Henry the first where had I been I told them I had been catching up on my beauty sleep after a twenty-four-hour shift, a twist of the truth soon shut them both up. I wanted now to know where all the drugs came from that they re-sell to the people who show up for a very liberated time at their weekend retreat a talk of some sought of deal for him and no mention about Henry the second. I was about to find out why. Their drug supplier was our very own police officer. Herbert (Herbie) Crayston uncle to Henry the second. I knew a Herbie Crayston who worked on the top floor what you might call a fixer for John Knight his rank was chief superintendent. I was to be honest trying to find this hard to swallow. Herbie our nickname for him, I worked with ten years ago with John Knight till he crept up stairs and learnt how to do a real job of back stabbing. I did ask Henry the first to repeat himself. I got the full life story about Herbie he even fronted the farmhouse on weekend retreat.

Henry the first real name was Jason Stirling I already knew this but I enjoyed playing along with henry the first, it made him feel easy and in fact I was his friend he had no idea how my mind worked. Henry the second who I am going to interview next real name was albert(al) Crayston. His uncle was the drugs. It was time to move on Henry the second now, with the current information I should wrap this up and be heading home soon. Everything that henry the first had said about henry the second and his uncle Herbie was true. For some unknown reason Henry, the second did think our conversation would be over, until I started to produce photographs of the grey bag, a mention of the jewelry and CCTV of inside "the sparkling room" poor Henry the second had come to realize that Henry the first "had open his big mouth," were the words Henry the second kept repeating. When I mention the four dead victims for same reason henry the second.

Did think that his partner, best friend and lover had pointed the finger at the four victims being killed by him. I had not mention any of this to Henry the second who did confess that the four victims were all shot by Henry the first. For some unknown reason they had thought there was a lot of money at the flat in Parap the brothers followed watch the four victims win after win with their betting. All money was given to Dexter Riley and Lionel Milo for safe keeping. Until the banks open on Monday a total of seventy thousand had been held by these so called four idiots would show up "The sparkling room" and people would be hurt. First Leroy Capon was asked, when he refused Henry the first just shot him, while I kept a gun on the other three. Will Oslo Jay Milton and John Sharm now all crying like little boys and telling Henry the first he did not have to do this terrible trying of shooting them one by one. I did then ask about the noise of the gun. Both guns had silencers on. The four laid dead then Henry the first told Henry the second to shoot each body in the mouth. I knew then that I would be just as guilty as Henry the first if he didn't, he was worried that henry the first would clear all debts in their life leaving the guns at "The Sparkling Room" that would point the finger at the owners Dexter Riley and Lionel Milo, so eventually after their trial they will the help of Uncle Herbie purchase the night club. It was in my mind a farfetched story then again it did make a lot of sense, it was slowly placing the pieces of this puzzle together. All I had to do know was to go back how henry the second had turned h cards on him. It did not matter really both of the Henry's rare just as guilty in the robbery and murder. The selling of drugs to the costumers at the farm in what I call "The icing on the cake now"

All locked up like a budgie in a small cage and singing his head off with words you would not expect from superintendent Herbert (Herbie) Craystine. He made a special request to talk to me mainly because I was acting top dog and his best make John Knight the very part time police commissioner had decided to do the vanishing act I had to inform acting set Billi Mayford that a lot of what you hear from "Herbie" is not to ever be repented. In the interview room, "I was trust up like a bloody Christmas turkey Aaron old mate by that young bread snapper. Chief Insp Frankie Turner, who fing promoted that gay prick?

"I did Herbie, he is a fine officer, and very good at his job" I replied

"Now listen being an old pal from the old days when Johnny, yourself and little old me used to run around banging up criminals left right and center. Some I know we fixed up just to get them off the street a little while then they would have been lifted by us. Now sign that bloody piece of paper and I will be off" Herbie told me.

I told him that. Then days are over Herbie," listen that boy I knew he looked underage in my bed sheets I paid him well he said he was eighteen and very desirable blonde hair young man"

"Anyway, he is the least of your problems now, your farmhouse was being used for wild sex parties and you were the one who was the supplier for drugs I have been told after that long lecture I could see that Herbie did look confused. Till was the end of the road for him now.

"Listen Aaron, she left me, sold that bloody house down by the marine and gone to live in some penthouse flat on the gold coast with her snotty nose sister!! So, you kept the farm and are living in a one-bedroom flat in Stuart Park now, a bit of a come down Herbie.

"Listen you can make all of this go away, if Johnny Knight he would was sitting in that chair, I know that he would have known of this listen if I go down, I will take him with me is that understood, I have enough to bury him"

"All I want is the names of the people you got the drugs from. I asked him and I did not expect to hear the words that came out of his mouth.

"Listen you F my supply from that bloody prick at the church that Berni Mackay the so-called financial adviser to that bloody Bishop and also down the road at that pub that Waltons place and that grubby little man will take. You cut off my supply chain Aaron!! I did not have much to say to Herbie expect enjoy the rest of your life in prison.

"You did not ask me if I wanted a solicitor"

"Sorry sir but I did ask you before the boss arrived act SGT Billie Mayford.

"Who is going to believe some black bitch up against a person with my years in the police force and I have risen like the cream on a bottle of milk" now shouting Herbie at me.

"I think the cream and the milk have now gone a little sour!! I replied and left.

I was running the show again the next day. My home was what you might say "spick and span" to the standard that my ex-wife Kate used to have out home always I arrived at work and headed up to the top floor. I had a few files to check over and then I would be back downstairs to my other real job that was active commander of detectives. Rachel Todd had already found out that I was on my way back to normal chilly egg sandwich no bacon today, the other day it was a little tough. Rachel made the tour of the bacon was just like me, being compared to an over cooked piece of bacon did not exactly make me feel like I was on top of the world. Yet I was everybody had worked hard today, with the results of the files on my desk all being updated Insp Beatrice Jones had settled in working with Frank Turner, Rachel my office manager, wanted a quite word in my ear. Her partner wanted a third child and I was the best stud in town to perform in this breeding programmed.

I felt I was a just a sex machine standing by to release my male juices at any call. I had a knock back Rachel yet again. I was in fact thinking about my four boys, what if fifteen to twenty years' time, and this offspring shows up in our life, telling them that he was their long-lost brother. All my honesty and credibility will be simply flushed down the toilet. I had to say "No" once again. You can imagine that I was not flavor of the month in the world of Rachel and her partner. I never ever said "yes" all I said was that I will think about it in the future. I had to explain this to Rebecca who did mumble the word of "wanker" when she left the office. I had request from Herbie, he had a Solicitor. Same old chook from the top end or down. Caroline Kelly, who I would not call an old chook. She had worn well in age. We got all the usual the introductions and an apology to act Billi Mayford from Herbie. The talk of a deal was in the air, but only in Herbies world.

I was told if I received some information would be able to crack a deal with the prosecutor and finally the judge.

I told Herbie it would have to be good, very good because you could end up fifteen years in jail, with the drugs and sex crime with a minor. I could see that Herbie was doing the old waving of hands, in other words, I did imagine that the young man took advantage of Herbie and lied about his age. This was put to me and I knew that Caroline Kelly must have got somebody to speak to a Kenny Turner who may change his statement. Really, I did not want to hear this and I could tell on the face of my side kick act SGT Billi she also did not have her marry face on. I wanted to know what did Herbie have an offer? A out of town drug production on a mango farm way past Humpty Doo. It was run by a Ryan Moore and a Allie Fuller. Both has previously I was to learn when I want back upstairs.

I told frank turner we are about to pay another drug production unit at on Filton mango farm, a Ryan Moore once a socialite model and his partner Allie Fuller, she herself has been off our radar for a while now. It was a good twenty minutes' drive down a dirt track at the back of the farm just off the highway to Kakadu. I got Insp Blake Kirby who would lead the charge with his top team of very experiences drug raiders was my term for these guys. I could see that Frank Turner has had his nose put out of joint by not being in charge today. A report of a lot of firearms so I did not want any of my team hurt I any way. Drones would be used, I was told that workers at the mango farm would tip off the drug operation this was nothing that I could do about that extra uniform would be needed, plus every detective from every unit would be up for what I called a fire fight.

The mango farm was easy only a dozen people working. The drone had been released and we were now looking at a farmhouse and a large shed at the back of the farmhouse. We would have some officers on trial bikes just in case anybody made a bolt for the open ground and into the woodland, beyond. We had cloud nine a bullet proof machine and followed by cloud ten on the other side of the property rifle fire was bouncing off these two bullet proof machines. I was still waiting back watching it all through the three drones up in the air. There did seem at least six people inside the building cloud nine had gone around the back of the shed and there was nobody shooting at the machine. I could hear Insp Blake Kirby giving the order for a demolition of one wall of the shed.

This was like a Hollywood movie, the driver of cloud nine just drove the vehicle right into the shed and then reversed automatic gun fire from cloud nine team four suspects were down, no causalities on our side were the message and so I decided to move forwards with my team behind cloud ten. There was automatic fire from the main house now and I could tell we had the upper hand. Somebody tried to escape on a trial bike a police sniper took him down with two shots. More fire from two automatic weapons was holding back anybody who tried to get near the house. It was solid brick so only the windows were where the team of Insp Blake had to fire at. The return of fire from the house slowly came to an end until the siege was over. Inside, three other drug workers all had been shot in the back trying to flee.

Looking like she had seen better days was a wonder allie Fuller across the room was Ryan Moore who had been hit four times but was also still alive. It was a silly mistake made by the first police officers that did enter that room because allie had a handgun and shot Ryan Moore twice in the head. She threw her gun down.

"He betrayed us and shot three of our friends in the back they wanted to surrender, if they did Ryan said "He would shoot them and Ryan was always a man of his word.

"Allie spoke in a broken voice with tears running down the side of her face. She looked at me and said, "Not you again, it must be a good ten years since we last met; where is what was his name Alf Jackson?" He has moved on to a much better place now I told Allie, who then took her last breath.

It did seem to be an endless day at work but I did manage to get home and have dinner with my boys, a seafood and potato pie and salad, the meals were done in individuals bowls there was more than enough. The boys almost licked their bowls clean, ice cream for everybody except me but I was thrown down a challenge at a game of pool. I did let all four boys beat me once again. It was the first time in months we felt like a family once again. I must try to spend more time with them, they all are growing up so fast, these days. I noticed one thing that their vocabulary had what I call street level words had been added. I did notice the boys had learnt not only to wash their dishes but also to place them in the dishwasher. At breakfast, the first I have had with them in weeks. I did notice that the kitchen was left clean and tidy. The Twins Tilde and Sofia mad already made a influence on their lives, which made the very pleased.

On the way to work with my driver Amy I got the call from our head clown to meet him in his circus ring on the top floor. John Knight was stuffing his face with an extra thick bacon and egg sandwich. I found that John Knight police commissioner had learnt at last to do was to multitask. He could talk, eat his breakfast drink his paint stripper tea and hold a conversation with me all at the same time. I could see that he had already taken a look into the files I sent to him.

"All the old bishop, drug lord and a bloody murder now that was a shock, Aaron me old mate and my golf partner Andrew Walton, doing a bit of drug production beside his home brew beer operation at the pub" He had to take his breath at last.

"So, you solved the shooter at that black stone handyman store, he came the gun to the bloody bishop, I never did like that will take, I did remember when I went to the wedding of Kate. I thought he was a bloody low life and he must have a huge cock to interest Kate!!"

How the mind of John Knight worked had always left me gasping for air and thinking how ever he came to that conclusion. The best he left for last his old mate Herbie. Poor old John Knight found it hard to believe that superintendent Herbie Craystine, Herbie to us and at one time we all worked close together.

"Drug pusher liked to that bloody Bishop and to the Walton's pub, he was doing right under my nose, I expected he did plot deals up here on the top floor instead of doing his police duties, and on top of all that sex with a underage school boy, caught butt naked between his bed sheets I would of love to be a fly on the wall when you kicked down the door, anyway I never liked the gay prick and now being caught out as a pedophile will not help his legacy"

"Did he want to do a deal, to let it go all always?"

I just nodded at John. I knew he wanted to say more but I jumped in to tell him that I got a lot on today. He did not mention or hint exactly where he had been for the past four days, anyway I thought today is Friday and he will have the weekend off. A brief mention of lunch with Carol Kelly the police minister id put the hairs up on my neck.

I headed downstairs to give my team another praise for their hard effort over the past couple of weeks. In the midst of the morning, I had my coffee manager Rachel come with her tail between her legs and an apology from a breeding partner for her wife. They said they had found somebody else. She did not mention his name and it was better that I did not know so I could not be involved in it anyway. I was very happy with that thought.

CHAPTER 4

"A FAMILY RIFT"

I was in my own comfort zone. Deep in sleep and my imagination was just running wild in this dream. I was in the wild west a sheriff in what they call a one-horse town. I used to be the deputy but I took over from sheriff John Knight who gave up work and purchased the local saloon. Where he got the money from now that is another dream. The local bank had been robbed by two strangers after two days in fact both found with a hole in the back of the head the money could not be found, strange event in the wild west John Knight went off on the stagecoach to Dodge city and returned with exactly the same amount of money that was stolen from the bank. He pinned the sheriff badge on me and said, "Just do ya best!!" Dr. Rebecca Mitchell who was the male version of Dr. Rebecca Mitchell except he was not only the doctor but all so the undertaker. In always locked twice at red, he had what he called a moustache under his nose, to me and most people it did look like two dead caterpillars. We road at to the waterhole to pick up the two bodies, why John Knight could not of brought the two bodies back into town I had no idea, which would be for another dream. My deputy was a first nation woman they call Billie a poor choice for a deputy, a woman and a bloody redskin. I heard a mobile phone ringing in my ear, this was crazy, they did not have mobile phones in the wild west,

I open one eye to find my personal phone with a life of its own. My police phone, I had switched off.

"Boss I'm outside. I know its early, we got three bodies down at the garages at Cullen Bay"

I did surface, talk about trying to put one foot in front of the other, I even fell down the stairs and I had not been drinking any beer.

"I got a coffee for ya boss and an egg and bacon breakfast roll from Maccas. I will just have the coffee thank you Amy." Boss I have eaten two rolls already this morning waiting for you" we set off, I looked at her with a roll in one hand a coffee in the other and Amy driving at a high speed.

"I hope you realize what you are doing is highly illegal Amy!!"

"It's ok boss we are police we are allowed to bend the rules in an emergency, and this is an emergency boss" We pulled up at the crime scene. Dr Rebecca Mitchell with no caterpillar under her nose was ready to give me her version of events. I had to pinch myself again trying to see if Dr. Rebecca had even a moustache.

"Anyway, two dead over there, both teenagers and armed did not have time to defend themselves both shot in the chest, over there the person who I believe was the shooter. He died trying to run and was hit by a doctor on a motor coming home from the hospital.

He simply flipped in the air, landed on his head broke his neck and was dead. He was believing it or not one leather bag full of money and the other bag full of cocaine. O I did not stick my finger in it to taste it, just like in Hollywood movies, I used a sample and my special little bag that turned the powder into a dark colored blur. Almost pure I would say Aaron!! Thank you, Dr. Rebecca, I will check in with my team who are very active led by the Chief Inspector Frank Turner who seem to love the sound of his own voice. I mention all cctv from the far tower blocks, interview anybody who was around at the time and I do want the money and drugs taken to the cock up in the watch house maybe SGT Billie Mayford could do that whatever I said to Frank Turner, it was all under control. I went over to the two bodies on the far side of the garages. An Insp Charlie Target new to the team had found cut who these two teenagers were. A John Reed and a Freddy Reed. I knew once I got the name of reed, where they came from and who they were related to.

It was time to go door knocking I started to walk up the hill to the tried tower block where Cyril and his brother Stan Reed lived, they both had a penthouse on the top floor. Both had been a little quiet on their later years. They owned the "Coco Club" a private club for the rich and the people who live on the dark side of life I do know at least over the past ten years the "Coco Club" had been raided for laundering and it was a plate to wheel and deal drugs for the local top end town.

In his silk bedroom gown and just like a Hollywood gangster in the movies it was seven AM but Cyril Read met me smoking a fat cigar and drinking a large malt whisky. I got to the point of telling Cyril that his number one son had been shot down in the garages along with his cousin Freddy. I did not mention the drugs or the money at this stage Cyrill left to tell his wife, who I heard screaming in the doorway stood Stan Reed, he heard the noise I had to break the news to him, Stan Reed showed no emotion and turned around and went back to his own flat and slammed the door behind him. I left both families and left the message that I will return later in the day. I went back to the car park,

I learned that the doctor who drove the car had had a panic attack, he was being threatened by ambulance staff, he refused to go to hospital.

The doctor was trying to explain that he just missed the first one running up the road and came around the corner and this guy was carrying a leather bag in each hand, stood no chance of getting out of the way. The doctor did try to bring the man back to life but he was already dead. The victim was a Levi Taylor, once a person who did work for the Reed family many years ago, he was what you might call an enforcer he had been in and out of jail most of his life.

Cyril Reed and his bother Stan had run what you call a dirty pie for many years. Now their son's get mixed up in drug dealing were they in fact breaking out on their own. Going back to Dr. Rebecca, for a catch up and in her words, "It was a drug deal that had gone wrong 'I look at her and wait for her next opinion.

'This forty-five-gun lying next to Levi Taylor, I believe was used to shoot both teenagers" it was then that I did mention a fourth person running ahead of Levi Taylor up the hill. I was not going to wait till later, I went back to visit Cyril Reed and his brother Stan was now on more of the cigar smoking and malt whiskey drinking.

"A celebration of the lives of our sons" I mention the drug deal going wrong and a third person unknown at this since was involved he was hit by a motorcycle and died at the scene being told by both the Reed brothers that they will take care of this their way. I thought of many people beaten to a pulp who would know absolutely nothing about this deal. I did not mention Levi Taylor because I knew that the Reed brothers would be hunting down his friends and many would die because they knew nothing. I left the Reed brothers in their misery in their own little world of plastic gangsters, mumbling to each other. I went back downstairs to find SGT Billi talking to the night porter of the third tower he said he knew nothing and also there was no CCV working it was all for show that was how the Reed bothers wanted it, they own the building. All other CCTV had been given to the team. I did ask SGT Billi why she was here I thought that she was with the drugs and money back at the police complex she told me in what I call a reluctant way that chief Insp Frank Turner jump in the car and just drove off without any explanation to her. I told her not to worry.

I had the call to see the "Top Dog" John Knight who wanted to know the low down on what had gone down in Cullen Bay. Although Cyrill and Stan reed had driven us mad for years, there were still parents. John Knight was showing no person for their grief "They are, and remember I told you this Aaron, Cyrill and Stan are behind this and now they are finding their sons to do the dirty work for them"

I just raised my eyebrows at John Knights comments, this man had no humanity in him except at the end of my cock. I also was to learn that Insp Beatrice Jones was out of my care now and is now working under the watchful eye of Chief Insp Derek 'hard" steel who was another man who lived up to his nickname 'HARD." Derek "Hard" steel had been running the integrity unit mad and had got nowhere on an investigation. Something that did come at of our conversation that "Hard' had some information on my "Aunt Candy."

Across the desk he passed me photographs at the Turf Club of Aunt Candy having a drink with stan reed on several trips she made to the V.I.P Bar. In the twisted mind of "Hard steel" he did suggest that I was crying information were going on and she was giving the information to Stan Reed. I just looked at John Knight and thought you are a bigger nut job than "hard steel' if you believe all of this rubbish. Then in his very own little way John Knight asked me if there was any truth in this story, I then was handed twenty pages of notes that "Hard Steel" had put together about my private life. I did then really tell John Knight where he could stick my job where the sun does not shine anymore, then again I did think that John Knight could be the very exception!!

When I was going down in the left a horrible thought had come into my head, that John Knight word of known about this investigation, Chief Insp Derek 'Hard" steel would have had to get his permission to run the investigation into my Family through monkey bullocks himself John Knight. I went into office and closed the door it was not long before Rachel Todd my office Manager slip through the key mole with a bit of a squeeze. She gave me a mug of coffee, I simply reached down to my desk and pulled out a bottle of brandy and soon there was more brandy than coffee in the mug. I showed Rachel the photograph of Aunt Candy and Stan reed at the races each Saturday I explained that the shooting in my driveway may not have been a warning to me. But a warning to me. But a warning to Stan Reed, it was something that more I thought about more I came to that conclusion. I had to admit the final stamp of approval came when "Hard steel" had information that Aunt Candy had spent her final night in Darwin after the races at the: Stuart hotel" which is owned by the Reed brothers, I produced a photograph of Aunt Candy giving Stan Reed a goodbye kiss at the airport.

It was time to come up with the date of the three deaths down to the garages at Cullen Bay. First up was a search warrant for the flat of

Levi Taylor in Stuart Park. I was very surprised that Wayne Bunnings the night porter at the Reed tower block without any CCTV open the door for my team. Now this whole crime was making sense Wayne Bunnings was the missing person in the drugs for money deal. He had bolted once the shots had been fired. He came to admit there and then that Levi Taylor lost the plot and shot both the teenagers who did not offer any resistance. I looked at Wayne Bunnings and told him that he will need protection in jail the Reed brothers will put a bounty on your head back at the watch house Pia Plaza the solicitor threw one of her regular tantrums about the interview with her client and how I forced him to confess. Poor Pia had got it so wrong and when Wayne Bunnings gave his account it did seem the air had covered and with Wayne jumping into a swimming pool like a little boy he had to admit he did confess even before I had asked a question.

For the next hour I got another version of the drug deal going wrong. Where did the drugs come from, I had to swallow my tongue the now very much dead Alf Jackson of the Royal Oak Pub fame had stolen them from the Reed brothers and then sold them on to Levi Taylor.' Now I did think that this was where Levi had got the million dollars from did seem a mystery. It was the two teenagers who were tired of living off the family money they wanted real money for themselves. I had to think that if it was successful drug deal it would have made what I call a "full circle" the drugs had ended back into the hands of the Reed family, yes, a different generation. It was time to confront the Reed brothers Cyril and stand what we know. Cyril is like a fish out of water but with the creep Zack Johnson a long-time legal mind for Cyril. I open up to let Cyril know by not giving his son John more pocket money it may cost him his life in a roundabout way. Cyril was having none of this nonsense.

When I threw the final bone at Cyril and let him know the drugs were the same drugs that Alf Jackson from the Royal Oak Pub fame had stolen from him. I knew Cyril would sit there with a no comment Zack Johnson the solicitor tried to tell me that the Reed family do not deal in drugs. I knew they built their so-called empire on dodgy drug money. Being told by Cyril that Alf Jackson was long time dead now and so I had no case. I did mention that I had a witness who would testify to everything that I had said. I was not going to tell them the name of the person, they ca wait until the trial.

"What Trial?" shouted Cyrill

"You for fuck's sake, you are just drawing at straws!!" I did need more proof for this to go to trial.

Cyrill left giving me the 'Finger" I made no comment in return. Stan Reed rolled up like he was off to a tennis match. Andrew Benton another lowlife solicitor sat beside stan, who was drinking one of those "pump you up" drinks.

I took the same road and got the same answers from Stan Reed. Now Stan did seem sad to the death of mission. He knew Freddy Reed hand some ambition beyond the family.

"He was trying to run before he could walk" Stan told me and I did see a tear in his eye. I wanted to mention my Aunt Candy to Stan which world of been the lit candle on the cake but I thought it was best to save that for another day. Out of the blue came another name from the past and the Royal Oak Pub another bar person. A Jewel Lockhart her DNA had been found in the flat of Levi Taylor and Wayne Bunnings. Now I had the connection to the drugs. I issued a warrant and sent my team off out to try to locate her the team are good within two hours she was found staying down at the new hotel and the waterfront simply called the waterfront I did wonder how any meetings they had to decide that name for the hotel. My team told me that Jewel Lockhart had been splashing the cash and getting new wardrobe ready for an overseas trip I could tell when she saw me walk into the interview room and being told that I was her "worst nightmare" Alf Jackson said if you see him at your interview, you are simply "fucked"!! plead guilty. While you can. Was to learn that alf Jackson gave the cocaine to her for safe keeping and it was their holiday money in the future. She had bump into another old lover Levi Taylor and she got out of her head one night and told Levi how she wanted to cash the cocaine in and simply bugger off out of Darwin. But this was the plan except Levi was now dead and she will dream. Handling drugs, she could get five to ten years or this amount of cocaine she simply sad 'bring it on!! I just didn't feel quite right about all this I still felt a part was missing.

I was about to have an even bigger problem that i never expected in my office Sgt Billi Mayford had discovered that the million plus dollars, had not yet been counted and when it had it was a little on the slim side. In fact, there was only half a million dollars in the bag in the custody lock up Det Sgt Billi did remind me that only Chief Insp Frank Turner was the last person that she knew had handled the money. My memory served well also; he drove to the city with the money in the car when I had told Det Sgt Billi to take the money. This was a big, big crime, small I call in Chief Insp "Hard steel" head of the integrity until or go to top dog John Knight himself. I closed my office door and told

Det Sgt Billi and Rachel with Insp Charlie these were the only three people I could trust I phoned for a search warrant with the justice department. Chief prosecution Ivan Deakin told me over the phone "Best of luck with this one Aaron, I do not want to know any details unless it is a huge success!!"

I got four uniform offices and with Billi and Charlie headed out to park to the home of Chief Insp Frank Turner the front door open to find in his underwear.

"Hey guys it is my day off" say what for, trying to crack a few jokes is this April fool's day"

The so-called bag was found at the bottom of the wardrobe Billi found three hundred thousand. I did ask him where the other missing five hundred thousand "I will not talk without legal advice' was the only reply they got from Frank.

Poor Charlie had to put the handcuffs on his boss frank was taken away and Billi stayed behind with two confirm officers trying to locate the money that was missing the alarm bells were ringing from John Knight and told him I will explain later. Which did not go down well and John Knight told me that he is coming down to see me. I thought then lucky me. A few strong words from John Knight and being told this did not look good on my leadership it did show that I was a weak prick" I just turned my shoulder and I did go a little bit too far and showed John Knight the finger. I thought I have been given the finger today and so I shared it with John Knight it is "Finger Day all round!!"

With the last word from John Knight. He told me that Derek "Hard" Steel is going out to Berrimah prison to interview somebody who used to work for the Reed brothers. He will be taking Insp Beatrice Johns only for educational purposes. I really had no idea what that meant. I went back to my desk to try and control my rage.

I really had to take control, the two most senior police officers having "a barny" in front of the troops was not a good look. Anyway, I wanted to look like I stood my ground and John Knight was the clown. A nice young lady named Anne showed up with the files from the top floor office that did need my signature today. I was surprised that John Knight had sent them down within ten minutes. Four chocolate biscuits and a cup of tea the young lady left with a cheeky smile and a "thank you assistant commissioner Aaron Brown!!

The rest of the afternoon was what I call normal I was about to tell Amy my driver to get the car when I had a phone call from Insp Rita Malifax of the sex crime unit "Aaron its Rita, you need to get ya ass over to the hospital Insp Beatrice John's had to defend herself from being raped by none other than Derek "Hard Steel" he is in custody in the back of a paddy wagon heading for Berrimah watch house. I could see that Rachel Todd could read bad news without even been told.

"Derek Hard Steel had tried to rape Insp Beatrice Johns" who miss a sexuality or miss celibacy back in my younger days. My personal phone rang it was the police minister on the other end, "I am on my way Aaron, I will meet you there at the hospital." I phone Dr. Rebecca I gave no details except meet me downstairs in reception now and bring a rape kit." My car was full of Amy at the wheel, I was sitting in the front and Insp Rita and Doc Rebecca were in the back seat. I ask Insp Rita to brief Dr. Rebecca on what she knew so far. I could see Amy was sitting there shaking her head without making any comment. I put my hand on her shoulder to show support. We pulled into the rear entrance of emergency tactical support were already there and were acting in protection for Insp Beatrice who was with specialist doctors who deal with rape. Dr Rebecca joined them after an introduction.

I did not have to turn around to look to see war herd of elephants were coming down the corridor led by police Minister Carol Kelly. She came over and gave me a hug something I was surprised about when she said the words. 'I am glad you are here" there was no mention about John Knight and me now in two minds about shall I phone him? I did want to the interview with Beatrice. I did express to Carol Kelly that it may be painful but we will only have to do this once and I need to know exactly what happen while it is still fresh in the mind of Beatrice and of course before I can make a move on Chief idiot Derek Hard Steel and work at what charges should be laid. I tried to explain it is little more complex with the other person being a high-ranking police officer for many years "You mean you want a bloody cover it up" shouted Carol Kelly at me.

"Far from it, he will not get away with this his police career is finished"

In what I would call Insp Rita took control the information was that Derek "Hard" steel had been trying it o by touching Beatrice between the legs when she was driving so much that she stops the car and told Derek to drive and leave her there. She was not comfortably going at to Berrimah prison with all those men looking at her. She would stay in the car and let Derek go inside on his own. He did agree but within minutes he asked her for a blow job. She told him that she was "a sexual" he had no idea what that was she then said she was "celebrate" what twenty-six and never had sex this all my sexual fantasies come true he screamed and tried to force her to go down on him, now that his one-eyed rattle snake was hanging out of his trousers. When they pulled into the car park, she jumped out of the car and ran to a middle ace couple screaming 'He is trying to rape me!!" Derek being his normal slimy self, denied and said he was a police officer and the young lady is delusional she has been under a lot of pressure lately. Derek trying to be a father figure instead of a sexual predator, grabbed Beatrice on the arm tried to pull her back into his car, she gave him the elbow and in fact her martial arts training had served her well, she actually broke his nose and Derek full to the ground which all of this was going on the couple had phoned the police and also two prison guards whatever Derek said in his story of events, my team had the evidence from the prison back at the office already. I got Rachel Todd to send me the highlights today, it does make my job so much easier and also myself better at my job, although I had no idea myself how to work the technology, which is why I employ people like Rachel Todd in the position of my office Manager.

I took Carol Kelly into an empty room and showed her the footage from outside the prison. I did tell her that what I am going to show you is highly confidential and you must not discuss what you have seen. Carol Kelly was taken back; I could see tears in her in her eyes. Then silence "where the fuck is John Knight when you need him, fucking heads are going to roll for this!!"

I thought that I am glad that ii am on your side and showing her the footage of the incident was not exactly the right thing to do. Deep down in some ways I do hope that this is the final curtain. I about had my pressure button pushed one too many times.

Dr. Rebecca came and took me back into the empty room. "She was not raped, she was still a virgin " I did not understand what Dr. Rebecca was trying to say "Listen he still attacked her and did suggest a little bit of sex to make the car ride more enjoyable" Listen Aaron what does that mean he tried to have sex with her in fact on her neck and on her arms and between her legs there are bruises, and I imagine his "DNA" is all over the clothes that she was wearing, if you had close contact with somebody. "Hey Rebecca" I said "Listen we got this and we are going to hang him at to Dry The media are going to have a field day, and our police minister will be blowing this incident sky high it was her niece. If I was John Knight I would have to say "Pack ya bags Matey no good hiding under the desk and getting a blow job anymore "Dr. Rebecca tunned to say the whispers are everywhere and the only person that the female member of the police force in the top ranks, are you I just had to say thank you Dr. Rebecca!!

I was now on my to see Chief Insp Derek "Hard" Steel, he had called for help from a family member his brother Action Steel a well-respected in the high court in his legal work. I was stop in my tracks by a phone call from commander Alex Greaves of the Federal Police who is caretaker of Chief Insp Frank Turner. An update was about that John Knight had sent a few of his team over to sniff around to see if they could locate. They were turned away by the team leader because they did not have any clearance to enter the part of the building that the federal police did occupy. There was a small problem from Frank Turner, he had eaten a bar of soap". Vomiting and a large bowel movement and he had nausea. The doctor said he is starting to become suicidal. No soap, toothpaste or brush no toilet paper. He will be just in his underwear and I will paper. He will be just in his underwear and will have to use water to wash his rear end. No cutlery although plastic will be given at mealtimes. I was sad to hear that Frank Turner had come to this, Rather than give up the names of the other people who have been involved in his drug Rachel and money laundering from seizer of drug crimes.

I did imagine that Derek "Hard ''Steel would be glad to clear his chest. Instead that bitch Beatrice the bloody niece of the police minister who was throwing her virginity into my face. "Somehow, I did imagine that Derek sitting next to his older brother Action Steel who was dressed like he was going to what I would call a gay dance a bit over the top in fashion for an interview room in the watch house I had to break the ice and the footage of outside in the car park out at Berrimah prison, well the ice was slowly melting. Poor brother Action Steel did ask why he wasn't informed of this secret filming. I just took that like a pinch of sale and threw it over my shoulder I went back in time to talk about and I did hope in a productive manner about the incident the day before when Derek wanted at bit of body contact in his office with Beatrice, in fact time to talk about and I did hope in a productive manner about the incident the day before when Derek wanted a bit of body contact in his office with Beatrice in fact if it was not for entering the room Sgt Hilda Metcalf told Derek to take his hands off of Beatrice.

I could see after having his brother alone for two hours Derek had not mentioned a word about this. I showed a photograph of the bruises on her arms where Derek tried to hold Beatrice down. We had no proof that Derek did commit the marks on Beatrice and Derek did commit the marks on Beatrice and Derek said Sgt Hilda Metcalf is a liar!! I went into details of Derek touching Beatrice driving in the car and he did try to put his hard down between her legs.

"False evidence Beatrice again was making all this up another twist of the truth, Derek called the episode I got down to the martial arts example of defense where Beatrice broke his nose, she attack me, "I was trying to calm her down" Derek had an answer for everything and really none of it was the truth. I ended by saying that Derek was lucky that the couple were there because Beatrice did use full force to defend herself, poor Derek could be in hospital now with broken ribs!!

I was then told by Derek that I had never liked him. Now I ever ended up being assistant police commissioner I must be sleeping with the commissioner John Knight when he started telling he that Aunt Candy was sleeping with the mafia brothers Cyril and Stan reed, I knew it was time to call it a day. I said that I will see you in court tomorrow!!

"Tomorrow Alton Steel told me when he will apply for bail, being a senior police officer and locked in a cell out at Berrimah prison is not a healthy place for my dear brother Derek who has health problems"

I almost said Derek's biggest problem id the control of his cock around young females, I just let it go, and another fine effort of biting my tongue. My grandmother always used to say that every dog has its day!!

I went back upstairs to the office, where I was met by chief inspector Diane Watkins and commander Stew Brackus, they both sat and listen to my speech of how now that I need some very experience senior police officers to join my team. The real time was now. I did introduce them to Rachel Todd who was going to fix up their office space. Insp Charlie Todd, Sgt Billi Mayford

"These staff or should I say team were my most trusted" I then sat Steve and Diane down and brought them up to date with our big case of the two teenage members of the Reed family shot in a drug deal that had gone very wrong both Steve and Diane knew. A lot about the plastic mafia family my term for the Reed family. It had been a long day and it was time for Amy to drive me home it was good to spend time with my four sons. Pool was on the agenda and once again I was well beaten. There has been an upgrade of the food. Now there is a choice of readymade meals for dinner just defrost what you want. The boys did enjoy this idea. Not only that but the twin's world only has to cook twice a week with a selection of choices I also enjoyed this choice. The boys had already named their top ten choice of dinner, so I must say the choice of the twins was a good result although I did have myself in the beginning of the exercise.

The next day with commissioner Steve and Chief Insp Diane who did seem to be on top of everything. I went up to the top floor. I shut down John Knight office and also my office. John Knight guard dog want to work in another office, my Crystal Fulton somebody new again sitting at the desk that did guard my office I told Crystal that she is now relocating downstairs to my world. Behind my office there is another room, never used, it does have a bathroom, a couch, but no office, furniture this was where she will set up her operating, I got Rachel Todd to come out to welcome her to our team. I was now acting commissioner of police cell until John Knight does have the balls to show his ugly head again. I got Crystal to send out an E-Mail to all concerned and the location of the temporary office on the first floor within the detective room. I did imagine those who I would call the old guard would not like to lower themselves to come downstairs to see me, only with an appointment Crystal told them. I had hit the nail on the head hard and files to sign. All mail that did concern office business is now sent to my office. If I was not careful, I would get writer's cramp after signing off a three set of files and most of them still saying the same thing. Any news about extra parking places for senior officers and what color should we paint reception, well sad to say put on hold until our once fearless leader John Knight did start feeling a little better and in back in living color to take control once again.

I had to say I was not experienced Chief Insp Derek "Hard Steel to be granted ball, conditions of an ankle bracelet, quarter of a million bond that his brother had put up within was far more than needed the judge did comment on, plus a daily visit to the nearest police station at nine AM each day. Derek was going at to the country to live with his brother Acton at the family home in Humpty Doo. The Humpty Doo police station would be his daily sign in. I felt a right kick in the guts for Beatrice johns. I had the police minister breathing down my ear about that fat judge should be replaced. She never mentioned about I have everything under control now I am doing the job of John Knight on top of everything else.

On top of everything else Insp Rita Malifax from the sex crimes who was leading the downfall of Derek "hard" steel broke the news that the case has been put back six weeks.

"He is going to get away with this, I can tell you know" Insp Rita told me.

I asked the reason and I got what I did not expect that poor Insp Beatrice Johns had suffered a setback and to be honest she could not fail in court. I thumb my desk and at the back of my mind with all Derek "Hard" Steel has done to not only try to destroy my career but also down grading my family. I told ins Rita to stay close she had a huge bunch of flowers, chocolates and smelly stuff from the whip round the team of detectives hard to show Beatrice that she is not alone. I had to admit what she was a right pain in the ass when she joined us, but she turned out to be a bloody good detective inspector and she got the job done. I watch Insp Rita walk away and before I could mention her name the ever blossom office manager Rachel Todd was in my office to catch up the gossip that she did not know about!!

I sat down with a bottle of water when commissioner Alex Greaves from the federal police gave me the sad news that Chief Inspector Frank Turner had hang himself with a bed sheet from the bars on the high window in his cell. I was the one now who will have to try and explain to some sought of cowboy enquiry how Frank Turner died in the custody of the Federal police; what was their connection to him. I must say to commander Alex not to blame herself. Frank could commit suicide than give up those who he was protecting. Chief Insp Diane Watkins had discovered in the lost few hours that frank turner had hid hand in a lot of money over the past few years and he was selling on drugs. Giving false amounts were shown in the records. I told her that there was only one man who could have trained him and that was Alf Jackson who held the position of drug inspector before Frank Turner showed up bright eyed and bushy tailed on arrival. Could my day get any worse; I was glad that under the watchful eye of Rachel my office manager Crystal Fulton had been successful in moving my office downstairs. With only for files to sign off on. It was time to "shut up shop" and everybody went home. I made it for dinner with me the boys and I had seafood pasta, and two of them eat beef and mushroom pie and two eat some chicken and rice. I gave the ice cream a miss but they all got stuck in with their own individual toppings.

I watched the news on TV the boys played pool and then went to bed early for once. All for had exams the next day. I was restless and not tired. I put on my dark black outfit, black coat, cap and beach sunglasses. I went for a walk along the nightcliff foreshore. I had left my work hone and my personal phone back in my bedroom. In my right pocket was a thirty-eight and a silence, I had six bullets and I knew what I had to do to put their cars in the driveway with the keys still in the in the ignition. A ford escort I rolled back at of the driveway and before I knew it I was an my way to Humpty Doo.

I had to move fast. I did not want to be caught by a stolen car when you are assistant police commissioner. I forgot about the other titles for this month. I drove past the house on the hill aimed by actor steel. The lights were on and it did seem over a quick peak through the windows nobody was in. strange Derek should be tucked up in bed at six o'clock one of the conditions of his bail. I drove down to the shops on the corner stood a wine bar that was owned by Acton Steel, I do remember last year I had an invite to the grand opening. I knew John Knight and a few of his cronies but if I went, I did imagine that I just might end up knocking a few of the teeth of Derek "Hard' Steel at the grand opening and the local police had to shut or down due to noise complaints. I would have loved to be a fly on the wall with Derek and

John throwing their rank around to the local police it did not matter to them. I did enjoy the actual low down on the event the next day.

All those who did not go from my team all had a joint smile on their faces. I could see across the car park Derek sitting there at nine thirty drinking at the bar. 'Is this a fucking joke" I thought to myself yes, he still had his bracelet on his ankle so where were who call the ankle police checking upon this prick!! I got to a point I almost went inside the wine bar and dragged fat Derek out by the throat. I thought that my head would roll tomorrow. I was going to remain calm and when Derek just came out on his own. He looked up at the night sky and headed home. He had about three hundred years to walk. I put on a pace and I got within ten years of the Derek waddle. I called out his name "Hey Hard what you are out eaten after your curfew?"

He turned to see me; I know that bloody voice. F off mister police man Aaron, F off" I told him I wanted to discuss what he has on my life for John Knight to use against me. I did expect something intelligent from Derek who was head of the integrity unit well if he does return to work.

"You are fucked Aaron. Good old Johnny has this in the bag, you are fucked, that bitch Beatrice John's cannot handle the pressure. So, I am going to just walk away from that so called sex crime"

There was a silence before I get up more steam to talk, he was like an old train engine "My brother has a plan to destroy her in court!!" this was the green light to me to do what I needed to do deep down. I was going to save Beatrice and to save my reputation with just one bullet. I pulled at my gun with the silencer on.

"You aren't got the balls to shoot m Aaron!!" with that I simply put a bullet through his right ear on was it his left anyway he was missing a bit of his ear, he was bleeding and started to cry like a little child telling me I will pay for this with my job. I did not think that Derek had cotton on to the fact that I want to kill him so l I moved closer and all I could see was that big mouth of Derek Steel open and shut and what he was staying I had no idea so the next time his mouth open I put a bullet into t. I thought I had missed my target twice now a Derek rolled his eyes while trying to reach at to me while holding on to his bleeding ear, his legs buckled and the weight of his body brought him down into a heap on the ground. I reached for his wallet and took a fine hundred dollars out for a rainy day. I was wearing gloves. I looked around and I did hope nobody saw me shoot Derek. I made it to the car and drove the opposite direction I wanted to go, within five minutes I turned around and drove back and even past Derek still laying there on the ground. I took a sharp left and ended up on the Stuart highway back into town. I did need to slow down I took the old route back into town. I kept my black cap and sunglasses pulled down at each traffic stop. I eventually reached nightcliff foreshore once again; the area was empty of people the petrol can that I had filled up at home before I left, I sprinkled all over the inside of the car. I set the petrol a light and took of the hand brake and pushed the car went down towards the beach before crashing into the fence and bursting into flames, I had jump clear just like a stunt man in a Hollywood movie. I was three blocks from the home. I took a couple of short cuts and over the back fence across the green before I was panting inside at once I went upstairs, I got undressed a put my clothes in to the wardrobe three large malt whiskies were needed after a shower I said to myself good job well done!! I hid the gun again at the back of the wardrobe. I found it hard to sleep. In fact, I had to drink the other half bottle of brandy under my bed before I simply passed out and I was woken by the boys going downstairs for breakfast.

I had no calls on my phone when I turned it on. I did expect some sought of message about Derek my personal phone was the same. I got dressed, the boys left for school. I wanted the twin who drove off and the other twin to arrive to do the housework. Good morning, Aaron I am Tilda, Sofia doing the school run this morning. It was a good start to the day and then I got the toot from my driven Amy Fuller who did see bright and cheerful and full of life. it was then that a body had been reported near Humpty Doo shops. It is believed to be Chief Insp Derek Hard Steel or it is superintendent Derek Hard Steel now that did depend what job he is doing at the time. I did try not to laugh but Amy had a smile on her face!!

I arrived last of all Dr. Rebecca was hard at it with her forensic team. I could see Commander Steve Bracken heading my way with his number two Chief Inspector Diana Watkins. I told Steve after a quick low down on what he thought had happen. "Steve it's all yours" now I made my way up to me crime scene all the locals had been interviewed Barry Rodgers found the body well "Digger the greyhound" did declined to let out a bark and then it was then that it was not a drunk sleeping in the hedge the body of the brother of their neighbor a Derek Hard Steel a police person brother to Acton Steel a very nice gentleman. Who does give a Christmas knee up for his neighbors at his wine bar. I was now getting much more information now from Barry Rodgers because Digger the dog had not even had his breakfast yet!!

A cyclist Ray Togan had passed the body twice and he thought it was a homeless person who was drunk Diane Watkins has sniffed out the local idiots in my eyes.

I told her I needed her support. We have to break the news to the brother Acton Steel. There were no lights on in the house. But the front door did open to see the Acton steel in an extra-large dressing gown. Never mind a good morning all I got from Actor was "what do you want are you responsible for all the noise this morning up the road?"

I had to stop the man who loves to hear the sound of his own voice. I slowly explain we found a body and we do believe that it was his brother Derek. I was shot down, "Derek in is bed, I know he has locked his bedroom door" with that Acton banged on the door. Being told I could not enter his home without a warrant. A spare key from the pocket of the dressing gown did reveal in fact Derek Steel had not slept in his bed. Once the door was opened. What can you say at a time like this to a man who has lost his only relative still alive and somebody who does hate your guts!!

I did notice the Acton return with a bottle of brandy in his hand and took a couple of large "Gulps" from the bottle. It was time to press on and I was not holding back. Derek was in his care and the curfew was at six pm. Derek was watching television when the Acton went out for dinner to be with an old friend and his wife. He would not disclose who these people were but that was Acton Steel a man of many secrets it must of run in the family. He was just like his brother Derek Steel who could also never give a straight answer to anything you ask him. I pressed on that Derek was under curfew and yet the moment you went out he simply made his way down to your wine bar.

I was stop in his version of event. "I gave Derek five hundred dollars pocket money but not to go out to my wine bar and have a little drink poo!!"

"May I say if you were home keeping an eye on your brother I have to say if you kept to your word just maybe and I say just maybe Derek would still be alive.

"May I say if you had not created these trumps up charges Derek would not even be staying with me under false charges false arrest. I had to set him free"

The actor shouted at me between mouthfuls of brandy. Well, I did expect that I will be the cause and if not the blame for the death of Derek "Hard Steel."

I left saying my officers will be in touch Derek you will have to identify later on with me front door slammed in my face I left with Diana.

"Well, what can I say he did seem a little odd, he shed no tears, in front the expression, on his face did not change when you told him that his brother was dead"

I made no comment to Diana

She went on to say the wallet was found in the hedge minus the five hundred dollars

"So, it could be a robbery gone wrong Derek asked to hand over his wallet, instead a lecture about the life and times of his life.

Being a high-ranking police office, then he met his fate. Diana stopped to say, "I did notice how calm you remained when that cane toad Actor Steel starting to shout at you."

An old tip Diane it will be something to remember even when you are interviewing somebody if you stay calm, they will very slowly eventually explode. Diana just laughed at my explanation. It was time to say good day to Dr. Rebecca. I explain that commander Steve Bracken will be in charge of this case along with Chief Insp. Diana Watkins "You are not going on holiday Aaron bloody hell who will be running this damn circus?

Dr Rebecca always had a way with the one liner. I did not even ask Dr. Rebecca about how Derek died or anything else to do with his death. I got Amy Fuller my driven to take me to my offices in the police complex.

Dylan Black was a choice to lead the integrity unit only an inspector and I did explain that it was only Acting Inspector of the Integrity unit. If you never wanted two people with different parents could be so a like was Dylan Black and Derek "Hard" Steel. In a nutshell I wanted Dylan Black to take over where Derek "Hard" Steel was on the investigation into the Reed brothers which world would help our investigation to when shot the two teenagers I already knew who shot them both a Levi Taylor but I was not going to tell him that I had Wayne Bunnings the night porter, locked up in a place that few can enter. I did expect Dylan Black in his role to be off at the starting gate, but with him closing my office door, I could tell that Dylan Black by name and nature, just about in his life everything was black and dark in his world even the light at the end of the tunnel had always been out in the life of Dylan Black. He produced a file and started to place photographs, of name other than my Aunt Candy and Stan Reed at the Turf Club. He had very thick written file that I did imagine was the life and times of Aunt Candy and Stan Reed and I do expect that Aunt Candy and was living with me at the time I myself would be mentioned. In fact, Dylan Black did have that black cloud above his head. While he spread the photographs over my desk, while he was asking me the head of the police in the northern territory some very personal questions. I thought that I do hold this very important position but could I get away with leaning across my desk, smacking him in the head a few times and they maybe stomping on his ribs and with around about eight weeks in hospital just may bring Dylan Black to his senses. What would happen to me, who would watch over the four boys? I had to be sensible here.

I had to stop Dylan Black who was slowly getting out of breath. I reach down to the lower part of my desk and produce the identical folder to the one that Dylan black was holding

"You already know" Dylan told me

"Yes, John Knight gave it to me." Dear old dead Derek "Hard" Steel had given him a copy, so simply in a nut shell where the fuck did you get this copy from?" there was a silence and slowly without me even waving to lay a hand on him.

"I got the file. Well, the file I found in a sealed envelope on my desk, when I arrived today for work Dylan was simply in what I could only describe as fear.

"You been set up matey. Now gather up this rubbish and go out to the prison to interview the person that Derek "Hard" Steel was going to interview. It was then that the phone rang and it saved what I would call the ass of Dylan Black. It was chief prosecution office.

I had Dean 'O high Aaron just a heads up a Charlie Reed cousin to the Reed brothers and one time heavy for them. Been doing twelve years in prison had been granted leave. Simply lung cancer and he has just six to eight months to live. Now I do believe that this was who Derek Steel was going to see until he decided to have sex in the car park. Ok mates stay in touch I sat and looked at Dylan Black and told him that there is no need for him to go out to the prison to see Charlie Reed because he had been released on medical grounds, he has lung cancer and only around six months to live. Poor Dylan Black was speechless until he said "that was the deal, spill the beans and he will get something off of his sentence, who agreed to this behind my back?

"Listen ass wipe you only been in the job five minutes, nobody has gone behind your back. I myself and so did John Knight did know that Charlie did not have long to live but we let everyday events carry on. It was then I had to point the door to tell Dylan Black was direction was simply 'out" of my office. After he left, I told Rachel Todd to get some fresh air spray in my room, it smelt that a cat had shit in every corner. In fact, I had to leave my office and go for a walk around my team to see what was going on in their would today. Ten minutes later I did return to a much more pleasurable smelling room "that was that dirty manager Insp Dylan Black who I will call cat shit from now on, "laughed Rachel. Bacon and egg sandwich extra chilly will keep the flies away," laughed Rachel.

She almost returned with Chief Insp Diana they had worked at where actor steel was last night while his brother Derek was breaking curfew. I could see that Diana raised here eyebrows when Rachel told me that she had to break the grand rules to find where Acton Steel was by tracking his phone. I looked at Diana and said that we may be the top unit in the police force now and then we just might have to just have to bend a few rules to achieve old goals. She did seem happy with my explanation.

"So, what have we got ladies?" I was told to sit down

"Actor steel was having dinner with judge Alec Namborton, who is the judge at the case of Derek "Hard" Steel and Insp Beatrice Johns, well he is no longer because Derek is dead, but this still hits the nail on the head that Acton was trying to fix the trail so his brother would simply walk away with a slap wrist.

"This is big. You will not know that both Alec and Acton are masons at the same lodge. This Diana we have to fight this behind the scenes the trouble is now do you prove that there has been some sought of deal done before or during the case. I told them to leave it to me and do not mention this to anybody. I mean anybody expect commander Steve in private. I told him that have to go out for a while

"Amy get the car please!!"

Twenty minutes in morning traffic and I was standing in the garden of police minister Carol Kelly.

"Why in the garden Aaron, I hope you are not going to resign?

"No, no we have a problem, well even and I say it that Derek Steel is now dead. His brother let him break curfew and go to that wine bar that actor does own. Get drunk, made his own way home around nine thirty PM.

Where he was shot one hundred yards from his front door. All the time Acton who was supposed to be doing supervision over Derek was having dinner with none other judge Alex Namborton of all people

"I stop then to listen our police minister waited for a reply I had just told her they were fixing the bloody trial behind the backs of everybody" shouted over the top of fine the police minister.

"They are masons from the same lodge, now I cannot take this on, first up we found this at through some tweeting of phone signals last night may I have to say without a warrant, I knew we are naughty very naughty, but sometimes you have to bend the rules.

"I waited for the reply" Aaron we have not had this conversation and I will take care of it on the four PM news"

Deep down I did not expect her to go public I wanted it for a lever again it the judge Alec Namberton.

The next hour was quiet. I went next door to become the assistant police commissioner to catch up with what was going on in his life. nothing special I had a meeting tomorrow to discuss the updated wage increase four police at all grades. Three long years and the cost of living going up everybody was struggling these days. I sign off on a few files and I did not exactly agree on but I must keep the wheels rolling on my wagon. It was ten to four in the afternoon. I did imagine that the boys would be heading for the swimming pool it is swimming trials again today. My personal phone rang and it was the police minister Carol Kelly.

"Put ya T.V on at four o'clock it will be interesting" the phone went dead and I turn on the T.V in the main office. I thought hold on to ya underwear team its judge Alec Namburton. He has resigned because of ill health. The pressure of the case of Derek Hard and Beatrice Johns had taken its toll on him.

There was no question time. He just waddled off like a duck with a broken leg. Standing in the rear was Acton Steel for all people. He turned and left when a reporter came too close. This legal mind had been stood down by the law society. I thought Carol Kelly you killed two birds with one stone. Smart bitch, my phone rang "there you go Aaron I took care of things thank you for your update, I will ask that all cases which went before judge Alec Namburton, now get a review. I sat back in my chair and shouted out "Yabba Dabba do there is real justice in this world!!"

My team were all gob smacked so I told them everybody go home early today. A quiet night at home except the twin's Tilde and Sofia paid me a visit with what was for me some shocking news. Dear Aunt Candy had been can we say had her hand in the till with the housekeeping money. Our weekly cost was far less now than it has ever been, yet we are buying more food and my I say with the blessing of the boy's better food.

What could I say except Aunt Candy had come to my rescue three years ago when my wife Kate left us. Stayed until I got a bad choice of housekeeper an Asian woman who could cook noodles one day and a rice meal the next, she spat the dummy because I would not let her mother came to live here. The boys were happy even Aunt Candy return what could I say about this life must go on. Now came the pinch line the twins who would be in my book became terrible twins in time, wanted a bonus on the money they had saved for me. I had one word, ladies or no ladies it was simply "Bullocks!" so after what did slowly a tearful discussion but not on my point of view. I will pay them an agreed amount on housekeeping expenses anything just to get ya bloody bonus. They wanted to hug and kiss me; this was not mentioned in the housekeeping rules I said.

I did at work bring the stuck in the wild people on the so-called police budget. I did demand that we also increase police recruits. Being told by the four financial wizards from the government that was for a later date. I banged on the table just like a dictator in the older days in the old we will set here until it is. I will lay on sandwiches and cake and beverages. Nobody had ever spoken to them like this before, the police minister Carol Kelly wrote on a note and passed it to me well was she in love with me. Was I her secret dream lover because everything I said she did agree on "The times are changing and we need a modern police force, paying modern wages with job security and a strong future, crime was growing we need more police, we will not get them unless we pay a decent wage" shouted Carol Kelly at the four stuffed pigs.

There was not a sandwich left on the buffet or a cake. I was lucky to grab my two at the time. Did think that these four stuffed pigs had not been fed for a while. It was all over just after lunch and Rachel my office manager did arrange four afternoon tea, scenes and cakes. I did notice none of the four pigs left until their plates were left empty. At four PM the so-called television was on with an update by police minister carol Kelly. The negotiations about a pat rise have been very successful on top of that we one hundred extra police recruit to this year at the police college. There was one almighty cheer from the floor or detectives, I got a lot of thumbs up from the team,

It was time again to go home. I was pleased that all four boys had reached the finals on the second night of swimming trials. They laughed and said they put it down to all the good food.

They are eating today; I just smiled and thanked the twin Tilda for taking care of them. I had to be careful in use she took my compliment the wrong way.

At work the case that did involve the reed family had develop a twist I was to be told by an out spoken bird on the grape vine that in fact Cyril and Stan Reed had secretly bank rolled the boys with the money and in the other hand in fact had obtained the drugs so it was going one hand to the hand and still was in the hands of the Reed family. It was a test of how the two teenagers could handle the big wide word. It backfired and it did understand why when they found out what went wrong with their teenage sons now both dead!!

There would be only one thing that the two brothers would be interested in and that was the name of the person who told the police.

Jewel Lockhart, one time bar maid to Alf Jackson in Royal Oak Pub. Even now the name of Alf Jackson was risen from the grave. I told commander Steve Bracken and Chief Insp Diana Watkins I found this hard to believe that se like the Reed brothers Cyril and Stan were playing both sides of the fence. I still believe that somebody told her and she passed it on and eventually ended up in front of Steve Bracken. Deep down I know there was only one way to end all of this madness. I knew now what needed to do.

It was going to be risky, but I was ready to take on everything. I got two spare guns from him secret hiding place. I made the call on a burner phone to Cyrill Reed and told him that I will tell him who gave the police the information they needed to put him and brother Stan away for a very long time. I knew that Cyril did know we were closing in on him now.

On the woodchoppers farm down past diggers rest turn off. I will be waiting for both come alone or I will not appear. It was rural and a friendly neighbor had parked his UTE in his driveway and put the car keys where they would be hard to find tomorrow in the ignition. It was around nine o'clock there was not a full moon tonight

The sky was pitch black I parked a hundred yards away and wanted for Cyrill and Stan to arrive. It was two against one so I had to get in first to survive. I knew both Stan and big brother Cyril would have no hesitation in shooting me. I set myself up behind a pile of logs both marched around looking everywhere Stan had a torch and was told by Cyril, to put it out. I could see that Cyril had a gun in each hand, Cyril had a small automatic pistol. I decided to take out Cyrill first with a shot to the chest, he fell and told Stan to shoot back, Stan was lost he had no idea where the shot had come from.

Next target was Stan, now firing into the trees but not in my direction.

"I think there is more than one Cyrill, it's a fucking trap, I told you to bring back up!!" shouted stan.

Cyrill laid on the ground he still had a gun in his hand, I took a pot shot at the shoulder of Stan, and I do not need to go to the police target range. Down Stan went. I slowly crept up behind them and simply said "Good evening gentleman are you for an evening stroll?"

Cyrill went for his own gun again and like in the old western movies I simply shot it out of his hand. Stan laid in a heap and told me to get it over with!!"

This is the end Cyrill and Stan, one thing I have to say to Stan "that Lady called Candy you used to meet at the Turf club guess what she is my Aunti!!" I told you Stan that bitch was no good" shouted Cyril with that I decided that Cyril had said his last words, two shots in the head, and I turned to Stan who simply said "If I was not married, I would have married Sandy she was what I call a fine woman" with that I shot stan in the head twice.

I could have left them there, but instead I passed a wood chopper on my way here and I pointed it at to the river. I strip both men and started up the wood chopper. I kept their rings and watches and wallets. Now the rain came and it was heavy but nothing would put a stop to my plan on went the woodchopper and Stan went in first, it spat and champ but at the top and pouring into the river was the last remain of Stan Reed I turn to Cyril and he ended up the same way. A huge amount of red pulp and the insides of Stan and Cyril were now flowing out of the top of the machine I heard splashing of the crocodiles looking for something to hang on to I picked up some before I shut the woodchopper down. With the clothes and their phones, I drove in the direction of nightcliff on the way home I was thinking of all the lives that I will save and the families that will not be ruined with Cyril and Stan Reed not selling them drugs anymore. I then took out the sim card and threw their phone into the river. I threw in their watches, both had money in their wallets I kept and then threw the contents into the fast-flowing river, the plastic cards I kept for later. Their clothes I dump into a waste bin, and headed home. I gave the UTE a real burn out in more ways than one

I made sure that the cards were slowly burnt without a trace before I pushed the unit down towards the cliff. Through the wooden fence and over it went crashing down on the night cliff beach and crashing into flames. I quickly made a Tom Roberts and was out of there. I noticed some people rushing over. I took another route home and sat on a wall to see if I was followed. I was not proud of what I have done, yet again I was thinking once again about the lives I would save from people not buying drugs from the Reed brothers anymore.

The next day a missing person was put out for Cyril and Stan Reed. Their car was found near a wood chipping and logging business. I got Insp Dylan Black in my office; I ask what he was up to on the case that involved the Reed brothers.

I got chief inspector Diana Watkins and commander Steve Bracken to witness this meeting between Insp Dylan Black and myself.

"Well, um nothing to report sir, in fact, I am getting nowhere and that Charlie Reed is too sick to be interviewed his so called Solicitor told me three times already.

"Well missing persons Dylan" sorry I do not do missing person, I am in charge of the integrity unit, you did appoint me sir"

I had to count to ten then start again

"Missing persons Dylan" I raised my finger to stop him talking.

"So once again the missing persons was Cyril and Stan on their list, but another twelve hours had to pass before we can act. Now I thought you could get a head start" I wanted for his lips to open with something constructive to came out.

"So, Cyril and Stan Reed are missing I will get straight on to it now!!"

CHAPTER 5

THEY TURNED THE TIDE

It was going to be a normal day for me with a few problems that I could not handle. Little did I know the reception that was waiting for me at work. I was taken back when a simple request for a meeting on the top floor. I thought I had put a stop to all those time-wasting meetings. Into the conference room and I was met by a Jenny Green a new assistant police commissioner but that was the start of a bad day. Carol Kelly the police minister was also sitting next to her and strangely was Chief Insp Diana Watkins of all people. There was no time wasting here straight to the point.

A lot of words that did not rattle my cage until I was told that I was unfit to hold the position of assistant Police commissioner never mind the stand in for John Knight as the commissioner.

Hello so where is the punch line and there it was "suspension" until further notice, my conduct and bad attitude had left a large hole in the detective division of the northern territory police.

I just sat there and look at all three of this none of them are really wise monkeys. Jenny Green an ex-girlfriend of John Knight who has suck a lot of lock to get the position of assistant police commissioner and then you got Chief Insp Diana Watkins, who did a lot of talking while she knifed you in the back. Last but not least the Police Minister who I thought was my friend, well I was wrong you do not have any friends in politics, well you do until you do not need they any more they had to be careful with their words Chief Insp Diana did enjoy to tell me that she was been working undercover for the integrity unit that she now does head I did wonder if anybody has told Insp Dylan Black that he is no longer a contender for the job of Boss of the integrity team.

I just had to ask Chief Insp Diana that question. Which did not go down very well a bit like a lead balloon on fire.

"He will be told in due time" Chief Insp Diana told me with a red face a bit like a pig's ass in my eyes. It was then that Jenny Green who had the nickname of sucker in some circles. Sorry to say that I have never been in that position of having her head between my legs. In fact, I did look at that as a bonus point, something I would not go near with a barge pole was those pump-up lips. I could see that both had been active again on her face. I was feeling quite bitchy, then again Jenny Green was mumbling about me not playing the part of the leader of the team of detectives. I could see almost a smile on the face of Chief Insp Diana.

There was no reason to doubt that the source of this information came from sweet Diana. My house will be search in my presence. My phone's lap tops also those that belong to my four boys. Also, the phone and laptop that belong to my housekeeper Aunt Candy is down on her farm for the past two weeks. I found it funny that they are up to date on my home life. I was asked for my fire arm my Police phone and my personal phone.

My work laptop had already been seized in my office. I thought sneaky buggers!! I was worried about my boys; I was told that they will be greeted by a special team who will be waiting for them when they get home. The time of four o'clock was mention. I just nodded because I did know it was the swimming finals today and I did not expect them home until at least six o'clock. I wanted nothing to upset them racing today they always have done well in the past in their swimming finals. So, I just said to myself that "These lips are served".

The last word from Jenny Green was that I will need a solicitor and all charges will be given to me as a later date. I was told not to leave the country with my four boys, just in case our passports will be seized during the search of my home a quick mention of over a million dollars in my bank account got a mention and where the funds came from?

I simply said "good House-keeping"

Around half a million was left by the parents of my wife Kate, and also the payout that I received for a victim of crime another five hundred thousand when Kate passed away with the attitude of a squashed cane toad that had been run over on a road and asking "Who did that?" Chief Insp Diana wanted to know what happen to Kate.

I just looked at Diana and refused to answer "Listen you will have to answer in court, if we feel you were taking it all back!!

I had only two words for Diana "Go and Fuck yourself" which I gave her with a huge smile on my face

It was then that Carol Kelly silent until now had to step in. "That is enough Aaron Brown has been through enough pain, with the death of his wife, who was run not once but twice in a car park at Woolworths. It was then I got up and walked out. I was in an explosive manner. I went down to my office to collect some personal items. Nobody talked to me I had the face of a raging bull. I was out of control. I stop to say goodbye to Rachel Todd eight years she stood by my side through thick and thin. I looked at Amy my driver and told her that I will not be needing a lift home. I could see tears in the eyes of Amy and Rachel, I gave them both a hug and said "Goodbye and thank you".

I got taxi home from across the road. I arrived home to find the twins Tilda and Sofia just on finishing the housework. Dinner selection was already in the fridge.

"You home early Aaron will you be at the park pool for the finals today?"

I will try, I got a bit on today" I replied.

I had decided that whatever goes on this afternoon I will be at the park pool and nothing will stop me. I went upstairs to make sure there was no space gun hanging around. I normally throw them into a river once I use them for my police gun was going to be my excuse for them. The twins shouted "Goodbye Aaron!!"

It was about to have a rest before the sniffer dog arrived with the drug team and some so called detectives that I thought would never be searching my home Sgt Billi Mayford and Insp Charlie Todd and Commander Steve Bracken.

It was almost lunch time, so I went downstairs to find my kitchen in a mess and told them to put my kitchen back in the way they found. Like a guard dog ready to pounce was Chief Insp Diana Watkins. Somebody who I will never forget till the day I die. They were what I would call people who had been waiting for this moment. The door bell went and I thought can this day get ay words. I open the door to see John Knight I put my finger up to my mouth and lead him out to my outdoor office under the mango tree. He had arrived with a dozen ice cold beers. I told him I did not want a drink then he saw an empty malt whisky bottle laying under the tree.

"I take what almost a month off and the whole police complex does a belly flop!!"

"So, they search your place did they find anything you didn't have any files at home did you?"

"I have never brought a file home from work all the time I have been a police person" I replied downing my bottle of beer in one hit.

I needed that so I will not ask where you have been, because you will not tell me anyway you have been, because you will not tell me anyways. A lot of mumbles from John Knight who wanted to know my side of the story. You know Frank Turner hung himself with a bed sheet. Federal Police were I say were looking after him. Derek Steel got shot that is still an ongoing case. Insp Dylan Black has been feeding Chief Insp Diana Watkins with a load of crap. Somehow he got hold of those photos and notes of Derek Steel about my Aunt Candy and Stan Reed.

I had your copy in my desk and the only person who I knew had seen them was Rachel Todd my office manager. Dylan Black started to tell me in confidence and I was almost falling asleep, then I produced my copy and told him that he was being set up. This copy was given to me by John Knight who liked me said it was "CRAP!! I knew that Dylan Black day could not have any light within the hours he worked it was all "black". John Knight laughed.

I went on to say that Cyril and Stan Reed have gone walk about and their Car was found out near Berry springs near a wood chopping business owner by Philip Philip's you remember good old Philip he was a champion football. I do believe that Dylan Black and I will not use word Inspector because it will be an insult to all other Inspector's in active duty. Anyway, the last I heard before I left the office that day from Diana Watkins that Dylan Black does believe that Philip Philip's may have been the person that they were meeting. John Knight started to laugh and almost choked on his beer. What I have done or have not done in my police duties they are being a little "Catty" about before I walked out of the semi-trial, I was asked about Aunt Candy and I simply said "she left for south Australian she is back on the farm with the cows and pigs and chickens.

Poor Diana face did look like a pig's ass she had not been keeping up with the details of my home. I mention Tilda and Sofia being twins. I did not expect the comment from John Knight that it was a sexual fantasy of his to have sex with twins at the same time.

I did not even comment on his remark. I grab another beer, and then he told me that he will be back at work tomorrow in living color. Then he went on about the house full of bugs. I did mention that I have no phone they wanted my police phone and personal phone. They are going to show up later when the boys got home and take their phones. They took my computer and also all four of the boy's laptops, they even took Kate's laptop that has sat at her desk for over three years now and nobody has touched it. A bit like her clothes, her wardrobe was giving a share up and the boys gave some of her outfits to the "OP-SHOP", all the good stuff they wanted to keep most of it is designer clothes.

"Yes, your Kate always looked like a million dollars". John Knight told me I decided to switch the conversation to his wife.

"Going to divorce me and bloody sell the house and going to live in penthouse with her sister Marg!!"

"I do expect I will find a small place for myself one bedroom, a flat in a quiet area"

I did expect the tiny Violin player to be standing on his shoulder now, playing away a sad tune!! John Knight did mention that I got six bedrooms here and was garden cottage I just shook my head and said "I do not think so join with that he said you need a bloody good solicitor to help you come at smelling of roses!! With that he left. I went for a snooze on the garden lawn of all places. I woke not feeling any better than I was before I had my cats nap

The clock on the wall read three o'clock and I went to get the four-wheel drive and head for park pool. All of my four souls did shine once again. Everyone a champion and got a medal. I think the BBQ will be fired up tonight. We arrived home to see two police officers and two detectives sitting outside the house. They wanted to know why we were late home. I told them it was another swimming final at park pool. I did not feel sorry for them who had sat in their vehicles for over two and half hours. I asked the boys for their phones. I gave them to Insp Charlie Todd, who told me it was nothing personal.

I simply said to him "What goes around always comes around again"

He tried to explain he was only doing his job. I smiled and led the boys inside the house.

I went inside and the boys wanted a BBQ to celebrate their win today. I hit the BBQ and let the boys take control of dinner themselves. It did turn out to just fine. I must have been hungry; I eat three burgers and three sausages I was told by the boys "you must have worms dad!!" into the pool room and one by one I let all four beat me. I was told that I will have to lift my game if I was going to play against them. I thought if only they knew the truth that I let them win!! It was then all off to bed.

In the morning the boys went off to school. Tilda one of the twins came into the house, and then I explain that I am taking a few days off from work. I left her to her work and went upstairs to my bedroom. I put on same old seventies music and listen through my wide head phones. I must have fallen asleep it was almost eleven o'clock in the morning when I heard the doorbell ring it was John Preston the solicitor a very close friend and his wife Jade was cousin to my Kate. I put my finger over my mouth and led John out to the mango tree to my outside office.

I could see that he had arrived with a dozen beers. "Johnny Knight had phone me and said I was up to my neck in bullshit and needed a hand or even some protection".

I simply replied that a lot of this mess was due to John Knight not being honest and truthful. Over the next hour and a few beers, I told John about the situation. I made the point of them demanding the phones and laptops that belong to them, also they took Kate's phone and laptop that has sat there on her desk and not used since the day she left us. I mention the death of Derek "Hard Steel" and of course Dylan Black throwing his six words into the mix on the missing Reed Brothers Cyril and Stan that led me to Aunt Candy. The relationship with Stan Reed did make John laugh your Aunt Candy with a so-called mafia figure now that is unbelievable. He laughs even more when I told him they have photographs of them at the Aunt Candy and Stan Reed got between the sheets in a motel room on her last night of her stay in Darwin.

John said he will try and get a meeting to sought this out but first up the family had to have their phone's back. I needed my phone I would have to rush to a neighbor for help. John handed me a burner phone, I did not even want to know what he was doing with one, and He was very strait laced. I was pissed because I wanted to contact my "bug man" to remove all the listening devices in the house. John mentions his wife Jade, who still found it too overcoming to come to our house. I mention it's been three years and mind you her bedroom office is still there and two wardrobes of clothes and every night I go to sleep I turn to my left and say "Goodnight Kate don't let the bed bugs bites, I love you".

I could see in the eyes of John I did need support just before he went out the side gate to his car. I had to tell him that I was not keen on keeping my job. If they sack me, I will sue a very large amount after twenty-seven years in the job and I had risen to the top of the tree.

He wanted to know what I wanted them. Acknowledgement that there is not one piece of evidence that they have on me is true with that I will be happy to stick this job up their rear end where the sun does not shine anymore. John wanted to know about John Knight and how he fitted in all this whatever came out of John Knight's mouth you would have to take with a pinch of salt. John Knight is only looking after one person and that is John Knight himself. I did mention that he is about to get a divorce.

"How many times have I heard that story, he even came to me last time and I told him I do not do divorce, but put him on to another member of my staff. One week later and God forbid the marriage was back on!! I left John laughing. I phone my close friend Alex Myers my internet man. I told him to come to the rear garden gate because there is a team in a blue van watching the front of the house. I had six beers left on ice for Alex I will do some egg and bacon sandwiches for him.

Alex went through the house and found eight little bugs he put him all together on the kitchen table. While I put the eight bugs in a small pot with soy sauce and let them slowly get a relationship going between themselves and the soy sauce, I then put in some honey and tomato sauce. We eat our egg and bacon sandwich's and drank some beer out in the garden under the mango tree. I did not go into the details with Alex Myers, who does sell some information and even bug the phone of your mother-in-law if need me. Alex had done a few small I say illegal jobs for the police and I was the only person who knew where I had got my information from. I could trust Alex but only up to a point. I did wonder if he had any info on the missing Reed Brothers, Cyril and Stan.

"Out near Berry Springs they say "James sharing the same bookmaker?" I asked.

Yes, he is a shifty bugger, think they were going to do a drug deal with him, I do find that hard to believe" Alex replied.

I heard a knock on the front door and then the doorbell rang it was Insp Charlie Todd and Sgt Billi Mayford. They had a box with all the laptops in and phones. I just thanked them and left them on the door step I did imagine that they thought we could all sit down and patch up a few of our problems between us now, this was not going to happen on my side anyway. I know they were only doing their job. So, suck it up!! I thought to myself I only like people who are my side of the fence. I was going to show how much I trusted the police I got Alex to check over my laptop and it was a winner they had put a bug inside. I went outside and walked up to the blue van and shouted that I have found another bug in my laptop, "Don't you people ever give up playing games!!" the two officers in the front of the van tried to make out that they knew nothing about. I just walked back to my home and the van simply drove off with the sound of the van horn. Maybe this was Goodbye I thought all the phones were safe Alex told me.

He left and I phoned John Preston the solicitor to say we got all our electronic gear back and they even put a bug into my laptop. John laugh, "you have to give them half a tick for trying Aaron, also Jade had decided to come to the home tonight to see the boys and of course you. I really thought that my life was slowly turning around.

"We have a showdown tomorrow at ten am top floor police complex. I will pick you up Aaron, come with an open mind please" said John laughing at his own comment.

I decided to defrost some fish and chicken and have a super BBQ tonight for John and Jade. The boys I did not tell them we had guest they all ran to John and Jade to greet them. Everybody was talking at once. I could see on the face of Jade how much she had missed the boys. Into the pool room, John was taken and after dinner there will be a competition.

The boys had missed John, then I was going to team in with him in a double match. Poor Jade was having one of this she wanted to take on all four boys herself. The poor faces on the four boys when Kate wipe their back sides" I thought Jade you are supposed to let them win. I stood back and they took on Jade and John and John let down his side. I did enjoy the banter; it had been so long since we have had company. I look at my watch and it was ten pm, way past the boy's bed time. It was a grant night and they did promise to do it again but not on a school night. I told John I will be speck and span for or meeting tomorrow. I was very surprised that I slept well, maybe that half bottle brandy did the trick. I saw the boys off to school, Tilda was about to give the lounge a tidy up. Well, I am the only person who does use the lounge these days the comment from Tilda was "had bit of a party last night then".

I was ready to go when the doorbell rang. It was not John Preston my solicitor, but the very last person I wanted to see John Knight. Me pointed to the rear garden and we both sat down.

"Listen I am prepared to give you an excellent character reference in return I would like those photographs that Alf Jackson gave you".

What could I say except that I had no idea what he was on about

"Those photographs could put me in prison for the rest of my life"

John Knight was what I would say was "Out of control".

I asked him to explain and slowly I got to remember that seven almost eight years ago. With John being the senior officer, myself and then came Alf Jackson being my right hand. We were going to arrest the king pin Glen Matlock at Madison gardens. Room sixty-two on the sixty floor I took the stairs, my lift was not working, John took the lift at his end of the building while Alf Jackson stayed down on ground level.

We told John that we should wait for back up and special operations the heavy job back in those days, no John had a plan we will surprise him. Somebody must have given Glen Matlock the thumbs up because he was out of his flat. He saw John and they had a close encounter although it was six floors up Glen Matlock was going to jump. John pulled him back and gave him a Scot's man kiss (head butt) Glen fell back, another body contact and over the wall went Glen landing on out car. I do remember rushing back downstairs and to the car.

"Is he dead?" shouted John

"Well, he will have a bit of a headache with half his head split open" I replied.

Alf Jackson said to me "Well that did not go down very well, we should have waited for back up!!"

"Never mind that we will need a new car, well first up a lift back to the office later on" I replied.

"He tried to push me over the wall" shouted John at both of or I think he must have said those very words about six times" he was sounding like a parrot.

I took his phone out of the pocket of Glen Matlock and on the phone was a text "There is a burner phone I later discovered I could see that John was pretty shaken by the order. In fact, he was lucky to be alive himself Glen Matlock was a good foot four tall and built like a Brick shit house.

"Listen Aaron about a month before he died, I went to see Alf Jackson in his beer garden. He told me that he had photographs of me pushing Glen Matlock over the balcony"

I just raised my eyebrows at John.

"You know he said call off the hands and that does include Aaron Brown or I will send copies of those photos of Glen Matlock and you helping him to learning to fly"

I would not believe a word that Alf Jackson said, anyway what was that got to do with you Johnny!! "My name is John not Fing Johnny Alf said he gave you the photographs just in case something would happen to him. You could use them as a lever to protect yourself from any problems in the future"

I just replied "Pure fantasy, all crap John!!

"I want those photographs that is why I gave you the assistant police commissioner position I needed you close to me" it was then I had to put John back into his box of tricks.

"I never wanted the job; I told you that at least six times and you still had my name placed on that office door next to your office. To think if I stayed active commander of detectives, I would not be in this Fing mess now. I would just be plodding along trying to catch criminals, I was never one to sit behind a desk and play with bloody paper clips, and nip off in the afternoon to play golf or have sex romp!!"

"That was a bloody mouthful Aaron, I am sorry that you are in this mess, and may I say a lot of it was your own doing!!

Saved by the doorbell John Peters had arrived and I had the call from Tilda the house keeper. John Knight stormed ahead of me just like a raging bull, just stuck his finger up at John Peters who asked me what he had done wrong. We got into the car, "What did knightly want Aaron"

It is a long story and I will tell you another day, let us get this day over with.

"Listen I have to say they have got nothing on you, I hate to say it but you are squeaky clean. We arrived and took the lift to the top floor. We were shown inside a conference room. John Knight was already there talking to Chief Insp Diana Watkins I thought two idiots together there, Carol Kelly was also there talking to Jenny Green the upstart Assistant Commissioner who crept into that position by being an old school friend of Carol Kelly many moons ago back in south Australia. Jenny sat down and behind her sat Diana Watkins.

Either side of those two what I would call "Wankers or dick heads" legal advisors to the Police of high ranks. What you can do and should not be sitting in judgment on me.

"Try not to bite your tongue during questions in my ear".

There was no holding-back straight into action time. My Aunt Candy and Stan Reed. Photographs, details of what Chief Insp Diana Watkins had classed as a relationship. All I said was they met at the Turf Club Aunt Candy had no idea who Stan was and Stan had no idea that Aunt Candy was a relation of mine the so-called rumor started by the deceased Insp Derek Steel was giving Aunt Candy information that Stan Reed could use in his so-called criminal ways!!

The death of Derek Steel was still an open case Jenny Green asked me way. I had no idea Commander Steve Bracken was leading the case along with Chief Insp Diana Watkins, if she had got her finger out instead of spending time spying on my family and myself maybe the robber would have been caught by now. A whisper in the ear of Jenny Green by Diana Watkins fired up my legal man John Peters who said that this whispering is not helping in any way in fact whatever is said should be said "Aloud". Jenny Green in reply said how did I know it was a robbery?

I simply replied that it was a known fact that Acton Steel the brother of the deceased was given five hundred dollars to Derek who later flashed the money in the wine bar that he did visit while being under curfew. This was something on the face of Diana Watkins had not any knowledge about the money, so this was what commander Steve Bracken had led the investigation which to his death over the robbery going wrong.

I said to John Peters, what is the chance of having Diana Watkins removed from this room. John Peters raised the point to Jenny Green being told that she is head of the integrity team she should be here. I asked who did appoint her because she was supposed to be the right hand to Commander Steve Bracken. I was told that John Knight himself put her in the position. I just had to go for a Brownie point and mention under-cover very sneaky!!

We were back on the Aunt Candy case, and I had to explain to them that she is down in south Australia and running the Dairy Farm with her brother. Then they mention of Cyrill and Stan missing person could they have gone down to stay as the farm. I did not want to answer that question instead a rear of laughter came out of my mouth. At such a stupid question. What was the latest on the two missing brothers?.

Deep down I was getting tired of this crap. I stood up and said "I have no idea I have been under suspension any have no contact with any Police Officers or wish to except and I say except John knight who has paid two visits to my home, where we sat under a mango tree. Jenny Green did ask what we talked about. I simply was going to be a

"Ass-hole" and say you better ask him that question, it has nothing to do with this meeting today.

Poor Johnny Knight was asked the question and he simply said that his wife is seeking a divorce and that was why he had to take time off work to try and save his marriage, he went on to say I was a trusted friend and he found comfort in my words of support, that I had given him in the past I wanted this to stop right now, they are fishing without any bait, they do not even have a hook on the end a the line.

John sat down and I stood up, I wanted to comment how my four boys had been traumatized. Having their mobile phones taken away and then personal laptop from out home. Also, the laptop and pone taken from my bedroom from the desk that my wife Kate called her office. Who the F are you people, you found "F all" if you had it would be mention by now. This searching of my family is far beyond any belief or any Fing justice that police force stands for. I tell you people I will be seeking compensation in the way my family has been treated".

I sat down drank almost a jug of water and listen to the next question about my family bank account almost a million dollars. I was about to let the vein in my next burst, but in a control manner I said "Six hundred thousand was left by her parents to Kate in their will.

Also, five hundred thousand was a payout from victims of crime at the death of my beloved Kate. I was again I decided to set it aside for the finance of my boss through college of university. I suddenly thought then being so bloody noisy into my bank account they did not pick up my two wages one for active commander and the other Assistant commissioner to the Police Commissioner, so much for their so-called perfect search records. I wanted to finish in what I would call a "big bang". I produce out of a box of glass jar with eight bugs inside. I explain they had been boiled in soy sauce, tomato sauce a splash of ginger and garlic "They are bugs" not the bugs you can ever but eight bugs in my home and even one in the boy's pool room, to listen into our private life. This police force and its standard has taken a downhill slide and the way I have been treated is a prime example.

I stood up and told the panel I am going now any further contact with the police it now will be done through John Peters my legal adviser. I do suggest you either lay charges or stay out of my life!!

I got up and left much to the surprise of everybody in the room.

John Peters only had two words to say when we sat in his car and headed back to my house "well done"

"Do you think I stuck it up um?"

"You certainly did, they had nothing half them questions should not have even been asked. I did love the glass jar of cooked bugs!! You did keep that a surprise even from me."

"It was the game changer John it was the game changer".

I gave John a hug outside the car and he simply said "There is no charge for my services"

The twin sisters Tilda and Sofia were just finishing up and off home. They made me a coffee for what reason I had no idea I was about to find out if they were doing a "good job". They did ask because they spotted Jade coming out of the house. I simply explained that she was a distant relative and she had not been to the house in three years since Kate died. I went on to say that she was very close to Kate they went to school together, studied law. I had given them both a hug to say that I was very happy with what they are doing looking after the boys. I was then reminded that next week is the start of school holiday. I told them that we will be going camping, if it rains, we will stay in a motel but still go fishing in the rain. They did laugh and I do not think they realized that I was not joking. I had to mention that just because we will be away, I will still pay them as normal. Another body contact with both of them and a kiss in each cheek at the same time. I made myself a bacon and egg chilly sandwich after they.

I even sat down under the mango tree and feel asleep. I was woken by my neighbor who had decided to cut my grass. I went to the main fridge and got a six pack of beer and left it in the fridge in the pool room. Which was payment for cutting on grass. I went upstairs and I do not know why but I did fall asleep on the bed. I was woken by my solicitor John Peters. He told me that Jenny Green had contact him about the laptops and mobile phones take from the boys. She was not impressed with the so-called tactics of Chief Insp Diana Watkins throwing her weight around being head of the integrity unit. A meeting was the plan for next week in his office, they wanted to touch on a few points and they did want me back but only on my terms. I told Peter next week I will be down at Lake Bennet fishing and will not have time for a meeting there between catching fish. Peter laughs but did not believe that.

I was serious with my intention of going away with my four boys. He asked when shall we hold the meeting. "Never" I told him. I want them to sack me so I can go for wrongful dismissal, listen if I do not show up for work. They will have to!! There was a long silence before he told me he wanted to get me back on the same page with the Police department.

"Do not put all your eggs in one basket please Peter" I replied and told him not to forget that we are   coming over with Jade for a BBQ this evening.

"We will be there in living color Jade will bring some salads ok".

I went downstairs and I heard the cracking of pool balls in the pool room. It was my neighbor.

"Hope you do not mind, but it does give me some space away from the wife who is at her bowls club right now".

"Whatever catch you another time, I left after I declined a game of pool with him".

I wanted an old black and white movie on television it was a western. I must of watch this a dozen times years ago as a young boy knee high a grasshopper. I still enjoy watching it. The boys arrived home. No football training, they did see happy. They are headed to their rooms to do their homework. I made four thick blueberry shakes when they came down, to go into the pool room. I told them in one large shout. "Fire up the BBQ" John and Jade are coming for dinner tonight. It was what I call   a good night the only thing missing was "Kate". Jade did manage to get he under the mango tree to burn my ear about my job.

"Now if Kate was here. She would tell you to pull your head in wouldn't tell you to pull your head was right. I had to think of the future or think about what I was going to do if I do not decide to be a Policeman anymore.

Nobody had spoken to me like that before and the use of Kate to turn my head around and think positive I will go back only on my terms. I did not want this paper work of Assistant Police commission playing with paper clips was never my go I told Kate I knew that John had set this whole thing up with Jade and at least I had listened to her. One more day of loading up the four-wheel drive for our holiday I told the boys we will leave Friday afternoon our BBQ that night was and I make to say the best ever Jade did honour the food with some beautiful tasting salads, plus she had made some mango slices and a blueberry cake that was covered in ice-cream by the boys.

I slept well and the boys had gone off before I had risen today.

I was woken by the doorbell. It was a surprise, standing there was Jenny Green and Carol Kelly of all people.

"We are going to catch you before you vacate to Lake bennet with the boys late today" Jenny Green told me with a smile.

I knew John Peters must of phone her to come and see me and try and get this matter soughed at before I won't away. Danish Pastries, were in a basket and a bacon and Chilly roll that Carol Kelly had got up early to make for me. We sat at in the garden and under the mango tree we dealt with the matter in hand. I explain assistant police commissioner is not for me, I do enjoy active commander of detectives I still like to feel my feet on the ground, I would be allowed to choose my own team after I did explain that those who had been placed under the spell of Diana Watkins I could not work with again. In fact, I did name only two people who will survive my driver Amy Fuller and Office Manager Rachel Todd.

I could see on the face of Jenny Green that this was not what she had expected or even hope for. She did mention Commander Steve Bracken who was heading the team in my absence. I was simply not interested in moving my number two anymore I wanted to say that deep down he was pretty average, who did seem to take a while to lead the team to just get anything done. He did lack leadership skills which was no good in a major crime unit. Unexpected news does seem to catch me with a mouthful of food. I was told that Chief Insp Diana Watkins head of the Integrity Unit has "Spat the dummy" and it did look like a Insp Philip Requiem will be running that show now. All I said "The penguin" that is his nickname, very old school but a very good detective that does sometimes lack what I call speed and urgently. They both laugh and ten told me they will expect me back in my office.

In just over two weeks. There was no mention of John Knight, so I raised the subject on their way to their car "John Knight is something that we will deal with in our own special way".

That did make my mind boggle. I started to load up the four-wheel drive. I did turn to expect Kate to be standing there holding some boxes to go in the back I was mistaken, she was not there, it was only my imagination. This being Kate's four-wheel drive, the boys will tell me that their mother is still with us on holiday. It was something special to them and I just hope they never let go of that thought. O Of course it started to rain, but it did not stop us heading down the Stuart highway in the direction of Lake Bennet. I told the boys it might be rough sleeping in a went tent but we will survive. Five minutes I told them that I had rented a family unit for the two weeks anyway so no camping this holiday just fishing.

Chapter Six

BACK TO THE GRIND

I arrived for a new chapter in my life. I of course had no identification to pass through the security door up to the detective first floor. I went to the reception, I did not expect to be given the cold shoulder and asked to drive who I was I simply said "I am nobody important, so just give me a day pass, so I can go up to the top floor and then to the detective office on the first floor". I just stood there with the humiliation of having to be escorted. I got my visitor's badge and away I went upstairs to the top floor. I headed for the office of John Knight his kennel was empty so I turned to visit the home of Jenny Green, who quickly jumped up and handed my gun and police identification plus my police phone.

"Welcome back Aaron, I hope you settle back in well and choose a brand-new team" I shook her hand and headed downstairs in the lift alone this time. I went to reception to introduce myself the jump up idiot standing at the counter.

"Here I am ex assistant police commissioner and simply old Aaron Brown Active Commander of all detectives. I found out later that the so-called desk Inspector had set up the young lad who only started the position about one hour before I arrived. I went to the security door and my old pass did work I arrived to what some would call a hero's welcome, a very loud cheer from the thirty or so detectives on duty. I headed for my old office Amy Fuller my driver had already placed my box of office jewels on my desk. Rachel Todd was first to greet me, no holding Rachel back today with a huge kiss on the cheek which got one almighty roar from the other staff. Coffee was presented to me while I got the so-called jewels out of my box. A picture of my four boys, plus my pens and collection of bits and pieces that have survived my eight years in this office. I did notice Crystal Fulton my ex-aide for my position of Assistant police commissioner.

I told Crystal that her position as assistant to Rachel Todd is open if she is interested. I could see on her face that she was pleased to remain under my shadow. Rachel set her up with a desk next to her. I had no even sat down and Berti Wagman with his electric screwdriver to put the new name on my office door.

"Hello Aaron you came back, because I got a new office" sign saying commander Steve Bracken.

"Wrong office he has gone down to Alice springs" laugh Rachel, in fact he spat the dummy when Jenny Green told him that you are now coming back Aaron!!"

"Anyway, which sign am I going to fix on this door. I even got a gentleman's toilet sign if you like Aaron?" how about active commander Aaron Brown, the old sign, sitting on this cupboard a little dusty but it will do the job. I finally sat down and now somebody from my past was waiting to see me it was Insp Phil Requiem, simply known as the "Penguin" to most people mainly because how he walks and sometimes talks always wearing a black bow tie in all weathers.

"Can I intrude please commander Aaron Brown?" come in Insp Phil what can I do for you?"

"I have been given the position of Insp in the integrity unity and I have to say it's not my cup of tea"

I just looked at him and decided to give any of my personal thoughts on him"

Listen Phil, it's what twelve years you have been creeping around these corridors of power and now you want me to be your friend, you do not even or should I say "Give me the time of day". Jenny Green made the call; I will phone her now to see if I can have any impact on the matter. I asked him to leave the room and close the door behind him. I simply phone Jenny and told her that the Penguin has not got the balls for the job. In reply was or well you find him a position in your detective team. I had to say on behalf of his bow tie a big thank you. I called Phil back in and told him to sit on the leather sofa. I was just about to order my breakfast egg and bacon and a splash of chilly toasted sandwich.

I did ask Phil if he had his brekky yet. So, Rachel did order two lots of sandwiches. Then she told him if you want tea or coffee, you can make it yourself. Phil and off to the so-called beverages station. He returns and I told him just to sit there and do make a comment about anything. I did offer him a position to tidy up and old cases still outstanding.

"I am not a cold case Inspector "replied Phil" listen you been watching too much television Phil but one case the disappearance of Cyril and Stan Reed in the Berry Springs area about five or so weeks ago. I will get Rachel Todd my office manager brings you up to date and I will also give you an Abbey North a new detective who will be your Assistant.

"But I normally work alone"!! Phil told me.

I simply told him "Do not make a comment and you are part of team now, no more solo work Phil"

He breakfast had arrived. I could see on his face, sitting in the office of head of detectives and eating breakfast with me. Everybody will feel that he is very important happy lines arrived for duty he was my new right hand, I introduced him to Phil, Chief Insp Harry Lines my number two, you will repeat to him on everything you do is that understood. Phil stood up with a mouthful of egg and bacon sandwich and shook the hand of Mary Lines then he sat down. I told Rebecca to find Harry a desk and also Insp Candle Pickin who will act ay number two to Marry Lines. Again, Phil still with a mouth of egg and bacon sandwich stood up to shake the hand of Candle when she steps into my office. Slowly the rest of the major crime team took up their positions out in the main office. Phil greeted each member of our new team and introduced himself. He did get a few raised eyebrows before he did enter my office to take up his position on the leather sofa, just like a half dead bird on a swing on his last breath of life. I did think that in his mind he was going to sit there for the rest of the morning. I gave Rachel Todd the nod and she just pointed to a desk for Phil and gave him the files on the missing Reed Brothers Cyril and Stan.

I had to go at for a while and left Harry Lines to give his formal speech and to tell his team what he did expect from them. I almost got out of the office when I was met by Jenny Green. She did inform me that John Knight a person who I had known for almost twenty-seven years had been charge with a murder that he did commit seven years ages. She showed me some photographs that had come into her procession. I had a smile on her face. Maybe she was just passing wind I did think at the time.

"I was there up the other end of the building"

Insp Alf Jackson had taken the photographs of John Knight throwing another man off the balcony. Being Jenny Green, she did not say how she came of these photographs. I simply said it was Glen Matlock who I found out in later years was a close friend of Alf Jackson then an inspector and head of the drug unit I went on to say that, I still do believe today that Alf Jackson did warn Glen Matlock the text to alarm him of an arrival. I suppose Jenny Green did want to know how I found this out. Well, I thought how did she end up with these photographs that only a couple of weeks ago John Knight had question me about the so-called photographs while I stood there in silence.

"Any way he is at on bail, at home wearing an ankle bracelet".

Again, I thought why is she telling me this, does she expect me to show up at his house with a case of beer.

"I only worked with him; we were not that close in fact my wife Kate could not stand him. She said that he is creepy and I should never turn my back on him"

I told Jenny who was quick to snap just like a crocodile back at me. "Yet you were his first choice of being his number two his right hand which I do know you did not want, until he twisted your arm, what did he have on you Aaron?"

"He had Fing nothing on me and that was what annoyed him, I was and still are bloody clean just like a new born babies bump just before bit has its first shit!! With that Jenny Green stormed off with all of the detectives looking at her.

Amy Fuller had my car ready, and I did phone Alex Myers my personal telco man we met on a park bench near night cliff swimming pool. I explained to Alex who had trusted me up that point. I wanted to know who was paying him to watch the bookmaker James Harding who was in the area of Berry Spring. The night the Reed Brothers Cyril and Stan went there to meet somebody and were never seen again. The only evidence was their four-wheel drive.

"I cannot tell you who had me employed at the time Aaron come on man!!"

Listen this could be a murder enquiry and if you do not reveal the name, I will lock you in a prison cell in the watchcase until you do,

"OK but I will say this does not destroy an old friendship, it was John Knight your Boss, I had been working on and off for about two years now. An old mate of yours Alf Jackson put him on to me and then John Knight had me spying on Alf Jackson himself he was just a bloody nutcase in my eyes!!"

"Who was Alex?" I asked him, well if you must know both of them were Fing weird, I mean John Knight has me spy on Alf Jackson at the same time; Alf Jackson wanted to know what John Knight was up to".

"Anyway, that day I spotted John Knight and that Diana Watkins having an afternoon delight in the Bridge Motel, I was following John Knight for Alf Jackson. Both of them used burner phones all the time"

I mention the photographs but did not tell him what the photographs were of. I had a light bulb moment that maybe John Knight did mention the photographs to Diana Watkins who in turn told Jenny Green and this was a chance to remove John Knight and take his job. I know these high-ranking police unit on the top floor is a back stabbing collection of oversized bells and not one of them could ring a decent tune. I did think of a Jewel Lockhart one time bar maid to Alf Jackson at the Royal Oak public house. I did wonder if Diana Watkins had paid her for the photographs?

It was like doing a puzzle and slowly now with Alex opening up I can see the real picture. I had decided to keep all this information close to my chest and simply trust nobody in the police force. I looked at Alex still sitting on the park bench. I found that it was time to lay down some ground rules with him. I updated him at least three times about John Knight at on bail with an ankle bracelet, but this will not top him turning on all those who are so called "connected with his past". I explain that I have at least three teams who will end up kicking down his front door very soon. He must remove any files he had on John Knight, I also advised him to make no contact with John Knight in fact I told him to get out if Darwin, I would not be able to save him otherwise.

I watch Alex get into a taxi and head up the road to nowhere. It was a time to return to the office and set up a meeting with all those who are connected to this case. The Penguin tried to look important again with a , Chief Insp Harry Lines plus his right hand Candace Pickin.

Rachel Todd was there to add any extra information that I may have "let slip".

The subject was James Harding the bookmaker for the rich who wanted to laundry money. Insp Angus had been on the trail of James Harding for six months now. The Wellington club is alive with members who do not like to pay tax and wish to lau   to

mention to all concern that James Harding was at o   an

bridge near Berry Springs on the night that Cyrill and   wo

also there we know on the grape vine that James Hard   th

to the Reed Brothers for a few million. Word on the st   if

going to be in a drug deal with the Reed Brothers to c   old

It was then that this meeting had gone pear shape   co

had been found shot dead in his flat down near the w   ou

time for me to head down to the waterfront to view th   ard

We had CCTV of the shooter, but I was heading

Mitchan to listen to her thoughts. He was a person of   tha

I told her. "Shot almost at blank range two bullets in   tir

to stop to catch a text to tell me that John Knight h   rol

bracelet and was on the run. We did have a team each   nex

he lived in, plus a couple idiots were on the job watch   Ne

told Dr. Rebecca. "O dear our Johnny has done a bolt   bu

could see that this news had put a bit of shine or even   mo

life today. I was above her sense of humour when C   mo

Lines told me that the suspect killer had been caugh   is r

it was John Knight of all people. Dr. Rebecca had hea   goi

from Harry and was no longer smiling.

"He is now wanted for two murders" she said   you

I walked over a have a whisper in her ear to tell he

we only know about these two murders so far!!"   for

I wanted to view the CCTV myself downstairs. V   His

Knight to a stolen car that he had used to drive across   rep

he is back on the run. I told Harry to contact traffic cor   esc

know who's that blue ford is heading in what direction. Somehow
somewhere, he had picked up a female and with facial recognition
rking it was a match for none other than Diana Watkins, I was under
impression that she had spat the dummy and was heading south,
ot to Alice Springs, for a stop over, and maybe on to Sydney her
stomping ground. I just had to put a loud over the day of our new
nmissioner Jenny Green. Who had little to say after I explain that
lead in a case is now dead, shot by John Knight who is running
und without his ankle bracelet like new born baby "lamb!!".

The comment that heads will roll because of his escape. I did think
maybe she should have it printed on a "T-shirt" and wear it all the
es she is at work. Once more she had to tell me that "heads" will
over John Knight doing a bunk!! The only good news I had in the
t hour was from Alex Myers, he had booked a seat on a flight to
Zealand for this evening. I told him to stay low "head down and
up" Just take care Alex, he said that he was going to live with his
her in Auckland. Strange I thought he was already living with his
her. He explains the women who he does call Mother in Darwin
ally his girlfriend, the one in Auckland is his real mother. He was
g to take his girlfriend with him that made me happy. I did think
tever you do my old friend stay safe and remember always to watch
r back and keep your head down and bum up

John Knight was a smart cookie. Twenty-eight years in the police
e, he would know what we will be doing to try and track him down.
first move was to dump the blue ford car. No other car had been
rted stolen so I know that John Knight had planned this so-called
pe, a long time ago just in case his career was going to come to an

end. The car was found near Humpty doo shopping Centre. There was one person who lived out there and that was the solicitor Acton Steel. I had the local police day him a visit. They were told that his four-wheel drive was in for a service and had to use his old ford truck to get around.

Going into the local car repair shop and asking the right question the two police officers were told that Acton Steel must have got his wires crossed the so-called service was last week. The two officers return to Acton Steel on my advice slap the handcuffs on him and he was in a paddy wagon and was expected for afternoon tea with me in about an hour this interview was something that I will enjoy I told to my team.

Acton Steel was eventually charged with helping a fugitive after I spent two hours listening to his bullshit and he kept wanting to return and talk about the death of his brother and why haven't we found the killer. I decided to leave Acton Steel in his own state of mind and call in to see the crime scene of James Harding. I just needed to wrap my head around a few outstanding questions I found a large amount of porn that did surprise me. An open safe and I do imagine that John Knight will now have the contents at the bottom of a wardrobe in a suitcase was almost two million dollars very neatly wrap in plastic. Underneath the money was a kilo of uncut cocaine. I found a large amount of ammunition and three illegal silvers handled Amedeo Rossi thirty-two caliber pistol with one hundred round of ammunition his deep freeze was full of different variety of ice-creams. The main fridge did contain some bottles of ice coffee. Two packets of chocolate biscuits and a half-eaten tub of chocolate ice cream.

With a very up to date wardrobe you could call James Harding a trend setter even at his fifty-year-old age. Various so called slimming aids in his bathroom for him to watch his figure. There was nothing to show that he had a partner male or female. I looked at Insp Candle Pickin simply said "It was time to close the door on his lifestyle". I left with Amy Fuller my driver doing her silence is golden mood we ended up in the police underground car park. I told Amy to stock up with plenty of Ammo, Guns, protection outfits. I do believe we will be heading for the outback, "we will go ahead on a helicopter anything better than a high speed drive for two hours out to Mary river caravanpark. Tactical support will follow us in their own helicopter. I had to look at the so called take off of six members of the tactical support that just did not happen. Amy joked about did they manage to put some fuel in the tank? I agree when we were off and going!!

With bad weather, there was a very heavy rain storm but I told the pilot to carry on whatever he did do not turn back we did land just when the rain stops. The sun came out but there were dark clouds ahead. Out pilot took off, poor Amy was dressed ready for World War three. Even wearing a bullet proof helmet, a little on the large side for her. We made our way up to the office sign when a man jumps out and wanted to know what did we want? He was the manager with the name of Dexter Gate a onetime Bikie Boss who went to jail for sixteen years if my memory does serve me well. He did not remember me, a Charlie Gate his rather came outside to say they had no trouble here and there is no need for the police to be here. "Got a Fing Warrant" asked the manager Dexter Gate who was still wearing his old Bikie waistcoat. I looked at the list and notice a couple of ex-drug dealers had decided to settle down in the caravan park. I did want to crack the joke "so this is where all the ex-drug dealers finally retire". I do not think that my sense of humor would of gone down very well. I did notice that James Harding did aim the huge luxury caravan at the end of the line.

I had to point this out to Dexter. "He is not here, has not been for a while". I knew deep down this was where I think John Knight and Diana Watkins might have been staying. I got the word from Dexter "It's Fing empty, some friends of his were staying on, but moved at two days ago". This was upper nonsense John Knight was in fact back in Darwin and wearing an ankle bracelet. I wanted to visit the caravan myself. I could see on the face of Dexter and his father Charlie this was not or the cards we started to move up to the caravan and it was what I call a bad freezing that made me turn to look back to see Dexter and his father Charlie pointing guns at us.

I shouted to Amy and said "behind us Amy" in full emotion Amy turned and tat pump action shotgun had a life of its own in the hands of Amy.

I did fire six shots only to catch Dexter falling and his father Charlie trying to run away but Amy pumped a dozen shots that blasted into the caravan they were standing outside. I went over to check on both of the bodies. Both had decided that this life had become too much and had moved on. A creak from a door two doors down and falling out of the caravan door was out third victim a Fred Bradon who was still alive when I stood over him. A onetime very known Pedophile in years gone by he was what I could call in pain, gasping for air "I thought you came for me; I have been a naughty boy with the local black children".

I looked at Fred Bradon and simply said "It is taking no prisoners day today Fred".

With that I shot him in the head. We finally made it to the James Harding caravan, it was unlocked. Some vodka bottles laid on the floor. There was an ashtray with the same brand of cigarettes once smoked by John Knight I did imagine.

"Johnny Knight was here Amy, now has he gone or is he still around?" I said three barns up I heard a lot of shouting and out the barns up I heard a lot of shouting and out the barn at the top of the hill came a four-wheel drive. It was heading towards us at rapid speed. I told Amy to "Take it out, shoot the Fing driver!!"

I fired four shots and hit the driver only fifty yards us. Now in all those television shows the car nowadays does a specular flip and sometimes it will even land upright and will carry on but no this vehicle had hit a tree stump and did the old flip in the air but did land upside down. I rushed to see if I could free the driver now hanging upside down, and may I say I can still hit a target, although I had not been to a target range for a while. Diana Watkins was the driver, in pain, she had even had her hair done for me, cut and dyed black.

"Nice to see you Diana, such a shame that we have to meet under these circumstances"

Um I was simply lost for words that came with emotion for the woman who simply tried to destroy my career. She did something really stupid she reach for a gun that on her hand, and maybe I put my foot on her hand, and maybe she was being naughty. I bent down and asked her to say "are", well at least open her mouth. Being told to go and F myself I shot her in the head anyway through the mouth. I leant over to see a brown leather bag on the passenger side. I went around and open the passenger door. The bag was full of money a little more that my housekeeping budget. I put the bag on the ground and told Amy I can hear or back up was simply arrived. I told them to go through all the caravans, watch out for gun shooting residents high on drug.

Amy was going to slowly move up the far side of the outside of the barn. I would simply go straight ahead. I told her to watch her back I also mention that I would like to take John Knight alive!! I slowly made my way forward until I saw John Knight step out of the shadows. "Lot of bloody gun fire Aaron trying to clean up a bit of a mess, and I say Fuck you Aaron Brown you have always been a thorn in my side all these years" well I must say it has been a time what I would not call boring. I replied trying not to laugh at the situation that I was in now. "What happen to Diana Aaron?"

"I must day that Diana is where all good things that pass your way end up, she is dead, hey I forgot to mention did you know that Diana was a girlfriend of your old mate Alf Jackson years ago back then, she must have been under age, I do believe that your mate Alf did introduce her to drugs and this was before he put on a police uniform. She did fellow him up here police exams!! There was a silence in the air. "I gave her five hundred thousand dollar that was a gift from Frank Turner of all people" I always knew that Frank was under the spell of John Knight and also in the early days of Alf Jackson, after he took over the so-called drug Inspector position". Listen Aaron you did give my bloody chopper pilot a fright, so turn away I got a million in this bag, take it, I got a boat waiting for me for a connection to a very long one way trip to another country!!

"So where did the million came from John?" I picked it up from the safe of James Harding and he also had it hidden inside his fridge.

"You missed out another two million John plus a kilo of uncut cocaine. I think that came from the drug deal that went down in the back roads of Berry springs with Cyrill and Stan Reed.

"He bolted James, the week prick, he heard shots fired, so he simply shit his pants and bolted. He was supposed to meet me in Berry springs car park with the drugs and money. If the plan went ahead, he was going to double cross the Reed Brothers, I think he shot them, pushed them into the river and the crocs simply had a nice supper that night!!

It was time to forget all the cheap talk. I did ask John to give himself up, and we can out an end to all this crazy life style that he is now leading. I took off my radio, so nobody could listen in. I told John I would put down my gun and I wanted him to do the same and let us leave together like old friends.

"Who better to arrest you than me John? I spoke.

"You always were a Fing Dreamer. I stood at into the light and tossed my gun on the ground. John pointed to the bag that he said contain a million dollars.

"Listen Aaron just over that hill, my bloody helicopter to freedom".

I did hope just for old times' sake he would not shoot me dead. It was a big chance I was taking and I stood there with John pointing the gun at me. I told me to step back and throw his gun over to me. I did exactly what he said. He bent down and picked up my gun and threw it in the night air!!

"I'm going now Aaron if you follow me, I will shoot you dead. I know how much love your boys so I do believe that you will not do anything stupid. Let us part as friends. I was watching John bent down to pick up the heavy bag he put it with the long strap on to his shoulder. There is a rule they teach us when we are training in fire arm practice and that is never ever take your eye off the ball. It was that vey split moment that John took his eye off of me to adjust the strap on his shoulder. It was then I simply reach around to my back and grab my spare gun and fired two shots at John. I hit him twice he fell to his knees, with the money in the bag. I put my hand on his gun.

"You always were a smart bugger, Aaron. Good old Alf Jackson always said "never trust him, he will bring you down one day without even knowing it". I could see that it was no good now John Knight waiting to medical attention we are just too far out in the sticks. I did decide to um give a confession to John. I did not want him to die with the belief that I was "Squeaky clean". I told John that I had taken "Derek Hard Steel" out he was out to destroy my family, all those details about my Aunt Candy were simply crap!! I then went on to say that in fact all that shooting out at Berry Springs was me, John I had to take care of the Reed Brothers Cyril and Stan. I started to laugh when I told John, I strip them naked and put them into the wood chopper.

It was a bit of a bloody matter but eventually they were shot out into the river. With the monsoon rain coming down I simply knew that the wood chopper machine would be nice and clean and ready to start a new day's work once the rains would stop. John just looked at me when I finished after my story by telling him I ended the life of Diana by simply shooting her in the mouth with her own gun while she was upside down in that four-wheel drive that he did borrow from Acton Steel who by the way has made a confession.

"You are worse than Alf Jackson and myself put together" I had to admit that to him with the pinch line "that I will never get caught" I could see Amy heading my way across the barn. By the time she had reached me I had put my hand across the mouth of John Knight and he had died. I was not proud of what I had done. In fact, in a strange way, I found it was my duty to kill all these people in the name of my law, to secure the safety of others. I picked up the million dollars and handed it to a very tired looking Chief Insp Harry Lines who did see happy that he had finally arrived with the team and coming up the rear was Doctor Rebecca Mitcham who told me "You can never be surprised who you might meet out here in the bush late at night!!" I pick up the bug from the Diana Watkins car and pointed to an empty car and just told Amy that it was time to go home and she can drive. When we reached my home, I open up the bag and gave her fifty thousand dollars. I told her that is my way of saying "A good job done Amy!!"

She wanted me to hang on to it for her sometime in the future. "I may need it she said. I had to be a bit of bastard and simply say if she does mention this to anybody that I will deny it. I left her giving me a shout "see ya tomorrow and don't let the bed bugs bite". I went inside to find Tilda one of the twins, watching television, the boys all wrap up in bed and a sleep. I thank her and went to check at what food was on offer in the fridge. I nice Chicken Pasta and three cold beers and even had a bowl of ice cream before I went to bed. I slept well and was ready for another busy day I had sent a report to Jenny Green telling her I will give a more personal update later in the morning. Most of my team were still travelling home after a very busy night out in the caravan park. They found nine out of the twelve permanent caravans were what I would simply prescribe as drug dealing. Now that their main supplier is no longer with us, I hope that would put an end to Mary River caravan park was the place to go to get yourself onto another planet. I had known about this place for a couple of years, it was strange that Alf Jackson of all people had pointed me in that direction. With my report up to date, I sat like a little boy in from of the head teacher in their office. I did notice that the coffee had not improved even with a new police commissioner. "Three down even before you found John Knight and Diana Watkins. Now poor Diana sitting upside down in her car could not face the music, infect she shot herself even before anybody could help her leave her car.

I had to point at that it was a car that belong to solicitor Acton Steel, who lent it to them to escape in. a lot of bouncing words off the wall then from Jenny Green when I talked about John Knight. "So, he shot Derek Hard Steel plus James Harding the book maker, and let us not forget Reed Brothers Cyril and Stan and you say he dump their bodies in the fast-following river for the crocodiles supper. I found I had to repeat myself on each fact.

I found that my story of the life and times of John Knight she did find hard to swallow. I had to explain m constantly used Burner phones so it was hard to trace him. Diana Watkins personal phone is in the hands of my team and we will use it to trace her movements and how she did hear John Knight escape right under the eyes of what is called "A protection Team" one sip more of coffee was more than I could take Jenny Green started to mumble about "where do we go from here?" it was time for me anyway move on with my life. I headed back to my office; I did not even have time to sit down when came Rachel Todd and her new assistant Crystal Fulton and followed by a frog-marching Harry Lines trying to look like that, he was in charge presented to me was a video of dare I say it Jenny Green without at any trousers on bare legged sitting on her desk and Diana Watkins with her head between her legs. I did asked Crystal a young lady in this modern world of what she had thought of this. Crystal took the words right out of my mouth and trying not to laugh she thought "Diana was giving Jenny a medical examination with her tongue". I kind of liked that brief but to the point of analysis to the situation. I found I was a little what I call porn being made up in the office of the police commissioner office. I had to admit the secret filming and commentary was being done by John Knight he must of down loaded it on to the phone of Diana. I myself had watch these times last night between.

Mouthfuls of lasagna washed down with a cold beer. Io had to make the comment that Diana Watkins did believe in being a free woman. First up was Alf Jackson for around five years but she was underage which Alf Jackson was involved. We had no idea about the relationship with John Knight but to nip off for an afternoon delight in the local hotel was still on the cards and now looking for promotion even before John Knight had gone, she was already giving pleasure to the future police commissioner Jenny Green. I could see that Harry Lines had not yet got used to my sense of humor. In fact, all Rachel Todd did was to laugh at my words and was joined by her new assistant Crystal Fulton, who I imagine that she would not find this morning viewing on her new job description!!

I thank them three for this information. What I will do with it I will let you know. I finished off my magical cup of coffee and headed upstairs to see Jenny Green. I have to say I have not seen a face change shape and lose all of its color, her eyeballs nearly pop out, and while I sat there sucking on a chocolate biscuit from her desk. I did expect a little more than "leave this with me for the moment, how many have seen this, Aaron; any idea?"

"Well, I have only just seen it, but I do believe most of my team around eight so far" so leave this with me Aaron, I will take care of it!!" with that I left.

If I was a betting man, I just knew that Rachel Todd my office manager would want a private word with me. She greased my parm with a bacon and egg chilly sandwich and a mug of coffee. I almost knew exactly what was going to flow in words from her mouth. "I think that Jenny Green will spit the dummy and quit she just cannot survive now, if old Carol Kelly the police minister just gets a Wiff of this, an old school friend or not she will have to swing the axe"!! Rachel Stood waiting for a comment instead I simply eat my sandwich and handed her the empty plate without making a comment. I was saved by the phone, and yes if I was a betting man, I could have got the double up today. It was Carol Kelly who had a visit from Jenny Green a few minutes ago with the offer of a resignation. "I always told Jenny to keep her sexual habits out of the eyes of other people when she is doing a performance" I just thought that this must have been Jenny Green's party trick from years ago. I did not comment and yes, I was up for the treble in racing three winners in a row.

"Do I think I could take over just on a temporary basis?"

I had to think for around three seconds and simply say "No, I have been there, done that, I have not got the T-shirt but instead I still have a bad taste in my mouth, about the whole time I tried to do best for the police force. It almost destroying me and I lost all faith in nearly everybody. I worked with and respected".

"So, your answer is no then?"

"I told Carol Kelly just in case she was deaf of hearing the word "No" once again".

Bill Skinner was a new appointment of assistant police commissioner, twenty years in uniform with the control of traffic, poor Bill was not really up to the mark, but Jenny Green knew he would not try to stab her in the back.

Bill skinner might just telk you to death about the flowers in the garden and how well his wife is doing at bowls, "She is now captain of the team. If my memory does serve me well, she had been captaining for the past twenty years since Bill had been directing traffic in the control room. Now weather the traffic actually was going in the best direction was offered there was a Major accident. Bill always like to have barrier, put up in the road to cause even more confusion to the public. I called back Rachel into my office to make her day that Jenny Green has spat the dummy and Bill Skinner is going to take over.

"What Bollocky Bill from over the hill" laughs Rachel very loud and left me alone to my files that Harry Lines had given me before, with what only I could say was his version out at Mary River being called the Rural Drug Capital of the Northern Territory.

I just thought how much worse could my day become Aunt Candy was on the phone things down on the dairy farm had got worst she had just shot the eighteen-year-old teenager who had moved on to take her place while she was up here. I told her to calm down "both barrels of that shotgun that Bill does use to shoot rabbits which he does fancy rabbit stew for dinner. I was at shopping and I did notice that the cows had been milked and were still in the yard instead of being let out into field. Will was on the floor, and she was stabbing him in the shoulder from behind with a steak knife. I had to remember that when Aunt Candy is talking about her brother, she never ever used the same name on the same day her usual term for him was "Dipstick on monkey bullocks" and even sometimes "dog breath" mainly because he never brushes his teeth. "She came at me calling me an evil old bitch, I fell back against the wall.

I grab Tom's shotgun gun, I told her don't came near me, she did so I fired the gun both barrels at once, I thought I broke her bloody shoulder she stood there with no face and half a head the rest of it was across the ceiling and wall. I was going to decorate this room anyway but not with any bodies half a head bloody Ted my brother told me I had made a right mess of things and new who is going to clean that bloody mess up? The ambulance is coming, bit of a way they might even send a bloody helicopter now that will frighten the bloody cows.

"Have you phone the police Candy?" That idiot local police officer said he was just going to sit down and watch the football, so could he come later? Um I said when I explain what had happen, he wanted to know, if I could just hang on till, he does arrive and I will also expect some Wankers from the b homicide detective gang!!

I phone inspector Rick Tompson of the motor crime unit. I once met him two years ago at a police convention. I should call him parrot face because he would constantly repeat himself. To a point of more beer, he drunk more he did slowly repeat himself. I was not to worry he had the phone call and will be or the way once he could locate his car keys. I phone Aunt Candy back and told her that an Inspector Rick Thompson an old friend of mine was on his way. I tried to tell her to stay calm, she could hear the ambulance helicopter above the house trying to find a place to land. She pointed to the paddock. I She then rushed at to see them, when the helicopter landed, Aunt Candy open the gate, but the cows pushed past and surrounded the ambulance crew when they were trying to reach Candy and the house six times her brother had been stabbed with a steak knife that he had given to Alice the teenager to skin and cut the two rabbits. Alice had decided we were going to have pizza not rabbit stew.

It did seem that dinner was either sausages, burgers or pizza since Aunt Candy was living up here with us. Now she was home again, she tried a few roast's meals and even some grilled fish, but Alice did not eat that "muck, it was dog food" in her eyes, Aunt Candy was told after they took Candy's brother Tom away eventually in the helicopter once it was turned on the cows bolted in all directions. Aunt Candy was left a long way from help and very alone. Her neighbors arrived after a phone call. They sold all their cows but will take up milking duties until a better idea can be put together, they were the words of Aunt Candy and not me.

Inspector Rick Thompson did arrive two hours later. I would have loved to have been a fly on the wall, not on the wall where the fragments of Alice's head were still situated. I only hope that Aunt Candy does try to stay calm. I told Rachel how life down on the farm has not gone well for my Aunt Candy. "Shot a double barrel shotgun at the same time" there was a silence before I got the punchline. "Well, she was a gangster's Mole!!" I deference to Aunt Candy and Stan Reed I could see the funny side of Rebecca's dry sense of humor. If was time to go at work the does go quick on the way home, Amy was looking a bit tired, and nor her usual self. When we pulled up at the house, she asked to speak to me.

She had a problem, and did hope that I could help her at her relationship her so called "Menage A Trois" had come to a end. The other two female police officers who Amy had introduce to each other now wanted to become a couple so it was simply "goodbye Amy". I did not know what to expect next but Amy did not hold back on facts.

"It is so strange that the lease on the flat will expire this weekend. The flat was in her name and she was not going to renew the lease, in fact she wanted to start a fresh!! The mention of the "Garden Cottage" I had empty and if she could rent it for a while. I had to tell her that the so called "Garden Cottage" is one bedroom shower, toilet, kitchen and lounge all together. It is fully functional, although it does belong to the boys, it is another play arena, well now the pool room has taken over that actual decision now. Will have to be more by them

"So, when"? Asked Amy

"There is no time like the present I told her the four boys were happy to somebody they called "Big Sister". I told Amy

"Well, it is it up to them they will have to vote"

I must say the reaction was of swift that Amy started to cry she was overwhelmed with emotion.

"Of course, you can, but how much are you going to pay us in rent" they asked.

I thought my boys are growing up. After a lot of negotiation, it was agreed one hundred dollars, but eating with us you will have to talk to the twins about food and cleaning and washing. I thought hag on I pay all the bills here and I am missing out. I was happy. I phone up the twins, who soon came down when extra money was mention. Washing cleaning and extra meals they agreed on eighty dollars a week. Amy went down to the cottage with boys. She wanted to paint the place and the boys did offer to help. She wanted new furniture and the bed, fridge, also the toaster, kettle and new bed linen. I knew where Amy was going to get this money from out of the ten thousand, I gave her after the Mary River episode for a rainy day. Well, this day had come!! She had only for suitcases, so she would pick them up tomorrow on the way to work and drop them off when she does drop me off her motorbike will go in the garage, she will ride to the Police garage to pick up the car as usual then return here to pick me up. I thought that there was no way I was going to arrive for work on the back of her bloody motorbike.

In the morning Amy told me that she had her four cases in the boot of the car. I did remind Amy and trying to keep a straight face that police vehicles are not to be used for personal use. We both laugh aloud at my comment.

CHAPTER SEVEN

"ANOTHER NEW BROOM "

What can I say to myself in the mirror it's almost midnight the alarm bells have gone off about multiple deaths at a teenage party.

I look at my phone to see also that another new broom Bill Skinner is now the new commissioner of police and acting in my eyes was the new acting assistant commissioner Violet Andrews (the stork) a six-foot five woman with the face of a cow's backside. If she did ever smile, I would imagine after sex with Bill Skinner. Five years working in the traffic control and has little respect from the ground troops. I almost have to stretch my neck when I pass her for a "good-day" whenever she is at in the canteen hunting for food to feed Bill. I heard Amy shoot off on her motorbike to the Police underground car park to fetch my car. I think now that she was got lost, it normally does not take her this long to pick me up.

I decided to make myself a coffee it may be a "long-night". Half a hour and Amy is not evening picking up her phone. I go outside to wait by the front gate. I see a car coming but it is driving too slow for Amy. The car stops and out of the window the head of Insp Philip Requiem (the penguin) in his little car a Volkswagen beetle.

"Want a lift boss I am going to the crime scene". I got in the car it was what I call a little squeezy ok if you are a teenager and in love but no place for two grown men in the front seats of Volkswagen beetle. I did manage to text Amy to say meet me at the crime scene. I have a lift in the penguin mobile. I imagine that she would have a smile at her face after reading that text.

We arrived at the scene in night-cliff only really ten minutes from my home in Coconut Grove. A lot of police and ambulance are here, I did find Chief Insp Harry limes and I got a update "A eighteen year old party for thirty people, we have ten dead, eight also in a bad way, what I can make out six uninvited guests showed up wearing the very same guests showed up wearing the very same sought of animal masks as the so called invited personal, the invited a six in the other and just attached the guests only seven got away over the fence into a neighbor's property. By the time neighbors came to help the invaders had made their way back to two station wagons and took off. "I looked at Harry who did seem a little over whelmed with it all. The team decided to take care of statements from anybody who was still standing. Trails of ambulances were running a shuttle service to the hospital. There were simply not enough ambulances to cope with the situation. I turned to see Doctor Rebecca already covering the dead bodies. She came to say that the deaths of another two teenagers were found on the far side of the pool.

There was no good news, four of my team had COVID so Harry had to make up his team with two from robbery unit and three from fraud and all four from sex crime unit. We also had a ten uniform on the scene, doing crowd control and trying to comfort the parents of some of the teenagers at the party. I turn to find Doctor Rebecca and she told me she did not have enough staff to cope with this tragedy.

"Head down and bum up" I told her without trying to smile when I told her ..

"She will have to manage it did remind her if a war zone in the middle east where she had done most of her training as a Doctor in the Middle East.

I took a walk around to see many officers trying to comforts the teenagers. I was very surprised that two or the invited guests did become taken prisoner by the teenagers one had been shot by the birthday boy himself Charlie Wayne and the other was still alive but he had a large spear stuck in his back. Paramedics wanted to move him, but they needed a Police officer to travel to the hospital with them, the point of the spear did remain in the victims back and the rest of the spear had been cut off by a paramedic. I could see that the victims had turned on him and he was in the eyes of the paramedic "lucky to be alive". I turn to see Amy standing across the room she came over. I told her to explain later we have more urgent problems with the dead and injured. Insp Candle Pickin was just doing what she does best getting on with the job working with a paramedic to try and find out who will be next in the ambulance due to their wounds. She had already one female die in her arms; her arms had been slashed with a sharp knife. Strange about life because I then found out it was the teenager uninvited guest who with a spear in his back was the one who cut her arms. I did take a few minutes to walk around the crime scene in three bedrooms place the living room and victims, some alive and some dead. In the so call entertainment room, I notice five people all shot dead. They laid between what I term as bongs, this was not a normal party. A BBQ and care it was a drug party A my came in and said there were drugs on the floor on the table where even she looked.

"No wonder there was a slow reaction when the killing started most people were simply out of their mind" Amy commented.

She was honest and true; this was no ordinary party for an eighteen-year-old. I met a neighbor who told me the actual birthday party for the family was yesterday and today at eighteen he was given the keys to the house so he could celebrate with his close friends. The parents a Max Wayne a financial know all and his celebrity wife Ann who used to do the weather on the television. Staying in a hotel on town I was told. I got Amy to try and contact them once we found at where they were staying, I made my way back inside to a room within the underground garage I found a pill-press machine capable of pumping at a few thousand illegal tables a rear.

I could see what the uninvited guests were after a rampage had happen in here. So, I thought this financial wizard is making cash on the side of his financial advice. He was giving to anybody who was stupid enough to pay him. Amy returned to let me know that the owners of the property are on their way to meet me.

"I will be here with open arms and handcuffs ready" I told Amy I went back upstairs to see Doctor Rebecca. I had to inform her we found an illegal drug pill machine in the basement. She did inform me without even taking any blood test some of the injured people had shown signs of drug abuse. Some of them could not even put two words together to try and explain what has happen. A lot of tears and screaming was heard with people sitting next to the dead bodies of friends. Amy returns to tell me the two station wagons had been found burnt out on the old Winneli industrial estate. A security guard actually had film on his security camera and on his mobile phone of six persons getting into two other vehicles before they set light to the two station Wagons. There was no number plate on the vehicles when they drove off in.

It was then I had the call the owners of the property Max Wayne and his blonde bombshell wife Anne stood before me. "What a mess your home is around twelve dead the late of count endless ambulances shuffling victims to hospital and please a lot of this was caused by your hubby of illegal pill manufacturing a side line that has cost many lives. I called two uniform police officers to take them to the watch house. Ann Wayne was screaming about her number one son. I told her that he is alive, he old manage to shoot one of the invited guests but now from being a hero he also will be joining you in the watchhouse after a medical examination by the look on their faces I will not be getting a Christmas card from them.

It was time now for Amy to try and explain what exactly happen to her. "A fing booze bus, I got done for driving at eight two in a sixty zone. Plus, they gave me alcohol test. A drug test before you say anything I showed them my identification and where I was going, I even said that Active Commander Aaron Brown head of the detectives will not be a happy Chappie we been called out to a multi killing of teenagers in Nightcliff"

"I was going to the wrong way" they said

"I tried to explain that I had to get the car, then they said that I had made up a trump up story because from now on all personal in the police force must be tested by order of the new assistant police commissioner Violet Andrews".

"You mean the Stork!! I told them That did not go down well, I was clean no booze or drugs but I got a speeding fine which I told them to stick it up whore the sun does not shine anymore. On the way back I should down put on the flashing lights and sirens and stuck my finger at them when I drove past!! I just laugh at Amy's explanation.

It was almost six am and I did need a coffee and even a bacon and egg roll from Macca's. Amy Fuller must of read my mind she showed up with a dozen coffees and some bacon and egg roll for a dozen people now coming to the end of all we could do here at the crime scene for now. All the known people who were involved had now been interviewed. The ambulances had stopped their carrier service to the hospital hours ago. I could see that the sun was above us and will soon full our day. I called an update for my team Chief Insp Harry Lines was speech maker I really do think that he did a good job trying to control everything in an orderly fashion. The Penguin was next he was not only in charge of himself but also had a world of knowledge of past crimes. He did mention the tiger tattoo on the wrist of the dead victim was responsible for some killings with his gun and machete. How many he killed I will have to wait until I get the report from Dr. Rebecca. She really did have her hands full today with reference to the tiger tattoo we have to go back almost ten years now. A local drug groups

All had these markings on their arms and also carried at threats with a machete, chopping off fingers and then sticking them into the victim's mouth was a regular party trick. A Wayne Tickner a lone wolf drug inspector had followed a suspect to the garages at the back of Mitchell Street back packers. The drug dealer was set upon by three men with tiger's tattoos on their arms. Insp Wayne Tickner would never back down from a fight even if the odds were what you might say "Were against him" a production of the three tigers to remove the fingers of the drug dealer who had ventured on to "their patch". The challenge by Insp Wayne did not go well for the three tigers. The first on came at Insp Wayne waving a machete almost in his face when Insp Wayne gave him a quick way to the next life with a bullet right between his eyes. The second tiger had not learnt from his friend falling to the ground he in fact also fell where he stops with a bullet I his forehead. The third tiger was not fooled by the gun on Insp Wayne and simply charged him hitting the third tiger in the shoulder before he left on top of Insp Wayne knocking him to the ground, almost overcome by the force of the third tiger Insp Wayne was fighting for his life ad it was not going his way until the original drug dealer that Insp Wayne was following simply pick up a machete and decided to go into the plastic surgery business. A couple of a simply chop in the neck of the third tiger left him gasping for air and fell on the ground, wiggling like a snake. He was not only in pain but pumping blood out of his neck like a pump at a petrol station.

The so called ran off and left Insp Wayne to phone for an ambulance which was just too late to save tiger three. Insp Wayne had placed a tracking device on the car of the right time drug dealer a person named Tommy regard a small person in the local drug trade but he did believe that he was a king pin. Traffic police picked up Tommy at the truck stop getting petrol at the Berrimah petrol station. There were no drugs on Tommy or in his car, sadly for him he left drugs in his flat that I did find with Chief Inspector John Knight back in those days. Wayne Tickner went on medical leave; some say he had a slight breakdown, well when I last saw him, he was in perfect health with his wife Jane who was an Inspector in the fraud unit. She was at the time the best-looking detective in our group of detectives. There were times when I had to remember at the time that I was married to Kate and was the father of four young boys. The sold their house to non-other that Chief Insp John Knight and his wife Bouncy Becky. Smart John did offer cash for the house where he had got that money from is another story that always led me to think that not only Alf Jackson an Inspector like me who was also known to except a brown paper bag full of money. Poor Wayne struck a bad deal and John Knight was about fifty thousand short of what he said he would pay in cash. The word was that John Knight would pay the short fall in a couple of months, when Wayne world be up in Queensland and owner of a small caravan park for tourist.

There was no love lost between Wayne and john in fact I did well out of the sale of the cinema the BBQ and pizza oven that the culture located on I was given at a very low price by Wayne I even got a motor mover thrown in which I gave to my neighbor and in return he would cut my grass for a six pack of beer whenever it needed to be cut. He also kept my pool clean and tested the water weekly. I never ever saw my four boys ever go to the toilet in the garden. They were swimming in their own urine my wife Kate used to say to them they are of course denied "peeing in the pool".

I always had good swim every day in the pool with four little boy's pee added to adjust the water level I used to tell Kate I always had to shower outside just like the boys had to with orders from Kate no pee smell at the dinner table. I did feel sorry for John Knight, it was not in the contract but he had agreed to take the house full furnished. It was two-bedroom one bed had never been slept on when John put the key into the front door and made a fuss of carrying his wife inside, it was simply almost a empty cave, a description John told me the next day. He was surprised that Wayne had even left the pool. The BBQ pizza oven was gone, even the pots and pans in the kitchen had gone, one broken chair in the lounge room looked really lonely. I do remember that I had to try and keep it straight face when John told me his bad luck. I do remember Alf Jackson had a good laugh at the expense of John Knight between us the Penguin and myself gave a update to the rest of the team. When the Penguin went out to the old industrial site in Winnelli he found the two burnt out het away cars and also one of the raiders of the party had been wounded in the leg and back by a unknown shooter, who was simply dump by the side of the road leading to the highway they burnt at four wheel wagons.

The victim was shoot twice in the face at a point-blank range. It did mean now that eight intruders wearing masks with now only five got away. I asked the Penguin if he thought that these were the sons of the old tigers out at Hepburn springs. I got a lot of coughing and even some spitting at the ground before he gave me a thumbs up to my opinion. It was then around eight am and I had a phone call from Rachel Todd my office manager. I was needed back in my office because the new police commissioner Bill Skinner and something that did resemble a "Giraffe"

it's a stork not a giraffe I told Rachel "Anyway the so-called acting assistant police commissioner. Violet Andrews who was actually sitting at my desk and trying to get access to my laptop on my desk. Rachel had informed her she did not know the so called "Password" to enter my private laptop.

They both seem to have stormed off now after comments about nobody in the office working. Rachel had tried to explain everybody who was available were out at the Nightcliff crime scene where at least a dozen people had been shot and more are on life support in the hospital. A vacant look by good old Bill Skinner and Violet Andrew did mean that has no idea where major crime unit was doing today. It was a great way to start your new position I did think to myself. The mumbling of that they better go out to pay me a visit and my team did put a smile on my face mainly because I was about to hear to that out in Hepburn Springs to see if the five young tigers are home exactly where their fathers once lived. Many moons ago I say it and to quote the Penguin in would be "pot luck"!! I did make the call to tactical support. I would imagine that they would bring "big bertha" an armored bullet proof truck"

That you could not stop in its tracks unless you hit it when a antitank missile. We stop just outside Hepburn spring in a lay-bay. We gave tactical support Inspector Alan Jenkins a update. Alan was just starting in tactical support ten years ago and did remember us two just ducking bullets because they were in a wooden barn and had not much protection from the bullets flying past our ears when we got to the end of the road. Insp Alan Jenkins used modern technology to launch a drone to fly over the property three farm houses still standing and two barns one I imagine would leak when it rained. There were small children running around. It was my call to go ahead on take it easy and slowly step by step. The last thing I wanted was dead children and woman on my conscience today. I did imagine old Bill Skinner blowing blood vessel in his neck or her first day in the job as "Top dog"

A new plan was given by Insp Alan Jenkins I had to just go along with it. The two barns were above a hundred years from the actual main house. The sound of our police tank was enough for that mother and kids run for cover inside the house. Automatic fire came from one barn without any hesitation the order was given for driving straight through the front doors and just maybe continue out the other side. Yes, it was like one of those American crime shows on television. With "a gun ho attitude" I had to admit I was like a spoils that you would find in Disney land, the Penguin was next to me with a steel helmet on. He was trying not to get any of his feathers shot at in big breath went and right at the back of the barn, I looked at the structure and it did not look like it was going to fall down. Tactical support also open fire and within it was sadly all over, I did not even fire a shot and the Penguin almost laying on the ground now had not even got his gun out of its holster. Five men arrived outside the front of the building hands on their heads and now down on their knees they were given some police jewelry to wear "handcuffs" all place in separation transportation. This was the old barn that we search and found no drugs but this time I saw a pill making machine plus plenty of drugs to mix together to give those dancers in night club a real bounce in their step. I needed more police officers here, all adults which did include the woman and mothers of the children had to be interviewed. At the very same time my phone was going into overtime. It was Bill Skinner a man who I had only given a fake smile to in the corridor of power not a word had even left my lips in his direction. "Where the F are you, Aaron?" he was at the crime scene we just left a house age in Nightcliff.

I did want to make the joke that if you want to keep up with me, you will have to move a little faster Bill!! I could hear the stork in the background flapping her the wings and giving orders to Bill who I thought at the time he should remind her that she is the puppy in this relationship and he was top dog. We did eventually agree that I will be here at this farm for at least another two to three hours. The last word Bill said "Don't move stay there. I need to catch up!!" I did think that I was having a bad day but when Bill did phone me to say that his car had a puncture what could I do but laugh after I put down the phone on bill. Large amounts of free-flowing marijuana were even growing between the tomato plants. "Eddie the drug dog" I did imagine think it was his birthday plus large amounts of cash and enough drugs to light up the whole of Darwin on New Year 's Eve even without the fireworks.

I was trying not to laugh at the six females trying to tell me that they had no idea about the drugs on the property in fact their comments I found really funny and to be bold they soon stop when I mention that they were living off the proceeds of money from the drugs and could end up in prison and the children will be put into care I told Amy to phone the child protection unit. I did continue looking over the three main houses. In a small wooded area, I found an old friend hiding inside her one-bedroom cabin. Iris Norton a lone survivor of the raid ten years ago.

"Well, well well if it is not bullock chops himself the big shot Brown!!"

"Nice of you to remember me, Iris in fact you do seem to be the only one left in the raid ten years ago".

"Listen bullock chops, yes, I am. You killed three of my sons in town and then put their two cousins into prison the they become old men, yes, I know you, bullock chops!!"

"So, what became of the other three females here then?" I asked.

"They went down south, never heard a word from then, the four children drag them screaming into a van, and put them into care. Now the four did return when they did turn eighteen and carried on living here and may I say they did bring a couple of young fellas from the home you had them cooked up in. I did try to see my grandchildren but I could not get any help from any Fing person who knew where they were. I stayed here self-sufficient I got chickens for eggs and grew my own Fing fruit and veg, I did not want any Fing government handouts.

"So, you get no pension then" I asked her still with what I would call a violent tongue.

"Yes, I get some money Fing peanuts, just enough to buy a few little things. I was tired of talking to her now Fing this Fing that everybody else in the world was a Fing rat bag. A low life in her eyes. I still had the team search her little house. I found some evidence that she still like to smoke the old marijuana I do believe she should change her name to cannabis!! She even had it growing in pots beside her front door. "The old puff weed is for my own personal use" I had to reply there is more growing here than you need for personal use.

It was the law and I got one of my team to charge here with her own personal crime. I looked down the wood to see even more plants she had the old ginger plant growing everywhere. "A mini plantation" Amy laughs at me, it was then that Insp Sally Morgan arrived, once a hero in the sex crime unit and now in her eyes demoted to the children's protection unit care of Bill Skinner and his side kick "the Wandering Stork". It did not take him long before who he described as "the waster" so he moved us around and today is my first day child minding"!!

I broke the news to Insp Sally "five kids all under eight years old have to be put into care until child services get off their ass and decided what to do with them. "Sorry but it is not really our problem we just "handball" them and simply pass them on to a government department who spend most of their days doing nothing" at least I got a laugh and cheeky smile out of Insp Sally.

"I look at Chief Insp Harry Lines who did seem to have now a new lap dog the Penguin"

"All the past is never far away, I just seen Iris Norton she is still alive and kicking" mumble the Penguin.

I simply replied "it must be all the bloody dope she is smoking and she is growing it for sale" I laughed.

"I had a fight with her, a machete she held it in hand right in my face. I simply ducked and punch her in the face, yes, I broke her nose" I could do nothing but laugh at the comment from the Penguin.

"Hey they did not even charge her with anything yet she was the matriarch of this family and now she has given inspiration to another generation to continue the drug dealing. Looking at Chief Insp Harry Lines who wanted to know how this family did manage to slip under the radar. I simply said the whole of the Darwin area and country side around here is full of people who are slipping under the radar daily, until they do something wrong, we do not notice them. I looked at Chief Inspector Harry Lines who simply said "so we are in other words short staff" a sign of the times not only in the police but in all social services, hospitals. You name it every area in our lives are running short staff. But we try and with a bit of careful planning do come at on top for a while.

Now it was time to return Amy said "The Top Dog and the Stork" have arrived.

Bring the car around to the south side of the property and we will make a quick exit. I told a sad looking and very tired Harry to get out team and go home it is now sixteen hours that we have been working. We all need a seat in a hot tub and few beers and some sleep. My phone rang and it was the Stork.

"So where are you Commander Aaron Brown we need to catch up"

"Sorry but I am at my way home now after a sixteen-hour shift, now maybe tomorrow when I arrive at work we can catch up!!

The pool old Stork just slams down the phone on me. I might be trying to avoid the Stork and her pet human Bill Skinner tomorrow. I have the Wayne Family to interview with them their drug manufacturing operation and of course we also have the Tiger gang to also interview. I was already eating my BBQ Tuna and a huge plate of salad for dinner or was an extra late lunch. I only had a bacon and egg roll in the last sixteen hours. In fact, I could eat a bloody horse the way my belly felt. Ice cream and chopped mango washed down with a couple of beers.

Amy soon joined me. She was going for a swim in the pool after her meal and then straight to bed that alarm clock was on time in the morning and I manage to catch the boys last night and this morning that did manage to put a smile on my face. Amy was waiting with me can I did ask her to drop me off at reception I am due for a showdown with Uncle Bill and the Stork. During a meeting I did wonder who was in charge was it Bill on the Stork. I did hear that she wore the pants when Bill was in charge of traffic amongst the uniform officers. I also knew that Uncle Bill could not run a "Piss up in a brewery" every minute or so the story would turn to Bill and let him talk.

In the end after a very boring conversation, I had come to realize that there will be changes that I will not agree on. I was told several times by the story. Who I did arrive with this speech lined up on my tongue. "Chief Insp Violet Andrews" your appointment to Assistant police commissioner has not yet been rubber stamp so I still out rank you and will not be taking any notice of one word you will say "The look on the face of the storm she was speechless. Her beak was wide open, yet no words were coming out.

"Well, I do have to agree with the Active Commander of detectives Aaron Brown that he is "Technicality" right my dear Violet. I did think if only John Knight was here still alive to see this, he would have roared with laughter and said something like "nice one Aaron and now take that in Stork and swallow it". I was not in any way going to humble myself to her in anyway.

Then I thought that Bill Skinner was also thinking of his sex life with the stork. She did have ruffled feathers, so Bill did decide to throw mid in my face "of course Aaron you were only the so-called assistant commissioner under John Knight and you could not handle the position".

I felt that vein on my neck about to burst. "Excuse me Bill old mate, I did handle the position under John Knight very well in fact I was doing his job also for a mouth, yes, I stood down and did not want to sit in the chair that you are now sitting in. After both John Knight and Jenny Green had sat in that chair. I did decide not to there up the position and it was decided that I did not want to be second best being the assistant commissioner of police. I came back to my old job as Active Commander of detectives. I then put it to an open mouth Bill who did look like me was just trying to catch flies that the Stork was feeding him with the flutter or her eye lids "Anything you want me to go Bill, you just give me the heads up, I will be very happy to retire!!!"

"Sorry Aaron this whole conversation was not trying to make you feel humble on even "degraded" in any way, I am more than happy for you to continue in your position leading the great team of detectives"

I could see that the look on the face up the story these words were not exactly what she wanted Bill to say to me.

It was time to leave, I did shake the hand of Bill but not the wing of the Stork who stood tall over me. She did offer her hand but I simple turned and in my very own little way I quick goose step to the lift and went downstairs for an update and plan for today. I did have a cheeky smile on my face I could tell that Rachel Todd my office manager really wanted to know about my showdown with Bill and the Stork, sorry to say that she would be out of luck I was not going to make a comment "ground rules today first up will be the matriarch Iris Norton then the Wayne family.

And finally, we will start to interview then charge the five teenagers well young adults we located here after their bloody killing spree. "I drank my coffee and gave everybody a list of jobs to do. I did not want anybody slipping through our fingers today!! That was the end of the speech. I did realize that we did not have all the facts so far but I had faith in my team to put their heads together and come up with the answers to the missing pieces of the puzzle and the real reason that set this chain of events Iris Norton did have Joan Freres the local solicitor of low life in my point of view.

"So, who is going to feed my chooks and the two goats" asked Iris to start our interview on the right footing. I simply replied "that I do imagine animal welfare, to be honest I had not given it a thought Iris". I could tell that this was going to be what I call a nonproductive interview. The next path Iris took was she had no idea what she was even doing here today. It was now for a big of enlighten for Iris. I gave flashbacks to ten years ago when she was given a simple slap on the wrist by the judge, due to health problems well she had survived another ten years so in my eyes she could not be on her so called "death bed". Iris did admit a suck on the bong for breakfast did put her in good health for the day. I could tell that Iris was not going to admit that this group of Tigers had been given knowledge from her in combat and of course the finer art of drug production, thrown in being a good sales person, while watching your back and keeping at the eye of the local law makers. It was in there hours a waste of my time in my life.

Apart from running the cultivation of her green plant marijuana I had nothing to prove that she had taught this team of young men, unless one of them does open the door to the real facts.

I could hold her for another seventy-two hours I would have to let her go with only charges of the marijuana production. Which I knew would only be a slap on the wrist. Iris would not face jail time at her age of seventy-two. So, I had a late breakfast egg and bacon roll extra chilly and a coffee thick shake gave my tummy a rumble and my back side to let some air cut.

I made my way to see Max Wayne with Lily Rodney somebody who looked like a cat walk model with the head of a crocodile snap snap went the lips of Lily about her client held twenty-four hours in a cell without a charge. How good was my patience today I think Lily was about to find out. Max Wayne was a much-loved person in society he helps the poor with his wife. I had the comment that did squeeze the air out of Wayne when I said he have food in one hand and drugs in the other to the poor and vulnerable people.

The mention of the party and every person there was tested for drugs and everybody had the green light. I went on to the Pill press down in his basement. I was very surprised he told me he had lived in the house for six months now and had never been down to the basement. He had a Gardner who used to keep all the pool chemicals down there and the ride on lawn mower the actual suggestion that the drug did belong to his Gardner and none of his family are involved. I had to throw right back into the face of Max that his son Charlie was giving at drugs like lollies to just make sure everybody "got high".

Being told that Robby who went by other names and was a hero. He shot and killed one of the people who invaded the party being told Robby fought off the uninvited party guest with his bare hands and got hold of the gun and shot the uninvited guest. At this point I wanted to know why these uninvited guests even showed up at the party. So, Robby Wayne is sometimes named Charlie Wayne.

I did have my own theory that it was planned and it was an excuse for a home invasion except Max the person they were looking for was not there. I did get a round of applause from Max for being a dreamer when I open up that I have already pick up a couple of local drug dealers who used to sell drugs for Max on the street. I could see by the look on the face of Max that I had hit a raw nerve. I could tell that inside his head the engine was now slowly running at of steam. Who did I have who has down a deal with me and simply thrown him under the bus to save themselves. A total of fifteen had died and another six are critical, three more are in a hospital ward and only six people did manage to get away by climbing a fence to safety to next door. We had statements to all those who could give them. Plus, endless hours of footage taken on a selection of mobile phones. Pictures of your son Robby handing "You mean Charlie, don't you? Max Wayne was eager to correct me.

The mention of Robby now eighteen years old will go to a man's prison for his crimes killing an uninvited guest will not save him from prison. My next person who you think looked like a "dog's dinner" without her makeup locked up in a cell and now listening to every word I was saying with her high class solicitor Elsie Walters the old "No comment" was simply used to everything I said to Annie Wayne once the weather girl on the six o'clock news until she showed up for work after a sniff of cocaine. Those was still traces of the powder on her nose a makeup artist blew the whistle on Annie just before she was going to take the step-in front of the weather board viewers were told that Annie had a medical condition and had been rushed to hospital, in fact she was sacked on the spot and booted out of the television studio I do think that Annie had not look into a mirror in the past twenty four hours. I had to tell her that the Police Doctor had given a drug report that read she will not be giving a weather update even in her cell.

I found the comment funny but I did not laugh in fact I had to come to terms with that Annie could be behind the drugs given to her son and not her husband Max. I did confront Annie with this thought of mine. I knew she would deny any knowledge of the drugs at the party for her birthday boy. I did feel this was much closer to the truth again only the Gardner goes down in the basement. The excuse that Annie does not like spiders was a very weak excuse for not going down to the basement. The Gardner a Wilf Epsom had not idea about drugs being manufacturing on that pill machine which stood next to the ride on Lawn mower. Wilf Epson was an ex-drug dealer, off the radar for five years and now in a paradise of drugs. Which I did deep down believe that it was wild who knew all about working the pill machine. It was in his eyes a bonus of the job. Yet to be interviewed by was on the Radar of Chief Insp Harry lines who had him in custody after he did try to do a runner towards a greyhound bus, only to be met by Harry who checked his ticket before pointing to a patrol car which would take him to the watch house. I was given a repeat on a piece of information that Wilf Epsom was throwing everybody under the bus and even himself. I locked at Annie and I slowly broke the news to her then she tried to tell me she never had any contact with the Gardner that was her husband's department. A large slice of apple pie and ice cream washed down with a blue berry smoothie. I was ready to at last meet the Wayne family hero Robby. I started the banter by telling him that he must of save lives with his hero killing of one of the uninvited guests. He also did manage to spear another invited guest in the back with a Large spear that used to be found on the lounge wall. I showed Robby footage of him handing at drugs. I do love it when they say that is not me it is somebody else. Until we got to the point some naughty person did mention his name on a video. The exact words "that of you want more drugs Robby has a large stash of whatever you want".

I told him you can never trust your friends to keep their mouths shit. Carol Williams the solicitor who was responsible for this way ward young man. I also enjoy the excuse I often give being told that we had doctored this tape to try and show that Robby was involved in handing out drugs at the party. I did try and get Robby to try and remember when he tried to give drugs to the neighbor's teenage girls for sex. Daddy Max Wayne had to pay off the neighbor with a holiday in Bali all expenses paid. I knew that Robby would not remember that incident Robby at school was the one to see after school if you wanted to get high the neighbors had not held back. I told Robby he would not be getting a medal for bravery but maybe ten to twelve years in the adult prison instead when the name of Alf Jackson being a close friend of Max Wayne and even shared a menage a trios with Annie and Max I really did not want to learn anymore about Annie Wayne. I did suspect now that my old friend and workmate Alf Jackson was the source of Annie Wayne drug habit before she went into business on her own Elsie Walters Annie's solicitor did try to tell me that the Ex-Police Inspector Alf Jackson was to blame for the so-called description of this family I simply said "Alf Jackson is dead" can we now move on. I am only interested in who was behind the drugs at the home of Max and Annie Wayne. I will not hold back until I get to the truth. All I got from Elsie Walters was she understood with the comment all those families now destroyed because of an eighteen-birthday party that ended in so, any dead and those who lived through it all will have nightmares of course Elsie Walters was right but Max and Annie Wayne were not going to take any responsibility for the deaths of the teenagers who got an invitation to an eighteen birthday party.

I had to return to my office, I had a cup of black coffee and realized that my shift was almost over. The day was not lost after all a Chief Inspector Steve Reed came to my office with a police traffic officer Ali Jenkins. I called over Amy Fuller my driver. I knew what this was all about in a strange why it was an apology to Amy and to me for the incident of the traffic stop with Amy on her motorbike. Ali Jenkins was only following orders from the Stork herself all officers off duty must be tested for drink and drugs. The speeding fine Chief Insp Steve Reed did rip up in front of us. I had to slip in and sat that I would have paid the fine not Amy she was only doing her duty, although I am always telling Amy to slow down. I did think if you do believe that you will believe that pigs do fly with Storks!!

I had asked before about the Penguin and I was told once again that he was back out at the Tiger residence and had requested Black Betty the sniffer dog of many talents. About one hundred yards from the home of the matriarch Iris Norton Black Betty would not move from a spot in the woods. A couple of people directed by the Penguin started to dig. I have to say that black Betty is never wrong, it was a body, buried with its head removed and one hand laid next to the right arm. Round the neck was a large gold chain with the "letter T" on it. There was only person who did wear a chain like that and had been off or radar for a few weeks now. Gene Tunny a very well-oiled thug who worked for Stan and Cyril Reed. dressed in a black suit with a bow tie on the door of their night club for some unknown reason Gene Tunny had done a vanishing act about two weeks before the Reed Brothers got put through a wooden chopper machine down by the river by me. I was well out of the picture in relation to the deaths of the Reed brothers.

I do imagine that Gene Tunny came here to the Tiger's den and started to throw his weight around and in return somebody threw a wood choppers axe at him that was the end of Tunny who had placed many people in a critical condition in the hospital over the years. Out of his forty years in jail. His last term of ten years I did help him point to the direction of a prison cell. Now I say give Black Betty a special treat now. A large commercial find of MDMA some ketamine and every strong LSD with even more money hidden under the cupboard in the kitchen of Iris Norton. I do know that she will say we planted the drugs and money there "trying to stitch up a poor old pensioner who is only trying to give a home to teenagers who have lost their way in life which did bring me to show time of this very extended family of Iris Norton. Eight males carried the Norton surname, plus five females and five children all named Norton.

I sat down with Doctor Rebecca to listen to the truth of who was who, and if I did not already guess none of the males or females and even Norton but also to each other in any way. Insp Candle Pickin had in fact had a quite word to the females about the children and they all blew back into her ear that none of the males here had been sexually active in the production of the children. In fact, four of the eight males were gay and were in a relationship with other males in the group. My mind was blown I have been and dare I say it "baking up the wrong tree"

The five females were:

    Crystal John's son Peter

    Willow Candle son Johnny

    Dawn Sharp daughter Yvonne

    Katie Weir's daughter Mandy

    Kathy Bright daughter Sally

The eight males were:

    Watt Smith

    Arty Jones

    Kenny Wilson

    Will Thompson

    Adam Wayland

    Lov Barnes

    Deacon Judd

    Andy Smyth

All eight came from broken homes and when Iris Norton did offer them a home with a roof over their head and more money that they will see in a lifetime they took a chance. I was to learn that the five females and eight males all called Iris Norton's mother and the children called her grandmother.

I was going to interview each of the males myself to learn more about their activities first up was Watt Smith, he boosted that he had shot five people at the Wayne property he did show no remorse his attitude was that it was his duty to protect the honor of the Tiger community. On the other hand, number two an Arty Jones who showed a lot of confidence but ended up with a spear in his back and was handcuffed to a bed in hospital.

Number three Kenny Wilson was shot in the leg and back of the head by the driver of the second car will Thompson, who decided that Kenny Wilson being wounded by a stray bullet from the gun of Watt Smith. Kenny Wilson did need to go to hospital and was going to make his own way there but Will Thompson had other ideas for Kenny Wilson. So, he just shot him. The body of Kenny Wilson was found in tall grass not far from the two burnt out vehicles in the old Winnelli Estate.

Number five was an Adam Wayland who had a habit of rubbing his eyes after crying about the crimes I was talking about in his little mind those people in the house of Wayne Family were all sent by Satan.

It was another twist to the background story and I do believe it was the teaching of Iris Norton had brain washed Adam Wayland. Number six was a Lou Barners the only half Asian in the group. He was evicted by his parents for the rape of his twelve-year-old sister and he was also already on MDMA at that time. Iris Norton found him sleeping in a shop door in the city of Darwin. She did take him to her home and seduced him regular "sexual activity with mother" was now normal for Lou Barners who slept with mother every night now. Number seven was Deacon Judd, another one who was proud of "chopping the mother fuckers up" with his machete. He did not need to use his gun he told me. last but not the least number eight was an Andy Smith, who did seem to be a leader of the group under the watchful eye of Irish Norton "the mother who made our dreams came true".

Andy smith gave details of the drug manufacturing. He also gave a insight to a couple more of the missing pieces of the so called Iris Norton puzzle. I was to learn that Stan and Cyril Reed actually bank rolled the whole operation. So, the two brothers kept their hands clean of the drugs. It all came to an end when Gene Tunny showed up with new grand rules. No more finance and he was fifty percent of the sales of the drugs he told Iris Norton who gave her answer when he attacks Andy Smith and knocked him to the ground, he was going to kill Andy Smith to make an example of him. It was going so well until Iris Norton placed a wood choppers large axe into the back of the neck of Gene Tunny, he fell, still with his head on and went to reach for his gun, when Iris Norton had not finished swinging the axe and chop off his right hand with the axe before he could fire his gun. Just to make sure that this was really the very end of Gene Tunny she hit his neck again and the head of Gene Tunny rolled down the embankment with two dogs chasing it. The body of Gene Tunny they buried. I did remind the mind of Andy Smith "six feet under" was a term in a church yard to burn the dead. They only bury Gene Tunny even four foot under and that was why black Betty the sniffer dog found the body. Two weeks later Stan and Cyril Reed went to Berry Springs where a Max Wayne shot them and dump the bodies into the river. Mother Iris Norton had told the young men that Max Wayne would be coming for them all. So, a party at the weekend at the Wayne's house for the birthday boy Darly Wayne would be a good time to strike first. There was one small problem to two people on the hit list Max his wife Annie were not there so the team took out everybody who stood in their way when the search the home for Max and Annie.

I was exhausted and sitting next to me was Sgt Billie Mayford now back in my good books. When we left the interview room, she only had a few words to say "Wow what a fing story that was!!". I did tend to believe Andy Smith. He had nothing to lose he would only ever see sunlight from his cell window and even out on the exercise yard. None of the six teenagers I had lunch a large piece of warm apple pie well a double serve if I was to be honest and extra ice cream.

In the afternoon and may I say early evening a meeting with Insp Candice Pickin the Attorney general and the so-called big head Stan Worrel acting Chief Prosecuting officer acting is a good term to use. Insp Candice Pickin was leading the charge to free the five mothers and five children to be released, no charges at all to be placed in witness protection.

Anew identity and to be shot to the five different locations in Australia under witness protection to start a new life child service showed up uninvited and were told by the Attorney General that they have no say in the future of the five mothers and their children. Having them places in a hotel until after the trial of Iris Norton and the six teenage males would not benefit anybody. Threats of action and even going to the press would cost a Shirley Williams her job in a couple of days in the position of child services. I did manage to have the Penguin with Black Betty our own star on four legs, do a search of the name of Shirley Williams home. Her husband Ray Williams was a drug addict and in the eyes of the Penguin and with his inner thoughts of his famous words once a drug addict always a drug addict. A disgrace Shirley Williams was caught smoking a bong herself when the Penguin and Black Betty beside him through the front door of Shirley Williams home!!

Shirley Williams still with more threats of going to the media, her mouth the size of a barn door was about to have a life change, not only suspension from her position as head of child services she was given the sack. It was not a good look for her picture of sucking on a bong ended up on the front page of the local newspaper. She had a large reception of mothers and their children waiting for Shirley to come home. Poor Ray Wiliams her husband was already on a suspended sentence due to my team in the drug unit the cell door was already open for him. I was given the call that Ray had some useful information to trade if he did not have to go back to prison. I went to visit Ray in the interview room "glad it is you and you have always been when I call a real man Mister Brown sir" I did sit down and to think I already thought that it might be a waste of time being wrong again. I did learn the source of the drugs that Ray Williams was going to be open with. It was something that he had never shared before. A mention of a property out at Hepburn Springs run by an old lady they call mother a group of teens worked in a production line. I waited for the name of Iris Norton to come up in lights. Little did Ray know that I was already up to date of the life and times of Iris Norton. Ray got a big fat "No" in reference to his freedom. Three years away from Shirley his wife was a bonus having to listen to her go on about her work day every evening when she got home, 'It was a bonus" shouted Ray once again taken back to his cell before he would have a nice country ride out to Berrimah prison, where he will be able to catch up with his old friends once again. I went back to my office when I got the call from Bill Skinner our new top dog my presence was required on the top floor.

I was met by the Stork no longer acting assistant commissioner it was hard to answer a question because they both seem to have so many questions for me to answer. I had to stop the Stork snapping her beak and flapping her wings while Bill was trying to put a sentence together. Finally, the subject was the five females and their children going into Witness protection. I did think then that Uncle Bill has a spy in my office. I was about to drop what I call "the perfect bombshell" I simply had no idea where the females and children are going. They are now in witness protection and are already on their journey. "You must have some idea where they could I say to her except that I am not privilege to that information or even will be. Being told that somebody must know what could I say except nobody in my office or even in this building would have a clue!!

I was told that I was being awkward and not very cooperative. I just shrugged my shoulder and with hat an almost violent Stork pointed to the office door I stood waiting for the lift to come up and I thought to myself "what a wonderful life that I do lead as head of the detective division". Back down stairs in my office with an over filling of jam and cream and a mug of reinforced tea which could be used as a paint stripper, if need be, Rachel Todd my office manager could tell by the look on face not to ask how did my meeting go with Bill and the Stork? Instead, I was told that Carol Reed wife of Cyril Reed a missing Mob King had received a phone call from Iris Norton of all people. I listen to the recording after I was told that Rachel had put the recording through voices, we had decided on a computer file. I was so surprised but even more with the conversation between these ladies was exactly right not to admit to anything over the phone. Carol denied that her husband was involved in some sought of deal with Iris Norton. He was a hard-working business man who worked hard for his family values. The mention of two hundred thousand dollars Iris wanted from Carol who still denied all knowledge of what Iris was saying to do with drugs. An investigation on going by the police still did not bother Carol who told Iris that the police are still searching for her husband Cyril and his brother Stan who had been missing for over a good month now. Iris had to have the last word, listen bitch give me the last money, your old man and his brother were simply croc bait and you can thank Max Wayne for that bitch!! Carol hang-up after she told Iris she was a dopey bitch; the bloody police ate listening in to all my calls just in case Cyril gives me a call!!

I looked at Chief Insp Harry Lines and simply asked "How the F did Iris get hold of a phone to call Carol Reed?

She was let at about two hours ago, I just only found out, the Covid problems the hospital does need the bed, Iris is in the Stuart Motel on Stuart highway there is supposed to be a team keeping an eye on her. I just did not whether to laugh or cry. I told Harry to get his ass in gear and get over to check on Iris myself. He did phone the team who were sitting across the road from the motel. Iris was walking outside her room stretching her legs she told Harry Lines when he showed up to question her. The phone he borrowed from a house maid and now she has given it back to her. Harry was making his way back to his car with Sgt Billi Mayford when a burst of bullets came from a very fast-moving car. Iris had been hit five times two in her Chest she would have been dead better she hitting ground was a fast opinion by Doctor Rebecca.

I stood over the body of Iris Norton while the good doctor pointed to the bullet wounds. Doctor Rebecca opens the mouth of Iris to show me that it was more than toothpaste on the teeth of Iris Norton it was cocaine. I just had to say to Harry Lines who look a little defeated now. "Was she high when she was talking to you?" I asked Harry who told me he found it hard to understand some of her words, she was mumbling she had been at the motel room not even three hours and high on cocaine. "So where did she manage to get the magic powder?" I asked him.

"Ah that bloody house maid she must have known Iris in the past and she might even do some business together" I looked at Harry and simply said "Done some business together!! The house maid had simply knocked off early the motel manager told me with the name of Maley Brent the house maid was on our person of interest pace. I sent the penguin and a team to her flat that was only a mile away the words that "she has flown the coup" was the last thing I wanted to hear from the Penguin. I sat on the motel wall and then I did realize that Iris had been set up, I had a couple of people of interest Cyril Reed who must have been very fast acting and of course Max Wayne who is locked in a cell but still could be getting so sought of freed back that he is behind the Reed brothers Cyril and Stan who went swimming with the crocs near Berry Springs. It was time to pay Carol Reed a visit first. I looked at my watch and realized that I have worked way past my usual hours in the day I did expect a rough meeting from Carol Reed who used to be a bar person working for Cyril. I could tell by her attitude that she had not lost any of her charm over the years,

"Have you found any trace of my beloved husband Cyril, if not why not and what the F are you doing about it"

I had to put my hand up to try and control Carol who did seem to have been on the old brandy bottle that looked a little lonely on the sofa next to her. It was empty a little like or now one-sided conversation. I did mention Iris Norton and the phone call "So you are listening in to my very personal calls. You should be out looking for my Cyril and his bloody halfwit brother. There was no love lost for Stan I thought. There was silence before Carol drop her brandy class on the floor. It was empty, she smiled and said "the prick Max Wayne could have something to do with my husband not being active anymore in my life?"

"There is so proof that Max Wayne removed him from your life; we found no evidence and certainly no body".

"The bloody crocs eat him" she screamed at me even before I had time to finish my answer

I went on to say that poor Max Wayne is still in a cell in the watch house and Iris Norton is in the morgue, she was shot about two hours ago, in fact about one hour after she phone you.

"I never met the bitch and Cyril had never mentioned her at home" I did expect that comment from Carol. On leaving I had to throw petrol on the fire.

"Whoever shot her we will catch and I do imagine they will want to do a deal with whom that Carol wanted to give me another blast of her acid tongue. I was happy to take the abuse and it did dawn on me that Cyril had rubbed off on his wife Carol. With the comment that I do expect to return at a later date, I finally left Carol walking to the drink cabinet for another bottle of brandy.

"Show ya fing self out, you were not fing invited anyway!!" I think I got the message from Carol Reed loud and clear.

Sgt Billi Mayford had little to say on leaving which was exactly how I like it. Just about to get in the car, and my office manager Rachel Turner wanted to give me an update on Maley Brent the housemaid. Her brother had the nick name of being called master blaster Bobby Brent a drug dealer who went into the drug trade at a early age he did like to sample everything. He was selling at the time he got more that he bargains for with a shot of heroin in his arm he did not ever take the needle out of his arm. The drug had been a little on the strong side, I was glad that Bobby Brent had not sold any to his costumers. We had no clue who provided the drug heroin to him. Even Iris Norton was on our suspect list, which must have been ten years ago now. Rachel told me that I had got my time line right so this world makes Brent around eleven years old back then I thought to myself. A long time to hold a grudge, then again, I have known some people who have held a grudge all their life and when cancer set in, they decided to repay the victim with a revenge attack.

Little you can do; trial is a joke they have less than a few months to live so they finally pointed a gun at the victim. Gave them a lecture about why they are about to die then pulled the trigger. I do remember that one old guy killed his very own wife, during carving up a leg of lamb at the Sunday roast dinner in front of his three grown up children, wives and children. The husband did believe his wife had been unfaithful forty-eight years ago. Both Amy and Billi at listening to my story in the car. We had a lead on Maley Brent. A family farm just before the now famous Humpty Do turn off, three miles down a dirt track. It was the last farm at the end of the road. I did decide to ask tactical support to join us, I was not going to be cut down in a hail of bullets before I had my dinner tonight, to die on an empty stomach somehow had always haunted me, all my life, the only person who was home was Maley Brent hanging on the end of a rope from a beam in the kitchen.

I could tell even before I made the call to Dr. Rebecca Mitcham that this was not suicide. She had been beaten to death crack ribs and marks on her back from being hit with a baseball bat that still laid on the floor. Sgt Billi wanted to know why somebody would want to kill her?

"She was the bread crump trail" I told her.

"She would of lead us to them maybe in a strange way. I called in the death of Maley Brent, then I was informed by Rachel Todd my office manager that Carol Reed had been talking to somebody on a Burner Phone in this area. Carol wanted to know is it done yet? That was all very drunken Carol kept saying over and over!!

I decided to call into the Stuart Motel and talk to the owner about what he knew about the lie and times of Maley Brent. I was to learn even before we arrived that the Stuart motel was owned by the Reed Family and this made, me think that Iris Norton was actually set up to be killed there. I did know deep down it was a stab in the dark on the other hand I could be right.

I do like it when people of interest do remember me, even from ten years ago. I knew the face and I must say he had given weight watchers a very wide Berth I was looking at Maley Brent manager of the Stuart Motel also uncle to Maley Brent the mention of the death of Bobby Brent then it all the past fame rushing back to me. if my memory does serve me well Rory Brent was a big-headed prick ten years ago when still holding the position as a manager at the Stuart Motel. I put it down to some thoughts of missing cells in his brain which asked questions like I will be doing today I knew he would try and change the subject with what I could only call "A bloody stupid answer". The death of his niece Maley did nothing to alter the muscles on his face not even a crocodile tear. "Maley could not take the pressure and with the death of Iris Norton she knew that she may be next the real fact was that Maley had used her used by date and was simply a long-term motor mouth in some eyes.

Rory Brent made one crave mistake that I will mention later. A rumble on of events about Iris Norton being raided again and her so called boys will end up in prison just like the last lot. I had to remind Rory that only two went to prison and the other three ended up in a shoot-out in a back Alley close to Mitchel Street. "Ambush by a bloody hit police mob I was told, the three teenagers stood no chance. I was not going to argue the story which was slightly twisted from the real truth and Stan Reed shot by Max Wayne and dump into the river on a monsoon rain event, Fed to the bloody crocs, Cyril and Stan Reed were decent business men. Rory went on to say that he was always well looked after by the two brothers Cyril and Stan. He had some kind words about Iris Norton running a home for females who got put up the spout, cared and looked after the mother and child, she took them under her wing. The runaway teenage young men. Iris gave them hope and future in a family business.

He did not mention the drug factory he did regret that Iris Norton was struck down in a hail of bullets outside her motel room. He did finish by saying that it was not good for business. At least four couples just packed up and left after the gun fire; again, he told me it was not good for business. I was about to leave when I did turn with one last question to ask. Rory "strange that you knew Maley had hung herself, how did you know this Ray". I knew exactly what he was going to say he heard it on the phone when one of the police officers told him. I told him "Ray listens nobody told you how Maley died, you already knew" with that I got two uniform officers place him into police charm bracelets (Handcuffs) a trip to the watch house, where I will put him in the care of the Penguin. I will wonder which of the two of them fall asleep first at the interview. I got Sgt Billi to turn his office upside down. All financial records, laptop, phones and whatever is hidden in the safe.

Rory had his own dog Kennel at the back of the front office so I told Sgt Billi to turn that over. "Have we got a warrant? She asked me.

I gave her the warrant with a half-smile. Amy went for the car and it was then that Sgt Billi decided to spring another what I would call a surprise and also none of her "Fing Business". In a nut shell the secret was at about Amy living with me after a lot of mumbling by Sgt Billi she told me that she was in love with Amy. I did wonder what this mad to do with me then Billi did ask was in a relationship with Amy in other words were we sleeping under the same bed sheets? There was two ways I could have given the answer one was on the way to burst the blood vein I my neck and the other one was the truth "No"!! I did enlarge the answer Amy does live in our garden cottage and apart from eating a meal together we had no contact at home. She does play pool with my four boys a couple of times a week she is like a big sister to them. With that I headed for the car, after I told Billi to get her finger out of her ass and do some work when she asked how will she get back to the office, forensic and confirm will be here for a couple of hours so catch a lift with them. I almost said that I will send Amy back to drive her back to the office but I felt that was simply rubbing salt in the wound. When I got into the car Amy did ask what all that was about, I told her to drive up the highway and stop at the first place where we can pull in. I just bit my upper and pared at the conversation that I had with Billi. In a nutshell she asked are we in a sexual relationship now that you have moved in with me. Amy did laugh that was what expected then a violent at burst of words she expressed about Billi was not exactly what I would say was warm comments we both laugh, got home. Amy took the car back to the Police Garage and when she got home, we sat down to dinner, then headed to our separate bedrooms.

In the morning Insp Penguin was bright eyed and flapping his arms in great joy when I told him that his V.W. Beetle is not to be used as a police vehicle, anymore. It took me three times to get the information through to the Penguins that John Knight once our fearless leader had in fact told the idiot in the office or the garage, an office the size of an extra-large toilet; in this little world you did sign in to take a car and sign out on its return. "It was a bloody joke". I shouted at the Penguin before I told him he has a new assistant Sgt Billi Mayford. A mention of the indigenous woman by the Penguin got my back up and I simply told him first nation person is the term that we use in this office. I did have six detectives of the first nation heritage and everyone was more than a good team member I did look at it flying the flag for the first nation people who had been here well over sixty thousand years.

I gave the Penguin the file on Rory Brent and simply said "he is hiding something hang him upside down and shake him by the balls till you are happy" Sgt Billi Mayford has a lot of information on Ray Brent, I did suggest a brief encounter with her word help him in his search for the truth from Rory Brent. I could see on the face of the Penguin that he was simply back in my good books. In fact, he could be top of the pile in his eyes. Sgt Billi Mayford well she was in her own world of a broken heart, after Amy caught her in the lady's toilet and read the riot act to her about her love life. I did not even get a mention Amy told me later in the car. Maley Brent knew a Steve Butcher wagon the word Spare written on the side about ten minutes heading south.

I have to think that this could get nasty so I needed back up at this time. Tactical support of six officers were needed. Insp Ryan Moore was leading his team today. I like Ryan, no monkey business with him, he had his boy scout head on the job and did not like anybody getting in his way. The location of a farm house just outside the best place to hide a criminal is in the outer region of Humpty Doo. A drone was launch and it did seem that Steve butcher and his sister at feeding the chickens are home today. Reamy Butcher always looking at for hawks when feeding the chickens had spotted a new type of hawk looking drone. So, she ran inside and Steve butchers only in his under pants came running at and with an automatic rifle tried to shoot it down I did say that Steve does need better target practice. A call from the office manager Rachel Todd did show that Rory Brent had made the call to Steve Butcher after a short call to Carol Reed of all people I thought this plot is almost getting thicker and it is not even nine am in the morning. I did ask Insp Ryan Moore if we could take them both alive. I knew how many times I have said those very same words to him, and yes it was in one ear and at the other "yes I will try" was his answer. I did hear him tell his team.

I did that what a waste of bullets from the Butcher siblings, we were one hundred yards away and bullet fire was already heading in our new direction. I was surprised when I was told that Insp Ryan was about to send over another drone to drop a small bomb on the house, they only do this stuff in police movies of the American nature I thought one large explosion but no white flags were flying from the Butcher home. Next another American police tactic, two motorbikes headed to the far side of the farmhouse sniper fire was not action from the far side of the farm house. This home was not the old wooden walls built solid stone; Insp Ryan told me.

I could see that for myself I thought with him trying to give me an update. The bomb did not work the snipers are just taking pot shots, so it was time for a full-scale attack. In what I called the tank bullets proof all over with bullets bouncing off the machine. Insp Ryan went right up to the front door and threw a smile bomb through the window then a gas cylinder within minutes the tank took hold and out of the front door was the Butcher siblings who were running at shooting in all directions it was like those old cowboy movies where the shooter does not hit anything instead, he is wounded falling to the ground. Reamy did the same, her body in pain after being shot three times in her legs. Her running days are over for now I thought her big brother had yet to show his face. A call for Steve to give himself up "There is no second prize here" shouted Insp Ryan Steve I did suspect was not only the shooter that took the life of Iris Norton by string Up Maley Brent after trying to get information from her about who she had been talking to. This was no way to treat you now with two deaths Steve if he was sensible, he should just walk out hand on his head. Steve was not a sensible person in fact he went out his own way in a blaze of glory only to be cut down in a hail of bullets. Something that is not really legal but Reamy gave a confession while watching for the ambulance Amy Fuller had her phone ready. The shooting of Iris Norton and the death of her close friend were given orders from Carol Reed who relayed them through Rory Brent who I knew was up to his neck in this. The drug connection to Iris Norton the connection to Carol Reed, now stepping into the shoes of her dead husband I had enough charge to put Carol Reed in jail for a very long time now and her pet manager Rory Brent.

CHAPTER 8

TURN THE OTHER CHEEK

With my team working flat at for nearly three weeks now and looking at this memo that is telling me there is no overtime payments I did decide to take things under my own wing. I had a meeting with Uncle Bill on the top floor of the building I was met by the "stork" who had the Fing cheek to ask me if I had a appointment? I did not answer but instead you could say "I spat the dummy!!" heading for the lift bank to the ground floor, a little voice called out "It's ok Aaron" poor little Billy is lost like a little boy in the arms of his mother. The "sSork" assistant commissioner Violet Andrews who was told to go to her own office with what I call Uncle Bill showing his authority with a stamp on the floor. I almost thought he was going to throw a tantrum. Well, I thought what a bloody welcome I now get cream cakes and coffee with a happy smile from Bill.

I had already sent a file to the office of Bill Skinner our new fearless leader. It did certain the downfall of Iris Norton and all her activities before somebody decided that she had pissed her used by date. A connection to the Reed Family Cyril and Stan who used the so-called Tiger Family in the production of drugs Max Wayne had got in the way of drug selling so the attack on his home at a birthday party did not go to plan as expected by the eight teenage Tiger members. Max Wayne and hit Ex weather person Annie were the target but instead they were sniffing cocaine with the top end of town on the other side of Darwin. I must say Bill was just like old John Knight. He wanted a simple explanation was all it took. A mention of the overtime payment ban. "Got to watch the budget I cannot have the bloody thing blowing out in my first year in office" I like it when they caught at their own jokes. I myself was not amused with the way this conversation was going never mind the cream on the side of his mouth and now has spread to his face. I did exactly what John Knight he did wipe his mouth on his sleeve. It was then that the "stork" made a entry with Bill wanting to know exactly what she wanted because he was in conversation with the head of detectives Aaron Brown. I was so pleased that Bill did remember exactly who I was storming at with her wings clip I told Bill I will give my team "Major crime" some extra time off over the next couple of weeks. I could tell he wanted to know exactly how much time. So, I did quote the hours that my three inspectors had work and the two first nation female SGT Billi and Kay plus the four detectives Pia, Cyprus, and Darren of course I could not forget my office team Rachel Todd and Crystal Fulton who without the information they kept ahead for the team very important team members. I almost forget Amy Fuller my driver Bill decided to put on a braze face and ask if she was living with me. I was not having an affair "I quickly put idea to rest". Anyway two days extra this week and two extra days next week, I told him. Um two and two is four, yes hat is ok with me, Aaron. Keep up the good work tell the team that I am very proud of them flying the flag for the detectives in this police complex.

I stood up and grab the last cream cake in the plate and headed for the lift. On my arrival I told Rachel Todd my office manager to sit down with Chief Inspector Harry Lines and work at a Rosta for the next two weeks and maybe three where all staff get a extra two days off. I must say it is not catching fly season with your months but both. Harry and Rachel stood there gob-smacked at my comment.

I had more than enough files to sign off from Harry Lines and the team before I knew it lunch time meant chilly bacon and egg roll twice and a thick blue berry shake. Crystal Fulton assistant to Rachel was happy to do the canteen run. I was the only person who eat in the office, all the other team members always bolted downstairs to the canteen, to see what exotic food they had an offer today.

A steam Jam sponge and custard was placed next to my chilly egg and bacon rolls with the cheeky comment from Crystal "you are not watching your waist-line are your boss?" what could I do expect I eat the jam sponge and custard before I eat my chilly egg rolls.

I was almost bursting my belt had to be given another notch when the phone rang, it was Adam Saunders from the prosecution office "bad news Aaron, Max Wayne and his wife Annie and that dick head hero son have got bail, five million big ones. How I have no idea, I rushed into the court room and it was almost done and dusted". My mind was out of control, I could tell that Adam could imagine how I felt we had been after Max for years. "The problem was Aaron that bloody pill press machine, he well Max is saying it was in the house when he brought the place two years ago" I had to stop Adam then and there.

We got video of his son Bobby or is it Robby handing at pills to the party going out of control and saying "Take more than one they were MDMA and Ketamine Mixture" and on top of that we got the room where Max and Annie doing a wife swapping party to find cocaine still on the table in that lounge of the hotel suite: in fact Annie Wayne still had some white powder up her nose when we did finally put the handcuffs on her@ heard it whisper going around that your team do believe that Max Wayne if he did not shoot the Reed bothers Cyril and Stan Reed and then feed their bodies to the crocs!!

"We got no proof, in fact um Iris Norton was spreading that word and it could of her shot, but then again Carol Reed had been charged with ordering that nasty business!!" the phone went silent before Adam simply but on my foot.

"You got to prove that Max Wayne had used that blood pill machine and then we got him for drug production!!"

I knew Adam was right we are on very weak ice and about to fall through it and get wet. I called in Harry Lines and the best sniffer for evidence Insp Philip Requiem" the Penguin. He had a nose that could rival black Betty the drug dog. I kept looking at the penguin who had standing next to him Billi Mayford who was in one of her silent movements. I told them I am going to place this idea into their basket.

"I am sure that you will be able to get to the bottom of that processing Pill machine. We need somebody who has worked it in the past year and above all will testify against Max Wayne Family!!"

"You mean somebody who has a grudge against then" remark the penguin who pointed to the door of my office and was led at by SGT Billi Mayford. I had no mention to anybody about the so-called conversation I had with SGT Billi and her love for my driver Amy Fuller who is now living in the garden cottage at the end of my garden.

Looking at Sgt Billi today with a guilty look on her face I did imagine that is how Uncle Bill Skinner heard about in on the all the way up to top floor. I knew that if I do remember right the penguin will return for advice within a few minutes about how he should tackle his new assignment. I simply told him go to see Dr. Rebecca down in forensic and ask if you could have one of her team to take some finger prints at the Wayne Residence. Within a hour of myself drifting off into my normal duties the penguin had struck "gold". A false panel behind a wall down in the basement next to the Pill press machine from floor to ceiling large bags of M.D.M.A tablets. The forensic assistant told the penguin and SGT Billi a few hundred thousand at least half a million worth on the streets with modern technology, you can take a finger print and place it into a scanner and just like magic a name will pop up of the person who left a finger print, pure magic is what I call it.

I had to say if I did not already know that Annie Wayne ex celebrity weather girl and also the son hero Bobby Wayne had left hundreds of prints on the outside of the pace and also on the inside. I had to go and take a look while this crime scene was still hot. Meanwhile my office manager Rachel Todd had been doing some digging into the previous tenants of this property who had vacated to Queensland. Two Chinese doctors a husband and wife who once worked in Darwin hospital and now they are working in Brisbane. A Darrel and Amy Judd not exactly

Chinese names. Born in Hongkong, I was told by Rachel who told me that Darrel was adopted by a rich American couple in Hongkong many months ago.

I made the call to a old working partner Insp Steve Wright. Who was now Chief Insp Wright. He ask about Alf Jackson "Dead" I said John Knight? "Dead" I replied and now I am the last man standing in our old team.

Without the boring details I did ask Steve if he ever crossed paths with a doctor Darrel Judd and Doctor Amy Judd and Doctor Amy Judd. Steve did imagine that I had not lost myself of humor and told me the couple are in the lock up and will be sensitive tomorrow. He did expect around twenty years each for illegal drug manufacturing. "You name it, they produced it". I explain the back ground to my enquiry. And what we had found in the Wayne residence he had read and seen o television, even me doing my old famous line "nothing to say" to the press. Files, finger print were sent to my office and I did promise that I will keep him updated and the progress of our case on the other side of the country. I had to inform the penguin and Sgt Billi that they might have struck gold with their investigation "if you want the job done right send for the penguin" I would not go that far but he could bath in the glory, for now!!

I was now sitting looking at the Rosia that Chief Insp Harry Lines had put together with Rachel Todd my office manager. It did seem that it would work "Everybody will have to pull their finger out!! Quoted Rachel with a cheek smile "I did ask if that did include me "I got no reply except a thumbs up from Rachel. It was just when you thought this week could be easy the alarm bell went off on my office desk "CPI had been shot at CPPI" means commission of police the one is Uncle Bill Skinner. Bullets fired at his car. I was glad his car was bullet proof. Driving home on a short cut near the casino and along what you might call beach road to his movie in the fanny bay. I made the call to my team to go into tactical support mode. Driving on the wrong side of the road, traffic police already diverting traffic away from the area, blocking off road a helicopter was already up and going.

I manage to get a very nervous Uncle Bill on the phone. He was about a hundred yards from his home. "It was a bloody good job that Violet (the stork) was not with me. She likes that rear window half way down I bent down to pick up my pen that fell out of my hand when five shot hit the car. Maxi my driver, told me to keep down it was going to get rough for the next few minutes. Tactical support told me to head for my home where they will meet me" we were about six minutes behind Uncle Bill. I then ask Amy to put her foot down with the answer "you asked for its boss!! Traffic lights had been switching to green and flashing a police car was at each traffic light directing traffic Uncle Bill phone me to say that he had a bad feeling and it was not just that he had "shit his pants" the automatic gate, his driver open and then the inner gate was open.

" It was not right" Bill keeps saying his driver quickly reversed and went up the road where I was heading for him and now tactical support were right behind him. I told Uncle Bill to staying in my car he was surrounded by tactical support. I got out of my car and made my way toward him.

"My Mia is home alone, something is wrong that back gate is always shut, always" I made my way down the road with eight tactical support officers plus Amy my personal body guard we arrived at Uncle Bill's mansion majestic sea views at into the ocean we heard two shots from inside the house, we hide behind the neighbor's brick wall within a flask out step a man who was wearing a black ski mask and holding a gun at the head of Mia. He demanded a car and safe passage out of Darwin. He was not from world where could he go and I knew that it was simply show time.

Snipers took up their position and this man in the ski mask was going nowhere in my eyes. I looked back at Bill now standing outside the car with the back door open. It was up to me to make the call. I turned to the acting head of tactical unit today and simply said "take him down". Just like on one of those American cop shows it went into slow motion. Our friend in the black ski mask was hit from two sides in the head by two snipers at the same time. His head exploded and he fell back then was hit again in the chest by a barrage of bullets. Mia was laying on the ground and was quickly held by Amy Fuller my driver Mia needed a female to hang onto. After being shot in the head twice and six times in the chest, I would see the victim was still moving his legs, nerves were twitching his legs but he was dead in my eyes. I pulled off the mask to find a first nation person who had already gone on to his own dreamtime. Mia told me there was another person who fell out with this man and ran off over the back fence into a neighbor's property. I told air command up in the helicopter and they saw nothing. Tactical support had been over the house before Uncle Bill was allowed inside the rear of the house. I did want Uncle Bill to leave so forensic would go over the place.

Finally, Uncle Bill went two hundred yards down the road to Mia's sister place tactical support had to search the house just before Bill went inside for ai extra-large brandy and then he went for a shower and change his manly nappy after he simply had shit himself. Units now with my team leading and searching for the other person who pled the scene. His description could fit at least a thousand first nation who hung around bench road during the day.

Homeless people were asked for some sought of identification. It was in a nutshell simply a joke. "A needle in a man stack describes Chief Insp Harry Lines. I felt for Mia she was taken to hospital; she was not in the best health on a normal day never mind having a gun pointed at her head. While Bill sat beside his wife Mia, he had a bad turn. Placed in a bed in a private room next to Mia I had a awful bad got feeling that the "Stork" was now in charge and she will now trample about what was I doing about this incident she wanted a update every couple of hours I was about to punch her beak, then once again I simply pulled my head in and simply showed "true leadership". I did not give her a salute but I felt that was what she really wanted at this place in time; just to make sure that she had my hundred per cent loyalty. I did think about "pigs can fly?"

"Then again so-called storks!! Also fly!!"

I sat alone for a hour in my office. Nobody came in and when u said "it's time to go home go F off you lot you have all earn your so-called dollar today. I got home and wanted till Amy arrived back on her motorbike before I eat dinner. I felt Amy sitting alone eating dinner on her own was not where her head should be after an excusing day of chasing shadows. We both had spinach pasta with extra cheese, washed down with four cold beers then my fifth beer I sat in the shower on my stool and turned on the water. I heard Amy had decided to go for a swim instead of a shower. In the morning I got up earlier to catch my four boys before school. They did remind me that next week is half term and will we be going camping down at some remote fishing spot. I told them that I will keep our destination a secret until we arrive. At work it was what I call chaos which could be the perfect word to describe my team. Some had returned on what you could call their extra time off. It did show loyalty to the job and how the team will soldier on no matter what. Our missing I can jump walls but had not surfaced a couple of residence had caught a first nation person pinching clothes off of the washing line which was not unusual in this street. Having so many homeless sleeping in the park overlooking the ocean just down the road what our suspect is now wearing is simply pot luck, red blue or black too. Blue or black jeans I had learnt from the DNA and fingerprints of our dead friend in the ski mask of Uncle Bill's driveway was a John Carrom who had two brothers from roper river they had been living down at the narrows for the past two years when the wet season cut off their community and they never went back. We had a address but it was old now two years in fact but with tactical support not having anything planned I decided to take them for a door knock on the Carrom residence.

Only a senior female who was the Auntie to the three boys who were long go a week ago "I could be heading back to Roper River now the dry season is coming!! She told me everywhere you look it did seem that there had been a party going on. Homemade drugs and empty beer cans in every room. The Auntie told me that she slept in the chair twenty for seven was her home she only got up to go to toilet and make something to eat. I could see that somebody had paid a visit to K.F.C more than once empty box's the word of personal hygiene and even housekeeping did not exist in this flat I got the team to venture into the other flats for information about into the brothers Carrom. I told them not to mention that John had moved on to his own dreamtime. "Sleeping rough not far from the beach" was what you might call a lead patrol in the area were step up to no avail.

Rachel Todd told me that she had some information that Andy Carrom used to do to spot of kangaroo shooting and pig shooting for a living back at roper river in the dry season. Will Carrom had never done a day's work in his life except steal cars for his brothers to travel in I did not believe that it was a lone shooter who fires at Uncle Bill's car. He must have had a plan because I spoke to Max Uncle Bill's driver said they did not travel the same root home every day. Then again living on beach road you either drove down left or right other the road to get to Uncle Bill's Kennel!! Calling Uncle Bill's home a Kennel I could see the sense of humor of Max they lived in the front lounge the rear lounge as a bedroom with an bathroom attach to it. Upstairs with the view of the ocean was two arm chairs where Uncle Bill and Mia used to sit and watch the scenes do down until Mia cooked their dinner.

I was surprised to hear from Bill in his hospital bed. He had gone to the toilet and was sitting on the throne talking to me. "I told Violet to keep her bloody nose out of the investigation, just let the people who are good at their job simply do it! I did think to myself well Uncle Bill has so called cracked me whip with that thought I heard the toilet flush and Uncle Bill told me that he was five pands lighter now and felt like a new born baby who had just exploded in his nappy!! Being told to keep in touch with him, six hours updates was the order from the toilet master Uncle Bill.

I went to visit Dr Rebecca who had no news from me except to confirm from some DNA match for Will Carrum who had been done at a young age for car theft and breaking into property, that even belong to his relatives Will had the attitude that everybody was lucky in life except him and his brothers. I did think that if Will had gone out and got "a real job" he may have not got himself into this situation in life we had posted a description of Will Carrum and also Andy Carrum to every police officer who was out and about in Darwin we did get a report that somebody who did fit the description of Will was seen with somebody else stealing a car from outside the corner shop in Stuart Park. The idiot driver left the motor running so he could keep the car running cool. A white ford four-wheel drive there must be a hundred like this simply driving around Darwin. Just to complicate the situation number plates had been stolen from cars parked near some offices now this could help us then again if the number plate did not match the white four-wheel drive. It was a break through with all police vehicles having vehicle recognition in their vehicle, even in my car but I have never needed it.

The white four wheel drive was seen on the other side of Palmerston, then another report heading for a special place on early for crime Humpty doo. The vehicle was found empty but a stop off at KFC on the way here. Forensic were soon in attendance within ten minutes this was the vehicle that the two brothers had been simply out and about sightseeing around the countryside outside Darwin. With the security cameras in action at Humpty doo shop they showed up with nothing of the two remaining Carrum brothers Andy and Will. It did make me think why would they want to take out Uncle Bill. He had no connection to them except he was our leading police officer. They must of track Uncle Bill to his home their mission was to kill him on the road or as home somehow the plan did not go well. Will had a huge argument with his older brother John and simply bolted over the neighbor's fence.

While Andy had driven around after he failed in shooting Uncle Bill on his drive home. They must have had a meet up plan later for Andy to connect to John and Will this had succeeded it but no John. No real reports with a published name of John on the television and the local newspaper. A picture of the house was not shown in the newspaper on or the T.V mainly because now you would get every not job out there standing outside Uncle Bill's house every time, they had a bad turn it was something that had not brothers me in the years that I have lived in my home again only at your Peril mainly because I would simply "Blow a couple of holes" in your head I do not take any prisoners these days!!

The penguin was flapping his wings and looking pleased with himself after the discovery of a so called "Tommy Rowe" the drug manager for Darrel and Amy Judd up in Queensland and before that he had active at the home of Max Wayne and his family. Tommy Rowe had simply vanished off the face of the earth. There was some brief interaction with. Iris Norton but there is no real proof of this only hear say from a couple of the teenagers who are facing some life sentences for killing at the Max Wayne residence that hosted the big bash birthday party for his son Robbie who is sometimes known as Bobbie in some circles. In my mind it was time to rattle the cages of the Wayne Family again the idea to secure all even to conclude the theory that Annie and Bobby was into the drug trade and Max Wayne had no real idea?

I had to admit that I was not is a good frame of mind to tackle Annie and her son, so I told the penguin to go for it in his own unusual way with the lock of knowing what he was doing. The penguin went into a positive mood, which I have learnt could be a very dangerous move for the opposition.

I had a free air zone and just when I did believe it was going to be an early night, I had a call "the Stork" was in trouble she does believe that her life was in danger tactical support were only two minutes behind me. Insp Jason Purley and Sgt Kay Coxley were standing there ready to move. I could not wait for tactical support; the stork Violet Andrews was living in the second penthouse that overlooked the waterfront. Her parents left her the flat and enough money to upkeep the property till her life came to an end.

I did not want this to happen to the Stork now with Uncle Bill I hospital and a real story that would mean that I was back in the frame of being the most senior officer at the police complex. The Stork opens the front door Amy we ended up in the lift to the penthouse floor. Her front door did look in tack. I bang on the door and went inside her flat when she automatically opens the door from her phone. "He was here with a gun, how the F did he got into Amy building I just don't know". "I told Amy to make some tea. "F the tea, pass that bloody vodka bottles" where the story just opens her beak and poured the neat vodka down her throat. The cctv footage of a first nation person that did look like Andy Carrum, he had breathed the ground floor, when two men were bringing in a new bed for another flat just like a rat up a drain pipe Andy Carrum was quick where did he go that is the question. The stork heard the lift come up to her floor but it was empty when the doors opened. Then bursting through the door came tactical support, I did think better late than never. After I was given the lecture about I should of waited for the very first time the stork turn to feel the leading tactical support office" if he had done what you said I might have been dead by now. Insp Jason and Sgt Kay had been down on the ground floor and had not spotted Andy Carrum come out at the building. So tactical support was going to each flat there was only eight flats in the building. They did try to restore their reputation but not in y eye and certainly not in the eyes of "the stork".

After one hour it was time to leave the stork did not want a police officer to stay with her SGT Kay Coxley was very relieved because she had heard of the stork love of the female body down in the staff canteen where all good rumors start and seem to never die. A bit like myself with Amy my driver "they are like rabbits with sex all night no wonder they both look tired when they come to work flashing eyes at each other "I did find that what I called a good one" even Amy joked about it in the car on the way when I knew that SGT Billi Mayford was behind all these childish rumors. I told Amy to bite her tongue because "every dog has its day" was a saying that my grandmother always used to say "you just have to wait a little longer" I told Amy

Uncle Bill was still in hospital and still trying to make out that he was still in charge. I finally crack the shits and yes. I did phone him, it was not what he would imagine that I would say "Bill I am taking over and to start with Violet Andrew is going into protective custody. Whether she dies like it or not I knew Violet would be stamping her feet and trying to tell me about her position of Assistant police commissioner but she was in a nut shell. The people around her at risk Uncle Bill made the call in not exactly I would have put it to her "shut the F up and do what you are told for once woman!!" I laid down the ground rules, curtains closed no lights on mainly because it will protect an image that could easily picked off. Sulking in the corner and I was about to leave with the front window of her penthouse just shattered into thousands of pieces.

Like a Jack Rabbit one of the protection team decided to return fire to a very fast-moving car heading out of the city on to the main road, he did manage to get two shots into the passenger side, whether he actually hit anybody, time will tell. The out of control headed for the highway I just hope that traffic cameras can be used to track this vehicle. Poor Violet had the old stomach problems, never been shot at before she told me. I was not surprised she had spent sitting in the traffic control room on her ass!! It was then I had to stop being the father figure because a off duty police officer who had been out fishing had stop at the Humpty doo pub outside bar for beers and a game of pool. Across the pool room and looking very relax was Tommy Rowe, he was looking like he did not have a care in the police officer not to be a hero, I am coming if I had wings I would be there in a few minutes.

I had no Amy to drive me I only had Sgt Kay Coxley so I decided that I will drive. Jumping red lights doing a bit of grass trimming along the way I did manage to do the journey in twenty-two minutes instead of thirty. A white-faced Kay who must have been feeling a little wet between those legs in that skin tight trouser suit. I was coming up the hill and with Kay talking to Zak Manton our new friend was driving a blue ford car I spotted it coming down the hill I simply told Kay to "brace for impact" I simply pushed Tommy Rowe in the car into a ditch and wedge up against a tree. I was glad that I was not going to pay for the damage on my car. Like a kangaroo a hop skip and jump just before I stuck my gun into the face of Tommy Rowe "slowly does it, Tommy", Kay who was still trying to adjust her trousers to show she had not really wet her knickers.

Tommy got out of the car after Kay released his seat belt. "Now Tommy Kay who is sitting behind you, is what I call um trigger happy in three years of shooting at the bad guys she has never hit anybody by all accounts, but there is always a first time with her gun pointing at the back of your head at this very moment!! Slowly Tommy hot out of the front seat and down on his knees. I did relive him of the face arm inside his jacket. Tommy did complain that his back was hurting and could he sit down on the ground again trigger-happy Kay did warn him not to make any sudden moves because her trigger finger could move. I started to ask Tommy about his connection to Max Wayne at first about his connection to Max Wayne at first I got no comment and I want a solicitor before I say one word. I did ask Tommy once again about Max Wayne home of the pill production in the basement. Very negative is what I would call Tommy.

I did throw the names of Darrel and Amy Judd, now awaiting a little more than a slap on the wrist, in fact around twenty years in prison. I had to confess to negative Tommy that I knew he had worked for them in the live. I went onto say we found a little stash of around three to five million of pills that he must of known about behind the false wall. Tommy did not have to say anything being silent and the look on his face did tell me on the right track, I had hit the nail on the head. I was told by Tommy that he was surprised in fact very surprised that I was still alive. I did know ask him what he meant although I did know he was trying to pay games with me. in fact, if I am holding a gun in my hand, you should always be very selective with your words. Tommy asked for a deal. I had to upset his relationship by telling him that I do not do deals!!

A mention about the name of the person who had decided to take down the main players in the police force in Darwin and even myself had a price on my head. It was time to inform Tommy that he did not bother me. Bill Skinner was a missed target, the hostage situation with his wife may turned out very painful for the hostage taker who had the exploding head problem. Tommy stops me there well what about your four boys, would I risk their lives. I was about to put a bullet between his eyes. "Don't shoot me I am only the Fing messenger I am the go between the main man and those idiot Carrum brothers who had screwed up everything. I did cock my gun and asked Tommy the name of the person who is a bank rolling this attack on senior police. I was going to count to five, ten was too hard for me at my age. I did not have enough patience I got to three and Tommy told me it is "May Wayne the money man"

Now Tommy wanted to stand up his back was giving him pain. A local police unit arrived to take Tommy to hospital for a checkup before he would end up in the watch house. I did know Tommy did not have much live for even a future other than prison but to pull a knife on me from his leather boot did allow trigger happy Kay actually hit her first target, no one but two bullets into the head of Tommy. I still had more questions to ask him tomorrow but then again Kay did save my life after all!! It was then that Amy did phone me, she was at the house playing skip a beat when she told me she just seen the officer at the front of the house take a nose dive to the payment with a knife sticking at of his neck. She saw a shadow try the front door. I told her to get the boys upstairs into the left.

My day was going from bad to worse I was at least twenty minutes away from my home now Amy was there all alone and she was all there was between my boys and the gun man. She was already wearing two protective vests. I did not question why she was wearing two protective vests. "I am on my way, hang tight". I told the officer I will drive Kay would stay and take care of everything with stay and take care of everything with his partner. I shouted help is on its way. Don't panic Kay just don't panic. It was time to see how much gas I could pump into the engine. If this van had never flow, I will try and make it. "Strap yourself in constable Ricky" was his answer for his name. yes, I did break every rule in the driving book, I had to tell Ricky that the person who you are going to help is Amy Fuller and she is normally my driver, I do not normally drive well I do at weekends in the family four wheel drive but then again not at high speeds mainly because I am with my four teenage sons. Ricky ____ was on the radio to control and was saying exactly what I was telling him.

I finally took the last corner to my road on two wheels up in front there was six police vehicles at least twelve of them you thought was an a "fing Sunday picnic" "Sir it's ok your boys are ok, they are good, Amy she got hit eight time but only two bullets hit her left arm she is fine. In fact, she asked for a cold beer!! Laying on the ground was Amy and I bent down to her and she said "fuck this baby sitting" I would much rather be driving that bloody car, anyway boss I did well hit eight times and with two positive hits in my left arm"

It was a long time since I have had tears in my eyes. A police officer gave pushed at the way and he told Amy she should not be drinking you. In the Amy fashion she said "fuck you, do you know what I have been through today!!" In the back of the ambulance, Amy was still giving the ambulance crew hell!! Dr Rebecca Mitcham she did notice I was overwhelmed I started to show tears when I moved to cuddle my four boys one by one. It was decided with a protection unit they will go and stay at the home of the twins Tilda and Sofia. I said that I needed at least four officers at the home. We do not know if there are more killers at there who could be a threat to the lived of the boys, I made my way to Ray Brent the officer who was outside my house. He still had the knife not in his neck but his shoulder. I went to thank him and all he said was that "Amy had done the hard yakka"!!

I went back to talk to Dr Rebecca "I would never want to get on the wrong side of Amy ever" she had put four bullets into the head of his bloke and two in his chest bloody hell. Amy had fallen back when she was hit in the chest by the automatic rifle Amy did manage to empty all six bullets of her hand gun into Will Carrum. I did learn a couple of minutes later that Andy Carrum had been found in the front seat of the station wagon with two bullets in his head fired from the penthouse of Violet Andrews at that moving car.

I went through the house and I did grab a bottle of that precious malt whisky that John Knight gave me in a box of twelve, I have only ever drunk one bottle before in the past three years. The only reason John Knight gave me the case of whisky was simple he was not keen on the Scottish medicine I decided there was nothing I could do at my home it was now best to let members of my team do what they do best. I walked down to beach road and there were people just about everywhere with the pop up café's on the grass area that looked over the cliffs down to the waves breaking over the rocks it does look like a nice place to go for a late night swim, now that would be a mistake you would only become croc bait with all the beach in Darwin none are really safe. I walked up past the now closed night cliff pool. It was a place where I used to go when I was a teenager I turn to go back around the block and make my way home. I could hear in the high-rise flats, parties going on. I am now a bit old fashioned for this way of life. I just turn the corner and right in front of the me Sgt Billi Mayford pulled up

I had to stop and just tell me. I did not realize that she lived here after a few words and the story about not renting a flat to a "abo" on the seafront I could tell that the chip on the shoulder of Sgt Billi Mayford had grown a little more since I last had spoken to her. It was strange that with everything going on today I cannot remember seeing her in the background with the penguin, waddling along with her. I just happen to comment that Amy is ok I imagine heading for surgery about now waiting for those two bullets in her arm about to be removed, I was stupid enough to say that just maybe on the way home from work Billi could just pop in to my house to give Amy a cheer up!! It was the wrong thing to suggest and on the other hand it could heal the wounds that now exist between them. Still full of hate Sgt Billi had more than enough to say about my suggestion of popping in for a cup of tea. Full of hate and sacrarium, I could tell that the mate had fester into even something that I could believe get any worse. I learnt over the car window on the driver's side and simply told Sgt Billi to pull her head now, I was in no mood after what I had to witness today it could have been the worst day in my life as a police officer. I still had a smile upon my face and my family of four boys were safe and well. I did reach inside my jacket and pulled out my thirty-eight with a silencer already on. I decided there and then it was time for SGT Billi to depart my company I put two bullets in her head while I simply said "goodbye Billi!! I quickly turned and headed up the road. I quickly looked to see if there was anybody about who could of seen me.

I did not know that I could even walk so fast at my age. Coming up behind me was something with a familiar sound it was the Penguin V.W. BEETLE. I heard the cry "out doing some night walking" I felt my gun to make sure I still had control of everything. I stop to see the head of the penguin right up beside me, the sound of his beetle car was leaving me with irritation of trying to talk over the sound of that "Russian tank" he called his blue beetle love machine" I finally stop and without my word I simply said "so where the F have you been all day, I needed a experience officer like you to stand behind me. "I have been busy" the penguin replied "doing what may I say being your boss?" Um following us leads" I thought you are just human being of middle age and simply not being able to ask a question. I almost made it to my home when Chief Insp Harry Lines showed up. His attitude toward the penguin was similar to me with the smile on the face of the penguin did make you even more angry. Chief Insp Harry asked the penguin once again and all he got was the same stupid answer I got "following up leads" I had to step in between these two now with the penguin back on out turf. I was afraid it could come to a bit more than "angry " in fact it could end up in a real punch up. The penguin told Chief Insp Harry that he was going to report him for his conduct. I did ask who would that be somebody above my rank Insp Philip Requiem? You could say for once the Penguin was speechless. I had no idea for the past three days between the time of two pm and not only was the penguin not available but also was SGT Billi Mayford. The explanation when he was asked once again, we were told that he sorting a few personal problems at with SGT Billi Mayford. I did crack the whip then it was not the time and place to be having a discussion about this. Out of the blue we were told by the penguin that they were in love and working together had now made them even closer, if it was not serious I would of burst out laughing I did have a smirk on my face and so did Chief Insp Harry Lines who turn to receive a call. It was not good news the body of SGT Billi Mayford had been found in her car by a traffic patrol after a neighbor walking her dog heard the horn on the car of SGT Billi going off. I jump into the car of Chief Insp Harry, uninvited the Penguin jump in on the back seat and was telling Chief Insp Harry to put his foot down. Now coming from a man who has never driven more than eighty miles an hour fast in his life this was a joke I felt we pulled over and already a second team of uniform officers had arrived.

Right behind us was Doctor Rebecca I looked at the body of SGT Billi I could tell with tears in his eyes the penguin was overcome with emotion making the outburst he knew who had shot her "it was that bloody Amy Fuller my driver" I simply did what anybody would do and that was to see how much blood could come you can. So, I simply let fly it was one of those slow-motion moments you see on television. It did take Chief Insp Harry and two uniform officers from letting me get my second punch in. I held him by the throat and in a few words, I told exactly what I had thought of him over the past ten years in the police force. I felt sorry for Dr. Rebecca who had to go to the rescue of the penguin been told that he would have me for assault well unknown to me Dr Rebecca decided to put the penguin in his place Amy Fuller had defended my home and saved the lives of my four boys, she was in the fing hospital awaiting surgery, if not already in the process of having surgery for her bullet wounds. All the penguin could say he had no idea. In fact in the next minute the penguin had no idea about Bill and Mia Skinner and what had happen to them in Fanny Bay and also the stork Violet Andrews almost relieved a home invasion and myself at Humpty Doo following up a lead to find Tommy Rowe who was involved with the drug production at the Max Wayne home prior to them moving in an ambulance arrived and the penguin was placed on a stretcher and taken to casualty. I thought your big sook. I could tell that Chief Insp Harry was a little upset that I in fact got the punch in before he did even Dr Rebecca did turn to me and simply said "well done I would have done the same except I am a lady."

I raised my eyebrows to that comment Dr Rebecca with a smile on her face. I was allowed to sleep upstairs in my bed. I did start on my second bottle of Scottish extra strong water. I hide the gun back in a safe place. I did decide in the next few days. I must get rid of it just maybe it may come back to haunt me; one day in the future. It was decided that Chief Insp Harry Lines could not interview Insp Philip Requiem and to the point I could not either and now we have what you might call history a bit of one-sided boxing I would call it "the winner of the fight in Aaron Brown" I had just the person to interview Insp Philip Requiem a almost new lady under my wing on the block. A Chief Superintendent Alice Ducktown known as "ducky" to her friends she in fact has taken control of domestic violence and sex crimes under a new structure unknown to my team till tomorrow morning. Also, unknown even to me that Crystal Fulton had come forward and made a statement after she did learn that Sgt Billi Mayford had been shot. All I could gather from Rachel Todd the boss of Crystal Fulton was that Sgt Billi Mayford wanted to be moved away from the penguin his sexual demands were not what a normal couple would do. It did make my mind boggle and if you want any gossip around the traps Rachel Todd was the one with all the information. I sat alone in my office with a couple of swollen fingers from the punch I used to give Insp Philip and Cheap nose reconstruction. I was what you might say was "the talk of the town" down in the staff canteen some police officers who were not even there describe my arm like a leg of ham holding it in midair before it simple crack the bank of the penguin an extra because Rachel Todd told me that I needed to keep up my strength ready for my next boxing bout and maybe I should think of going for the heavy weight title in the police boxing tournament?"

A phone call from Amy to let me know she will be coming home today so can somebody came and pick her up. Who else to send was her replacement driver Sgt Kay Coxley. They will have a lot to talk about me. in fact, I would just love to be a fly on the rear mirror. I turned my head and somebody I had not seen since Kate's funeral it was Chief superintendent Alice Ducktown (ducky) to her friends. A passion kiss on my cheek and leaving her trade mark lipstick on the side of my face. A brief introduction to the team before some coffee, a quick update on my family like with the boys who had a four memory of her, stripping down to her underwear and doing a huge belly flop into the swimming pool in my garden at the wake for Kate. The two were very close and did remain so even after "Ducky" moved down south away from the wandering hands of John Knight of all her waist before she would simply blow his cock of with her gun in front of a dozen detectives in our team poor John Knight had her removed and she was shown the door that led to her going down south for the past ten years. I had to admit I was the last man standing, Alf Jackson left ran the PUB the royal oak after his mother fell down the stairs and laid for a hour a bar person did report before Alf Jackson decided to move her body. I was always suspicious about Alf giving his mother a little push to help her on her way down the stairs. I went on to tell "Ducky" that Alf did turn to what you could call the dark side, he did control and had a lot of connection to the drug dealers. I had to admit without too much detail I had to remove Alf from this world and I did end his life in a shoot-out with a bullet or two in the head of Alf. The rise and fall of John Knight she found most interesting he also went over the fence and it did turn out he was corrupt right up to the very minute I had to put him out of his misery with a couple of bullets in the head. "Ducky" could tell that I had no regrets" I also did mention after being told by Alf Jackson who ran over my wife back and forth in the night cliff car park it was to be

Alf himself. he did apologize and told me that it was his one regret of all the people that he had killed over the past years. Within thirty seconds I had shot Alf twice in the head "Ducky" did say she would of not have waited that long. Chief Insp Harry Lines sat silent he knew it was time to sit back and listen to us. He was asked his feeling about Insp Philip Requiem who we named "the penguin" "o another bird laugh Ducky a testament which we had in printed and also a recording of the last words of Sgt Billi Mayford to Crystal Fulford. I ask Crystal to came in and meet "ducky" who will be conducting the interview with Insp Philip Requiem. I could tell that crystal was still sad about the death of Sgt Billi. In her mind she did believe that SGT Billi was frighten for her life while in the presence of Insp Philip Requiem.

I had to make no comment, I did say that if quickly we could get this interview over and even if Insp Philip Requiem does not admit to killing Billi, it will still be enough to charge him. We had not found the gun and he could not prove where he was at the time of Sgt Billi being shot "Ducky" went next door to the empty office to listen to the voice of Sgt Billi and read the transcript of the conversation. I would sit upstairs with a video link to watch the interview. A Ryan Tarrant one of the top defenses solicitors was going to sit beside the Penguin. They are old school friends by all accounts. A union rep from the police union was told him the fing union had never done a fing thing for me and never will. It was what I would call a good fire ball to start the interview. I knew from the upstairs that the penguin would not enjoy being interviewed by a female especially somebody who had years of experience in dealing with every type of sexual criminal you could imagine in fact the strike rate for "ducky" would send shivers down the back of most people she would sit opposite from. Not the penguin he tried to go on the attack about who she was, what is she doing in the chair and where was Chief Insp Harry Lines. "I am your worst nightmare and under the code Harry Lines is too close to you being your boss to interview you Ryan Tarrant had to step in and calm the penguin down, who was standing up now and flapping his wings in all directions. "Ducky" had not changed at a interview although I had not observed her in ten years, she was one person who did like to be in control of the interview. Simple questions, with a stupid comment from the Penguin of "no idea" to question after question. His home had been searched and a lot of porn was found that did contain bondage.

The penguin did admit that he did enjoy watching bondage on his television. It was true that he tried to introduce Sgt Billi to bondage tied up with stocking her hands and feet to the bed post, while the penguin wore a stocking over his head. I know you are not allowed to drink anything stronger than coffee at work, but I had to reach for my bottle of malt whisky I my desk for a couple of hits that did bring me back to reality. I could not believe what the penguin was now saying he was madly in love with Sgt Billi and just could not keep his hands off of her the three afternoon seasons out at "Stuart road cabins" did cement their sexual relationship but then again not in the eyes of Sgt Billi she was about to reason today in fact with the doubt in the mind of the penguin "Ducky" played the recording of SGT Billi confession to Crystal Fulford this was a fake tap the Penguin told "Ducky" who was mystery woman Crystal Fulford the Penguin was told and just could not understand now how the so called relationship between Billi and himself had gone pear shaped Billi hated him and was not into bondage sex. The penguin did say that Billi did not express while he did perform anal sex on her. It was time for me to bend down and reach for my malt whisky bottle on top up my coffee cup mow!! A long statement about how he felt and was devastated by the death of Billi being asked by "Ducky" if he had lost control and shot Billi just in case she went to the authorities and exposed the penguin for what he really was. A grubby little man who had few true friends mainly because he was classed as a "whacko" and with these relations going to hit the staff canteen he would no longer be able to work in the police complex his position would be untenable the reply of "bollocks!!"

Was simply the final comment after two hours of trying to get to the bottom of the life and times of Insp Philip Requiem "Ducky" simply stood up and said "we are done for now" solicitor Ryan Tarrant had been caught what you would say was "off guard". It was a in fact the position of the future of Insp Philip Requiem being a detective was really over he could not recover from this. He should take the easy way put and simply resign his position. I knew the penguin and I had a very bad got feeling that he would want to fight on and clear his name so there was no doubt in the mind of people that he did not kill SGT Billi Mayford. I had to let the penguin go and he was on suspension full pay and all the other crap that went with it. On the return of "Ducky" to my office we sat alone and I passed her a cup of my special coffee with the comment that I still drink the best coffee in town I smiled and waited for the words that I did not want to head from the lips of "Ducky". "Toss a fing coin to decide if he killed her, we have no forensic evidence that he did kill her, we have only he was in the area we had his VW Beetle clocked not once but twice heading for the residence of

Sgt Billi, "Another sip of coffee then Ducky decide to down the cup of coffee in one swig" Aaron he is what I call a sex pest and yes, he may have just slip through on fingers now but he will be back one day". If you sack him a wrong dismissal case a public gallery will enjoy the show yet the police will not. They would be happy behind closed doors and even no court cases just agree on a payout figure and simply wipe your hands within your hand washing tactics" talking in riddles now I could see that "Ducky" was not happy that she had not broken the Penguin or even tried simply to simply flatter her eyes.

I made the call to Billy Skinner who simply said "we should call a vet and take Insp Philip Wanker Requiem out to a bloody paddock and simply shoot him!! I did think that Billy does not need to give me any more idea and finishing off any loose ends. His number two the Stork was back on the top floor and she is under the watchful eyes of two protection officers at all ties. He did thank me for taking care of what he did call the circus. "There are far too many clowns performing this day" I did not really know what Billi meant about a circus and clowns, maybe he was just talking about the top floor of the police complex. A mention about the email and only officer of no rank allowed to drive senior officers around was in the eyes of Billy "Bollocks another stupid John Knight idea I expect"

I thought this is what I was pushing for Amy Fuller can become a senior sergeant now, I know jumping a rank but it is long overdue and should he pay be back dated at least a year. I do believe so the decision was mine said Belly who went on to say that I was at one time being paid assistant police commissioner on one pay scale and then active commander of detectives on another pay scale. It was that too complicated to understand. In fact, Billy told me I do not have to pay any of the money back that was overpaid. In fact, I was doing two jobs at the time and so I should be paid a double salary. I did feel there was a certain shift and a warmness coming from Billy in my direction. Now I I could not wait before Billy does decide to call me his best friend now that I would know upset the Stork but put a huge smile on my face!!

Philip Requiem God bless his cotton socks did not resign. He is now downstairs in the basement running the file room. "Ducky" did mention that she could do with a good right-hand man I told her not to look in the direction of the penguin and she would not make a terrible mistake. In her mind to keep the enemy under your watchful eye is how you are going to catch them with their trouser down. It was not what or even think of that so called expression. So, Philip Requiem hand to "Ducky" in the sex crime and family domestic violence unit.

I sat there shaking my head at his request from "ducky" "let it be on your shoulder's old girl" I said.

Chapter Nine

"IN THE SHADOWS"

There are times in your life that can change in a moment when somebody was simply lurking in the shadows. What they saw can simply come back and haunt you. I took a couple of days off to be with the boys who were on school holidays. Amy Fuller my driver was home walking around like a one boy's explanation of her sling on her arm under their direction she had moved into the main house where they could simply look after her, instead of her looking after them. She took the Aunt Candy room it did need a really good spring clean but the twins Tilda and Sofia took care of that Bill Skinner was back at work cracking the whip in all direction. His so called second in command Violet Andrews (The stork) had her wing feathers been given a good clip. She was at last been put in her place. I did find out from the lips of Bill himself she will be acting as a support act not in the position of making rules and simply making everybody's life a misery security had been given an uplift on the top floor you had to phone ahead and go through a scanner the moment you put your first foot forward out of the lift. At the end of the first-floor Chief Super Alice Ducton had set up her office much against my advice she had taken Insp Philip Requiem under her wing. So I had the Penguin under the wing of a duck now during the past twenty four hours a Helen Brent had come forward being a neighbor of Sgt Billi Mayford the information that Sgt Billi was on a relationship with a Karl West a first nation person who had been released from prison only a month ago for drug offences, Karl West had left Darwin on a Greyhound bus for Cairns two days before Sgt Billi was shot then again her landlord a Deacon Donvale , another low life had plenty of money to splash around. Helen Brent had open up to the Ducky about threats from him against Bill who had Karl West living in her flat and had not informed Deacon Donvale who it was reported had laid down on the table a deal where Sgt Billi would agree to casual sex for a reduced rent. When she refused, he told her he did not want anymore "Abos" living in his flat it was not fair on the other neighbors. It was true that Deacon Donvale was a jealous guy with this information the Ducky simple obtained a warrant and kick down the front door of the penthouse flat of Deacon Donvale that did overlook the public swimming pool at Nightcliff. You could say he was caught in what could only be describe as female sleeping wear.

A few drugs not enough to really charge him with enough for home use. A twelve-hour interview left ducky upset that she could not prove that this law life Deacon Donvale was involved in the death of Sgt Billi. I sat there slurping on a banana thick share giving my ear to Ducky. I just had to mention the Penguin and he was only on administration duty; he had settled in very well with the other three female officers and two male officers in the sex crime and domestic crime unit. It only took the Penguin to set his own tail feathers that were burning with rage the security alarm was rung by Ducky and Insp Philip Requiem was back in a cell under the watchful eye of the police doctor.

In the Doctor's words "Philip's not exactly ready to perform police duties again the doctor did suggest that Philip had more time at home and a visit to somebody who could understand him and his problems. In my eyes he was one big problem and his bubble could burst at any time. It was on my mind but being her boss and her friend "I did not say I told you so!! The need for a person who did understand somebody who could understand Philip and his mental handicap. I was made to feel sorry for him by Ducky but deep down he was simply a nut job I hate to at it but I thought he was ready for a padded cell. It was taken home and given a cup of tea when he finally cooled down, a nurse and a doctor simply left him watching children cartoons on the television. In the morning he was found hanging by an electric cord from a beam in his kitchen. He did write a suicide note, I did not get a mention, only Sgt Billi did he told the world he loved one hour earlier driven to the car spot where Sgt Billi was found shot. He laid a bunch of flowers and a note saying "love to Billi from Philip". He drove back, the traffic cameras had tracked him back to his own home where he decided that enough was enough without Sgt Billi.

I could see that Ducky who had a huge heart but a body of steel was deeply moved while breaking the news to me. I held her in my arms and I did whisper in her ear "this is not your fault" Ducky did blame herself, if she had not given Philip that job, he may still be alive. I had to tell her again Amy again that she must not blame herself. Bill Skinner told me that I should not have allowed Philip to return I should or put my foot down and took control.

I did take Ducky home to my house and yes, the four boys wanted her to simply strip down to her underwear and do a huge Belly flop in the swimming pool. Their wish was granted and a roar of laughter from Amy and myself started the party night in the right love. In the morning I had a update by Chief Insp Harry Lines and I was very surprised that now a gang of school boys were infect in control of the local drug trade ducky into our back room which was full of monitors showing the local street and park from another view of this disturbing way of life that has crept into the daily lives of the residence of Cullen bay and did seem to be taking full advantage of it I pointed to screen one that did show a teenager boy on a bike to a teenage boy on another bike, finally after four boys involved the first boy did return with the drugs that the man must of placed on order.

All boys are known to us and are all under the age of thirteen this team of five boys will change every couple of hours on go over to this other area along the housing estate. I knew that Ducky had a dozen questions to ask me. In a nutshell these boys bring some financial gain into the home. All from a broken home, father left or is in prison. The mother struggling with another two and even more boys at home. Most of the boys who we call runners do go to school and also past on drugs to other classmates they also had a list of endless recruits if we do shut them down within twenty-four hours another group is in operation. It is the main man we want I tried to explain to Ducky the child protection and counting what other names of so called "volunteers" are making no impact the victims are too young to charge and when they are all they get is a slap on the wrist, within hours of leaving the children's court they are back at doing the same thing once again. We need to catch the "big fish in this drug ring. We have to set him or her up, put a trap in plate and nab ourself the "big fish" hook line and sinker. I had to tell Ducky who still was over whelmed with watch she was seeing. I explain instead of the use of a surveillance team and simply waste man power we have "the technology". I explain the use of drones on the roof of building with a camera wanted on the drone, which does contain even at night sometimes, we cannot just set up a van near a park on move into front room of a flat, those days are gone left back in the past. We have to move forward I had to tell Ducky the man that did purchase the drugs on the monitor one is one and our undercover people we have on loan from down south and even from Queensland we use our people over for a couple of their good undercover officers. I pointed to a Range Rover on the far side of the car park. It was the home of the "Big Fish" this one is called Frank Stroud a very slippery individual if he does suspect we are watching him he will shut down the operation and open it on the other side of Darwin we have tried and I have to say failed in on our quest to catch Frank Stroud the last time he had no drugs in his Range Rover In fact he was just sitting there watching a local night game of teenage football with parents with children cheering on their family members. I took Ducky to one side and told her I do believe that Frank Stroud has somebody on the inside of our office that is leaking the information about our drug operation that is why only a team of six is used in this room. All members are from various units around the country. Our normal team are not given access to this room that is why only myself and Chief Insp Harry is here. Not even my office manager Rachel Todd who I trust with my life has been involved. I knew Ducky was going to ask about our fearless leader Bill Skinner who does know it's a "hush hush operation" if successful he will be told.

I got a cheeky smile from ducky so I must say between us three we will go after this drug king pin Frank Stroud who has his very own fourteen-year-old son Jerry Stroud in command of the teenage boys. He does seem to show them what you could call "the ropes" each one has no real connection with the next one except passing a small plastic bag to each other. The money goes one way and the drugs do come back the other way before Ducky did ask, and I told her one month we have been running these twelve boys in front of a judge in a children court no luck with Frank Stroud or his off spring Jerry Stroud, both manage to slip through our fingers. I went back to my office and had a nice strong cup of coffee when I was so surprised to see Amy Fuller my driver being very bored of playing mother to my boys, she wanted a desk job until she is ready to drive me around. It was time for me to make the Major announcement. I did make the call to Uncle Bill who did show up with the storm flapping her wings. No wasting time Uncle Bill at once told Amy she is now at the Rank of Sergeant and will remain my driver and body guard. I could tell that Amy was overcome with emotion I read her lips that said "you did this!!" yes, she was right, I had it back dated for six months so she would get a nice pay check that she does deserve. A huge cheer went out into the room and a knock off drink down the Pub later was agreed by all. Amy went to her old desk and Rachel my office manager gave her some files that did need her special touch. I did believe that the team was what I would call getting back together to be their old selves once again after the sad news of the death of the Penguin. The atmosphere did seem positive until we got the call, a teenage boy had been shot just pass the school gate outside night cliff school. I gave the word to move, sorry for Amy she did stay behind to hold the fort with Rachel Todd my office manager. We arrive finally with Sgt Kay Coxley at the wheel trying to express the point we had arrived in one piece. Dr Rebecca had beaten us, so had Chief Insp Harry Lines and other members of our team. The victim was Alex Smyth a first nation teenager who was on our list of teenage drug movers working with Jerry Stroud and his father Frank Stroud we had CCTV footage other children were crying and screaming of a result of a boy on a electric scooter just flying past Alex Smyth and only slowing down to shoot him in the head. A quick turn left down a school lane and the killer were gone he was chased to the end of the lane by two other teens "he was like the bloody wind" one told me "He wore a Ski Mask, dressed in black but brand-new basketball red boots". I was asked to listen to a Clive Punter and a Trevor Wilson.

He was going to leave that evening job, he told us we also did it last year it was too risky so we quit that fatty Jerry Stroud was not happy and told us if we ever open our mouth we would be "dead met hanging on the school fence for all to see" Ducky showed up with two of her female detectives Chrissy Moore and Lizzy Tabler, they wanted to help I told her child services need to find some people to do some counseling we got a lot of very distressed kids out here. Parents were rushing to pick up their children once the media had given out basic facts over the radio. I could understand being a parent the safety of my boys in society today is something that is on my mind. Child services did show up with their arms open. Now it was more than I wanted to do but I had to go and inform his family it was only two hundred yards from the school gate. I arrived to find Gwen Smyth the mother of Alex Smyth being placed in the back of an ambulance she had passed out on the lounge floor. A member of the child services was there they had been keeping an eye of Gwen due to her excess drinking and the children a total of four that did include Alex being the eldest, Jenny the thirteen-year-old, Sandy who was eight. There was no sign of young four-year-old Benny. A nosey neighbor said "that weirdo who lives next door, I saw him take little Benny into that Chrissy and Det Lizzy was about to open a large can of worms. The front door was open by a Milly Stanton "listen he rents a room upstairs and yes, he has young Benny with him like two Gazelles up went the two detectives not a sound could be heard except some mumbling, with alarm bells ringing in the head of Chrissy she kicked the door in and found a Ralph Jackson performing sex on little Benny but also, he was like screaming it on the internet, Chrissy screamed and knocked Ralph Jackson to the ground. The video camera was still filming when Ralph Jackson picked up a baseball bat and went to attack Chrissy who screamed for help from Lizzy I rushed to the bottom of the stairs when Lizzy begin to move back down because Ralph Jackson had trip over his own feet. He fell down on to the landing where he went to stand up and Chrissy gave his the "Scot's man kiss" down he went he hit every stair, ending up what you could describe him being in a "little pain" he had done more that the old dance on the stair. He had hurt his left shoulder and his right arm. Lizzy simply told him "If you move just one inch, I will blow your fucking brains at all over the stairs". I stood back and thought if I was him, I would simply lay still, never mind the pain even if I shit my pants I would not move. Chrissy came down the stairs holding young Benny and locked at me and simply said "he was having sex with a four-year-old child, his little bottom is bleeding with that Chrissy must have had a nervous reaction because when she moved passed Ralph Jackson her foot slip at het Ralph Jackson right in the face. Ralph had another problem he had what I would call a "bloody nose". The ambulance had arrived from around the front of the school to take Ralph Jackson to hospital. "No way back now!! "This young boy has been suffering sexual abuse from that animal lying at the bottom of the stairs". The female ambulance medic took a very sad and crying Benny into the ambulance Ralph wanted to know when the ambulance was coming for him. Being told by the ambulance driver "I will make the call but it is at a bad time with more important needing our care!!

I thought myself I better keep right out of this argument those two detectives Chrissy and Lizzy are two people you do not want to get on the wrong side of them just now. Ducky arrived after a call from Chrissy I followed her upstairs to see what had been going on this rented bedroom. "Live sex acts on the internet, a pedophile delight was this sick human being Ralph Jackson" listen Chrissy this Ralph Jackson is known to us he is a listed pedophile who is normally over in Malak, I have delt with him years ago, he went to prison came out what last year and is now living in leafy Nightcliff just down the road from the school.

Mily Stanton tried to deny any knowledge until Ducky the move her up against the wall; "he was having sex with a four-year-old boy while you were sitting down here eating a hot cross bun and drinking bloody tea. You are trying to say you did now know anything or hear anything". Ducky looked at me I simply said "book her as his accomplish to start with. Deep down I was shaking the third ambulance arrived and realized now Ralph Jackson had a broken ankle a broken right arm a broken left shoulder at least his nose bleed had stop. "Gee that must have been some fall?" asked the ambulance driver. "I did see it he hit every step, he twisted and turned and when he hit the bottom step, he had a nose bleed!!" I said in a very firm voice of authority. I went to outside to phone Chief Insp Harry still around at the school entrance. He wanted to know what was going on around here? I simply said I will explain at a later time!! I did now think it was time to go back to the office and take control of all investigations.

Rachel Todd my office manager had put together the CCTV from outside the school. It did show when and how Alex Smyth was shot around fifty yards behind stood a Jerry Stroud it did look like he was standing still and waiting for something to happen. I think I was right when the shot was fired at Alex Smyth all the students ran for cover and back toward the school entrance that was everybody except Jerry Stroud who took a lazy wander up toward the body of Alex Smyth and just slowly passed the body, people rushed to help Alex Smyth except Jerry Stroud who showed no emotion and spoke to nobody even when he was asked the question about did, he even sees anything? You can see that Jerry Stroud kept looking back at the small fearless crowd of students standing over the body of Alex Smyth now, with a teacher telling his students to "stand back" the couple of students who chased the skate boarder around the corner to no avail throwing their arms in the air to show their anger.

From our sky view of the area given by the two drones on top the high-rise tower blocks. There was no activity from the drug boys running between each other. There was plenty of punters and even two of our very own undercover detectives. I do not feel the operation had been shut down in a show of respect of the death of Alex Smyth. I think the show of force and shooting of Alex Smyth does show they might of game over step the mark and had now drawn too many police into the area were we on to them only we know that. I went into the office of Ducky to catch up with her and her team. I told detective Chrissy Moore and detective Lizzy Tabler my full support. I explain that on my way here I had a meeting with Walter Cardwell a solicitor who does like to protect a pedophile and his rights against the police who are just trying to put him behind bars for his lust for children. Brutality of how his client Ralph Jackson was thrown down the stairs and beaten into a pulp and laid upright facing the stairs with injuries that had simply come from "pure police brutality". I did wonder how Walter Cardwell had come to this conclusion because he had not even spoke to his client who is still undergoing pain relief and having his broken joints placed back into the right position so he may function again back into daily life in society. I did think that the view of Walter Cardwell who I have had at least a dozen encounters over the years, his record was exactly zero to my twelve convictions. I tried to explain that his client did fall back on to the landing from the step down to his bedroom while he was attacking a female police officer with a baseball bat. I know I should of not of said "we got it all on a video and your client having sex with a four-year-old boy"> I did then realize that I may of "let the cat out of the bag" the look on the face of Walter Cardwell I could tell that he had only listen to gossip from the weird neighbors who had some hate for the police.

I told Det Chrissy and Det Lizzy to make sure they get their statement right I went to continue my thoughts when Ducky did decide to intervene, I stop Ducky in her tracks and told her that this is her case by I will oversee the conception and I do not want Ralph Jackson getting off on a technically and having his basic crime downgraded. I left them to ponder on what I had just told them. I would see in the eyes of Ducky that she knew that she had tried to over step her position. I mention to Ducky to screw down Milly Stanton the woman who owned the house and rented the room to Ralph Jackson. I just said "best of luck any problems, never mind how small, my door is always open. I headed back to Chief Insp Harry Lines to find out where he was with the death of Alex Smyth and what was he going to do about Jerry Stroud and his father Frank Stroud who is supposed to be the drug king pin in all of this investigation.

Rachel my office manager had already had the phones of Frank Stroud his bank account's all under her watchful eye. Jerry Stroud phone was of special interest he had open up to an unknown person about the shooting of Alex Smyth. The words of "you did a perfect job just one shot and I feel it sent a message to anybody else who will be bad mouthing out operation. "It was enough to simply make an example of Jerry Stroud the use of our tactical support, Black Betty the armored vehicle and to make a mockery of the so-called family home of the Stroud family. Drug dogs were standing by plus myself sitting in my car only for the fresh air and observation purpose only. There was no reaction from Jerry on hid father Frank who most of been inside trying to flush the drugs down the toilet and down the sink. We were on top of that we had a connection to all outfits this is two thousand and twenty-three. We are on top of this this day, within the second call from the first call five seconds before in went tactical support almost taking the front door down and the rear door down also. "Armed police drop to the ground". Poor Frank Stroud did want to make a good impression on his son Jerry, it did not exactly go to plan. Yes, the flushing of drugs down the toilet and bathroom and kitchen sink, right into our plastic containers down below we had got the head of the snake in our hands and was about to cut it off. They do say then the body will die. I stood and I watch Frank try to explain to Chief Insp Harry that the drugs were planted in his house. I could tell that his son Jerry was what you might call a little bewildering for the son. What did this mean was his very own father going to do what men do and that is throw people under the bus? I wanted to laugh at the conversation in fact I found the banter very funny.

Found in so many hidden places were a huge amount of MDMA a large amount on ketamine, almost a kilo of heroin and lots of little bags of cocaine; also, a pill processing machine found where you keep your pill processing machine these days in the garage. There was so much illegal equipment in that garage, poor Frank Stroud had to park his car out in the drive way. Within the Hour Trever Wilson the solicitor for the rich and famous was stomping up and down in reception demanding to see his client, Frank Stroud. I was letting Frank het used to a jail cell for a while when an Elsie Kelly another out of town with reality but was to defend Jerry Stroud with a member of the child protection office sitting in next to Jerry in what I would call a guardian. His father was in jail and the mother ran off with a very active nineteen years old toy boy around six months to a year ago.

I went upstairs to my office, I did need another screen to monitor Ducky tape or Milly Stanton and now Chief Insp Harry slap down

Jerry Stroud, who was not quite ready for the interview. Teenage tears from Jerry and how he wanted his father to support him. It did take a lot of education about the law before little Jerry the lost teenage boy who had no idea why he was here. His solicitor playing mummy did give Jerry a good cuddle and explain to him everything will be just fine, he will be back home and free and in the arms of his father. I did wonder what fing planet the solicitor Elsie Kelly I did need a something I had not eaten for a while a rock cake from the staff canteen. I even dip my rock cake into my cup coffee could not take the rock out of the cakes so I did dump it into the waste bin. When Rachel did ask about the rock cake i did say it did live up to its simply named "rock cake". Really the last thing I do not need was a hold up with the interview of the teenager Jerry Stroud the formation of tantrums and constant crying meant that a doctor must be called a Doctor Robert Holiday an old friend and not the one way back from the wild west.

After a heart-to-heart talk with Jerry Stroud, it was discovered that if he made lots of news, we would simply give up and send him home just like a naughty boy he did admit that his solicitor had given him this advice, I found that hard to believe which was just like the two duty officers wanted to rape him after he was strip search and his clothes had been given to forensic for a DNA search which was standard practice. The two officers on duty in the cells wore body camera and after looking at the film footage of his strip search, neither officer had made any sexual request to Jerry Stroud his solicitor had to be informed from her position and a Clive Mural did decide to step in at the very last minute.

Meanwhile back in the world of Ducky. Milli Stanton who owned the house where she had rented a room to Ralph Jackson and now with statements from the neighbors across the road led us to believe that Milli Stanton was even more involved than just letting a room out to Ralph Jackson. She always took a cash of wine around to Gwen Smyth and in return she would look after the young four-year-old Benny. Now the truth was known she used to hand him over to Ralph Jackson it was not to be today Ralph Jackson went to college the boy himself with Gwen laying on the floor it was Milli Stanton who did phone for the very first ambulance to this address. Now the ambulance had arrived for Milli Stanton at the watch house, poor Milli had more than a panic attack so Doctor Robert Holiday had her sent to hospital for an overnight stay. I simply told Chief Insp Harry to get stuck into Frank Stroud with Walter Cardwell sitting by his side trying to act like a solicitor who had some idea what was going on.

I had a call from an old friend Dougie Walters who owned a bike shop because they boys had spat the dummy about me not taking them away on Friday and were tired of waiting for me to take time of work, I did decide for me to purchase for electric scooters plus helmets to be worn at all times. Dougie Walters was glad to prove his daughter Sally to show my four boys how to ride them. I got the report back they were more than happy and even happier with Sally spending a couple of hope with them giving them the lessons. I feel I had been forgiven with a visit from Bill Skinner and the Stork he just wanted a update on the shooting at the school and that nasty business with a four year old boy being rape and having it flashed across the internet it was all going well, and with that he left with the silent stork also leaving.

The interview with Frank Stroud was going just like I expected "No comment"

To nearly every question he had been asked. We need somebody to throw Frank Stroud under the bus. He did deny having his son sell drugs for him. I did wonder how his son Jerry would feel that he was now being shown the door by his own father. We did show Frank Stroud pictures of him sitting in his Range Rover, giving supervision to the under the watchful eye of his son Jerry. Of course, he did deny they were what you call illegal drugs, more vitamin pills to give the body an energy boost especially on the dance floor, Walter Cardwell did make a noise what some would say was a comment. "You have no proof that these pills are harmful my client had told you they are vitamin supplements". Chief Insp Harry quickly shutdown the stuck-up idiot and told him some pills have cocaine mix inside the pill and some were laced with Ketamine some were well above the legal limits. The answer was simple the person who made the pills should take responsibility for that back came Chief Insp Harry "well old boy the person who is responsible for the pill production is sitting right next to you!!" I could tell just like Chief Insp Harry that good old Frank Stroud had not told his solicitor about the pill making machine found at the home of Frank Stroud. At the request of Walter Cardwell who could now like some time with his client Frank Stroud I would have liked to be "the fly on the wall" in that interview room. After a twenty-minute break a return back to our world came Frank Stroud still in denial about the illegal drugs he did still insist that the pills were for "A little boost to make you happy and even dance better" I did wonder if Frank Stroud was even on the same planet. In a touching line about his son can be a little out of control at times he did feel that he should of tighten the purse strings on his pocket money. I like Chief Insp Harry Lines had no idea where this rumble of words lines had no idea where this rumble of words and he did end up eventually pointing of the finger at his own son.

Throwing his son under the bus, while he denied being the drug King Pin so many have called him. The conversation did drag on for another two hours and poor Chief Insp Harry had in a nutshell got to a point that I would say was nowhere. It was time to pull our mastermind school boy of sixteen years old Jerry Stroud, into the for front of questions. Once he heard that he was simply on his own and his father had used him and now he had denied any knowledge of the real drugs that were being sold, not just "pep pills". We had no tears from young Jerry instead what I would say was a huge wakeup call from Jerry who pointed the finger at his father and how he was used to recruit his classmates at school, to deliver the drugs on bikes and electric scooters. I did not expect the turn of foot from Jerry and when he did open up about the shooting of Alex Smyth outside the school gate was not supposed to die it was supposed to be it blank in the gun and not a real bullet.

He did ask for police protection from his very own father in return he will open up and tell us anything we wanted to know. His solicitor Clive Mural was simply taken back after being on the pay roll of Frank Stroud to try and get Jerry off on a technicality of some sought. This interview has gone well for us but not exactly the way that Frank Stroud had expected or even wanted. Andy Sharply was a nineteen-year-old who does odd jobs for Frank Stroud he was the one who pulled the trigger that ended the life of Alex Smyth. He lived out in Malak with his mother the drug dealing out there was enough to give him a good living plus the odd job or two for Frank Stroud tactical support was called upon and with Insp Jason Purley and my driver Sgt Kay Croxley were sent out to arrest Andy Sharply. I heard on the radio that Andy Sharply had taken his own mother hostage and it was a standoff situation. Chief Insp Harry Lines was soon on his way to see if he could shine a light to end this situation before Harry arrived Andy Sharply took his own mother's life and then shot himself in the head. Only two shots fired both fatal, Harry phone me to say this kid Andy Sharply was terrified of going against Frank Stroud. I thought over the years a lot of young men have gone down that very same path. In many ways I did feel sad for for Andy Sharply. His mother had cancer and would be dead in six months, but this still was no excuse for Andy Sharply to take her life. I was to learn that Andy Sharply worship the grounds his mother walked on, he spent a lot of the drug money on the care of his mother and to make her life happy. We did need Jerry Stroud to tell us who gave the call to end the life of Alex Smyth was it in fact his own father Frank. For some unknown reason Jerry would not commit to saying his father had ordered the killing. It did lead me to believe that Jerry himself had crack the whip and he knew just the man Andy Sharply to carry out the mission of killing Alex Smyth.

I could see that Chief Insp Harry had in fact been blinded by the facts, he would end up with Frank Stroud saying one thing and his very own song Jerry saying the opposite. We do know that in court Jerry testimony would be cut into shreds by a good solicitor, in fact I do not believe one thing that Jerry has said. So, I instructed Chief

Insp Harry to bring in the other five regular boys were connected to the drug deals with Jerry Stroud. I did tell him to offer them a pardon if the information they gave was honest and truthful parents of the five all denied that their sons were involved in drug dealing. In fact, every parent told Chief Insp Harry that their boy was out "playing basketball". I thought at least they had the same alibi. Child services were called in the five boys Alan Jones, Steve Smith, Robbie Tyler and a Alan Cox and a James Hird. One parent was also in the interview room. There was silence with all five boys until photographs of them were shown.

It was only for extra pocket money and they got to ride electric scooters which they said was fun. The parents of all five boys had to bow their heads after Chief Insp Harry was accused of making this whole thing up!! Photographs over a week were shown and had been blown up to show the faces. No charges would be laid if they were cooperative with the police was explained once again. The father of Adam Jones said "it was a police trap, do not say anything Adam" the other four did admit to the crimes and did comment that Jerry Stroud a school friend had recruited them. During the evening that could change positions. They had a Walkie Talkie to inform the office what was going on. The term the office was the Range Rover where Frank Stroud sat in the drivers sent aid gave orders to his so Jerry on the price that the costumer will be charged form the handing over of the cash to the delivery of drugs took about six to seven minutes. Frank Stroud never spoke to the boys all directions and comments went through his son Jerry who used to get a little tongue tied at times trying to pass on orders to his fellow "movers and grooves" was the name Jerry gave them. Everybody was paid cash at the end of the night and the next day at school none of them made any contact with each other. They were also told not to splash the cash on people might just start to ask questions. The father of Adam Jones had decided to take the deal after all but it was a little too late, he was told we had got all the information we wanted now and his son will be given a caution and a record will be kept of his part in the drug dispatch operation. The other poor boys were given just a slap on the wrist by Chief Insp Harry child services were pleased with the outcome. Alan Cox and James Hird had managed to put away their nest egg and did purchase two scoters. All five boys were told to keep their heads down any never get involved in the world of drugs again.

A return of Frank Stroud to the witness room and being told that not only has his son been giving evidence against him but also fair boys who often worked as the dispatch team members. I was not in the room, but I could tell by looking at the monitor up in my office that this was the last thing Frank Stroud wanted to hear. The expression on his face did show shouting at Chief Insp Harry who did stand his ground again the mention of drugs found in the residence of Frank Stroud was enough to give him at least a fifteen-year holiday in the camp Berrimah prison. The recruitment of school boys to do his duty work would add another five to ten years. His very own son even now giving evidence against his own father could face five to ten years. The question of the death of Alex Smyth by Andy Shapley will be unable to testify against Frank because he took his own life. I could see a smile on the face of Frank now he had heard that news.

I finally got home to see my four boys enjoying their brand-new scooters. All wearing their helmets which made me very happy to see. A huge from each of them and the question how did I know they all wanted an electric scooter. I did ask if I could sell their bikes to help cover the cost. It was only a joke but I did get a very firm "No". The next day it was show time with the Pedophile Ralph Jackson, he was fit for a light interview in his wheelchair, in a vacant room that the hospital had found for us. I just wanted to find the fire escape and just push him in his wheelchair, from the top of the stairs to the bottom. A smirk on his face, the greasy hair and his constant need to consult with his solicitor Walter Cardwell. Today was going to be his of freedom in the real world. His hospital room is going to be given a perfect was for a room in the hospital wing at the Berrimah Prison.

All Ralph Jackson kept repeating was that the landlady Milly Stanton used to bring the young boy Benny to him and say "Hey look what I have got for you only one hour mind you and I want him back". A cask of wine and one hundred dollars was the demand from Milly Stanton. Ralph Jackson knew that Milly Stanton had known his past and been in prison for child molesting. In fact, her very own brother Richard Stanton did suffer with the same problem except last time he went to prison somebody took a Razor Blade fixed to a toothbrush and slit his throat. Nobody owned up and the word was that the prison Stanton death. So, I felt that Ralph Jackson will be in protective custody but will have to sleep with one eye open at all times. I was at last engage in the "I.P" address of those sick individuals living among us and do have a perverted some would say sink mind.

This was some information that I did not really want to know sitting opposite he was Chief Insp Harry plus my office manager Rachel Todd and her side kick a Pia Jackson. Sitting to my right was Ducky and her two sidekicks Chrissy Moore and Lizzy Tabler from the sex crime unit. I did feel that I did need a bigger office today but I tried to keep a smile on my face while I listen to the results of who was tuned unto the sex crime of Ralph Jackson and his crime against four-year-old Benny Smyth had done a live "sick" show. The first was a introduction was a naked Benny Smyth playing with the mad-hood of Ralph Jackson I did notice that Ralph Jackson was what you would call "under-develop" in the size of his penis. I did feel like walking out of my own office, now that would not be very good leadership through their "IP" address we had located twenty people who logged on in west Australian and mainly in mining camps almost one hundred and around the same in South Australia. I had to say when we came to Victoria and New South Whales it was over five hundred log on's the same all the way up to the top of Queensland "Ducky" let us know that some of the people they located in Darwin had already been in jail for sex crimes that involved children. One location was only one hundred yards from nightcliff school and across the road a preschool right opposite where this sick bastard lived. All will be arrested by the ducky team with uniform on back up. I sat there motionless the so-called interstate locations will be given to each sex crime unit in each state. Another piece of information was about Millie Stanton she herself had contact with around a dozen pedophiles in the Darwin area they were connected to her brother and she had kept the friendship going. I told Ducky to just throw the book at her and get her locked up for a long time. She was in my eyes just as bad like those who had committed the actual crimes.

I had to go for a walk and get some fresh air I did not understand how ducky and her team could deal with this every day. I did express my thoughts to all concern and what a good job but more a brave job they had done trying to filter out these sickos from our local society. A word from Ducky did take me back that some of these men are married with children of their own who are now listed as a personal interest who enjoyed watching sex crimes on children. I was heading for the canteen a double egg and bacon roll with fried chillis was on my mind when Rachel my office manager let me know that there was a Sam Jones father of Adam Jones one of the drug delivery boys was waiting in reception to speak to me. I did ask Chief Insp Harry to join me, it was after all heading this case. I have always liked people who get to the point they do want to make.

Sam Jones was a typical "big head" I did imagine he could be found most months in his local pub. Snapping his words and demanding why we did ignore his son's account after he told him not to make a comment. I thought if you want a piece of me, you have come at the wrong time Sam Jones. I slowly and I did choose my words very carefully. "There were six questions, all were a simple yes or no," your son was told not to comment the other four boys did give us the information. So, in the end we did not need your son to testify after all!! I kept a smile on my face, a rambling of words about he was going to the media with this story how we let the boys go with just a slap on the wrist. I had to tell him the director of public prosecution had decided not to proceed any further and I am governing by their decision.

"Going to the media they would not comment on a going case" Chief Insp Harry did finally fly in like a seagull after a hot chip that you are holding in your hand. I had to stop Chief Insp Harry because at times he does have what some would call "A short fuse" I had to give Sam Jones a history lesson about his son who had to tell him almost four weeks ago where the bundle of cash had come from you found hidden in his bedroom. He himself did admit to two of the other boys involved that you had found out about their extra activity in the evening and not playing basketball. You let your son Adam have fifty dollars a week and anything over that which could be as much as two hundred dollars over a week would now go in his pocket. Poor Sam Jones had no idea that we were on to him. I had to remind him that he was now living off the benefit crime and that itself is a crime and I will talk to the director of public prosecutor whether or not he will have you charged. I could almost see the skin on the face of Sam Jones fold in to his face. I pointed to the door and with a whisper in his ear I simply told him to "Fuck off and do not came back unless you are in handcuffs look on the face of Chief Insp Harry that he had not seen this side of me before in fact it did make him realize that I did not get to my position by being "mister nice guy" I hooded for the canteen got my chilly egg and bacon roll plus a bowl of ice cream that I did rip my chilly roll into with energy mouthful I felt like I was only twelve years old once again!!

I let ducky present the facts to Milly Stanton "no need to have a panic attack" ducky told her. We had enough charges for her to spend the next few years in prison and if she is lucky when she is released, she will be able to draw on her old age pension. It was strange watching her she never showed any emotion for Ralph Jackson. The end of this tale was not Alex Smyth the boy who was shot was giving up the drug run mainly because his fourteen-year-old sister could not cope looking after the other two children on her own. It was beans or toast on tinned spaghetti on toast and sometimes tinned curry on toast. Friday on the menu was "chip butties" fried chips from the chip shop in bread and butter these meals was all their mother had ever cooked them. At school they always got a free cooked lunch because they were poor to be poor children services did keep the three children together, one being little Benny himself a couple took them in while their mother went into a rehab hostel to try and help her with her drink problem. I did hear six weeks cater the mother given had died. The couple who took on the three remaining children had decided to adopt them full time. Little Benny did have some mental issues because of the sex crimes that were committed by Ralph Jackson my own four boys were good home life was always fun and laughter the electric scooters had given them a new jest in life. Sgt Amy Fuller was about to step back into the position of my driver she also was a blaming face of fun but no so much at work I began to feel the team itself had grown stronger Chief Insp Harry did seem to be on top in pursue of justice for the mother and their children and violent husbands.

In the morning ay my office I was met by Chief Insp Harry Lines he told me that first part of the trial of Ann Wayne girl on the six o'clock news and her son Charlie Wayne who dies have the name of Bobby Wayne he was with his parents I simply told Harry that I do not care what he called himself Bobby or Charlie Wayne he will still face the same charges. It did seem that Harry might have a problem on his mind and it may not be connected to this case. I did drop the hint of opening up and he said he was concerning that Max Wayne could walk free with his wife Ann and son Bobby both sticking to their same source of saying that Max was not involved in their drug business. He did own the house and when he went interstate, they simply pump up the pill making machine normally for four days and over that period that could produce thousands of pills that they would sell to different drug dealers. Bobby Wayne always took a couple of days off from school on the week that Max went interstate. Ann was facing on her return to public life with a deal that Bobby would be around forty years old then after the final sentence. I still could not believe that Max Wayne was going to just sit by and watch his wife and son go to prison for round twenty years. Max himself had moved into park gate motel on the edge of the city, he did own around fifty percent of the building. Now converted to holiday flats. The Wayne mansion was up for sale but nobody wanted to live in a home where all these teenagers had died. One real estate expert did comment that the Wayne Mansion "smelt of death". It was put on the table to bulldoze the property, then many did say they would not want to live on the ground so many died. A second-hand church yard" was the new title of the property.

Somebody when Max Wayne was interstate had decided to try and do a quick demolition job on the mansion. Petrol bombs and leaving the gas on did what you would call "only half the job". The strong thing now was eventually the insurance company would pay up to Max Wayne. I always thought that the fire was lit while he was interstate.

Chief Insp Harry Lines did inform me that there was not one day when Max would show up in court to support his wife Anne and his son Bobby. I had other ideas on my mind that I wanted to sought out with the leading hand of public prosecutions. I was to find out we got a new person now cracking to whip a John Williamson who told me straight away with his tongue up my ass it was a pleasure to meet me. if only I did feel the same about him. I wanted to know why we cannot charge Max Wayne with something in relation to this shooting at his house and the drug bust after at least five minutes of explanation and God forbid could this John Williamson talk, did he even take a breath? He had not answered my question so I did repeat my concern about Max Wayne walking free. I was to learn that both his wife Ann and his son Bobby had stood on a stack of bibles and even done a hand stand in a way saying that Max Wayne was innocent. When he flew off early on Monday morning and did not return till late Friday evening this was when the pill machine was in full operation. He had no idea I did find it hard to swallow. I gave him tom Chief Insp Harry and Sgt Kay Coxley to go over their findings. The Wayne duo Ann and Bobby had been in court only on a video link, now they would be there in living colour. It was very important that Chief Insp Harry had go hid facts right. I was told by John Williams who did seem to have a bit of a strange body odor that he left in my office. Rachel Todd my office manager came in to clear the air of what she said "smelt like wet socks". I did comment just maybe he might have pissed in his shoes in the men's urinal. I did not even get a smile from Rachel on that comment two hours later I got a limp hand shake from John Williams and he was gone like a bad wind from a cow shed. Rachel had to go and spray the office next door and left the door open so some fresh air could circulate around. I had too much paper work to catch up on and before I knew it Amy was standing at my office door waiting to take me home.

Amy did tell me that I looked tired, I did agree and I wanted to catch a good sleep tonight. I had dinner with the boys before they went off on their scooters just before it got dark. The pool room was busy before they finally went to bed. Amy did join us for dinner and may I say she was unusually quite tonight. Everybody was tucked up and a sleep that top step on the stairs gave out a creak in fact that top step had in fact had a creak in it since I first moved into the house. Now if you stand on the right side of the step, you do not get a creak it is only on the left side. It was eleven o'clock and I went to the top of the stairs maybe one of the boys is not feeling very well, I could not hear anything down in the kitchen but I did coo at out the window and down the garden his tongue a work out by Amy before he went inside the cottage. I did wake up early at six am to find Jay my eldest son who will be eighteen next week and will leave school a monthly later.

I did not mention what I did see during the night the boys went off on the school pick up with Tilda the twin driving today. Amy had left on her motorbike to pick up my car at the police garage. She returns and she did seem full of life today. I went to my office and it did seem quite today without Chief Insp Harry and Sgt Kay Coxley off to court today with the Wayne family. I was told they had another early meeting with John Williamson by Rachel Todd my office manager who gave me a strong coffee to get my body firing up today. I had a meeting with Bill Skinner where you sit like a school boy in front of the head master and for some unknown reason you cannot hear a word, they are saying the word budget and cancel overtime was all that I did remember by the time I did step out of their office and back into the so called "real world". I did in fact after I drop off some paper work in my own office I did decide to go for a walk about in the city, it had been a while since I had placed my feet in the city mall. Homeless people sitting outside shops begging for some money. I came across the top end café and sitting outside was Amy Fuller my driver no longer two old flat mates. It was their day off from uniform police duties I was asked to join them I knew that Amy would be our focus of conversation. I was so learning the so-called story that Amy had given me, was not the same story these two ladies were now giving me their version. They came home from a swim in Parap Pool to find Amy in bed and having sex like a rabbit with Chief Inspector Harry Lines of all people. The girls were not upset but, in their bed, where the three of them slept together. It was a extra-large king size bed I was to learn. I also found out and trying not to swallow my coffee that this romance between Amy and Harry had been going on for a while. Now if only I had kept my nose to the ground more instead of concentrating on my police duties, I might have put two and two together. I did wonder off in my own mind think about Jay my eldest son now.

Amy had gone on the attack against her flat mates and decided to move out it did suit them because they knew that the lease was up for newel. The next day when they got home Amy was gone with all her suitcases and sixties music CD'S. I did express how sorry I was, the three them had been together for two years in fact Amy had decided on the "manage the trolls" which was going so well and this was the first so called argument between the three of them. I got up to leave and the waitress gave me the Bill for three coffees. I turn to look at my two female friends and they were gone like the wind. I headed and Sgt Kay Coxley had just arrived from the court case with Ann Wayne and her son Bobby had been convicted. Ann did receive fifteen years after she did testify that she led Bobby into the drug business.

Bobby did receive ten years. The drug did take in account that he had shot one of the party invaders and stuck a spear in the back of another that would have saved lives. The judge did go on to say that Bobby was seen on a video handling out drugs like candy. Chief Insp Harry did say that Max Wayne was not in court there was a race meeting at the Darwin Turf club and he could be found there a reliable source had told Chief Insp Harry. I was pleased it was over and now Chief Insp Harry handed me a medical note from his doctor saying he did need a monthly of work due to stress at work and his marriage at the same time the pressure of the job being Chief Inspector had got to him I did want to say taking time out for work and shagging the ass of Amy Fuller must have been a lot of pressure during working hours. I simply bite my tongue for a later date Harry left without saying goodbye to anybody, I did notice that Amy did look a little relieved I like to act in a swift manner and between myself and my old wooden desk I did not expect Chief Insp Harry to return to his position. I called in Insp Jason Purley and told him that he will be acting Chief Inspector and he will be taking over all of Harry Lines duties from today. I had to throw in the cherry on top of the cake and that was being my right hand I did expect one hundred percent loyalty at all times anything he could not handle please come and see me; my door is always open. There was a rush of support for Jason Led by Rachel Todd my office manager. I looked over at Amy and gave her a nod. I did decide to keep my conversation with her two ex-flat mates a secret until I may have to raise its ugly head. Once again in the end it was really none of my businesses, I did get a comment form mother superior Rachel Todd doing her office manager duties when she did open up about Chief Insp Harry had been active with a few of the ladies in my team that had given a few of them more than a headache. I had to stop Rachel then and there. It was not my policy or never will be to show any interest in who is sleeping with who or even their sexuality. Mother superior Rachel Todd simply said "I do understand Boss and the matters closed and my lips are now concrete!! I could not have said it better myself.

I thought I then had our new Chief Insp Jason standing with an arm full of files, I did understand that they do need signing off on. It was something that Ex Chief Insp Harry always left to the very last minute. I could have told Jason to stick the files up his ass but it was only his first time in the job. I did mention that I have to counter sign them anyway, so he placed them on my desk within a lighting flash Rachel Todd did mention that I had enough to do today so she could forget y signature. I did think why not she had been doing it for around five years now. A good job done I thought to myself Chief Insp Jason was like a bad wind, he had found some notes that explained that the school boys are back moving drugs for a new leader. An old name from my past a Ted Malton the two cameras on top of the two office blocks that were sitting there on the drones. Due date for removal was to be tomorrow I told Jason to go over to speak to Rachel Todd the office manager and she will activate them and Det Pia Jackson under the watchful eye of SGT Amy Fuller will take control of the situation.

I went into the observation room behind my office to take a view at what we had on the screens. Yes, not three days have gone by and back on the scooters are the school boys selling drugs only three seem to be in action, they had done a slim down operation, the car that was the place to be handing at the drugs was owned by a Ted Malton. Within minutes if Rachel Todd did not have enough to do had some information that Ted Malton was in fact cousin to our Mister Jones father of Adam who did not want to cooperate in our last raid on that drug ring. I did think cheekily bugger passing the information on to Ted Malton who has been flying under our radar for the past two year since he came out of prison for drug dealing. He got an eight-year sentence when Alf Jackson and myself busted him in a midnight raid, we did not need any tactical unit, Alf a bit like me did enjoy the use of brute force back in those days. Ted Malton did rush to the kitchen for a extra-large kitchen knife when I just happen to step in to save Alf Jackson with one of my free plastic surgery on the nose jobs. I did not know the nose could blees do much with a little tap from a cricket bat that was handy in the corridor. I mean I could have shot him much meant of even more paper work and back in those days Alf Jackson and myself under the supervision of John Knight all had a massive dislike for paper work. I could see that both Rachel and Jason plus of course Sgt Amy and Det Pia all enjoyed my tales of the old days before I spent most of my time sitting on my ass behind a desk.

"We need the source" I said Jason gave me a blanket look, there was something I am eligible is to blank faces. "I other words' where are Ted Malton and his cousin Jones getting the bloody drugs from, we need their supply we need the source". I do not need to explain myself anymore I said. Phones bank accounts, person of interest connected to Ted Malton anybody who also had a past in the drug trade. At once Rachel put her team into action to gather information. I did hope that Jason would not be stupid enough to ask "shall we do a raid later on?" I had to think it's only his first day so go easy on him and bite your tongue big fella. "Jason, no raid, we want them all lined up like bloody Tin soldiers, before we move. It was one hour later. The name of Max Wayne was mention, my ears did prick up. A phone call from Max Wayne to Ted Malton had been tracked it was made when Max was the Turf Club and his wife Ann and son Bobby were being sentence in court for the very same thing, he is having a discussion with Ted Malton about drugs. The conversation did reveal that Max Wayne was the middle man in this relationship. I did need hid supply man that was something we had to trace the phone calls before a "Hayden Times" another name from my past. Mayden times was in prison the same time for a longer sentence than Ted Malton. Fifteen years he did serve and it was only one month he got out of prison to breath fresh air once again. We had a new address for Mayden times on fact he was staying in the motel park gate rundown joint that Max Wayne has a shape in and is now smacked up there himself. I did try to imagine where the drugs were hidden, I did not think that they are stupid enough to have them in their motel room. Ted Malton was staying in a flat in Nightcliff and only a short walk from the home of the Jones Family. I told Hason to get a couple of teams together to track the Jones Family and also Ted Malton. It only took one night until cousin Jones was handing over a shoulder bag to his cousin Ted, I needed to know once again the origin of these drugs. Where does Max Wayne fit into this. The phones were quiet and I did believe they might have got a switch to burner phones now my team found it hard to track them now. The night operation was again in full swing. I out an undercover officer in to the mix to order a large number of drugs to throw the cat against the pigeons. We were surprised that in one man they could be delivered. This was time to swoop on all concern Ted, Malton, cousin Jones, Max Wayne and Hayden Times. I did need around twenty officers that would include tactical support. I wanted all of them picked up around the time I did not want anybody getting an early warning and bolting like a wet rat down a drain pipe to hide. I told Jason that coordination of everybody is essential. Nobody should move until the dealing is in progress. I got a limp thumbs up from Jason who left a horrible thought in my mind should I have made him my right hand at this very moment I did not have very much confidence in him. I had to say to myself "well it is only his first day in the position once again"

The first pit fall was that Sam Jones the main connection to everybody was not in place. Sam Jones the plumber had been called put for a burst pipe in Stuart Park. A message to Hayden Times (Mr. Supply) was that Irene Jones the wife of Sam will be waiting for him with the package. Rachel explains that she thought the package was the money. True enough one hour later Hayden Times did not even have to get out of his car, Irene in an over tight jump suit was there with an identical bag to the one that Hayden Times gave her, a quick look inside by both of them and he was on his way back to the city along Dick Ward drive when some traffic police would stop him in his tracks on a routine stop, when two of my team would slap the handcuffs on. Next part of the exercise was Sam Jones who arrived in what look like a panic mood only to find he had not been missed. He was in his work van off to catch up either his cousin Ted Melton who was waiting in a car park, just up from the park where the drugs were to be sold. Video of everything was kept even Irene in her skin tight body suit handing over the money for the drugs.

Within twenty minutes two boys arrived on electric scooters both we had not come across before. Sam Jones was well gone now on his plumber's van. Only to be stop by the same traffic police who had now moved across to the other side of the road again police jewelry was presented to Sam Jones who had more than enough to say but my team were told not to do and request for answers in what was going on. While this was napping, I got Ducky to go to the Jones residence with a warrant and child services to assist Adam Jones while his mother taken into custody for her small part in two drug infested world sending many to their early death. A small number of drugs plus the usual Irene was caught puffing away without a care in the world until Ducky invaded her privacy. Money was flowing and drugs were exchange the two boys on their electric scooters were earning money tonight.

I was all about to go Belly up when acting Chief Jason gave a little tap on the window of the car that Ted Malton was very comfortable in silly Ted tries to bolt out the other door only to find two tackle support officers, throwing him to the ground. By all reports and by the body cam footage Ted Malton still thought he was still a young man and was ready to take in the world. It was not the first time, but now the second time poor little Ted Malton ended up with another broken nose. We did need some medics who were already standing by. I had a bad feeling that the number one on my hit list Max Wayne was not at his Park Gate Motel room. His phone was plus two other burner phones unused next to his bed on a side table we had a team either end of the motel yet he still has flown the coup. Some designer suits were packed in a suitcase for him to fly interstate tomorrow the tickets were one way, he did not have the usual return ticket for today.

I wanted the room to be left exactly how the team had found it. A few phone calls were made and he was not at any of his usual habits. So, it was the waiting game I did remember many moons ago there was a entrance half way along the back of the building, in the good old days when sex was cheap with a door knock, you then went upstairs by these stairs, through a doom just marked emergency exit. You did phone the nice working lady you were waiting to see she in fact would open the door from the inside. Where you would follow her to her room and the opening of the wallet before the fun would come and all your Christmas of pleasure would come at once. Everything was now in our hands. A Joe Walsk and Tony Beach were taken into custody by Det Chrissy Moore and Det Lizzy Tablet both working under the watchful eye of Ducky. Their parents a sleep Infront of the television both couples were very surprised at their sons had been what they called "naughty boys" they thought they were out riding their scooters at the bicycle track around the park. It was a long day and I went home. Amy had gone home on her motorbike, while I caught a lift with two uniform officers.

Everybody had gone to bed. I sat on the edge of the bed and looked at the clock if my thoughts are right my son Jay would put his foot on the top stair to get it to the next one down. Now right on que and I watch him be welcome into the garden cottage by Amy. I took a chance and decided there is some unfinished business to be taken care of at the Park Gate Motel in the city. I went to the taxi rank and took a taxi two blocks from the Park Gate Motel and walked the opposite decision until the taxi driver drove off on another call. I had my black look, cap, face mask, in my pocket my thirty-eight pistol my endless collection of hand guns. The silencer was already on. I could see a team of two detectives each end of the Parkgate Motel I took a walk along the fence o the school behind the Parkgate Motel. I found the alley way leading along the rear of the Parkgate Motel. I looked up on the top floor, and I could not see the light on in the room that Max Wayne had taken over it was not alone and I stood back and figure of Max Wayne passed me I did pretend to look for a light for a cigarette that I was trying to light up.

Max did step and produce a cigarette lighter to help me light my cancer stick. While he held his lighter still the wind kept blowing out the flame he did apologize and I did something stupid and said "that's alright Max!!" he looked at me, drop the lighter door, where he had a key and he did part own the place, he got the door old and I put my foot in front to stop him closing the door. It was coming for Max for a while now except I did not put my usual two bullets in the head, instead I gave Max extra one for luck. I then pulled his body out of the door way and looking around I pulled it between two cars and then I felt once again I had done my duty as police after walking up the mall I arrived home, feeling what I would call "Full of happiness". Deep down I knew this whole operation could have gone very badly for me. I must be even more careful in the future. I went to sleep and

I do admit I did not sleep well, only to be woken by Jay and the Todd step of the staircase.

I was editing my breakfast when Chief Insp Jason who was more than acting today. It did seem he was on the ball with a report that Max Wayne had been found dead between two parked cars at the Parkgate. "So, he never made his flight around seven hours Doctor Rebecca told me. also, he was shot several times at least three times in the head". I told Jason I will be there soon; I did look up to Amy and she was already gone off on her motor bike acting Chief Insp Jason had the theory, that somebody who knew him, finally had no more use for him and his money. Dr Rebecca said it was a professional hit three bullets at close range two in the back of his head and one in his mouth. "He stunk of rum" was the other comment she made, "so h was out drinking, we had a team each end of this building and he did slip in along this back-Alley way!!"

Acting Chief Inspector Jason was no longer acting, he had the bull by the horns and his mind on the game today. I did not want to interview anybody today so I left it up to Jason and Ducky. Jason took on Hayden Times and Ted Malton, while Ducky took on Irene Malton and the two school boys Jason (Joe) Walsh and Tony Beach both school boys were happy not to go to school today and did not realize how serious the trouble they were in now. Their parents sat quietly and a member of child services sat beside them for support. Irene Malton did deny she was involved in the drug deal until she saw the footage that was filmed from a room across the road from her house. She still denied that she knew that there was money in the bag she handed over to Hayden Times to say that she never even touches drugs, until she was told of her memory lapse with the bang on the table that she was caught puffing like a steam train. "It was for health Reasons". Being told that she could lose Adam to child services, after his involvement with drugs and her husband Sam both are unfit parents in the eyes of child services.

I did tell Ducky and Jason that it is very important that we do not tell anybody who is on their list today to be interviewed that Max Wayne id dead. I wanted to keep that detail up our sleeve. Irene Jones was trying to be a touch at of control with the situation. So, Ducky did try once again make her realize that her son Adam will end up in a foster home with both his parents heading for a long prison sentence, handing over a bag full of money for a bag full of drugs was not in the mind of Irene to be worthy of a prison sentence. We did have tears and after a cup of tea. Irene did inform Ducky that Adam came home from school one month ago with the news of how he could make some easy pocket money. This did mean this operation that we did bust was in operation much longer than we realized if only Irene's husband was more cooperative with Jason trying to act like he was the king pin and not the delivery boy did little to impress Jason acting his part as a Chief Inspector. We already knew that Ted Malton was the brains behind this just because Sam Jones went to his cousin with the idea, he was still a nobody in the eyes of Ted Malton he tried to give orders but was told he had done his part and now simply "F off" and let the people who know what they are.

Ted Malton opens up with information about the source of the drugs was Hayden Times and where the money was going to come from which we knew the money was going to come from which we knew was Max Wayne. In return Max would get half of the profit once the drugs were sold. One thousand dollars was paid to Sam Jones and half a kilo of marijuana. Max Wayne had decided over a few beers at the Turf Club that two thousand dollars was enough for Sam Jones, if he did not like it, we will use somebody else in the future for being the exchange person. The face of Sam Jones went from being the touching tough guy to a humble servant of his cousin and Max Wayne who was cracking the whip from a distance.

A total of eight hours before we had all the facts. Ted Malton wanted to know who pointed the finger at him. He did suggest that it was his own cousin Sam Jones because he did not make that much out of the deal. "No, it was not your cousin Sam Jones, we already had intel and used the information from the bust we did a few days ago "Chief Insp Jason told him.

I did phone up John Williamson the head prosecutor and told him we have a new collection of people not unlike the last mob we busted a few days ago. He had already heard that Max Wayne was dead and will not be standing up in court trying to convince everybody of his innocent.

I went down to see Dr. Rebecca on her findings about the death of Max Wayne point blank range, shot just inside the doorway then pulled out and drop from ground level down on to the car park, where he hit his head on a concrete protection ramp to stop cars bumping into the wall. His neck was broken from the fall then Max Wayne was drag between two cars and with the owners not attending their car till eight AM when he was found. There was no trace of the killer, she was waiting to see if the gun had been used in a similar crime before, she did live in hope for a match to try and link this murder to the other unsolved murders she had recently. I did try and look a little surprise at her comment I put on my innocent face and my team it was more than a good job done, it was brilliant!

CHAPTER 10

"OUT IN THE OPEN"

I was almost a sleep when I had a knock on my bedroom door it was my son Jay and Amy Fuller my driver. They wanted to talk to me downstairs so we did not wake up my other three sons. I must say it was not what I was expecting standing in the sun room I was simply told that I am going to become a grandfather. I felt like a lost fart between my ass cheeks. "We are going to have a baby" Jay told me that lead balloon had fallen from a great height and hit the ground running in the opposite direction that I had wanted. I looked at Amy and she just stood rubbing her stomach. "We thought that the side Verandah next to the mango tree, we could close in and make it the baby's room". I had to stop Jay there and then, that mango tree has termites so it must come down, each year we have been getting less mangoes!!

I told them I did need to talk to Amy on her own. I could see that Jay did look puzzled at my request. They kissed goodnight which I thought was a nice touch in this moment in time. We went down to the garden cottage. I had to put a stop to this dream right away between my son Jay and Amy. I got straight to the point in telling Amy I did know that the baby did not belong to Jay. "You two only been together a few weeks, so come clean and tell him before he does make a real fool of himself and tells the world his three brothers will be calling each other

Uncle. "You got it wrong Aaron, Jay is the father" at this moment in time, the cast thing Amy wanted to become a liar in my eyes. It was time to open the box of words and disclosed what I know and suspect, I mention that I had simply bump into her old flat mates and the story was that they came home early and found you with Chief Inspector Harry Lines banging away like two rabbits Harry is married has two children and a third on the way and this moment in time he is moving back home to be with his wife and kids to try and save his marriage. "That is not true Harry is single, once married years ago" Amy cried out to me. I had to tell her that she was not the only one who he had a bit of body contact with. He was also seeing Sgt Kay Coxley who also is in the mood of morning sickness. So, this is what is going to happen, you will tell Jay that he is not the father also due to this development you will have to move out from the garden cottage. I cannot have you pushing a pram around the garden, it will be in my eyes rubbing salt into the wound in the eyes of Jay also your job you cannot do if you are expecting a child, if we got into a confrontation, I would never forgive myself if you got injured and lost the baby. I will give you time off to sought out your life I will catch a cab to work tomorrow. With that Amy gave me the car keys and simply said "thanks for nothing Aaron". "I am only protecting my family just like I have always done!!"

Then I got the door slam in my face. I made it back to the main house. I went into the lounge to find a stiff drink; malt whisky and I did notice Jay standing in the kitchen doorway. He came over and held me tight, I did likewise he had tears in his eyes while he thanks me for the love, I give him and my moto is "That the Family always does come first". He did laugh and said imagine if Mother was alive what would she say? "Well, she would have given you a good talking to about keeping your trouser snake under lock and key and besides your brothers are just too young to become "Uncles" and you are just too young to become a "Father".

We both went to bed and for the very first time I sat with my eldest son and had a very large couple of glass of Malt Whisky the first sip he did cough and turn his nose up but the second and third glass of Whisky he was in command.

Jay had decided to take the day off school. I did blame myself he had never had a hangover before and now he was trying to fix a broken heart full of his dreams. He still had a job filling shelves at the local supermarket till Uni starts for him in the New Year. When I finally got to worn, I had to break the news to the team that Sgt Amy Fuller will be off for a few days. The wise owl Rachel Todd did mention that she did hope it was not morning sickness there has been a bit of that going around the team "Only in the females" I did reply to a roar of laughter I did phone my twins the housekeepers to keep a eye on Jay today he was under the weather I do remember when I broke up with my very first love, my Mother did say she does look pretty but is a bit thick in the head. The next date two years late was my Kate the love of my life that I did eventually marry.

I was glad to see Crystal Fulton back on the team. I had missed her. She had an abortion and needed time to recover. I look at Rachel who was keeping her mouth shut but I did read her lips "Harry Lines". I just nodded and said in a large laugh, "Well do not stand around talking, you got work to catch up on Crystal and I do know that the Mother Rachel is very happy on your return. I did not give Rachel any air in the speculation about Amy. It was then an Sgt Penny male arrived with the introduction of "Sir Commander Aaron Brown I am your new driver and I am the replacement for Sgt Amy Fuller. I looked at Rachel and now the Dustin Lid had been blown off of the Dustin and the rubbish will not be able to keep up with it. I did order a coffee and then I sat alone in my room and I felt the eyes of Rachel watching every move I made even while I sat in my chair day dreaming out of the window.

A chilly egg and bacon roll with a kiwi fruit thick shake did put a smile on my face my new driver Penny Maze must have been given the direction of Rachel my office manager I handed over the car keys to her and told her to watch out for grumpy George the garage manager who does like to stick his nose into matters that do not concern him.

"So, he is a true gossip in other words !!" Penny simply commented.

She had hit the nail in the head right way. It was then my personal phone rang and Tilda my house keeper was telling me news that I never expected.

"Listen Aaron everything is under control and Jay is on his way to hospital he was tried to commit suicide" I looked at Sgt Penny Maze and simply said "get the car at the front of reception I need to get to the hospital".

I could see Rachel come bouncing in, I simply said that "Jay has tried to commit suicide he is on his way to hospital now" I could see her eyes well up in tears.

"Go Aaron go for F sake now!!" shouted Rachel

I could tell that Sgt Penny did know how to put foot down and burn rubber with the lights and sirens. I did have to close my eyes when we went through the red lights on the way to the hospital. I have to say at this moment in time of that I always thought that Sgt Amy was in control of this car but Sgt Penny has found wings on the car. I had no idea even gave more excitement to this journey. I arrived to be greeted by Sofia the house keeper. She handed me a note when we reach the room where Jay laid motionless.

"He will survive, he was lucky to be found, he had taken in a large quantity of drugs that can be very harmful."

A doctor came over to tell me once again he said "He is lucky, very lucky somebody found him. I read the suicide note. Jay had written that all his dreams had come true and he loved Amy so much, a family we will become until she told him that the child was not his. What could I say and do Sofia put her arms around me for a hug. I did have tears rolling down my cheek. "We will get through this together Aaron, you are not alone we are with you!!"

I sat in the corner watching the medical staff do what they do best.

"He is awake" the doctor called out to me. I stood up and looked at my first son Jay trying to say "sorry" to me. I held his hand and told him "Everything will be fine". I was told he did need to rest for short while now so I went outside where I was not Rachel my office manager of all people with a cup of coffee in her hand for me.

"If you think I am not going to be here to support you, well you are bloody wrong Aaron".

He is sleeping he will recover. I told Rachel. I did not go and find a bench to sit on and wait to speak to the doctor when he was ready to speak to me.

"A very lucky young man who feel helplessly in love and it did now work out, now he does need love and it did not work now he does need your support when he does come home he will have to be under the care of a psychiatrist to make sure he in on a level playing field once again". I did think that he was his final exams in a couple of weeks which to me did not matter. His health was more important getting my Jay back to normal was the priority. My mind did wander to my other three boys and how was I going to explain this to them. In the next hour Rachel went back to work and I sat alone with Sofia there was no much I could do the doctor told me so why don't I go home and return with my other three boys later today. I always take the advice of a doctor something my grandmother taught me. I did go back to work it was no good just wandering around the house like a lost sheep in a paddock who cannot find the rest of the flock. Chief Insp Jason Purley had taken up his new position like a "duck to water" a new overnight crime had come in my direction. A fight outside "the flying parrot". A very down-market eating house that has had its problems over the years with drugs and fight illegal drinking after hours. A selection of owners that you would not trust to arrange a children's birthday party. The son of the owner Billy Reem when a Paul Reem had been struck by a beach chair in the car park by a member of the Adamson Family trying to protect John Adamson who had a knife placed in his face by Paul Reem.

In a very long explanation from Chief Insp Jason did family explain the situation to me with the liquor license did state till eleven pm the would-be manager Paul Reem did decide to close at nine O'clock. More than a few words were said and around thirty people went outside to wait for the taxi convey to arrive. Paul Reem did come out of the kitchen back door to have another go at the patrons waving a kitchen knife trying to cool down Paul Reem which was trying to cool down but he was like a bull in a China shop a Jimmy Adamson struck Paul backwards to the ground where he struck his head and died on the spot. There was around twenty witness who all gave the same statement Dr Rebecca Mitcham had notice cocaine in the nose of the deceased. I sat waiting for the punch line from Chief Insp Jason. This family of Adamson were known in the drug trade but have been off our radar for around seven years, now they are into property. I still waited for something from Chief Insp Jason to make me go for my Malt Whisky bottle in my desk. Finally, I got what I wanted some meat on the bone.

"This John Adamson who I do believe you know from a past encounter of more than once, he is the father of our Sgt Amy Fuller and he did ask for you in the interview in the early hours of this morning!!" I had to bite my tongue and wonder why now and not this morning was I not inform of this situation, "I have been home to bed and I had the John Adamson released on bail!!" I was feeling like one of those dung beetles pushing that ball always up that hill and went I got to the top and that I have pushed this dung ball up the wrong hill. "He did ask for your boss, I told him that you are tucked up in bed and will be at work in a few hours, I did remind him that I was in charge I am circus master in this moment of time. I did think of the face of a clown on the body of Chief Insp Jason. "Amy Fuller or should I say Sgt Amy Fuller in on sick leave at present and I will arrange to me this John Adamson who I do remember back in the days all at a constant war in the world of drugs with John Adamson.

Once a drug dealer always a drug dealer just because he is flying under our radar does not mean he is not still up to his neck in the drug trade. I did receive "I understand boss" from Chief Insp Jason. He handed me his report and went over to his desk. I called him back and told him to go home and catch up on some sleep, tomorrow is a new day and I have a meeting with John Anderson who does claim to be the father of Sgt Amy Fuller at home we had dinner and the boys were very eager to go to the hospital to show some support for Jay the eldest who just could not handle life at the present. In the car I did explain the reason why Jay tried to take his life all they told me that they will support him in any way they could. Jay had a great smile when his three siblings invade his quiet room. I went to see the doctor who simply said that "I could take Jay home with no time to relax he had done enough sleeping so it was off to the pool room when we got home. Once again, all four boys beat me at pool.

Jay I was surprised that he wanted to go to school and just carry on just like usual. I must say I was very proud of him. Tilda did go into the school and explain in a brief detail what had happen so the teacher I could keep an eye on him without him knowing. I got hold of Chief Insp Jason to get him to line up an interview with John Adamson. The ex-drug lord and now property developer. I could tell on the face of John Adamson that he was not pleased me the comment that I was the last man standing with John Knight and Alf Jackson both pushing up daises these days. I had already told Jason that I will do all. The talking he is to just sit there and bite his tongue at all the words that come out of the mouth of John Adamson. Next to John Adamson was his very long-time solicitor Clive Thompson, somebody who also should be locked up with the clients he does defend. "In a nut shell the public prosecutor office will not be laying any charges in the reference to the death of Paul Reem outside the rear of "the flying parrot eating house". I went to stand up with the words of "well thank you for coming today John Adamson. A personal matter that John Adamson had requested that we talk alone. I could see that the solicitor had the face like a pig's ass when he was told to leave and joined by Chief Insp Jason who also did look like he had just slid down a fifty-foot razor blade and did not feel he was cut up by it.

John Adamson wanted to discuss the life and times of Sgt Amy Fuller who was on sick leave at the moment and was not living in the garden cottage in my garden. I was so pleased that Daddy John had welcome her home to his mansion out at Bay View his wife Jill had not spoken to Amy for almost four years since she left home. A far too long explanation of the home life of the Adamson Family was not what I wanted to hear. At nineteen I was to learn that Amy the daughter of a distant cousin who was killed in a road race accident on the Stuart highway near Humpty Doo her husband also died in the accident. Amy was raised in a private boarding school down in Adelaide, before she broke her adopted parent's heart by telling them she wanted to join the police force to avenge her parents' death. Being top of the class she went on to become a detective doing an advance driving and protection course, she ended up being my driver. Going on for just over three and half years now. I knew most of this late information but I did not know that her adopted father was a leader in the drug trade in the northern territory. This was something that I will raise with human resources and my office manager Rachel Todd. I was taken back being told that tomorrow Amy was going to have an abortion in a private clinic. She will pay for it and will be twenty weeks pregnant. She has seen two doctors over the past month and did decide little over week ago to have the abortion. My mind was working over because Amy must have made this decision before she told my son Jay, he was going to be a father. There is a large part of the puzzle missing here was now at the front of my mind. All the time I was thinking this John Adamson was still talking I had to ask him to repeat what he had just said. The motorbike he did purchase for her, he wanted to buy her a mini cooper he also mention that Amy will be moving over of my residence and will move into a flat in the rear of his house.

He wanted to send a removal truck over tomorrow or the next day. They would use the rear gate of the property, he did believe that Amy only had basic furniture, kitchen ware and two cases of clothes plus her stereo and Vinyl collection. I just told him to go for it but phone you came to remove all the items. He went to share my hand but I do not shake hands with anybody except family and very close friends since could. I did watch John Adamson leave reception with his lap dog solicitor Clive Thompson snapping at his heels. I went upstairs where I got Rachel my office manager to join me after closing the door. "So please explain how Amy Fuller adopted father is the drug lord John Adamson manage to get a job in this office as my driver, now didn't human resources, check her out Rachel?"

"Boss she came with flying colors and did seem to fit your need".

"I am not talking about bloody flying colours I am talking about a "background check" Rachel!!

"Now some body fucked up" was the word I did want to hear from Rachel.

Well, she will not be allowed back into this office and into the main building well Uncle Bill and the stork can decide on that situation. John Adamson is a known drug lord for ten years, although the past few he has moved on to buying up properties doing them up and renting them out.

"A way of money laundering his drug money" Rachel was back on the same page with me.

"Fancy a chilly egg and bacon roll" boss? That will go a long way to heal the morning I have had so far.

I called in Chief Insp Jason to let him know we will be going out to "the flying duck" to visit Billy Reem another drug king who has been off on radar for far too long now.

I gave Harry a brief education in the drug war seven years ago where almost twenty people ended up dead that we do know about Billy Reem was a trigger-happy thug who enjoyed drive by shootings. John Adamson was one of his rivals both Billy Reem and John Adamson never got more than a slap on the wrist, due to lack of evidence. A yearlong drug war led by John Knight back in the days with Alf Jackson being my right-hand man both of them had a habit of "taking care of business" which meant if they did not have enough to school an arrest warrant at them instead, they just shot a bullet. Around seven mystery unsolved murders are still on file within my desk. I can tell you know that John Adamson took his group to that "flying duck eating house" and out of the twelve I have seen two drug dealers from down south Australia enjoying dinner with John Adamson, it was rubbing salt into the wound of Billy Reem to let him know that John Adamson is still around and open for business just like the old days. I watch the house video or the restaurant at the flying duck. I did imagine that the neck of Billy Reem was swollen with the vein in my neck just about to burst.

I told Chief Insp Harry Lines to give me a few minutes and we will be off to "the flying duck". Rachel my office manager. It was time to bring this long-time kind friend up to date I explain that Jay is coming home and does want to live life normally at school I went on to explain what I knew so far about my ex-driver Sgt Amy Fuller. She is going to have an abortion in the next couple of days, plus she made the booking two weeks ago. According to her adopted father John Adamson, so in fact if you really think about it, she sis not have to involve my Jay, telling him he was the father and they are going to play "Happy Families" Rachel was waiting for me to stop talking by the look on her face, something that I had come to detect over the years of working with her. "So, Harry Lines has been planting his sperm not into not one but three of my girls Crystal Fulton she has had the abortion and now Amy Fuller and following up the rear Sgt Kay Coxley still spending more time in the lady's toilet than at her desk with the so called "morning sickness". I wanted to comment by Rachel gave me the upright finger to let me know that she still had more on her mind.

"So, to save his marriage, he let a transfer up to the Cairns area with two sons and his wife expecting her third children a couple of months. No wander his mind was not on his police job he was too busy breeding!! Rachel always had a way of words that you were not expecting to come out from her lips. I told Sgt Penny to get the car, poor Chief Insp Jason was in the thought that he was going to travel with me on the back side. In fact, I had to stop him from climbing into my car. I simply pointed to a police car with a driver waiting to take him to the flying duck. We arrived at reception and it took a few minutes for Billy Reem to show his ugly head. He asked if we had a warrant, I simply replied what for have you been hiding drugs out the back in your humble flat "anyway I simply come over to let me know, we will not be laying any charges on John Adamson and his party for the death of your son Paul. We have it all on your CCTV in the restaurant and out in the car park.

"Listen Brown!!"

"Commander Brown to you Billy Reem!!"

"Well, they arrived in a group of twelve and started moving two tables of six together, somebody forgot to tell the waitress there was a group of twelve booked in. listen Commander Brown, I did notice some criminal element from down south, drug dealers so that Prick Adamson is still up to his old tricks.

"Hey you just stop right there Billy, you could have just given poor John Adamson a bear hug to welcome him and even tell him that you have missed him over the past few years!!" you always had weird sense of humor. Commander Brown, anyway you are the last one standing now old Alf Jackson who took over the Royal Oak Pub with money I imagine from money in brown paper bags.

"You got that wrong, his mother won the lotto so she did purchase the Royal Oak Pub that she has spent most of her spare time in". A silence before Billy Reem started on John Knight. I did expect that he was trying to remember his name to start with "So the coroner will notify when the case of the death of your son Paul will take place!!"

"He was attacked that Adamson set him up" shouted Billy Reem at me and slightly losing control of the situation". I had to but I did not enjoy telling Billy that his son Paul was on cocaine, the silver dinner tray was found in the back of the kitchen just near the door that Paul did come out, moving that long blade kitchen knife. If he had not fallen over and knocked his head, he would have gone to bed and never woken up he had the cocaine powder blowing in the wind out of his nose to put it in another way my forensic team did say that the strength of the cocaine he took would have killed him within the hour!!"

"Sorry my Paul never ever touch drugs; somebody must have given them to him or just maybe one of your mob stuffed the cocaine up his nose any planed that cocaine in the kitchen". Billy always had an answer for everything and just like the old days he had a twisted mind and did believe his family was holy holy.

I left Billy with a warning that if he does take any retaliation against the Adamson Family in any way I will crash this motel with a ton of bricks right on this reception area, there will not be any bloody slap on the wrist this time. You were lucky last time that your little gang did not turn on you, instead went to prison with "concrete lips" not saying a bad word about you. I think we are finished Billy I am only a hot skip and jump away with my team. Billy did not even say goodbye to me. I went back to the office and sat watching the clock to give the green light for me to spend time with Jay and his brothers. I was not going to mention how Amy played him and in fact there was no need for Jay to even know that she was expecting a baby. In my estimation Amy Fuller is not the young lady who I trusted my life with and also, I must not forget she saved my ass more than once!!

I had a good spring in my step the next day at work until I did notice the huge pile of reports waiting for the signature of mine. I sat there in a word of my own and if my day started in a up lifting way now, I felt I had just jump out of a plane without my parachute. Now heading in my direction was Louise Meadows commander in the Federal Police. Her specialty apart from listening to her own voice was the drug trade. She had busted so many drug dealers I felt that she should put a notch on the leather belt that she had to wear to keep up those skin tight trousers she has a habit of wearing and it does send the young male detectives into a frenzy when she does walk like a cat walk model.

"Well, hi Commander Aaron thought I would just pop I and let you know that I do believe that we are working together to try and stamp out John Adamson drug ring, of course old Billy was pleased to give his blessing and he did mention that he had no idea we are working very closely together almost intimate"

I just sat there and mumbled "are we?" who the hell is that tall woman standing behind Billy, everything he spoke she had to get a word in I mean who the F is running the show Billy or her she kept saying we". "We call her the Stork" I replied

"Does she lay eggs Aaron?"

I did not mention how many blow jobs the Stork must have given Bill over the past ten years to secure that position of number two next to him. I did think that it was not the appropriate trying to catch a breath was Commander Louise was soon to tell me that Phil Barlett and Joe Turner big time dealers from Adeline who flew to Darwin last week, came back to Adelaide three days or so ago and caught the next flight back to Darwin and have been staying at the home of

John Adamson. She heard on the grape vine that they will be going to the Turf Club later, this did mean to me she had somebody on the inside. She knew about the incident at "the flying duck" and wanted my update on it.

It was then that Rachel arrived with coffee and like two old hens who are celebrating laying and egg somehow, they both forgot about me sitting next to Louise was an Insp John Stafford who finally introduced himself mainly because he would see that Louise had forgotten about him even being there. The final word I heard come out of the mouth of Louise was simply "Eight bloody years you have been putting up with him, you deserve a medal!!"

I sip my coffee and said to Louise "So where was I, O yes, an alteration outside in the car park a Paul Reem staggering around waving a very large kitchen knife at John Adamson, hit by an old broken deck chair in the head, he fell hit his head on the concrete wall and he was dead!!

Um I took a breath, "O yes full of cocaine, enough inside him to kill him within the hour my forensic head Dr Rebecca Fuller told me. "So, the old chook Rebecca she is still with you? Another one who does deserve a long service medal!! I made no comment to Louise who took a deep breath and told drugs coming in a container from depth to the line to Darwin stopping off at Tennent Creek to go east to Queensland when as where now that is the problem commander Aaron Brown?

With that a simple drinking her cup of coffee in one hit and raking six chocolate biscuits to place in a napkin in her pocket. I will have these for lunch later she said. The sway of the hips and then she turns to give me the "V Sign" before she slowly got out of our life for a while.

"Did you expect her, if I knew I would not have showed up for work till after she had gone" laughed Rachel at me.

I said "Show some respect Rebecca to your very dead and lost friend Louise"

"She did ask me out for a date about five years now. I simply said to her that I already have somebody to sleep next to every night"

I did not want to know any more about the sex life of Rachel Todd and her partner who I nickname "The breeding cow".

Arriving like the second last thing you would want to see if you were busy was Chief Insp Jason Purley who said that he had a team watching John Adamson and "the flying duck". I simply said that John Adamson is going to the Turf Club with Phil Barlett and Joe Turner the two drug dealers from Adelaide.

"Excuse me boss, how do you already know this information?"

"Well young Jason we just had a visit from Commander Louise Meadows from the Federal Police. This is now a joint operation with her team. Mind you when it is over and if it is a success, you will be lucky to get a mention and so will I it will all be about the splendid job that Louise had done and her team with a little help from the local police in the northern territory. I must add that she will want us to keep her in updates but do not expect her to open up on what she has found out and even doing. Poor Jason just like a school boy found his way back to his desk after a lecture from his teacher. I went back to the pile of files that did seem to be growing after Rachel had made the trip around this large office. I could see that I had a message from Uncle Bill and the Stork on my computer it read" glad that your team are joined at the hip with Louise and her Federal Police drug team". I did think that do I know anybody who is good at hip surgery?

I think I might develop writer's cramp for all this endless file signing at home it was a normal night. I had curried fish and rice with a salad Jay my eldest did tell me "It was bloody yummy". With all the boys tucked up tight in bed, I had a message to say that the furniture truck will be at my rear gate to collect Sgt Amy Fuller home belongings. I did sleep like what they call a baby my phone rang just after ten past five in the morning and to my surprise it was Amy Fuller herself. "Aaron its Amy, listen we are under constant fire from an automatic weapon in a white land cruiser, no body hurt but every window in the front of the house is now helping the air conditioning, every window has been shot to pieces. I thank her and simply said "do not do anything stupid". I went to grab my work phone and I had a call from Sgt Penny maze on way to get you, Adamson house has been given a few bullet holes. Twenty minutes later and he wearing tuber out on my shoes, Penny did finally arrive, driving and letting me know the whole team are alive and kicking and also rapid response team. The heavy mob don't you mean tactical support" I replied whatever the bloody mob who get paid to get shot at are coming!! I thought O'Penny did you fall out of the wrong side of the bed. We did arrive after uniform who were hiding behind their car, tactical support showed up next and went in "to secure the location" they called it the Adamson and house guest were all out the back of the house, listening to Amy who did seem to have house charge. A simple well-done Amy, anybody hurt a couple got a few cuts from the glass shattering across the front bedrooms. I did not want anybody inside until forensic had done their examination.

"An easy morning" said Dr Rebecca "No bodies just a couple with a few cuts", well over one hundred bullets had been fired into the house I was told with John Adamson charging over at me like a bull in a bloody China shop. He was trying to tell me that Billy Reem was responsible for this out race. I tried to calm him down and told him that Billy was taken to hospital after a mild heart attack.

His two sons Donnie and Alfie stayed at the hospital all night with their Mother Jeanie, they are still there now. I have a team watching over them at this very minute. I had a call from Chief Insp Jason who said that two Federal Police Officers wanted excess to the property. "No way I said, not even my team are accused inside. They two Federal Police did have to guts to tell me they were simply parked up the road, until they drove off to Stuart Park to pick up a coffee and a take a way breakfast at around five o'clock. "Well, that was when for you to sneak off for ya Brekky, you could not wait till ya end of ya bloody shift. None of this would of happen, Chief Insp Jason directed them back to their car when a Albert Johnson who was head of the neighborhood watch in this Castlemaine close bay view. He told me that they say outside his house all night. I did wake up just before the shooting started and notice that the police vehicle had moved he did relay to me that he did think that the shooters were in the car. I just gave him a cheeky smile and told him to keep up his neighborhood watch duties. I told John Adamson that they will not be able to go into any rooms at the front of the house, it's a crime scene when forensic have finished we will arrange for a cleaning team to step in clean up the mess and board up all the windows, until to arrange for a glazier to come and replace them.

"Who the F is going to pay for those twelve windows" John Adamson shouted at me. I simply said "your insurance company". I could see that John Adamson did not enjoy in being the target, I could see him having a large brandy with Phil Barlett and Joe Turner the next move from John Adamson was about his two-guest catching the flight back to Adelaide, they only came up here to see their two races where both the horses had won at the race track in the early evening racing yesterday. I tried to act my ignoring and say I had no idea that there was a race meeting yesterday. "It was for a cancer charity which I am one of the directors". I thought that his two mates from Adelaide were simply drumming up more drug business at the Turf Club.

I phone call from Rachel back at the office did confirm that the two horses that won in two of the five races did belong to Barlett and Turner. It was then the female cow in the China shop did also finally showed up Commander Louise Meadows, demanding why her team were not allowed on the crime inside house until forensic have given me they all clear stamping her feet in the temper just like a school girl. I told her "Just maybe your team who were supposed to be watching the house, went off to Macca's fir their take a way Brekky when within minutes of them leaving the fireworks and gun fire started. I could see on the face of Louise that she had no idea her team had simply screwed up. I got Det Pia Jackson to find out exactly what time "the federal police master pick up two minutes past five Det Pia Jackson was told and was also confirmed on the CCTV footage. It was a good ten minutes before Louise came back and told me she had sent those two Muppets home. They had said they did notice at least a dozen police vehicles passing them at Maccas while they went for their break I tried not to laugh at the explanation that Louise had been given by her two Muppet's detectives. A burst of her tongue about Billy Reem is up to his neck for this episode. I had to even damped her mind tonight, that poor Billy had a heart attack and was in hospital, next to him was his wife and two sons. "Well, he could have hired a team to do this. It was then that traffic police had found the burnt out white four wheel drive out at Winneli waste ground on the old industrial site "it is my number one spot to local vehicles burnt out these days "I told Louise who was not interested in taking a drive out there. I did comment to Louise that the vehicle had been reported stolen from a home late yesterday!! I went to Winneli where already Dr Rebecca had a team on it trying to find some evidence. I felt that this investigation was heading in the normal direction of Federal Police only. I was not going to let her get one over on me once again to claim all the glory back at the officer low and behold just live a rabbit coming out of its home in the ground. I found Louise standing in my office door. I had to invite her in mainly because she would have stormed in anyway. "So, my people that your people gave a police escort to Paul Barlett and Joe Turner all the way to them getting on a plane back to Adelaide, you see I had plans to interview them!! Louise had to catch a breath so I jump in just like a kangaroo to get the next strike in. "Well, if you did interview them, they would sense that we were on to them. I did feel it was best to just kindly let them go to dig themselves into a bigger hole. May I say simply that after a one-on-one conversation with John Adamson that shooting at his house might even be aimed at our two Adelaide friends and not him. Just one more thing John Adamson does sleep at the back of the house overlooking the pool and he does have bullet proof windows across the back of the house. I could see that I had caught Louise off guard with my comments, all I got from her was that is my theory and in no way does she believe a word of it. No time for coffee or chocolate biscuits Louise had word to do and try and crack this case. I did try not to give a cheeky smile when she left but I did find it hard not to.

There was no DNA or prints in the burnt-out wreck of the car in Winneli. Dr Rebecca did say we should put up a sign to say "Burnt car please park in an orderly fashion!! If my memory does serve me well this is the sixth car in so many months dump here and set alight. I was about to order my normal feed or an egg and bacon roll with extra chilly, when I had a call that Billy Reem was still alive and kicking and would like a one-on-one conversation with me. I must say that Billy did look ten years younger after the doctors and nurses had to get control of his life. it was not long before I wrap my lips around a hospital cup of tea and now, I do realize that I will never ever complain about the police canteen "Thee Pain stripper" ever again. Billy would like me to know that the shooting at John Adamson home was nothing to do with him or any of his family. He had lost one son his eldest Paul and did next want to lose any more family members and friends. I did wish Billy well and then again; he did not have to open up to me. I some way I did give him credit on the other hand Billy was a born liar and could have hired a couple of sharp shooters to do his dirty word for his family. I did keep my meeting with Billy from Louise. I can play games just like she has and in the end nobody has really won. I was just about to leave the hospital when I had a call that somebody had prepared sprayed bullet into the reception of "The flying duck".

The receptionist was wounded three times but would live to hide more secrets about the Billy Reem Family. A gun man on the back of a motorbike we had some CCTV and found the motorbike burnt out in an empty home being renovated in Stuart Park. Nobody was on the building site today. A neighbor did rush to put at the fire but did not see the two people who lived in there leave. Rachel got on to traffic to look for any traffic CCTV that could help us. I had a strange feeling now that a third party was involved. They had stirred the pot between the Adamson Family and the Reem Family.

Anne Maria the receptionist at the flying duck motel receptionist had been wounded twice. Once in the left shoulder and arm. I went to inspect the damage and I was glad that I did not move to clean it up after forensic had door their job. We do have what we call the "Crime scene team" who do a really good job of mopping up blood and anything that does need to be seen to around a dozen shots had been fired already. Dr Rebecca did mention that it might be the same gun a bottle of red was up for grabs here. On my track records I know that Dr Rebecca will be up to grab the bottle of red wine from me. Steve Reem did arrive back at the motel only to go into what some people was a meltdown. The only thing he did not do was bang his head on the wall or on the ground. At once he did suggest that it was John Adamson had got a couple of his bean heads to do this. I did try to explain to Steve that John Adamson had every window in the front of his house blown out in a hail of bullets. "It's all a fing cover up and you let are helping him try and get the upper-hand!!" Steve shouted at me.

It was like talking to a brick wall what even I said to try and calm Steve down he had his own train if thought. I left Chief Insp Jason to try and talk a little sense into Steve while I ended up back in the office. A warm cup of coffee and just some plain minute dry biscuits well they are called minute dry biscuits until I did them into my coffee. I looked at the clock and thought that the boys will be home from school soon. My personal phone went and yet to my surprise it was Sgt Amy Fuller "Aaron it's me again Amy has just been shot at along dick ward drive, I was out getting fresh air on my motorbike when I notice two men in Ski Mask following me and one was carrying an automatic rifle, one got away and one does need some medical attention, just near the first nation community, along that straight. Please come Sgt Penny got the care while I gave Rachel a breakdown of what Amy had told me.

Traffic Police had stop traffic in both directions and were slowing turning people around. Both side of the roads were crime scene Amy was standing covered in blood and shaking. "One is over there and the other ran into the tall grass and got away". A person who had been watching a little too much late television American Police shows was soon to show me on his camera in his car. I could tell she that woman, turned her bike around and drove up on two wheels straight at those two when then jump lanes into traffic and their bike wet one way and they both went off in a separate direction, one even went over the roof of that on coming van before he braked and the rider fell of the other one was running for hid life from thus had bitch riding at a hundred miles an hour, up on one wheel like a bloody circus. I almost had a bloody heart attack. We also had the motorbike control freak was a Kylie Davey who had a small criminal record we did believe that the one that run away was Nicky Coxton, the two of them are joined at the hip even a relationship Rachel gave me the update from the office.

I had to send Chief Insp Jason to the known address of Nicky Coxton and Kylie Davey with a tactical team. I did remind Chief Insp Jason that Nicky Coxton had an automatic rifle that can fire a few extra rounds when you are not expected it. I did want my team and tactical support team to all came home safely. Kylie was on her way to hospital Det Cyrus Newton was her escort. A broken arm, a couple of broken ribs plus the usual bumps and grazing you get when you are flip off a motorbike, over the top of a moving van and land upside down. I stood holding the hand gun that Amy did want to unload into the mouth of Kylie Davey. I thought after what Amy had been through vision from the upcoming van and car. All I can say is that Amy was lucky a mention that Amy picked up a hand gun and went to fire it but there was still moving traffic at the time. Instead, she went over to the person driving the motor bike and stuck the gun into the mouth which much to my surprise when the Ski Mask was taken off it was in fact a female; dare I say it she was in a little pain after flipping from a motorbike on to the roof of a small van and then on to the road. Medics were soon on the scene it was in one word 'Lucky'. I did want to go and give Amy a cuddle but I did not think that this was the time and place. Det Pia did give Amy some support. I did ask the usual stupid questions and all Amy kept saying "This bitch and her mate just try to shoot me off my motorbike like trying to knock of an coconut at a side show at a fair.

The past couple of days moving back in with her adopted parents being shot at through the front of the house and I almost forgot she had the abortion, which was a lot of weight off my mind and also my stomach, it was not the way that I would have put it but again Amy was always one who liked to let her words fly out in all direction with footage from four different vehicles, all I can say was that Amy had guts to turn her motorbike around and drove straight at Kylie Davey firing her automatic rife and not really hitting anything was Nicky Coxton another one time drug dealer at school and used to work for John Adamson of all people. Her father Frank Coxton was given leave on the last two years of a drug sentence due to bowel cancer. Frank Coxton took the blame for a drug deal and got seven years and only served five years. I did turn information on some other people for a reduced sentence but once again not one word was said about John Adamson who would and should have been implicated. I tried to go on and reason with Kylie Dasey who only wanted to be alone. I tried to tell her that her friend left her laying in the road, so Nicky Coxton could not really care about her. "Nicky in only interested in being a survivor and I must say that I am so pleased at least one of us got away. Mumbled Kylie Dasey from under the bedsheets. Next door was Amy Fuller, still a litte shaken but very stirred up inside. Meeting me did not help with her blood pressure.

"The say I can go home to be at the wedding tomorrow" Amy tol me.

"Wedding what bloody wedding Amy?" I asked.

My so called sister Wendy, well my adopted sister is getting marring to Duke Newbury, yes Duke Newbury son of Frank Newbury it will being the two criminal families to together. "I just had to ask where, I did know it was a stupid question. I got the answer I did not want to ere. The wedding was going to be in the rear garden under a Marquee, only forty guests now instead of a planned two hundred. John Adamson had got a little but of sense inside his thick head after-all I did not expect question time from Amy who was asking about getting her old job back. Two words from my mouth "No chance!!" I did know that she did understand being a Police Officer in major crime while living with a person of great interest to the Police her father would not sit very well, around the coffee machine up in my office. I had to give another large "No" to the next question of who we had next door who tried to kill her.

"We have no proof of identify and who sent her to shoot me?" one word to pass my lips an John Adamson would have his feelers out to try and locate the actual shooter. I had a light bulb moment and went back into the room of Kylie Dasey. I simply told her, shooting at a Police Officer is about twenty plus years, firing on the Adamson house and also the flying duck reception would be around another twenty years. So when Kylie would come out of prison she will be due for her pension. That is if she does live that long take her guard down and her throat would be sliced open with forty years to take care of business.

John Adamson would be in no hurry for sweet revenge. I will place her into Federal Police care in their cell until the trial, after that I cannot offer any protection, even in solidarity confinement, somebody will be able one day to get to her. A mention of some information could help her in the future. I wanted to know first up where was Nicky Coxton hiding, I did know that she had not gone to her home, we are already watching her family home. I wanted to know who hired them both to "Stir the pot".

"You got to be joking, anyway we got twenty thousand to shoot at the windows on the Adamson house, ten thousand to shoot up that reception at "The flying duck motel" that bitch just stood there and screamed she never ducked down four cover, no wander she got wounded, lucky she was not shot dead. Now that Amy Fuller another thirty thousand just to put the shits up her. Amy her bloody Fathers money could be picked up in that little park in Fanny Bay, in a bin a brown paper bag before you ask instruction was by a burner phone!!

He contacted us, we had no way to contact him to us it was easy money and nobody I do say nobody was suppose to get hurt. Nicky Coxton I know in on the run and will have to shoot her way out. She will not surrender. Could be living with some of her first nation friends or even headed out to the sticks we has no plan together after we did the business!! In some ways I did tend to believe her and on the other hand the story is a little far fetched why even choose Kylie Davey and Nicky Coxton. I could only think of one reason and that was Nicky's father Frank Coxton, although he is terminally ill with bowel cancer, it was one last chance to Pay back John Adamson for the years he spent in prison and never once mention John Adamson to anybody. It was time to pay Frank Coxton a visit. With the welcome of "what the F do you want policeman, your lot have been here and turned the bloody place upside down, looking for my little girl Nicky with no bloody luck" laughed Frank then with his wife telling him to shut his big mouth" from next door.

Karen was Nicky's sister looking after Frank Coxton and his wife Tracey who has dementia not a job would want myself both living in separate rooms. Frank watching horse racing all day and Tracey watching the soaps on T.V. I just pop into just to see Tracey who was quick to tell me to F off she does not do sex anymore now that her husband is back out of prison. I did notice both of them had a seventy inch television both had air plugs so not to disturb the other, Karen sad it was hell trying to live here once again, herself only out of prison for prostitution just a year now. She also had a seventy inch television I did think to myself that these televisions must have been in a sale on simply stolen!! I spoke to Karen and did not expect any sympathy for Nicky who was on the run and if she is not careful her next stop could be the morgue!! Karen told me that she has not seen her or her girlfriend Kylie Davey. "O I know where Kylies is in hospital awaiting jail!! I said with a cheeky smug of a half-smile.

My next stop was to see John Adamson and how he was going to stop this wedding becoming a disaster waiting to happen. When I mention to him how Amy will be ok for the wedding, mainly cuts and grazing on her body but her huge ego was simply bruised. I was to learn that Amy had told the hospital that she had no Family. That was how John Adamson was kept in the dark. He did blame me for the interference into the life of Amy. Kicking her out of the garden cottage and getting her stand down at work. I had to stop John Adamson right there and then and tell him by looking right into his eyes "All of this is on you John Adamson your Amy cannot serve in a major crime unit while you remain a person of interest, for god's sake John Adamson just pull ya bloody head in for once please. I went on to say this Amy left the garden cottage because she ran a tall tale about my son being the father of the baby. I had to put him right and straight with Amy what was the right thing to do now.

I could see that John Adamson also had no idea of the real truth. He had down sided the wedding from one hundred to only forty people. Everybody will have to go through a scanner to enter the white marquee. No church, just married under the blue sky and the sound of the white cockatoos up in the trees. All I could do was wish him well I had notice that the all the windows in the front of the house had been fixed up and already I could see these security personal already laying at the landscape in their minds. I headed back to my office and just maybe I might barricade myself inside and disconnect all the phones. Rachel my office manager was very surprised that the Adamson and newborn families are joining together that will me most of the city of Darwin drug trade and also the outer suburbs will be under their control. I had to remind Rachel that according to John Adamson he has put all those bad day behind him now.

My biggest problem was to get my handsome Nicky Coxton before she does try and kill some other innocent person. Rachel was on to the phones of her family members and anybody else that has passed our way in the past few days that could be connected to her. The CCTV footage from the shops at Fanny Bay was not helpful it did not show the bit of park where our first nation people spend most of the day and night. If they starting fighting, local uniform show up, calm things down and in a few hours the fights are back on, normally about who has the grog and who has nothing to drink the money package to Kylie Davey and Nicky Coxton was always placed in the same rubbish bin. This lot me thinking that the person who is making the delivery must be able to see that Kylie Davey and Nicky Coxton do in fast pick the package up and no local first nation person goes to the bin looking for food. With four take away food, pieces of chicken, half eaten pizza etc.

I got Crystal Fultom to go over the CCTV we had from the last drop of according to Kylie Davey. While Rachel kept me with a update on the mobile phones, a unlisted number kept coming up and it ws coming from near the Fanny Bay Shops or even one of those flats near by at the back of my mind I did not want trigger happy Nicky Coxton making a surprise entry at the wedding. I did not sleep well that night, dinner with my four boys then I had to let them beat me at pool again. Sgt Penny picked me up at seven am and I got her to drove over to the John Adamson property at Bay view. Parked in the drive way was a mini cooper a present for Amy Fuller who was just about to take it out do a spin. She gave me that hums up when she passed me. I went down to John Adamson who looked his normal mister cool. The Marquee was up and all that did need doing was the tables to be set up for the guests. A separate bar area and behind the screen was a mobile kitchen.

I wished John Adamson a nice sunny day for his daugther's wedding, it has then that Wendy the bride to be showed up about to go for a run which I did not advise on her wedding day. She did take my advice and did some lap swimming in the pool. At my office, I did a quick check on every member of my team, just in case they had come up with some new information. Chief Insp Jason Purley had gone behind my back and put two teams of four heavy armed men each end of the road that the John Adamson home was situated. I took a step back and gave him the chance to show his true colors. Unknown to me, he had got the invitation list of people coming to the wedding. A total of forty guests plus the bride and groom and both parents. A top table of six and four tables of ten guests. Seating arrangements did include Phil Barlett and wife Judy plus Joe Turner and his wife Brenda, special guest from South Australia. I had a visit from commander Louise Meadows who had great pleasure in rubbing my nose in the information that she did think that she had over me; till I pointed to the seating arrangements on a chart on my office wall. A tip off from South Australia Federal Police had given Louise the heads up!! If I do recall that Louise did leave faster than she did arrive not even for a coffee but she did arrive not even for a coffee but she did pinch six chocolate biscuits for himself on leaving my office. Left on the biscuit plate was one very lonely chocolate biscuit so I quickly picked it up and stuck the whole biscuit on my mouth, much to the amusement of Rachel my office manager, who quickly went to her secret chocolate biscuit supply in her desk. I kept thinking while the wedding was going on and then the reception party where was Nicky Coxton was hiding. With no sightings and not even a whisper of his where abouts, I soon settled in to my signing off on the paperwork. I did notice Chief Insp Jason was on the phone to his two teams every twenty minutes, he kept looking over at me, I expect should he owe me a update was on his mind. I left early for home everything was okie dokie!!

Dinner with the boys, and we all sat in the lounge watching the rugby together while stuffing their faces with ice cream and toppings. I was in a deep dream when my Police phone was activated and then Sgt Penny Maze told me to give her fifteen minutes before she would arrive at my house. I was to learn that a high tacking of a truck lay-by about a hours drive South on the Stuart highway. The driver and his mate had guns pulled on them while going to the truck stop little boys room. Made to open up the truck and find a black case and give it to two very outspoken females in Ski Masks who ended up locking the two truck drivers back up in the rear of the container. It was a hour for a second truck pulled up and heard the cry for help. No description of the so called get away vehicles, they did believe that the driver was a man who kept on telling the two females. If they move shoot them in the knee cap, just in case they breath too heavy.

According to John Peters the driver, both were on their way to hospital the second driver of the truck was a Sam Riley. I was to learn from Rachel Todd my office manager that Sam Riley had a past connected to the drug Trade. I did suspect then that it was what we call "A inside drug job". Somebody must have told the two female's what to look for and where it was hidden inside the container. Out in the sticks we had no traffic camera's only when people did enter within twenty or so kilometers was the first traffic cameras checking for some speeding tricks and some motorists. All cameras were checked and we had nothing out of the unusual Chief Insp Jason Purley did finally show up and give me the report did finally show up and give me the report that the wedding and reception went well. I told him to get his head down and bum up now this robbery was our main objectives we do, I said we with the intel from Rachel what we knew about the special drugs could be heading for the Adamson, Barlett and Turner drug deal come undone, another what I call a inside drug deal gone wrong.

I do not think that John Adamson will be making a report that his drugs had been stolen from right under his nose. Sam Riley was a close friend of John Adamson and was sent along to make sure there was no more "cock ups" John Peters who we did know owned the truck. I sat down and laid down what I thought about the heist to my team. Who every was wearing those Ski Masks the two females were well out of their debt pulling off this drug raid. Who would they sell the drugs to and they blow up in their face down on the parkland in Nightcliff a white van had been torched a stolen blue van was also torched in a back lane in Stuart Park. Only people out running early gave us a brief description a man and two first nation teenage girls. Wandering alone and it did look like that were carrying a large brief case. We did belong to people of interest we were now monitoring. We had nothing to show for our effort.

The people of interest was Nicky Coxton who must of dump phone but her Father Frank Coxton did fit the profile, a little bit of cancer would not stop him from getting his hands dirty once again, the third person maybe a first nation person who had now taken over the place of Kylie Davey. Teenagers will do anything to get their hands on some easy money with no DNA or even finger prints around the "Robbery of the century". It did mean we had got nowhere; in the enquiry I did feel that maybe I should go around and maybe rattle the cage of Frank Coxton. The only thing that Frank Coxton was really interested in was hid little girl Nick. "She could be laying in a ditch somewhere raped or eve shot, I found a total of six times I had to listen to Frank Coxton. After he finally settled down he did let his part of the conversation slip a little to tell me that he does still drive, he wanted to take out his wife on a Sunday drive and that did not work at work her dementia, she did think that he was going to take her away and leave her out in the countryside with the wild creatures there like kangaroos. I was to find out that Frank's wife when she was a child her parents use to just go out and dump her cut bush.

Somehow she would find her way home and when she was return with a stranger she would get a beating for running away again. For me it was hard to believe which part of the story was true. With all the people walking around the container that was robbed, the remains of a rolled up cigarette with some ginga inside, tested for DNA and I did not believe that my luck had simply changed with a phone call from Dr Rebecca down in forensic "we got a match and it does belong to a Frank Coxton!!" it was enough to welcome Frank into the interview room for a cup of tea and a little conversation. It was only one hour before a Terry Bandon a solicitor and also a first a nation person who finally showed up. I think that Frank Coxton did know the game was up, he may of only drove the far. The car that did belong to Frank Coxton was in his driveway of his house it would not start it had a flat battery then with a change of mind set I never even mention to Frank that he had his own car in the robbery. "Don't take ya phone, the bloody police can track it and it will lead you back to prison "Frank was given a education on what to do and not want to do with technology being used by the police.

Find the cigarette butt with his DNA on was a poor excuse he might of stop there last week sometime for a rest he went out to drive on his own. I did think to myself the only reason that Frank was out there was to survey the area where he had the idea of robbing the truck. Somebody must of given him the inside word and surley Frank did not want me to believe that he is sitting on a few going to get rid of it?

"Rid of what?" Frank asked.

I simply said the cocaine, I hope Frank didn't do it for a small fixed fee? Frank knew I had something on him, his best bet was to say nothing was the advice from his solicitor Terry Brandon kept telling him to say no comment to what ever I asked. I knew with only the cigarette butt would not convict Frank Coxton. I had to let him go, the solicitor Terry Brandon made the comment to go on record that I was trying to fix up his client. I might have ever planted that cigarette butt there myself Terry Brandon did go on to say, that "I could of taken it from his informed that no more interviews unless Terry Brandon was there himself in living color!!

Duke Newbury the bride groom was spotted at his flat lurking around like a lost dog with his new bride not up in a luxury room at a hotel but up in the grubby little flat where Duke Newbury lived, across the green lawn outside the shops at Fanny Bay. He must have been hungry because on his wedding night he ended up in the pizza shop, I did feel this was strange with all that food at his wedding buffet. It was not a pizza that Duke Newbury walked out of that shop with but a brief case. All this was caught on the roof of a office block across the road by out "night vision drone". I made the call to tactical support and before I knew it I was standing in the bedroom of the new wedded couple and the black brief case. I was on overtime so I wanted to get this over and done with. I asked Duke Newbury to open it, and it was Christmas in my eyes full of cocaine to think that he has this brief case stolen from his new father in law. His new wife just could not shut up even when Duke told her to being told to "shut ya mouth bitch" was something a new wife was not going to take. I did learn that Wendy Adamson had open up to her future husband, who went t his father Frank Newbury who put the plan together to high take the truck, none of them would be involved because they would simply be at the wedding. It did sound good and might even be good o paper but Frank Coxton always wanted to get back at John Adamson and Frank (without her ski mask) did drop off the black brief case to the pizza shop, trying them that somebody will be along later to pick it up. We had run a photograph through our system and the name of Suzy Tanton another close friend of Nicky Coxton who used to deal drugs while at school for Frank Coxton. It is what you can say it is "keeping it all close to your chest". A honeymoon in a separate police cell was not a good start to a wedding of Duke Newbury and Karen Adamson with no time to waste and it was nice to see that the new relatives were still enjoying what was left of a wedding celebration. I had to say that I almost choked on my words when I broke the news to John Adamson and Frank Newbury. Also not far away was Phil Barlett and Joe with their wives.

I do have to say that our friends from South Australia had been named by Wendy Adamson who was a little dunk and no idea what she was saying according to her new husband Duke. I had a large team of uniform officers who love an invitation to a wedding but then again they did not even have time for a piece of some wedding cake before the handcuffs went on John Adamson and Frank Newbury with Phil Barrett and Joe Turner shouting a lot of verbal abuse at John Adamson and his big mouth daughter Wendy. Both the bride and groom are tucked up in a separate cell in the watch house. I sent a team at the time to the home of Frank Coxton where I found Suzy Tanton the missing member of the team laying naked next to Frank Coxton and she was giving his old Fella some stimulation with her mouth. There was no sign of Nicky Coxton. I did at least ask if she does know that Suzy Tanto was putting a smile on her Father's face. The some of one hundred thousand dollars was found in a black plastic garbage bag the so called payment for stealing the black Brief case from the container on the back of the truck. Another twenty thousand was there to given to Sam Riley. I did think that he had no idea what was in the black brief case. This operation had what I call a "snowball effect" going down a hill and slowly picking up even more when it went down the hill. "Sam Riley did not believe that somebody had "dobbed" him in. he did believe that it would come from the Darwin . "Too many people knew too much" Sam Riley shouted out loud so everybody could hear him in the watch house.

I was on top of the world and to think we did all of this and nobody had the time to phone commander Louise Meadows, who did storm up into the main office like a cyclone and ended up looking a little girl I would of told Louise to go and wash her mouth out with soap in the little ladies room. Some of those words were not very kind to me being the active commander of the detective division of the Northern Territory Police. I did feel that the word of "Bollocks to you Aaron Brown" would have been quite sufficient!!

It took my team another two days to track down Nicky Coxton. A splash of cash with her picture right across the media just was too much to resist for her so called friends of Nicky Coxton. I must say it did not end well for Nocky. After a six hour stand off and her very own grandmother being held hostage. Nicky did decide to end it in the only way that she big spectacle what she did expect one sharp shooter with one shot to her head ended her life. Nicky must of fired off around thirty shots in all directions, till I sadly had to give the word "take her down!" nothing I was proud of, she could of spent the rest of her life with Kylie Davey and Suzy Tanton could all of grow old gracefully in prison.

Chapter 11

A KNIFE IN THE BACK

I was really feeling that in was on top of the world, I felt that I was invincible until I had to enter the Love nest of Uncle Bill and the Stork, who was may I say attacking like a vulture waiting to rip pieces of skin off of my back. Luke warm tea and a stage biscuit that you might give to a dog only if you were thinking that the dog was hungry. They both looked like death warmed up" Neither look that happy to see me. I did notice the file I had sent him about the John Adamson Family and friends being hi-jacked by his future in-laws and of course the very future of Sgt Amy Fuller and her position, can she return to major crime. I did express a dozen reasons why not and not one of them did really register with these two out of touch senior Police Officers. There was no magic wand to wave, Amy was the daughter of a drug lord and is now living under his roof.

Well, I do know he will be in prison for the next fifteen to twenty years, but it is a risk that Amy would pass on information to her Father through her mother visiting him in prison. The two of them with a smirk on their faces that a swing with a baseball bat could be removed very quickly, you can tell that the Stork is back in Billy's good books. Most of the questions did come from her, which had already given what I did call a perfect answer. Being told something that was already on the grape vine back in the detective's main office was that Amy will be sent to traffic control, running the direction of where an when uniform should investigate in Major crime this would not be a problem. I did feel not exactly ok with that she would still have excess to any information o the main police computer. I did point this out but the Stork quickly told me to simply "lighten up a little Aaron, simply lighten up!! A smile on the face of Billy relayed do not try and simply argue the point, the Stork had won the race and past the finishing line even before I had left the starting block with the sound of the starting gun going off between the cheeks of Billy's ass, in my view.

It was time to leave, I step out into the corridor to notice Sgt Amy Fuller giving me a welcome smile, across the hall was a unexpected Chief Inspector Jason Purley with a face on him like he had already "Shit his pants"!! I did not want to ask him what he was doing here before I even open my mouth just to say "good day" Jason told me that it was at the request of the assistant police commissioner Violet Adam who I do call "the Stork". I simply said to Jason "If they do offer you my job just simply take it Jason". I could see that comment of mine did put a smile and a burst of laughter from Amy who I must admit did put a smile on my face. I stood in front of the lift door to see Amy go into the ring of fire to meet Billy and the Stork to hear what she should take simply as "good news". I got back to my office to find that Rachel Todd had her ears pricked up like a race horse going past the winning post.

I simply said "Jason is boot licking for Billy and the Stork".

"Yes boss he got the call earlier".

"I told him to quickly jump for my job if it is on the table!!"

I could see that Rachel had lost her sense of humor and in reply "I hope Fing not!!" apart from that I had to explain who was going jail and who was not and they would ask why. It was like trying to explain to children that the ice cream had melted and there is not anymore. I went on to say that the best kept secret in this Police Complex that Sgt Amy Fuller is going to traffic control will be living with her mother and the sister a bride with no honeymoon, husband going to prison for around fifteen years like his Father and also his brand new Father in law John Adamson, they can all play happy families inside those prison walls. A strong coffee and a whole packet of chocolate biscuits was presented to me by Crystal Fulton assistant to Rachel Todd. It was a good hour before Jason did arrive back at his desk, he treated me with contemp by simply ignoring me, so I called him into my office and asked if there was anything to report. "No Boss we simply caught up on what a good job I am doing in being your right hand. They even used one of my famous sayings "head down bum up!!" I was told by Jason.

I left Chief Insp Jason to play with himself for a while at his desk. I had the call of day light robbery at a local food store in the park area. So I put my team on robbery to investigate Sgt Penny Maze was first out of the traps and burning rubber all the way to park. We had some CCTV from the shop and also the so called get away car, three idiots in the care I watch the CCTV and notice that they had guns and the actual money from the till was a cover up for a bag under the counter I did ask what was in the bag to a Rowan Adams the shop owner, simply money to be taken to the bank in the city. I could tell by the look on his face that there was more than money in that bag I got Det Cyrus Newton to escourt Rowan Adams to the watch house so we can have a little cosy that about the life and times in his food store in park next door to his shop was a take-a-way food shop, greasy food for all those who are not watching their weight, pizza, fish and chips, kebabs, burgers, you name it. This Greasy Spoon is selling it eighteen hours a day next door was a second-rate monthly load office simply called "All the funds you need I had a update from Rachel Todd who told me that all three business are owned by a Gerald Hazelgrove, he has no previous record but he is a person of interest. I was about to find out who was interested in Gerald Hazelgrove and it was my old mate Chief Insp Duckworth or simply "Ducky to her friends" good morning boss, we had these three joints under our watchful eye and yes we were about to make a move until your bloody heavy mob charged into the grocery store, some sought of robbery was the reason? Ducky was careful with her words. "A Rowan Adams the store manager was not being co-operative with me, on the CCTV there was a bag taken from under the counter, he said it was money for the bank and did not simply believe him. The bag was a little big on the large size for a few day's takings" I replied.

I wanted for the air to clear and I went t o sit on a wall under a tree. My driver and protection officer Sgt Penny Maze had been to fetch a couple of large white coffees for Ducky and myself. "Yes, I know that drugs are a side line in that take-away and maybe this Grocer shop, all owned by a snake in the grass Gerald Hazelgrove, his overall manager is that ass wipe Paul Hazelgrove, has been in the watch house a few times but always with the help of a solicitor and his father's money had walked free. I sip my coffee and waited for the punch line from Ducky. "Human Trafficking" local females abducted and sold for sex, just like out in the far east and middle east, we are searching for Avalon Charlotte aged sixteen went into that grocery shop and never came back out. A carton milk and a loaf of bread was her mission, it is four days now. No CCTV working in shop nobody did remember her, the best friend a Maxine Sutcliff waited on this very wall. No luck with the staff in the shop, they all denied that she even came into the shop, she went home reported it to Avalon'S Mother, she came down with guns blazing in all directions in a matter of speech, next she showed up at the office waving arms in all directions. It was not the first time that Avalon had gone for a walk about last time it was a week she was found out at Jabiru Town four hundred Kilometers away, she was still dazy and had no idea how she even got there. She was infact found asleep in the back of a truck which was delivering to the local supermarket out there. The driver was innocent, well? He had one other stop at Bark Hut Inn so either Avalon climbed into the truck there on was in the truck when it left Darwin. The more Ducky spoke to me another twist was soon to develop, Avalon had been raped several times and could hardly walk after a lengthly period of being raped in her rear end. I almost swallowed my last bit of coffee in one hit then. Wait before you go at the park market this Saturday just gone two sixteen years old females a Charmine Fry and a Scarlett Bates both are known for shop lifting at the park market, both went for a walk about last seen sitting outside the Greasy Spoon, drinking coffee a white truck pulled up and shut off our vision from CCTV across the road, when the truck left the two girls were gone. Parents took till two o'clock the morning to sound the alarm, after they all got home from the weekly pub crawl in the city. I did interview the parents and did not get much help from either of the parents of the girls. I went to ask about the white truck and it was making a delivery to the Grocery store and also the Greasy Spoon. Now take this with a pinch of salt or simply you might call simply coincide but the actual driver of this white medium size truck was a Callum Langton, who was the same driver who found Avalon Charlotte a sleep in his truck out at Jabiru on cloud nine. He has done what you might call a "bunk!!" simply no sign of the truck either until we got it at traffic lights heading towards Humpty Doo. "And on the way to Jabiru" I have to gate crash Ducky on her very long explanation. Chief Insp Jason did look pleased with himself, we had taken control without even being told and get all the statements, from the four people in the supermarket come poor man's grocery and also two working in the Greasy Spoon. The manager Paul Hazelgrove would not be located, nobody had any idea where he was. The load office was closed I walked over with Ducky and Sgt Penny Haze followed by Chief Insp Jason who was acting like a lost dog. "Sgt Penny open the door to this shady place. Within two minutes after a few twists and turns she did open the door and of course the alarm went off, that did not stop Sgt Penny with the use of her phone played around till she came up with the code and turned off the alarm. "Bloody hell Penny I hope you never become a bad guy we will find it hard to prove that you did the brake in" laughed Ducky very loud.

Within ten minutes Gerald Hazelgrove showed up being mister big shot, wanting to know what we are doing in his office "simply looking for his son" Ducky replied.

A very negative Gerald Hazelgrove simply said that he had not seen him but he did hear him leave for work around six o'clock this morning. I did ask in what I would say was in a polite way if he could phone his son. I got a look of that could have started world was three from Gerald Hazelgrove. It was a look and a sound of silence before he made the call on his mobile phone, he tried twice and simply said "he could be driving right now mister policeman" I had to walk away that vain in my neck was about to burst. I did turn around to ask our new found friend Gerald Hazelgrove if he knew a Callum Langton. A explanation was needed of who he was and the answer I got was that he employed people to handle deliveries maybe I should ask his son, I had to reply "well that is why we are seeking your son Paul to help us without enquires. I finally walked away and went back to sit on the wall again. I phoned Rachel Todd to let her know that I would like Gerald and Paul Hazelgrove phones tracked and had she had any luck in the location of Callum Langton. Last know area was in Humpty Doo. My favorite place on earth. It was within minutes a report of the write truck that Callum Langton was driving had been found near Humpty Doo and also the body of Callum Langton was inside the driver's cab. I told Ducky, phoned Dr Rebecca to meet us there, I got the answer that she was galloping down the stuart highway on a white horse towards humpty doo. Sgt Penny Haze decided that her driving skills needed to be put to good use today.

I saw Dr. Rebecca arrive just before me and was making her way towards the cab on the truck. I did not have to be told "I think he is dead". A sharp knife was sticking out of his ear and a bullet between his eyes and his tongue had been removed and left lying on the dash board for the world to see. We know what it meant "keep your mouth shut and say nothing!!" three hours was the time of death. Forensic had already gone into the rear of the truck to find some blankets and a bucket used for a toilet uniformed had picked up Paul Hazelgrove in Palmerston. He was asleep in his car. He explained that he was not feeling well. He did not have his phone on him to call anybody for help. He did have several marks on his hand to show that he had been in a fight. He was on his way to hospital even before I had time to talk to him. On our arrival I was told that he had been drugged and had no idea what he was even doing all the way out here. I made the call to his father and said he was in Darwin Hospital and not Palmerson Hospitaal and was now under medical supervision. I did not even get a thank you from Gerald Hazelgrove. I had Dr Rebecca send a couple of her team to go over the inside of the car that Paul Hazelgrove for any extra DNA that did not belong to him. I was very surprised that the DNA from Avalon Charlotte was found in the car of Paul Hazelgrove, it did seem that she had been sleeping in a blanket on the backside of his car. Also the results of inside the rear of the truck Charmine Fry and Scarlett Bates DNA had been found. There was also plastic ties that can be used as handcuffs, we needed to put together a route that Callum Langton had taken before and after he was killed out here a public call was given to see if anybody had any dash cam footage that would be useful.

Normally in this truck there is a log and a tracer to tell where the truck had been, it had been disconnected since it left parap market almost three days ago now. It was time to have a real conversation with Ducky and how long had she been on this case and why didn't she inform me before about her suspicious. All I got was about a week ago. She first heard about "young female slaves" I was just too busy at the time, she wanted advice about how to spread her wings, I had to laugh at that comment from Ducky. I am never too busy, I told her that she had lost vital time in shutting down this operation and even finding these girls. I had the word from the hospital that Paul Hazelgrove had slip into a coma and he will not be talking to anybody except maybe his god.

We did venture back to park, the grocery on would be a mini market was busy and so was the take-a-way food shop the Greasy Spoon. All the staff was tight lip and nobody could remember the last time they saw Paul Hazelgrove although he was there at the opening today and talking a lot to Rowan Adams who we had in custody in the watch house. A mention of Callum Langton not that we did mention he was dead, more about when was the last anybody saw him. Describe as a creep and could not keep his hands to himself was the word from female staff of both business.

Before the mini supermarket could re open after the robbery, forensic did find some work that did prove there was some cocaine behind the counter and I did suspect was in that bag. I know it was pure guess work on my part. Rowan Adams had got some legal advice a man who would spend a great deal of time in front of a mirror a Noel Jones and his bill was being paid for by Gerald Hazelgrove of all people I got the old "Don't comment on that question Rowan" I did mention traces or cocaine behind the shop counter and underneath the counter where that bag was kept. "All I had to do was hand it over when they showed up, I did not expect any guns" nobody was going to be hurt, but that idiot was waving a knife in my face. I wanted to know who instructed him to hand the bag over. Being told it was there when he arrived, he did not close the shop last night it was his night off. A Dazey Bruce was the assistant who shut up shop, so I had him brought in to the watch house well that was what suppose to happen. Dazey Bruce was found shot in his flat across the road Dr Rebecca put up a bottle of red wine that the gun that was used on Rowan Adams was also used on Dazey Bruce. I had lost so many bottles of Red wine to Dr. Rebecca, yes she was right once again. Dazey Bruce had been dead around five hours. There was no false entry so he must of known his killer. Why kill Dazey Bruce, did he simply know too much. I was surprised to find that Dazey Bruce had a drug problem and was high as a kite on cocaine when his blood analysis was return, the results were very high, not enough to kill you but to put you in your own little world of dreams for a while Dr Rebecca did try to explain to me in her own little way. The only other DNA found in the flat was in a beer can and that did belong to Paul Hazelgrove all people. He had been a very busy boy in the early hours of today. On my mind and the number one issue was the two missing teenage girls Charmaine Fry and Scarlett Bates it was time to seek the help from the public now. Ducky did show up and wanted to know where she could get that add on the phone of Sgt Penny Haze. I told her I had no idea "anyway it will be illegal Ducky and you know I do like to keep everything above board like all good police Chiefs "What like Alf Jackson and John Knight" Ducky snapped at me when I felt was a little below the belt even for Ducky!!

I was wasting time in my head I wanted a warrant to search all there properties owned by Gerald Hazelgrove plus his name. I could see that Chief Insp Jason had something else on his mind today, just by his attitude. In fact I am the very last person on this planet you want to show some attitude in your job with regards towards me. I explain he is not getting much sleep with a new baby at home. I thought he kep that one a secret. I just smiled and told him I had to go on with four boys who all had early sleeping problems. A phone call for Chief Insp Jason made him leave my company. I was joined by Ducky who did inform me that he caught the Stork and Chief Insp Jason in one of her interview rooms having a really intimate and cozy chat. I joked and said to Ducky "O that is about my job, the Stork would like him to move into that leather chair in my office". A look of have you gone mad from Ducky, who replied "I am next in line for your Fing Job Aaron and they better not forget it, the job was promised to me when they caught me on the fishing line to lure me back" I had not reply for Ducky, but I did think at least she is being honest with me.

I was very surprised when Insp John Mitchell and Sgt Andy Moore showed up with the search warrant, I did not need one for the grocery come mini supermarket, billed as the smallest supermarket in the Darwin are, I did not need a warrant for it, mainly because I already had found some cocaine spillage on an under the counter during the robbery. Gerald Hazelgrove walked away throwing his arms into the air, demanding to know what the "F" was going on. I did ask him to explain, then I asked him to join me at his home so we can make a search without knocking down the door. At the front of his house I was to find that he had two rather large doors you had to go through to get in before you step into the main hallway. Black Betty the drug dog who I have not used for a long time was on hand to give the house a good sniff over a bag in the room of Paul Hazelgrove and talk of the devil. Det Pia Jackson was on the phone to let me know that Paul was not in a coma after all a reaction to a mixture of drugs that he had taken had left him to have what the doctor called "blackouts" not a coma that the nurse had passed on to Pia.

I did decide to break the news to Paul's Father Gerald, who was another one who had a lot on his mind. I do know if it was one of my boys I would be up there in the hospital sitting beside his bed. I pointed at the bong with the cheerful comment that Paul does use it to ease the stress having almost half a kilo of some of the best dope that I had smelt in a long time, I felt the overdose on drugs and not remembering how, why or when did Paul end up in that state in his car. The thought that just maybe Paul had decided to take his own life with a overdose on a happy trip or drugs. Dazey Bruce had been shot and also Rowan Adams with the confirmation by the same gun. One bottle of red wine to Dr. Rebecca was on my must do list. The bottles of red were given to me by John Knight for my birthday many months ago and I kept them in my cupboard in my office. I love my beer, red wine is for Cane Toad's in my eyes. I had to come back to reality because Black Betty had broken loose and gone a little crazy to find two kilo of M.D.M.A tablets plus a kind of ketamine and half a kilo of L.S.D hidden under the bottom of a false floor in a spare bedroom. I told Gerald Hazelgrove who was trying to explain that he was not into drugs, although they have been found in a bedroom next door to the master suite. I just stood shaking my head and not saying a word while I listen to the handler telling Black Betty that she had had a productive day. Apart from shitting in the hallway on her way out of the house on the way to the garage, where she was sitting up straight I was amused and poor old Gerald Hazelgrove still denied that the shed inside the garage to house the ride on lawn mover was also the home of the finest marijuana this side of town. I could tell by the face of Gerald that he had no idea about the drugs in his house or in this garden when he saw Sgt Andy Moore walking towards him with two uniform officers. I did like Cody who did think he could out run three police officers around the garden pool. I did think a tactical attack on Cody by Sgt Andy that did end up with them both taking what I called no need for swimming lessons today.

I just gave Sgt Andy the thumbs up and told him to go home to get changed into some dry clothes. It was then that Chief Insp Jason showed up and wanted to know why was Sgt Andy taking a swim in his clothes. I found the answer to the question just too stupid for me to even open my mouth. A report that some traces of marijuana was found inside the so-called Greasy Spoon. Our fearless Chie Insp Jason had decided to shutdown the gate the Greasy Spoon and arrest the three staff on duty. A few M.D.M.A were found in the back office of Rowan Adams in the mini supermarket, this was enough to charge him with the handling of drugs. When Insp John Mitchell told his new boss what he had located in the Hazelgrove home that sought of put a damper on the face of Chief Insp Jason. I told my team it was back to the watch house and let us leave no stone unturned in charging all those involved in the drugs in Parap. I did feel that is was a productive day in some circles but I had two murders to solve and two missing teenage girls Charmine Fry and Scarlett Bates!!

I had to stand back and look at this from another view, even another explanation. Finding Avalon Charlotte D.N.A on a empty thck shake container from Parap market was a start. Avalon was quite respectful she did not show any attitude towards me, unlike the conversation with Ducky. "So no fat cow today then, only you and this first nation female" mumbled Avalon to me. Her name is Pia Jackson born just outside Alice Sprigs and she is one of my best officers I have to work with. I mention her D.N.A being found on the front seat of the car Paul Hazelgrove was driving. "O him, took me out to the back lane and he already had a mango thick shake to give me," A quiet moment while Avalon got her thoughts together "well next thing a drug drive in the country, we smoked some gunga down the Stuart highway. I must of passed out and woke up with Paul pulling down my knickers to my ankles, we were parked in this wood "I told him there and then, hey Matey you better stop here and now because you do not know who my Father is Freddie Charlottle just out of prison for beating a man up who just put his arm on my Mother in a bar.

Now my dad can fight and to finish it up he put a bottle in the face of that innocent bloke who was only reaching over to get his beer, my mum had stood right in front of it. My dad was not going to let any man put his hand on my mum. Mind you have to day y mum had a different man in her bed most weekends while my dad was in prison. Talking about poking a wild bear, I kept quite. My mum could not so without sex she told me. it was then after a long statement of the life and times on the front seat of Paul Hazelgrove car. I asked what happen she said he gave her a pill to wash down with a warm beer, she passed out and next thing she knew she was sitting at the bus stop in Parap across from the Cheese Cake shop, she had no idea of the day or time. One other person did come to mind was Callum Langston the truck driver he kept sliping in and out of her memory. There were words spoken between Paul and that Prick Callum Langston who told Paul to dump me and hope that she does not have a conversation with her father and she does accidentally raise your name in the confession to Freddie Charlott who had the nick name of "Bottle O" when I was in prison a few years ago, yes, I did know him!!

This was enough talking and there he was "Mr. Bottle O" himself Freddie Charlotte". Got any news then have just a whisper in my ear and I will take care of the rest. A light bulb was starting to flask inside my head even if I was trying to breath with the smell of beer fumes coming from Freddie, who did explain somebody just happen to walk into him trying to rush and put a bet on a horse. The horse won and when the punter went to pick up one hundred and fifty dollars from the office, Freddie told the punter he will be taking that for dry cleaning his clothes. There was no argument according to Freddie. My light bulb flashing in my head, did put a case together that just maybe Dazey Bruce the assistant manager at that mini market come grocery and also Callum Langton had both crossed paths with Freddie Charlotte and both ended up dead. I keep my theory to myself. I got Rachel my office manager, to track the phones of Avalon Charlotte and Freddie Charlotte that is if he does have a phone! I was to learn that the Charlotte Family so most of their shopping at the mini market and always end up going next door for some take-a-way food.

I call in Ducky to put my theory about Freddie Charlotte and to let her know that I had what I would call a very Civil conversation with Avalon Charlotte. A mention about the mother Agnus who has a cleaning job in the early mornings at the offices in park. I had to be pulled up by Ducky who told me that she does her office cleaning in the evening. I raised my eyebrows and told Ducky "That will be all for now but stay close".

"O by the way one of the officers she does clean is the office of Gerald Hazelgrove, plus I do believe that she also does his housekeeping". I stood up from my desk and quietly said "well that was why Avalon so easy she in fact must have known her mother does clean his home". "Well, I have to say it has taken you a while to realize that boss". Squawk like a parrot Ducky was pleased with herself having one up on me. so, I thought that whatever is on Ducky's mind I will bring it to the surface. It was that Chief Insp Jason Purely had been promised my job by the Stork of all people.

"Do not count the chicken before the eggs hatch" Ducky I took a deep breath.

"Anyway, the way things have been gone around here just lately, the Stork and even Uncle Billy could be looking for a new job a very long time before I finally say "Goodbye and stick the job up your ass Matey" at least I got a smile from Ducky and then she came over to hug me and simply said "Thank your old friend, anyway you are always bloody right everything, it is just so annoying in a loud sound of laughter. I did notice that Rachel was giving me the thumbs up behind the back of Ducky.

Within a few minutes of Ducky leaving Rachel arrived with a large slice of chocolate cake and a strong mug of coffee. We were joined by Crystal Fulton her assistant who had been extra busy with the phone monitoring of all who are on our interest list. A conversation with Gerald Hazelgrove pouring out his heart to his sister Kira, who married the black sheep of an English noble family, purchased four mango farms and a racing stable. Living out at Humpty Doo was the background I got from Rachel who did seem to have my piece of chocolate cake today it was if my eye sight is correct a much larger portion. Crystal did notice that I have observed this master.

"It is ok Crystal I am watching my waist line anyway" Rachel just kept talking until she got the audio just right. "so my dear brother what the F is going on with you?" where ever do I start, even try to here we go the bloody shop got held up, police came watch a CCTV of the robbery and god forbid it was in their eyes a cover up for the taking of a packing left by somebody it contain cocaine they only got five thousand in taking, next thing that top dog detective office and even my home all of this while my son Paul ended up in hospital bombed out of his mind, O I forgot the night manger well I mean the late manager that good hard working Dazey Bruce somebody put a bullet in him, when he open the door to his flat and that mister know it all truck driver Callum Langton somebody shot him out your way so they found drugs well all sports in that shop in that bloody take-a-way that I am not surprised at I told Paul to get rid of those two cooks, both bloody shifty then they bang on my door with a warrant to search my place. I did know about Paul and his bong, on top of that some tablets in his room hidden. Now the next thing that spare bedroom you call your room they found some cocaine and various illegal drugs. I had no idea the last time I went in there was Christmas day when you came to stay for Christmas without your husband my I say!!"

"Um he was having one of his usual depression moods because his bloody race horses, three in fact did not win in their races at the Turf Club, strange they all bolted in for a win a week later. So how is Paul what did he do overdose, I mean he did that on Christmas evening I had to phone for an ambulance, they had to pump out his stomach, all that booze and drugs did not what you would call a good mix. Before I forget that Charmine Fry and Scarlett Bates, we have them secure and out of sight!!"

"You will have to decide what to do with them first the police are looking for them".

"Listen Rowan my husband would like to fuck them a few times before we pass them on to the highest bidder!! That was the end of the phone call.

"Well, that has solved a mystery for me. where the two missing teenage girls are!!"

Rachel looked at me, "we got enough to go after that Kira and her husband, who might even be implicated in the death of that truck driver Callum Langton and even Dazey Brice well that gun was used to kill both men. I did mention that Paul Hazelgrove could be involved with both deaths. Dazey Brice knew about the cocaine in that blood supermarket under the counter, I mean he was on duty, then we look at Callum Langton who just might have become the end of the road in this so-called kidnap of young girls from Parap market. I knew that was a big call. I did need those traffic camera's CCTV to see if Paul was out in the area as the same time as Callum Langton. The last thing I had to mention that whoever took the drugs was not the person they were intended for. I could see Crystal was following my train of thought with a gentle nod of her head in agreement while Rachel was still finishing her chocolate cake with mouse size bites. I needed a warrant to search the property that is owned by Kira and her husband

Peter. I did need tactical support also my full team and also the drug dog black Betty at last in living color Chief Insp Jason had arrived and wanted to know to know what was going on when he saw me trying to fit into my protection vest just like all the other staff. "We are going on a raid in my number one place in the world Humpty Doo, well just past. Humpty Doo, we got a witness a lead Jason". Well so have I, well I got a witness who did see Paul Hazelgrove knocking on the door of the flat of Dazey Brice, he will say he actually saw him enter the flat. "What do you mean he will say, well did he or didn't me, this is a murder enquiry Jason. I could Jason off guard then with the whole team just waiting for him to answer "well when the woman turned to go down the stairs, she looked back and Paul Hazelgrove was no longer standing outside the flat" it was time to get this show on the road, Insp Arden Thompson was going to lead tactical support. A veteran even could be called "old school" he played by the book and would not take too many chances I have found in the past. We top at the end drive way to the Mango Plantation; the house was a good mile down that dirt road.

We will be spotted a long way of our arrival point; I am some somebody working on the Mango Plantation would sound the alarm. We had no reception committee. A house keeper named Cecelia came out to great us. I produced the warrant and stood back while Arden Thompsom a proud Inspector took control. The house was empty. Being told that Kira and her husband could be down at the Mango packing rooms it was a false lead, the manager of the packing room did say that he had not seen either of them for at least two hours now. I wanted to know if he had any ideas of where this couple could be. "Could have gone fishing" about two miles down the mud track, you will find the flowing river. I was more interested in other buildings around here. There were four homes all together, what did belong to the various owners of the mango farms before they all became one. We were told that there is a sign down the track pointing in direction of each home. Deep down I was to think that we were being given the bloody run around by this cockhead I pointed my gun at his head and simply said "which homestead do you think they could be found Knucklehead?"

The very last one called spring cottage they would be there if anywhere. I got Detective Cyrus Newton and Detective Pia Jackson to stand and make sure nobody will use a satellite phone to warn or suspects. I mention to the five staff standing there "Do not move quickly because both these Detectives are what you would call "trigger happy". It was another ten minutes until we found Spring cottage and Kira our main suspect decided to come out to great us. She was painting first nation dot paintings and what I would say simply passing there of "Aboriginal Art" which is illegal to start with and it does deny the first nation people from making a living from the art that has been passed down for sixty thousand years, Kira had no idea where he was, she had not seen him since breakfast. Insp Arden Thompson did decide to use drones to try and find our missing person Paul. Down this dirt road was a river and a cottage on the other side. There was a small boat on the other side in front of a cabin.

I did ask Kira about this cabin and all I got was that it was "His man cave and yes, I did go into have a look around only to find the walls are covered with crocodile skins and the heads are wanted on the walls. My imagination was drifting in all directions, this damn river is crocodile infested. I felt like making Kira made into the river just to see if the crocodiles were hungry today. I am not that mean; I did ask if there was another way to the cabin. "Simply drive up the highway about twenty minutes. A turn off at the sign Summer cottage and about twenty minutes down the dirt track you will be opposite. I had the call from Insp Arden Thompson that a vehicle has just taken off and headed up the dirt track to the highway. I phone Det Pia and her side kick Det Cyrus and told her to get her ass into gear and find the entry to Summer cottage block off the road and stop anybody from leaving. I did wonder if I was doing the right thing if it did turn into a fire fight poor Det Pia has a poor record at hitting the target a size of a barn door. Never mind somebody shooting back at her. An inflatable boat was produced, not out of thin area but it was risky in taking it into a croc infested river two of the tactical support put their hands up. The plan was to get across, fetch the tinny and return we had no choice and it worked like a bad smell Chief Insp Jason had decided to join us in our decision making. I see put him in his place and told him to take Kira back to the watch house and lock her up, then pick up Paul Hazelgrove from the hospital he can go into a cell. His father Gerald had been freed under bail conditions but not anymore, I have new charges waiting for him, Rowan Adams manager of that turkey shoot mini supermarket. He can be given another twenty-four hours to get his mind set before he is question tomorrow. I could see that Chief Insp Jason was not happy that he was not going to be in "the fun today".

The two officers heard voices calling out they looked through the window and saw five females locked up in cages. They were told not to try and enter; a bomb has been placed to explode if they try. I caught Kira just before she left to find out what life in a cell was really like!! I asked about the females they were her husband's play toys, I had to mention the so-called bomb placed inside, "O he was back in the army bomb squad back in England. We no longer have a sexual relationship, so he needed the teenage girls and I almost forget his is a Tranny himself, he loves to dress up and wear a wig. I thought that this woman is very sick in the head she does not find anything wrong with the kidnap of six teenage girls in his care, "What about their families?" I got no ready except she just spat on the ground her trip back to the watch house while all of this was going on Insp Arden Thompson had made a few telephone calls to secure somebody who could save this situation with a bomb disposal. One of his team was up a ladder and on to the roof and had placed a camera down inside to see what exactly was going on inside that cabin. I looked at the footage we had six cages in the extension, five females in a separate cage, I was to learn that Kira husband Peter had taken Charmine Fry as a hostage, she was in that old farm truck that was now heading up towards the main highway and I did hope that Det Pia had reached her destination. She had and was wearing a headset, so sign of anybody yet I was pleased to here. Sgt Penny Maze never one to back down, did volunteer to go down a rope and inside the cabin. I was shaking my head and telling her it was not in her job description. She got to the floor and could see wires running to the front and back door. Also, there was one to each of the window on the front and back of the cabin. "Creepy in here, all these croc heads looking at me and wondering which one is their skin on the walls!! A phone hook up to a person who does know about how to defuse a bomb was talking to Sgt Penny who was concern that she needed to pee. One red, one blue, one yellow and two green wires were located on the bomb. She told her new found friend in the bomb disposal squad. He will be there in about forty-five minutes; he was coming from Roberson Barracks. Our police bomb disposal unit was at least over an hour away.

I told Penny not to do anything stupid do not try and be a hero. All the time the distraction of the five female's shouting at her and demanding they be let free from the cages "Shut the fuck up bitch's or we will all be dead within a puff of smoke, so keep quite while I talk to the bomb disposal officer on the phone, he will be here soon. Myself not having anything to do why bombs in my career except when I sat on the toilet after eating extra Indian curry now my cheeks on my back side do have a habit of causing explosion. My sense of childish humor did bring Penny back down to earth. A mention of going out for an Indian curry after all this mess is soughed out. A lot of talking going on with Penny who did seem to settle down now. My calculations should be right and they were the bomb disposal officer gad arrived. I told Penny and to that information she simply said "well I will open the door for him and let him in the front door then!!

Before I had time to say whatever you do Penny do not open that front door. It was too late she had defused the bomb and now wanted to use the lady's room. When she came over to me, I told her she was a bloody idiot but I am very proud of her. "A perfect job I could not have done better myself in fact you deserve a medal for this effort. A Scarlett Bates me who was kidnap at park market and we did suspect Callum Langton. A Nicky Todd and Lucinda Clark, Freya Meek and Layla Lines had all been missing persons over the past few months. I was to learn dressed up like a female and a good sniff of cocaine their hostage keeper Peter, used to like a different female each time. It was simple if they did not, please him, they would eat up being croc-bait. Layla told me a Janet Marsden and Mercedes Pickton. The conversation led to "The Tranny" they called him, killing the croc when it attacks the victim, shooting the croc, skinning out. Cutting off its head and the croc meat was fed to the survivors.

Three ambulances had arrived and were on the other side of the river. It was then that I had Det Pia on the phone, telling me that the old farm jeep or wagon whatever, had stop and pointing a gun at the head of Charmine Fry this twisted man named Peter by some and Tranny by others was shouting about shooting his victim Charmine if they did not remove themselves and let him drive past, he would shoot her. He was just sounding like a bloody parrot Det Pia said he kept repeating himself. I did ask what Det Cyrus was doing. "I think he has shit his pants if the truth was known". I did learn that Peter was prancing around and had fired while into the air and once at the police vehicle. It had a silencer, his gun "So listen Pia you are down that target range you have told him you are down that target range you have told him to put down his gun now" I heard Pia shout out "drop that woman you mother fucker". I told her to take aim at his chest, you will only get one shot now hold your breath and simply pull the trigger, if he does not fall, shot again!!"

I had the confidence in Pia and I simply told her "You can do it girl, go for it" I heard the gun fire and the scream that she had hit him but he is still standing and the hostage is running towards Cyrus who had not decided to play a part in this game Pia Fired again and this time, she had a head shot after aiming at his chest. Peter fell in a head and she ran toward him and took away his gun that was dangling on his fingers. It was a little late but the cavalry had now arrived Ducky and her team. I told Pia to go to Ducky and put out your arms and she will hold you tight and tell you it's all over now. I just wanted to talk to Ducky who said that Pia was still shaking. I told Ducky to hold her tight the hostage was ok Cyrus had her in her arms. I did mention that Pia could not hit a Barn door, bur today she has proved us all wrong.

I sent my new bombs disposal come driver the hero Sgt Penny Maze up to get the car on the other side of the river. While "Ducky" arrived with that look that I had seen many times before over the years. "I am not happy chook!!" Det Pia had been taken back to the Police complex after medics gave her the all clear. I was to learn from Ducky who had spoken to Pia that Det Cyrus Newton had just froze sitting behind the car, he had not even produced his gun out of its holster. This was not what I was expecting from the six-foot four man built like a brick toilet. He only moved when the hostage Charmine Fry made a break after Pia had placed two bullets into our suspect Peter. I did think that was enough for me to contend with until she met Chief Insp Jason Purely on the road heading back to town who could take time to ask her what she as doing up here now. It was all over and there is no need for her to be here to investigate any sex crimes? Ducky told him in no uncertain terms that six females being held in cages was not a sex crime. With that Chief Insp Jason quickly burnt rubber after raising his eye brows. I simply said that he had in fact just "lost the plot". I just wanted to focus on these five females now being given medical treatment before being taken to hospital. I put them into the care of

Ducky and her team. I gave Ducky a quick walk around and I wanted her to maybe come back later after forensic who had not yet arrived, giving this place the once over!! Still sitting on the table in the middle of the room was the Dismantled bomb.

"Is that safe are you sure boss?"

"Yes, my driver Sgt Penny put that baby to rest after climbing down a rope from the roof. Both doors and windows were connected to the bomb"

"One minute she is picking locks, next minute dismantling bombs and of course in her spare time being your driver!!

I had to laugh at the comment from Ducky who had now finally got back her sense of humor.

Ducky was happy with her team to help the remaining five hostage teenage females into the three ambulances and go with them to the hospital. I told Ducky, statements can wait until the hostages are ready to talk Sgt Penny was up at the main gate with the car, I caught a lift back up the dirt track with Ducky. I passed Dr Rebecca on the way with her forensic team heading down to the cabin. I told her no bodies down here, only the one body of the suspect up at the entrance of the dirt track. Dr Rebecca had a brief look at the crime scene and had already notice the gun with a silencer on and the mention of a bottle of red wine that the gun was the same one to kill Dazey Brice and Callum Langton. It was not a betting day in fact I told her I have thirty bottles of that red wine in a cupboard in my kitchen, she can have them all whenever she would like to collect them. Being told that the red wine was very expensive I told her the three cases were a present from John Knight of all people, who also does not drink red wine.

Being told that in the Bottle shop that wine is for sale at just under ninety dollars a bottle. What could I say to Rebecca except she had got herself a bargain!! I was waiting for Ducky to make a comment that she also liked red wine and not to mention but am I having a relationship with Dr Rebecca Mitcham. I had to say "simply not that I know of". I got out of my world with Ducky, and got back into my car and headed for home. I asked Sgt Penny to stop the car a couple of miles down the road. I took out of the inside of my jacket, my little gadget what I call my bug detector. Yes, three green lights came on and I did locate three bugs "Listening Devices). I put them on the ground and quickly snap my heal of my foot on them. It was time to give Sgt Penny an explanation of who or why is somebody bugging the Commander of detectives. I told her a brief history lesson of having bugs in my home, even the lap tops that belong to my boys were taken away when I was under suspension, a few months ago.

"Well, I thought everything was simply Honky Dory with you boss?"

"Listen I found two bugs in the car two days ago so these three have been placed in the car overnight or somebody had placed them sometime today. I got a total of six in a jar of water at home. I found two members of the integrity unit parked down the road the other night. I got two cups of hot chocolate for them and poured both cups over the front window screen before they simply drove off into the night. I never spoke anything to my previous driver Sgt Amy Fuller except good morning – good night. Time of pick up or where I am going to before the office three years, I played that game and will continue that attitude so please do not feel in anyway in do not want to talk to you. I do but now understand that some sick bastard could use my messages to my driver in the I could see Sgt Penny get out of the car and head across the road to be alone and think about what I had just told her.

I was not expecting what I heard come out of the mouth of Sgt Penny. "Listen boss I have had an above average day, would you mind if I finished off the day by fucking your brains out it would be the icing on the cake, for me so to speak".

I looked at Sgt Penny and not having sex for over three years since my wife Kate got killed in the car park by a car driven by Alf Jackson. I really thought that it would be an offer I could not refuse. Her flat, her bed, drop me off, then she would return on her moped. I was on my third cold beer before she did finally arrive, I was nervous I had not been with another woman since I first met Kate. A shower together was the idea of Penny and I must say I did feel good. Sex was more than I had expected Penny had another hidden quality other than driving a car at high speed, picking locks and dismantling bombs, she was a sex expert in many ways.

I was to learn she had no current partner, male or female but had no problem in having a one-night stand with who ever took her fancy. I was old enough to be her father I did mention. "But Aaron many a good tune was played on an old fiddle" I did laugh at the comment from her and slowly fell asleep. I was woken up by her with my car downstairs and she was going to drop me off to shower and out on some clean clothes. It was good for me I was back in the car and on my way to the office with an extra-large smile on my face. I could see Chief Insp Jason looking his usual sheepish. I explain that Ducky with be giving her personal touch to the six hostage and will interview them when they are ready. I wanted him to interview Rowan Adams the Mini store manager, plus the two looks from the take a way next door Bellamy Tweed and Paul and Gerald Hazelgrove and Kira the sister of Gerald Hazelgrove.

Paul Hazelgrove who had tried to take his own life according to the doctors at the hospital. He was what I would call well out of his depth running the mini mart and take-a-way Greasy Spoon for his father. I had a witness statement saying that she did see him enter the fact of Dazey Brice on the day he was found dead. I had to stop them when a Maurice Egon a solicitor from the top end of town was to represent him. I could tell that Paul had no idea about this. Paul was asked a couple of hours before if he did need a solicitor and his reply was "why I have done nothing wrong". I left Paul and his new found friend an hour before I came back. It gave me time to go over all the information I had on my desk in relationship to this case while I did much through two egg and bacon chilly rolls. I was hungry today, and I do not know why, well it could be the energy I used up with a bit of body contact with Penny last night.

Somebody who did catch my eye was Det Cyrus Newton who I asked him to step into my office. I did want to give him the benefit of an explanation for his conduct, he knew he put Det Pia Jackson in danger and he did expect some discipline action to be taken. All I had to say was pack up your desk and walk out of the main office and never look back" I then finished my chilly egg ad bacon roll and headed for a confrontation with Paul Hazelgrove and Maurice Egon another person who did believe that his "shit didn't stink". I went back to Paul with that I had an eye witness who saw him enter the home of Dacey

Brice within hours of him being killed. He did admit that he had enter the flat and the nosey bitch neighbor across the hall way of Dazey was the one that saw him. The door was in fact unlocked and laying on the floor was the body of Dacey Brice with a hole in his head. He ran out of the flat, and closed the door behind him. He knew that he would be a suspect in his death. So, he fled down the Stuart highway and was swallowing a handful of pills, he just wanted his life to end, it was an easy way out, he tried to explain yet again he could not explain why he didn't report the death of an old school friend Dacey Brice, who led a homeless life sleeping on the floor of a friend, "I am just a couch surfer" Dacey called himself until Paul did talk his father into giving Dacey a job in the mini mart. Eventually he worked hard and become the late manager. Paul explains excepting the parcel from Callum Langton might have lost him his job, also the life of Callum Langton after a very lengthy explanation Paul did not think that his Father Gerald was behind this. With the comment "My old man never gets his hands dirty in anything" this man almost an admission that his father was up to some shady practice. Maurice Egon the solicitor if he could then did sleep in to say that Paul had lost control and has no idea what was now saying to me out of the blue Paul simply told sweet talking Maurice Egon simply "F off" several times, he will get somebody else to watch over him in a legal way.

It took another hour before the old chook Tammy Williams showed up to represent Paul. Another two hours went by before I did continue the interview. Being told that Paul does now want to withdraw everything he said in relation to his father Gerald who is an innocent man I do remember the phrase of a "innocent man" was what

Tammy Williams was famous for when her client was found guilty and sent to prison. We went back to Paul taking a handful of pills, passing out and he did admit that he did not expect to wake up. I went on to mention Peter husband of Kika who only use their first names. I did quote Peter Monmouth seventy earl of Oxford, is his correct title. "He should be called "Lady Monmouth" with all that dressing up like a woman". He had over the years tried to get Paul into bed until his Father Gerald did tell Peter "Old Girl if you touch my son I will cut your cock and stuff it down your throat!!"

His aunt Kira had a lot to put up with and always on a birthday on a special occasion Aunt Kira would show up without her husband Peter and stay a couple of days. I did mention the missing teenage girls, Paul did know about the whispers but had no idea who was now celebrate since his mother caught his father and Aunt Kira having sex in the spare bedroom, to be honest this family are so mixed up, I did not want to learn anymore about the sexuality of the family members I wanted to mention the six teenage females we located in his old Peter's cabin next to the river, I also wanted to mention that his Uncle Peter was dead. I kept all this from him, he will find out once it is public knowledge in the media, I had Paul taken back to his cell, I still do not completely believe his story. Paul could have killed both Dacey Brice and Callum Langton the truck driver, then given the gun to his Uncle Peter before he took the overdose of pills.

I went back to my office, to meet Ducky sitting in my chair "trying t out for size Ducky?" I asked her I had a weird relationship with Ducky with what some would call "dry humor". A report from all six victims and also the disclose that a total of four females had ended up being "croc bait" I knew that I should have eaten a double breakfast today of chilly egg and bacon roll I was about to feel sick. I was old by Ducky that she has found a camera with film on it hidden behind a shelf in the cabin. It did show four different females being pushed into the croc infested river, naked just with a rope around their necks and slowly attacked and eaten by the crocodiles. The screaming echo the walls of my office and I did reach for the waste paper bin but I kept my stomach contents inside me. in the film it showed Peter "The mad Earl of Oxford" shooting the largest crocodile. Then with a cable and the land rover he pulled the croc up the river bank film of him cutting off its head skinning the poor crocodile. Then I did wonder who the hell is actually filming all of this? then I heard the voice of Kira "well done husband another trophy for the wall!!"

So, Kira was part of this I said to Ducky. "I have to say it commander Aaron Brown she was up to her neck in this crocodile episode and of top of that, later on in the film she is filming her husband having sex with the teenage girls I hate to say it but she is a sick bitch. Four girls have given a statement saying that they had to perform lesbian acts in front of her on each other after being told it's that or croc bait girl's!" by Kira I had so much now going on in my head before I started the interview with Kira, I really need to search for my bottle of Malt Whisky in the bottom of my desk. Instead, and out of luck in which way you are now looking at the moment when Dr Rebecca Mitcham stood in the doorway of my office. "I do hope I have not caught you in a bad moment boss, but I do need to have a private conversation with you. With the closure of my office door and Rachel Todd my office manager throwing her arms in the air.

What could I say "Please take a seat" sit down I did I imagine she was about to split the Dummy and resign, I have not thrown in my face for a while now. I was wrong once again I did sip my cold coffee and asked Dr Rebecca to speak her mind, which could be a good thing or a bad thing depending on what way you look at it. To my surprise the conversation was about my garden cottage being vacant. I was trying to digest all of what she was saying and even asking in a nut shell, that she wanted to move in to the garden cottage and rent it from me. I had to step in and simply say that the garden cottage did belong to my four teenage boys and it would have to be passed by them. What was I leading myself into. A long and very over length explanation about her flat is now too noisy with a lot of young couples now moved in. I did say that living with four teenage boys is not exactly what you would call "Quite as a church". That was a poor explanation, my four boys are good. Loud at times they have the right to be, it's their home, I simply replied to her. The sound of money filled now filled our conversation. Once again, I did press that she will have to negotiate with my four sons. It will include electric, use of the pool and garden. She will need a bed, T.V and whatever she needed, I almost forgot a small oven or microwave. Being told that she does live on take-a-ways. Toast and coffee are the only cooking she does, if you want to call that looking. A fridge for her fruit and ice cream. I gave her a smile, then tonight or tomorrow, but check that I am there first. I did get the feeling she wanted to give me a sloppy kiss, but myself holding my rank and manhood together, just shook her hand. Within a dog's breath Rachel came in with a hot cup of coffee and just stood there like a lemon waiting to fall off a tree until I like her what the hell is going on. I simply said "she is moving into the garden cottage" with that statement all that Rachel said was "You better lock your bedroom door at night or prepared to become a overaged toy boy to the head of forensic medicine Dr. Rebecca Mitcham!!"

I did think that the comment from Rachel was a bit below the belt even from her. Round two of the conversation from Rachel did state that Dr Rebecca had her eyes on you for a few years now!! I gulp down my coffee and headed for the sanity of an interview room with Kira who did look well after a night in the cell and no time to get any make up on today, where was I going to start. I did imagine that Kira would have a answer for everything I did notice a change of solicitor, a Bill Awkward. I did not know why and to be honest I just did not care why I had a large file on Kira to get through and first up was the cabin that her brother called a man cave. The six females held in cages by her brother and straight away before. I had even finished my sentence Kira denied knowing anything about what went on inside that cabin, except the crocodile skins on the wall and the trophy heads of crocodiles on the walls. She had not been into the Cabin for at least two years, she told me. So, all I did was start to read the statements that the six teenage girls had given to Ducky.

Talk about swallowing your tongue poor Kira had no defense except "Those bitches are all talking rubbish and lies! More I read from the statement and when I got to the poor female who was used a "croc-bait". I could see in the face of Kira that it was now good shouting at me across the table and telling me I was making all this up. I did decide to have a break let Kira cool down and take some advice from her solicitor. Stunned by what I had said so far it was not long before I went back into the interview room with an all-out attack. I produced the videos of her brother and Mercedas Picton being stark naked with a rope around her neck and in a few words thrown into the croc. Infested river. I had to stop the recording and go back only one minute before Kira could hear her own voice saying "Push the bitch into have to play the tape once again. The truth was and if you wanted to believe Kira her husband made her film this very awkward scene. Those were the words of Kira not myself "it was an awkward scene!!"

I had to repeat her words "A awkward scene". Next in line was the so sex tapes of the teenage girls putting on a show for Kira, even watching her husband having sex with the teenage girls while he was high on cocaine. A close up of his face did show the white powder still on his nose. With encouragement from Kira while her husband was having sex with the teenage female's was more than enough., she said once again that her husband did force her to video the sex scenes. I did comment and go back to the statement from Lucinda Clark and Layla Lines that Kira would offer come into the Cabin alone and demand that the girls "get down and dirty on each other Kira just looked at me and told me. I was a sick bastard and asked did I get off on sitting alone and watching the videos. I had to be honest and tell her that I had not had the honest and tell her that I had not had the chance to do such a thing. I was feeling never mind the Botox lips and cheeks on her face this Kira was an evil bitch. I had another ace up my sleeve, her relationship with her brother after a well-drawn-out battle of the real truth and I did fell that I was well in front. Her solicitor Bill Awkward a fully paid-up member of the "port nose" brigade did little to help Kira even when she did turn and look for support. Bill Awkward was a close friend of her brother Gerald Hazelgrove, so when I did ask about her relationship with her brother, I could tell that Bill was not really into incest. Kira did shout at the top of her voice that they had been having sex together since they were teenagers and still do whenever they got my information from the ass wipe son of Gerald, that little fat prick Paul. I made no comment of how I found out of the sexual adventures of Kira and Gerald. It was in fact none of my business but I just thought I would rub some more salt into the wounds of Kira. I had to finish off our meeting with Kira and telling her that she will be charged with several crimes as being a compliance to her husband's crimes and will be ending her life in a prison cell. Poor Bill Awkward did ask about some sought of deal. I had to admit I knew everything so Kira had absolutely nothing to deal with me.

I left the interview room with Det Pia Jackson who had sat all through the interview now telling me "that Kira is one hell of a sick bitch a raving "Nymphomaniac" told Det Pia with a very cheek smile I replied "that I could of not describe Kira in a better way! Deep down I had a bad feeling in my stomach that this would not be the last of Kira that I would see in my life. with a mop and a skip was Bill Awkward who I had only just left with Kira who did seem to be pulling out his hair during the interview. "Commander Kira has some vital information that I think you should hear" Listen Bill, I told you and I told her that I do not deals, she is going down because of the part she played in the death of Mercedes Pilton being shown on camera! I looked at Bill and told him, nine am tomorrow, back in the same interview room and I just hope that it is not going to be a waste of time. I looked at Bill rushing back to his client Kira and with Det Pia raising her eyebrows at me I knew I had enough of a day. I want to go home and find some sanity with my four boys a goodnight to the team all except Chief Insp Jason who was on "A walk about" the reference that Rachel Todd my office manager told me. Sgt Penny Burnt some rubber in my journey home and sitting in her car outside my home was Dr Rebecca Mitcham. I had forgot about our meeting to do with the Garden. "Got yourself a date boss?" laughed Sgt Penny when I got out of the car. "See you tomorrow Penny another day in paradise". I replied. Dr Rebecca walked behind me to meet my four teenage sons. An introduction by me and then I wasted no time in telling them that real reason Dr Rebecca was standing in our kitchen Jay my eldest son, did mention it was his last day at school today before he walked Dr Rebecca up the garden. "Wow a pool I love to swim" she said. The cottage was empty no furniture, not even a cockroach had taken up residence. "Just basic furniture, tv, toaster, kettle, bed, chair ad that is all you need o yes a fridge" Jay told Rebecca. 'I will take it, how does three hundred a week, electric id included am I right? Rebecca turned to see the other three boys arrive and I would see there was no more fun any negotiation. "Seventy-five bucks each," shouted Jay. I gave the ice cream a big miss and had a cold beer. "She does remind me of him except she had shorter hair "Jay told me after Dr Rebecca left. Tomorrow afternoon she did hope to move in unless her work got in the way, "all those dead bodies and crime scenes she must be a busy lady" Jay mention.

"Well, we had worked together just over five years together. I replied with a smile before I went for another beer and watched some television. The four boys were in their pool room and all I could here was "seventy-five bucks each wow" coming from the pool room.

At work I could see Rachel Todd did want to know if Dr Rebecca will be moving into the garden cottage. "Today I told her unless we find a couple of dead bodies to derail that plan, and yes, the four boys did like her, it will be having another mother around was the final outcome from them. Det Pia was quick on her toes and told me that Kira is waiting downstairs with her solicitor to continue our interview. I grab the coffee off of the desk of Rachel and headed downstairs. What I was about to hear from her did leave me questioning her motive. She was facing life I prison with the charges slowly growing overnight. "If I am going down, I am not going down alone police man!!"

A tale that started at one point and did seem for a while never to end. Her husband Peter had told her he instructed Paul to get rid of the loose ends before we all end up in prison. Dacey Brice the night manager in the mini mark had a big mouth.

Just like Callum Langton the truck driver who also knew about the drugs and did help kidnap a few teenage females that Peter used for pleasure. After Paul had "taken care of business" he drove out at the farm property and handed the hand gun with a silencer to Peter telling him he had taken care of both of the loose ends. Peter did admit that Paul was not himself and left in a bad mood. It was then that he must have tried to kill himself with a handful of pills. It did not work, and Gerald Hazelgrove did question Kira if she knows anything about this of course she did now and Gerald told her if Paul dies, he would take care of her and that sub human Peter who see is married to. She went on to tell me and with the ears of detective Pia now burning with facts that Gerald knew nothing about the kidnap of teenage girls by Peter who had used them for sexual pleasure. The final nail in the coffin came when the mention of Reg and Andy Willi, who were behind the finance of drugs and yet kept their hands clean and used rather other dodgy characters to do their dirty work. A history lesson that I did not was raised, he was introduced to Reg and Andy Willis by Gerald Hazelgrove of all people. Unknown to me that Alf Jackson was the number one man if you wanted to get into the drug trade, he was the man who would point you in the right direction for a percentage cut in the profits. I felt my heart had skip a beat when I heard that after I shot him dead Alf Jackson was still pulling string from the grave. Kira had no idea of the connection I had with Alf Jackson over the past ten or so years. I had nothing to do except thank her for her time with this new evidence I will speak to her brother Gerald and son Paul once again.

It was time for a team update everybody who should be there was there except Chief Insp Jason. He had phoned in sick was the message that Rachel Todd my office manager told me. so, we had a positive conversation and we made more progress that I had imagine. There was only Gerald Hazelgrove and his son Paul to be interviewed once again. Reg and Andy Willis, I had a update that they had seem to have gone to ground in a penthouse in the city and a horse property out at Humpty Doo had both been searched. A lot of personal drugs had been found; both did seem to have a cocaine habit. Six different burner phones unused had been located, plus two burner phones that did contain the home phone of Gerald Hazelgrove of all people. Traffic control was also looking for them who were involved in an accident two days ago and fled the scene. Deep down I did wonder if somebody had given them a tip off that we were looking for them in connection with drugs and murder. I could write down half a dozen names and most of them worked in the defense solicitor position. I did notice that four of the solicitors all worked in the same building, Rachel Todd was quick to point at. After the meeting it was time to meet Paul Hazelgrove to give him a pat on the back for giving me nothing but lies in a previous meeting. He sat with his eyes almost popping out of his head when I told him I have a witness who did tell me that he shot Darcey Brice and the truck driver Callum Langton with a confession that he was guilty and went to see his idol Uncle Peter at his mango farm with the intention of shooting him and that would end in a sense to get rid of all the loose ends, but Paul did admit he did not have the balls, to pull the trigger, his Uncle Peter just walked up to him and just took the gun out of his hand and called him "A weak prick just like his father". This did lead to Paul trying to take another over dose of handful of drugs, that made him feel sick and took him on a journey in his mind, until he came back to reality in the hospital. He did not mention anything to do with his Uncle Peter and their very private relationship that Aunt Kira and exposed to me.

I told him in a brief sentence that, taking the drugs was nothing compared to a double murder which will result of him never living outside a cell in this lifetime. He did admit that he was sorry but that would not bring back Dacey or Callum. His Uncle Peter told him everything will were out just fine. The police have nothing on you, believe me one thing that he did not know his Uncle Peter was dead and the other life he lived keeping teenagers' girls in cages for sex. If they did result, he would strip them naked and feed them to the crocodiles. I explain we had a video of everything and even the part that his Aunt Kira played in all of this. I think once I told him that he just knew how evil both Kira and Peter were. He did ask to speak to his Father, I did explain that will not be possible because he is now facing charges of trafficking drugs being the finance behind the deal. I was surprised when Paul did mention the names of Regie and Andy Wallis being involved he had met them having a few beers with his Father.

My next part of call was to see Gerald Hazelgrove and another new solicitor Agnus Taylor a man who likes you to digest his words slowly when he is talking just in case you wanted to fall asleep listening to the boring tone of his voice Gerald in a nutshell looked like a dog's turd. Somebody had and dare I say forgotten to give Gerald his makeup bag. He was still wearing some dark shadow eye market but it did seem dark shadow eye market but it did seem to have run a little over his cheeks. A middle age business man who dies like to wear eye market is somebody that I would not trust or even ask to borrow money from. Whether Gerald knew had been going on in the big wide world while he sat in his "Holding Cell". I did decide to give him an update and get his reaction. The number one son is up for murder of two people, I gave a brief explanation and I got no reaction. His sister Kira was also up for murder of a female who was fed to the crocodiles, I just added a bit of cream and cherry on top when I did mention the six females that were found in sages in a log cabin on the property of her husband Peter who called it his "man cave".

Walls covered in crocodile skins and the head of the crocodiles. I just had to mention that Peter is in the morgue where he was taken up residence since he was shot trying to escape with a hostage. I looked at Gerald who showed no emotion to whatever I said, to him. So I decided to go even more on the attack, I did mention Reg and Andy Willis who he introduced to Alf Jackson who was a close friend to Gerald through our very detail conversation I never did raise the topic of Alf Jackson and myself were very close until he decided to venture into the pub business after his mother won the lotto and got Alf to be top dog in the pub, with the death of his mother who was drunk and feel down the stairs, it was never proved whether she was simply pushed by Alf or did she fall. I did know she laid upside down on the stairs for two hours before Alf did phone for the ambulance an ex bar person told me she tries to comfort Alf's Mother but was quickly told to get back behind the bar ad serve drinks it was "Happy hour" Alf told her.

I got no real answer from Gerald the Willis bothers were also in the money lending business like Gerald, except they did venture into the drug trades under the guidance of Alf Jackson. I did not even get a smile from Gerald who was motion less except when he moved his head to lock it his solicitor who had the very bad and what I would call a bad habit of shaking his head without even the mention of a word from his lips I was leading to the package of cocaine left in the Mini mart under the counter to be picked up, just under a million dollars the price on the package. Being taken by the fake robbery of the Mini Market and was to be found in a bar fridge two days later by members of my team in the property that was used by Bill and Andy Willis a training center for their race horses. I had to explain all this to Gerlad so he did understand that we have now learned that the driver of the white delivery was had made the call to Bill Willis about the package they require is waiting for them.

Under the counter at the mini mart. This eventually cost Callum Langton a bullet in the eye, fired by a gun given to him by uncle Peter to tie up loose ends by your son Paul of all people. I did get a reaction from Gerald who only said he had no idea Paul was in the drug trade and working with his Uncle Peter. Kira was up to her neck in everything that was on the wrong side at the law. A very surprised comment from Gerald that Kira used to go and stay at the Bill and Andy in the Penthouse and end up in what you must call a "ménage a trios" at least once a week I had come to the conclusion that nothing in the sex life of Kira would leave me surprised anymore. I did joke to myself was there anybody of interest that I had met who hand not had sex with Kira. I went for a sip of water and almost swallowed the glass when Gerald told me that Kira was very close to Alf Jackson, who did introduce Kira to cocaine, who did introduce it to her husband Peter.

I was drugging the end out but now it was to lay down the new ground rules for Gerald. He will be charged with letting his mini mart and greasy Spoon take-a-way being used for drug trafficking by the people who worked there. He can argue his case in s court of law. I was very surprised that he did manage to get bail and was walking around Parap shops just like nothing happen. He did put the mini mart up for sale and Greasy Spoon take-a-way. Within a month some body splash the cash. His shop that did act what you could call was an office a local estate agent took it off of Gerald's hands the weeks passed by and Chief Insp Jason Purely was still off on sick leave. So, I had to bring up Ian Dusty Gilmore from uniform. We did work together eight years ago. Dusty never said but I was told on the grapevine that Alf Jackson pushed him out because he was not corrupt. I have never discussed this with Dusty, who had a more than few grey hairs.

The reason being was he had been working with Uncle Billy and the Stork of all people. They said "Jump" and Dusty said "How high today". I could tell that Dusty had not lost any of his sense of humor. First task was to try and locate Bill and Andy Willis. Three weeks my team had been sniffing around without any luck. A half-sister called Petra who used to run a up market clothes stall at the Saturday Parap market was now a new lead. Why nobody in my team had crossed the path of Petra before left me dumb struck. upstairs in a back room of the old brother was where the Willis brothers had been hiding. All this time "waiting for that mister make up man Gerald Hazelgrove to get a safe passage set up out of Darwin. I thought that poor Gerald has not been what you could say in his best condition just lately with his empire crumbling and members of his family heading for prison.

Traffic made the call and located the Willis much sought-after four-wheel drive heading for the truck stop at Berriman. Reinforcements were called and before they arrived the Willis four-wheel drive was heading down the hill to the traffic lights at a major intersection that lead to east arm. An eye witness said Willis's vehicle passed him with shouting going on the light was red but the four-wheel drive could not stop across the road to hit a road train which sent their vehicle into a spin like a circus act across the road only to end upside down before another road train coming the other way simple in one huge crunch finished the lives of Bill and Andy Willis, they ended up just like sardines in a can. A very lengthy investigation was to discover that somebody had cut the brakes. Nobody could of stop their vehicle with the brake lines cut. I got Sgt Penny to drive me out to the crash site it was not something you would want to see on a full stomach. We did retrieve their mobile phones to let us know that Gerald Hazelgrove had been in contact with them only hours before they started to make a run for it.

Gerald did deny the phone conversation until I showed him his phone calls. Out on bail, and knowing the where about of two known people of interest that the police were seeking. I had to laugh at early and his excuse after excuse when I told him the actual for wheel drive was once owned by the mini mart manager Rowan Adams of all people who had lent it to Willis's brothers, been a very old friend. It was my old friend Dusty who had talked the sister Petra into giving him the car registration number that was eventually traced by traffic control. I had the pleasure of keeping the very same call open for the return of Gerald Hazelgrove who did expect had something to do with the brakes on the four-wheel drive. Just like everything else that Gerald had contact with he had an alibi and had cleaned his hands of any involvement in their death. I always thought that just maybe the Willis brothers knew something about Gerald that I did now know.

CHAPTER 12

THE FINAL STRAW

It was that time again, when I have to make the trek up to see Uncle Bill and the Stork but first, I must go for a walk about and meet John Williamson Chief Prosecutor. I know he has a large work load, listening to him going on about it, once again. We met on the esplanade. I got the coffee and a couple of sticky buns for us to enjoy while I put my questions to him. I gave him a list of people that he will come up against in court and a brief note of how naughty they had been. I did not expect the answer I got from his vicious lips "of course in the old days they would have hung the bloody lot of them O no, not now, a slap on the wrist from the judge who look like he had been sucking on a bong all night and kept awake by a hooker demanding even more sex!! I felt that poor John had just got out of bed the wrong side. But no, he just went on about me and my team tracking down the criminals and he does a successful prosecution. F Even when they are found bloody guilty and the judge gives them a slap on the wrist.

This was the second or was it the third time poor John had mention a light sentence. I did feel that he was what you might call a little pissed off with the judges he was to come up against. They never listen to him or the any advice from him. No there was no "tears" but I felt that one man standing on his shoulder" we finally reached Gerald Hazelgrove being told he will walk just because he owned the two buildings the minimart and Greasy Spoon where drugs had been sold. He has more than one witness statement from those who were into drug selling, God forbid he was innocent it was his son Paul. I had to admit I really had nothing more to present to John. Being told that Gerald was in a cell now and in two hours he will apply for bail. The old ankle bracelet will be applied. John did admit that he was a fight risk. They did apply for bail late last night but the judge was at the opera and will hear Gerald sing for his freedom once again.

There is an awful lot that goes on after I prove the person of interest is guilty and does confess was the final lecture, I had from John today while stuffing the sticky bun into his mouth so he could not even talk anymore. He spat some out and a couple of seagulls were quick to clear up his "left overs". "Only if the bloody judge was as quick as that bloody seagull!! Shouted John walking away. Throwing his arms in the air. I headed for the lift in the Police Complex I reach the lift to the top floor, no I did not have an appointment I told the watch dog on the office door to Uncle Bill, who I could hear laughing and joking with the Stork. The silence suddenly hit the room when I made my way in without even knocking. Being told by the Stork that you should always knock before entering a room with a closed door. I just hope that the Stork could open the door on her own. I just hope that the Stork could read my mind because I was saying "Fuck off". I looked at Uncle Bill who did look tired. I sat down, I decided to give the coffee a wide berth.

Much to my surprise and even more to the surprise look on the face of the Stork, she was told to leave the room I did think that this is good, it will cut my time in half I will not have to repeat everything twice so the Stork could understand what was really going on in the real world. I went over the activities with Uncle Bill and I kept getting the comment from him "what a great job you are doing down there, cracking the whip keeping those Billy goats active. Uncle Bill talking about Billy goats was hard to swallow. I just tried to follow Uncle Billy's train of thought. I just got left at the first railway station, I was not even on the same train that Uncle Billy was on. A mention about Gerald Hazelgrove and yes, I could not believe it that Gerald (Mr. Clean) does in fact not only belong to the very same golf club where they offer play golf together but Gerald is also a freemason and does belong to the same lodge as Uncle Billy. I had to try and bite my tongue then.

Being told that Gerald Hazelgrove was what you call a decent fellow, a strong family man and has sent his son to college to learn business and now runs a supermarket and take a way food shop. I knew then that Uncle Bill had not even read the charges that I had mention the son Paul is facing. It was a sudden move from Billy who did display the passing of wind between his rear cheeks. What you might call an apology from Uncle Bill did follow some even more useless inside information that Chief Insp Jason Riley will not be joining me back in major crime. Uncle Bill simply said "It was not his cup of tea" I had to hold my breath and bite my tongue; I could have said I did not think Jason was any bloody good at the job the team will be down the pub later to celebrate him leaving. I had old Dusty now who used to be man backed by the Stork and now had gone back to where he started being a bloody good detective. I just gave a thumbs up to Uncle Billy who I knew he had no idea what it meant by me with that Uncle Bill pointed to the door, so I thought this does mean that it is time for me to leave his office. I did open the side door quickly and I had to judge people but I did believe that the Stork was listening to our conversation. I gave the Aaron Brown fake smile when I passed her, trying to make me believe that she had dropped something on the floor that was very she was bending down? I headed back to my office with a spring in my step, I was like a school boy I could not wait to brave the news "goodbye Jason". I did not get a cheer or an applause from the team not until I said "the first pint of beer is on me". I got a cheeky smile from Rachel and a thumbs up from Dusty, who I told "it does look like you are staying old friend".

"I have no problems with that" replied Dusty.

It was time for my egg and chilly, "no bacon today the canteen had forgot to order anyway from the supplier" Crystal Fulton told me, with a cheeky smile.

I have to call her big ears but if you want to know anything that goes on within this building you should just ask Rachel Todd my office manager who closed my office door when she told me that Chief Insp Jason Riley is going to head the integrity unit. I had to put a damper to this off the press information that Jason is not the first and will not be the last to take up that position from this office floor. I turned to Rachel and gave her four hundred dollars to put behind the bar for drinks, she just looked at me and nodded, since my Kate had died, I had never been for a team drink Kate herself would always show up uninvited and be the bell of the ball. The only dancing, she only did not do was at the policeman's ball at Christmas many did enjoy her antics both a woman with four children should not be expressing herself like that. I am a father of four should have not let my wife carry on like an out of controlled teenagers. I loved every minute of it and so did my close staff member.

I had to break the news to Sgt Penny Maze first, yes she could go to the knees up at the pub just down the road and second she did not have to take me home first and last but not least she had the choice of a week off work while I am off on holiday, if not come in to work with Rachel Todd my office manager. She took the week off Dr Rebecca Mitcham did save me a phone call when she showed up at my office with her findings on the death of the Reg and Andy Willis they were floating in a world of cocaine while Andy was driving also an ounce of the cocaine was found in a plastic bag inside his jacket I passed this information on to Dusty my new right hand who will be running this circus as the ring master acting Chief Insp Dusty Gilmore I told him whatever happens and even the building does get hit by a earthquake do not phone me I am going camping with my three boys Joe, Jim and Jack the eldest Jay will be working night shift filling shelves at the local supermarket. Turning to me Dr. Rebecca turned to me and simply said "give me ten minutes and I will give you a lift home and maybe we can have dinner with the boys".

Talk about trying to catch flies with her wide-open mouth, poor Sgt Penny had not been told that Dr. Rebecca is the new tenant in the garden her up to date with all the gossip that does surround my private life these days. We had dinner with the three boys then Jay joined us before they all ended up playing pool with Dr. Rebecca once a teenage pool champion many moons ago, she told me. She was relentless and she told all four of them that she would give them a chance to replay me at a later date. I started to load up the four-wheel drive, it did start first time I knew Kate was still looking down on us and taking care of all the little points I out family. Jay was happy with his three brothers being away he could catch up on some sleep, in fact Jay had moved into the old room of Aunt Candy who I had not heard from for a while. I went upstairs to bed I had a big drive tomorrow, down south to wherever we decided to camp. Deep down I knew that I had some unfinished business after I got a late call from John Williamson the public prosecutor.

There will be simply no charges laid against Gerald Hazelgrove. I was feeling "gutted" so I went out for a walk and to my surprise I found a car parked in a drive way with the keys left in the ignition. I let the car roll back started it up and I was off to Parap to visit the home of Gerald Hazelgrove. With my surgical mask on and a black cap, a hand gun with a silencer ready I made my way up the side of his home. I could hear voices in the garden. I took a peep and I could see somebody standing in front of Gerald and pointing a gun. It was time to get involved and I told the person to put down the gun. He did turn and it was Rowan Adams once the manager of the mini mart. I was careful not to use any of the co called Police orders to drop your gun, face down on the grass. An explanation that Rowan Adams was here to take care of Gerald Hazelgrove. Waving that gun around I almost said "You beat me to him I am afraid"

I could not wait another second and put Rowan Adams out of his misery with one bullet in the head. He fell and I walked over telling Gerald not to be naughty and go for that gun on the ground. I had the offer of cash and would you believe a large amount of drugs just to walk away. I said to Gerald "You cannot buy me, just like you buy other people". With that he went to say who I was but the finger on the trigger of my gun took control. One bullet in the head, not dead in a way I would of like he was wiggling so another shot in the heart and one shot in his mouth. I open the mouth of Rowan Adams so his tonsils could feel a piece of hot lead. I left walked around or a while find the car, took it to the Nightcliff football field and simple with a sprinkle of petrol and a spark from a of match, any trace of myself ever being in that car was now gone. I walked home went into the kitchen for a cool beer. I did look up to see Dr Rebecca sitting outside her cottage, I went up to join her.

I did explain that I had been for a walk along the seafront, something I always did with Kate my wife at least once if not twice a week to be alone with her was the most I missed about Kate. Five am the alarm clock went and it was battle stations "we are all going on a summer holiday" we all sang the three boys I did stop off at the first petrol station to fill up with petrol and Litchfield caravan park was our first port of call. If the fish are biting, we will stay, if not find another fishing spot was our rule. It did rain in the dry season at Lichfield so we took a family cabin. I did not watch the news to see if the two bodies had been found at the Gerald Hazelgrove residence. It was three days and a nosy neighbor who normally cuts his lawn, did discover the two bodies. I saw Dusty on television giving an update about the police are on this case and Dusty did think that it was a gang land killing.

In the background I could see members of my team and also Dr Rebecca looking busy with evidence bags. I did expect an update on my return. The rain did stop and the fish still kept biting we had a full freezer load of fish in our four-wheel drive for our weekend BBQ's when we got home. Jay was so pleased to see us sitting alone and eating I the kitchen was something new for him. He did love the constant banter of his three brothers while eating their meals. He had not spoken to De Rebecca who did seem to work strange hours waiting for Sgt Penny to bring the car, I sat on our garden wall. I high five from Dr Rebecca before she drove to work a message in reception that Uncle Bill and the Stork would like my presence some sought of "did you have a good holiday" instead all I got was a complaint from Uncle Bill about even going on holiday at this time when his close friend Gerald Hazelgrove had been killed. I did not expect from Uncle Bill point of view.

His side of the story about "Dusty" being not up to the job, he does lack the skills was what Dusty was sent to me by Uncle Bill himself. My ears could not handle much more of Uncle Bill who kept looking at the Stork for support I got up and simply said "Well I am back now so things should return to normal!!" with that I headed down to my office, while I waiting for the lift to came up to the top floor. I had to listen worse comments coming from Uncle Bill and the Stork that must have delighted the top floor audience. I arrived to see my team hard at it and I at once asked Dusty for an update. I also told him that the top floor are not happy that he has not caught the killer of Gerald Hazelgrove and Rowan Adams. I called Dr Rebecca and all three of us went out to the crime scene to go over the evidence so I could understand the crime even more. Much to my surprise on an arrival I had some information about some "long grass person".

A term used for the homeless sleeping rough. A group of four had moved into the house on the Monday night. Stolen all the high-end booze and later return with some extra friends to steal all the food and beer they could. They had been sleeping rough in a flat on the floor on that Thursday. Forensic had their finger prints on file, it was only a matter of time before they were spotted so the arrest could be made. A solo first nation man who was a suspect just happen to walk out the corner store, buying tobacco and was followed to a ground floor flat. Tactical support was brought in to supervise the raid. It was unknown id these were the killers of Gerald and Rowan, only one gun was found on the scene and that had not been fired, it was found lying next to Rowan. Both Gerald and Rowan were killed by an unknown weapon and an unknown person, the third person was the killer both Dr. Rebecca and Dusty both agreed on that point at least.

A brief explanation by Dusty, led me to believe that this was not the first time the four first nation person had help themselves to booze and food from the kitchen. The rear doors to the lounge were often left undone and open by Paul Hazelgrove when Skinny Dipping in the pool during the night. Another surprise was that the neighbors were not home at the weekend and did return late on Monday that firework display to celebrate Australia day was on their happy calendar a married Muslim couple with a strange connection to a religious cult were not that friendly to the Hazelgrove household. The husband did not notice that there was two dead bodies on the lawn and did not bother to phone the police or for an ambulance. He stood on a small ladder to look over the motionless bodies lying on the lawn and did nothing, Dusty did repeat in making this point twice in telling me. A bigger surprise was that they did share the same gardener with the Hazelgrove property and it was him after he cut the grass next door and went around to the Hazelgrove property and discovered the two dead victims.

He was the one who phoned the police. He did not go into the house to find it ransacked it was Dusty and his team who discovered the home invasion and clothes that belong to Kira were thrown to have been taken by the first nation female and was dressed in designer clothes when the tactical support kicked down the front door to the flat. The neighbor did not believe in helping others outside their religion. Not reporting the death of his neighbor and the other victim will be debated whether any charge would be made against him for not reporting the crime. I just shook my head at what I was hearing I had to listen to two points of view what finally happen with the two victims ended up dead. It was a gangland killing that Dusty kept going on about there may have been even two or three suspects that walked away from this crime scene, while Dr Rebecca did decide to press on and say it could be a single killer or even a falling out between them.

The three of them ending up with a mystery person shooting Gerald Hazelgrove and then Rowan Adams a change of story that Rowan Adams would have been shot. The time of time death was on late Saturday. Both bodies were covered in flies on her arrival and some wild life had chewed at the face of Rowan Adams, she did believe it could have been rats by the marks on his face. I knew what really happen but I had to be smart and just play along with this circus show that had been put on for my own benefit. I let Dusty and Dr Rebecca leave and stood alone with Sgt Penny watching my every move even put on a face for Sgt Penny to show that I was feeling sad for the loss of Paul Hazelgrove who I had wanted to end up in jail and not dead on his lawn. I made no comment to Sgt Penny who simply said "welcome back boos another day in bloody paradise!!"

She was right at the office I sat and read all the details from the four first nation people of interest. Petty crimes liking being drunk, stealing in shops there was no violence in any of their crimes I did see that in a biscuit tin in the kitchen ten thousand dollars, cash I was very surprised that all four of them did not go away down south with that money and live it up a little. Being permanently drunk for three days after drinking all those very rare and expensive spirits, they had feed themselves on very expensive cheese and olives some pickle a cooked chicken and sliced ham and some frozen party pies and sausage rolls that the female manage to cook in the flat they were staying in while the owner was in hospital fighting lung cancer. Coffee was presented to me by Rachel Todd my office manager, plus my usual chilly and cheese bacon and egg roll. "I have been living on fresh BBQ fish for the past few days I told her, yes we had a great time and now I am back to sought out this mess". I got Dusty in to go over her theory of a gang war.

Who else could it be with the drugs being stop from that sex machine Peter and Paul Hazelgrove out of the pictures some people may have paid up in advance for the drugs and now they had been let down, with Gerald Hazelgrove the only one who is not in a holding cell he was the one to be challenge. I asked about what Rowan Adams part was in all of this. "Well, you always said that Rowan Adams was up to his neck in this rug operation, standing by and watching the mini mart team sell drugs I could not see him doing that. Rowan Adams was the only other person God forbid like Gerald Hazelgrove not to be charged with any drug charges. How that happen has blind sighted me the staff at the mini mart said that Rowan with all his knowledge had got his nose constantly into everything in that shop was a little blind sighted. Paul Hazelgrove got the drugs to the mini mart team and to the right people. I went along with the theory by Dusty then I asked him so who were the killers then?

This was a good distraction in my train of thought to help Dusty point the finger at somebody else. It is not the first time I have stood by and watch an innocent person being rail road into being accuse of a crime that I had been involved in. Dusty was very busy looking for a lead with the team going out their way to solve this case. Time did pass by and before I knew it, time was ready for me to go home. Dr Rebecca did come into my office to express her anger about Dusty not excepting her thoughts on the double murder. I had always listened to and excepted her point of view and it had led me to finally catch the killer many times. I told her to go for a swim in the pool to cool down before dinner tonight. I hope you do come to dinner I told Dr Rebecca that sent a sudden sound a silence on the major crime detective office. I told Sgt Penny that I am ready to go home, it had been a long and somewhat adventures day in the world of crime for me today. Rachel Todd gave me a normal thumbs up and said just like always "I will see you tomorrow bright eyes and bushy tailed boss!!" I gave a cheeky smile back to her with a wink of my eye.

I sat next to Jay my eldest who joined us for dinner, but it was his breakfast today all boys choose the tandoor, chicken curry. I had the spinach lasagna and we were all joined by Dr. Rebecca last of all. I think that my boys do believe that Dr Rebecca will be the one who will step into the position of Mother for the boys and a wife for me. The boys do feel how lonely I seem to be these days; I have lost a lot of my weird sense of humor I was told by Jim my second eldest ad now the new leader of the school skate boarders. Skate Boards shooting up and down the path outside my house with the neighbors honking-out the window and wonder why children are out playing at this time of night, really, they should be in bed with a cup of warm milk. I hate to shout out loud but "its school holidays". With my voice the curtains were drawn and I think they related to their quite life at the back of their house if I am not wrong I will expect a letter through my post box telling me about their silent rights. The last one was about the noise in the pool after seven O'clock at night mind you it was a scorcher of a day. The idiot next door who does cut my grass for a six pack of beer and couple of games of pool just to get away from his battle axe wife had never said anything about my boys to my face.

Dr. Rebecca joined me for a beer at in the garden. I do not discuss work once I walk at of that reception door. So, I could tell by her face that the conversation about Chief Insp Dusty did have a continuation but it will be heard tomorrow. I did drop the hint and that sent Dr Rebecca off to fetch myself a beer and she drank the red win out of the bottle that did not stop me from showing my sense of humor to her. The conversation did drift to my four sons; Jay, Jim, Joe and Jac all named by my wife I told her if she had a girl, I could choose the name I had to admit that on nights like this I do Miss Kate for conversation and adult sense of humor. Dr Rebecca drank the whole bottle of red wine while I just sucked on my beer. In the morning I could see at breakfast Dr Rebecca was watching the world go by with only one eye open. Jay arrived home from his night shift while I listen to the car horn from Sgt Penny.

At work "Dusty" had located a Jimmy Watson and Peter Adams who was the brother to Rowan Adams who used to be the day manager at the mini mart and now famous for dying next to Gerald Hazelgrove when one door does finally close another door does open to the supply of drugs. Jimmy Watson and Peter Adams seem to be setting up a new drug ring. So. my thoughts on Rowan Adams being what you might call "drug involvement" he was just as guilty but we had not enough evidence like we had on the other members of the staff at the mini mart, we had come to believe and listen to all of their individual tales some were so much taller than others. Paul Hazelgrove was their supply man by all accounts. Like everything about this expanding case, I have come to doubt a lot of what we discovered under the umbrella of Paul Hazelgrove who acted like he was the king pin and took care of anything that had passes it used by date, normally people who I step out of line. I left Dusty to shake down Jimmy Watson and Peter Adams, he even locked them up in watch house overnight and after a lot of questions he had to let them both go. Dusty had the idea that the brother Peter was the missing person who just may have shot his own brother, in a rage of temper. Peter Adams had a very short fuse and was not a person you wanted to get into a fight with in a public bar. The beer glass was a number one weapon for Peter Adams, Jimmy Watson was the intelligent one of the two if there is such a thing in drug gangs, they also were in company of Joe Murphy and a Roy Teek who always spoke with their first.

I had cramp in my hand for all this paperwork I had been signing off on. I was glad to go home it had been a long day and I made the comment that I missed out on my Chilly egg and bacon roll today. I was told to excuse the comment but "if you want to be fed just ask" Crystal Fulton told me with the glance which gave Rachel Todd something to laugh about who made the comment "Excuse me boss but you are old enough and ugly enough to just squeal when you want feeding". I thought what is going on here I am the Boss and I demand respect if not at least feeing. Being told that Sgt Penny could call into "Maccas" on the way home if I was that hungry. I simply declined the offer and waited till I got home to eat dinner with the boys. After dinner, Tilda and Sofia took the boys with their two girls to the cinema. Jay went to work I sat alone looking at the pool but I did stop at trying to act like a fish tonight. It was late and no sign of Dr. Rebecca so I went to watch the television with forty channels to choose from. I dozed off and was woken by the doorbell. It was my ex-driver Amy Fuller and standing next to her was bird brain himself Chief Insp Jason Purely now running the integrity unit. I was asked to come with them.

Pointing their guns at ne, I had no real choice. Being told to leave my personal and work phone beside the television. I was what you might call "Hassel outside" I was put into the front seat of a unmarked car with Sgt Amy Fuller my ex driver at the wheel and trigger happy bird brain. Chief Insp Jason Purely sitting behind me and also a little reminder "that if I do try anything I will have a large hole in the back of my head!!" I did notice we were off to the direction of Humpty Doo and turned in to the property that Reg and Ray Willis used to train their race horses on. There was nobody about and I was asked to vacate the front passenger seat. The handcuffs were squeeze tight over my wrist. I tried to find out what was going on but simply told to keep my mouth shot. We made our way to a half-dug hole in the ground that did remind me of a grave. I had come to realize now that they want me to dig my own grave. I could have a better use for this hole right now and that is to put these two knuckle heads in it, there is only one problem and that is the cards are stocked very high against me achieving that goal!!

I was going to try and talk myself out of this situation I am in, I mean I do have the gift of the gab trying to convince Jason that Amy was only using him for her own grievance of not being allowed back into the Major Crime Unit. The main reason was that her father was head of drug Cartel and she did tell a "big porkpie pie" on her application form. I mention how she tricked my eldest son Jay in the belief that he was going to be the father of her child. Amy had an answer for everything I said about her. I even told Jason when all of this blows up in his face, she will be pointing the finger at him. Jason wanted to know who was the father of her child. I had to shout out it was his old boss, Jason; it was "Harry Lines" who also was going to be a father to a baby with three other female detectives who all just like Amy had an abortion I could tell that Jason was what you might call "stunned" by this revelation. I did wonder where he had been living through all that drama in the major crime unit. "We would have to put up a nappy changing station next to the coffee station. I do not think my sense of humor did impress Jason who told me I was making all of this up just to shame Amy who is an honest person. I went on the attack and she has a twisted mind and everything she does is for herself and trying to secure her own future. I was getting nowhere except this hole was slowly becoming deeper. I looked across behind Amy and I thought I saw a shadow move behind her in the bushes. I was told to dig and then Amy did remind me that I gave her fifty thousand dollars out at Mary River Caravan Park. After I shot Diana Watkins who had crushed her four-wheel drive after she fled from John knight who finally told her that he was going overseas and there is no room for her in his life never mind on the private plane being told that I shot Diana Watkins in the head after she was dangling in a seat belt upside down in her car. I thought I was putting her out of her misery and settling a debt of misery that Diana Watkins had brought on my Family I was to learn that John Knight the upstart police commissioner who begged me to be his number two. Poor Jason was getting confused and said I was making up an excuse for shooting a senior police officer. I did mention that Harry Lines had stolen the fifty thousand out of a brief case that was heading for our money vault in the watch house. I did try to explain to Jason that Harry Lines had given the money to John Knight who passed it on to Diana Watkins "It was drug money, it started life with Alf Jackson many months ago. I was told to "shut my mouth" and simply dig". Amy had a good memory who went on to tell Jason how I also shot John Knight after I did admit shooting Cyril and Stan Reed of the plastic mafia fame and I fed them to the crocodiles. Jason did remember that he was working on that case and got nowhere. Next was the death of Derek Hard Steel, who I took care of out at Humpty Doo, not far from here, there were lot that Amy. wanted to inform Jason and even John Knight threw a man off a balcony and Alf Jackson and myself was involved in the cover up. I told Jason that Amy is making all of this up, I am an innocent man, I have a good strong police record Amy shouted at more facts and told how I placed six bullets into Alf Jackson to make sure that he was dead when I got him to admit that he drove over my wife Kate not once but twice outside Nightcliff shopping centre. John Knight name was to rise once again when I found out that John Knight had known for over three years that Alf Jackson had driven that car that ran over my wife. "This was no fucking loyalty between them who simply would take somebody out if they thought they did deserve a bigger punishment like a bullet in the brain. Apart from the direction of "Keep digging" poor Jason was now even more lost and confused. Not somebody who could keep a secret was Jason. When he told me that he had been to see Bill Skinner and Violet Adams known to me as Uncle Bill and the Stork. They had sanctioned my removal from the Police Force. I found that hard to believe. I mean Uncle Billy did not have the balls to argue to stop such a vicious idea, now the Stork she had balls and I do imagine would be much larger than most men and could be behind this whole idea I had come to realize in what well could be the last hour of my life now I was starting to became a little nervous to say the least.

I did try the soft touch with Amy, I did mention how many my four sons took her into their lives and treated her like a big sister. Being told by her that she hated them "Spoilt Brats" and had no respect for me. Now if I keep digging down, I will never get out of this hole in the ground. Well maybe that was their idea. Jason did decide to give me a lecture about all the bad points in my life. I had to admit, I have never heard him talk such a lot of old "Bollocks" and I used that worry to express my thoughts on his equation of my career. In his mind I was no different to the purpose we tried to convict criminals. I had led two lives one a Police Office and one a killer who saw himself as a Judge and Jury and a Terminator who would bring the end to a life who I had decided to have reached their used by date. I found this was pure poetry, in fact I could have not put those words together much better than Jason. I had to comment Jason and his use of the English language. He did think just like usual I was taking the piss out of him; I was trying to degrade him just like I had done always working with them.

I told Jason you got it so wrong; once again I was just trying to make you a better person and how to adjust to the pressure of the job. I put him in that job I gave him the promotion. With that Amy called out "Don't listen to his bullshit Jason let us get done what we have come to do and that was shoot him and bury him in this bloody hole in the ground. Jason went to say sorry but sadly he did not finish the sentence, a voice from behind a tree "armed police drop your weapons" I should of said "sorry" to Jason when I swung that long handled spade and tried to cut off his head, with one hard swoop, I went to stand over him and felt that Amy does not love me anymore the bloody bitch had shot me in the shoulder, I fell to the ground almost on top of Jason was not a good place to bed with him wiggling in pain. I heard three shots ring at and a voice cried out "you ok boss its bloody Penny I finally got here. I went to get up and found the gun that belong to Jason. I just picked it up and pointed it at him and simply said "sorry Jason but you are on the wrong side today". I put four bullets into his head. I turned to see Penny who did seem to be ducking and diving and finally "Gee you are a bloody dipstick to find shouted Penny at me, she did go and cuddle my right side where I had been shot. I fell to the ground and just missed falling into my own grave. "You have been hit, we must get you to a hospital" Penny shouted I look to see another figure rushing over towards us, I thought what the "F" is this showtime? Next thing a marching band will appear It was Dr Rebecca who did explain that I must go to hospital, I told her that she could use her medical skills and patch me up here. All I got was a lot of abuse from Dr Rebecca and a part explanation of how both Penny and her got here. In a nutshell Dr Rebecca saw Jason and Amy march me out to their car at gun point. Shoe phone Penny who was quick off the mark with instructions to follow the car and she will catch up with her in her own car. It took twenty minutes and almost reaching the Humpty Doo turn off, become in a state of emotion Dr Rebecca. Also followed Penny who now was following the Jason and Amy car I was dizzy now was it their extra-long very detailed explanation or just the loss of blood Penny help put me in the back of her car and before I knew it I was under the emergency sign at Darwin Hospital and being poked around by two doctors and a nurse telling me that I will be alright once they get the bullet out I had to admit I did feel no comfort with her comment.

I told Dr Rebecca to phone Ducky and she will come to help, she is the only one you can trust at this moment in time. I was worried Ducky would go to the Stork and Uncle Billy but following my instructions I gave to Dr Rebecca. "Ducky" voice I could hear filling the walls outside my treatment room. It was then I felt a sharp jab and being told "Goodnight commander sleep tight its surgery time" I woke with Dr Rebecca and Ducky both talking about my private life and Penny just enjoying their gossip. "He needs a strong woman in his life, well he had never taken the bait, whoever it is, have to realize that this old boy does come with a package of four teenage sons".

I open up my eyes and simply said Well I made it and tell me when is the wedding going to be".

"Which one is the bloody bride" laugh Penny

"You could be laughing Ducky at Penny"

"Sorry I am too young for him, anyway he could not keep up the pace!!"

There was none of what I was expecting and how are you feeling, can I get you anything. It was a nurse and a doctor who asked these three females in my life to leave now. I need to rest. I woke up .

Two hours later, I heard the movements of my four son's lips. Asking me if I am alright? What could I tell them, to be truthful I really felt that I had let them down. Jay was off work for the next two days to take control of his three brothers. I also learnt that Sgt Penny Maze had moved in and was sleeping in Aunt Candy or was it Mandy's room. I had a real horrible bad dream that I spoke to Aunt Candy and she was going to stay for a few weeks over the Darwin Cup Carnival held at the turf club maybe I was just having a bad dream. I was asking if I would have a good-looking scar? It was then that Jay did step in and take control "Yes Aunt Candy did phone to say, that she missed her flight her lift broke down on the way to the airport. I told her what happen to you and the house is under protection from the tactual support police. Aunt Candy said she will come up next year and I was to give you her love" I did not expect a large cheer from my boys about Aunt Candy unable to come to see us. Within the hour they were gone back home there was once again silence and I was told to rest by the nurse and then by the Doctor. What Pill they gave me, put me into a good night's sleep except I could still fill the nurse taking my blood pressure and telling me to sleep tight and do not let the bug's bite!!

Breakfast was something I felt did need to be investigation tinned fruit Weetabix, 2 pieces of cold toast in a paper bag. I normally have a chilly egg and bacon roll for breakfast I told the nurse and all she said was "dream on". I drank the coffee and I have to say I will never ever complain about the so-called coffee at work ever again on television the breakfast news was on the television and I did not even get a mention just before I had a checkup from the doctor. "If you keep this up you might even be going home this time tomorrow". I was not having another bad dream when the Police Minister Carol Kelly showed up everybody left the room except her she produced her tape machine and I listen to a confession from Chief Insp Jason telling the truth about the plan of my abduction and finally to be buried it was supposed to let the world know just in case it did not go exactly to plan I was about both the Police Commissioner Bill Skinner Uncle Bill to me and her royal highness Violet Adams known as the Stork to me. I could not believe that they both agreed to Jason Purely and Amy Fuller disposing of me in a grave after they shot me. I just looked at her "Tell me what to do, I do know that they are both about to get their heads removed. I did remember that I in fact had tried to remove the head of Jason Purely and the long handle spade until Amy Fuller decided to bring me down with a bullet in the shoulder. I did now wonder about Carol Kelly and some of her comments after led me to think that she has been sniffing some white powder up her nose just like all politicians do when they become under real pressure.

I do not have anybody suitable to replace them both and I do know down in South Australia they have a couple of people who could step in, then again, the "Troops" I do know that they would not be happy bringing in outsiders!!" she picked up my coffee and took a sip, "God Almighty how do you drink that stuff?" I just tried to laugh without splitting my stitches, I had a horrible feeling what she was going to ask me next so I just looked up toward the ceiling "How about you stepping up again to a more senior role once again, now choose your own deputy, maybe the old chock Duckworth you know who you call Ducky Chief Insp Alice Duckling I should have called her by her full rank. Now Ducky had already step up by all accounts sent tactical support to guard your house and keep your four boys safe, I wanted to come but there was a dinner party at the Chief Minister's home and I was guest of honor. I thought did I really want to know all this crap? There was a long silence before I said "one month only I will take control, only one month I have been there and got screwed before I even didn't get a bloody T-Shirt, saying Boss on the front. Carol Kelly, I had not seen laugh so much before I did think that she was going to wet her knickers well that is if she did remember putting them on today? Mainly because she did seem a little out of control of gasping for the right words and trying to get me to say" Its ok I will step up and fill the shoes of Uncle Bill. 'Carol Kelly went out one door and in step Ducky through the other door. I explain her promotion she did think it was for my job but instead she had gone two floors up to being Acting assistant Police Commissioner. '' Yes, I except the position so when do I start? 'She asked in reply I told her she already had five minutes ago; She gave me a fake salute. I started to explain about Uncle Bill of all people being involved with drugs many moons ago. I had to explained that I had a very early visit from a lonely Uncle Bill laying down some new ground rules for the future with me.

I told her I had no idea, that Uncle Bill and John Knight were involved with Alf Jackson. Bosting that he had given them the drug dealers contacts. He was owed five hundred thousand if he kept his mouth shut and did not point his finger at anybody. I had to say that Uncle Bill thought he was better than the rest of us and now coming down to earth. He simply has the wrong end of the stick. He knew I was nothing to do with the so why even raise the subject with the threat of going to the press and sell his story was a threat to my future he wanted half a million and I got five days to get it. I told him to get out and do not come back. I simply told her, that he demanded half a million dollars or he will tell his story to the media and bring me down from this position. He always has been a nasty piece of work he used to hit his wife when drunk, Ducky left me ponding my next move in this situation. I got out a day early if the truth was known they needed the bed for somebody else. A good night's sleep at home after dinner with the boys and I was ready to fire on all cylinders at work in the morning.

Tomorrow around eight AM with a belly full of egg and bacon chilly roll and a large mug of the major crime coffee. I will go upstairs with tactical support and relieve Uncle Bill and the Stork of their duty and place them under arrest. Carol Kelly lent over and gave me a Sloppy Police Minister's kiss on the lips, in fact she did enjoy the first kiss I was having a second one, but when she tried to put her tongue down my throat. It was time for me to push back and simply say "Take it easy Carol I have just had surgery"!! she left with a guilty smile on her face with the look if "a naughty girl".

I had another snooze before it was time to see the doctor you out in about an hour, you will have to wear an arm brace to support your shoulder. I thank him for his good work and his bed side manner. Home was my first call I woke up Jay who was sleeping in Aunt Candy's old room. It was his day off and his brothers are driving him mad today. Sgt Penny was sitting in the kitchen and I could see the eyes of Jay light up when he saw her.

I did phone my office to let them know I am coming back to work. I wanted "Ducky to be on hand and also "Dusty". When I finally arrived, I did request that there should be no fanfare. I had placed an order for two members of tactical support to come upstairs to pay Uncle Bill and the Stork when I break the news to them. Waiting downstairs and trying to look cool was Police Minister Carol Kelly who gave me a cheeky wink of her eye. In the lift it was a tight squeeze I did ask Ducky to attend but Dusty I will speak to in a short while. No, I did not have an appointment I told the guard dog on Billys door, who was rushing to do up his trousers when I walked in the room only to find the Stork sitting on his desk. "Don't you bloody knock before coming into a room". The Stork shouted at me. "I will get to the point that you are both being relieved of your positions I am taking over". I look at Billy who did seem a little lost in what was going on. The voice of Carol Kelly was the icing on the cake "under my authority and I do believe that charges are to be made about your involvement of what happen to Commander Aaron Brown. Who was by all reports supposed to be simply shot and buried in a grave that he was made to dig. The Stork just looked at Billy who at this point had to sit down again, still with the zip on the front still undone and his shirt sticking out.

"No idea what is going on?" Asked Billy

"Where is the proof" asked the Stork.

"Um well Chief Insp Jason Riley and Sgt Amy Fuller I am afraid they cannot report to you about any sought of success. They both lay dead with holes in their heads. I told them both

"What both dead? shouted Billy.

"If you would kindly come down to the watch house where charges will be laid against you" I told me.

"Listen Violet, I told you it would not work and now look what a mess you got me into".

The Stork just raised her arms in the air and told Billy she had no idea what he is talking about. I knew she would just try to wiggle out of it and blame Billy, taken downstairs to the watch house and placed in separate interview rooms. I turned to Ducky and told her she is acting Commander now and also Assistant Police Commissioner in one swoop of my pen on paper. I pointed to her office next door to mine. "Only for one month Ducky, then back to being just Ducky the Commander Carol Kelly walked over and handed the paper work to her. I got on the phone and asked Dusty to come upstairs with Crystal Fulton. I need to see them both. Dusty had his usual blank look on his face of what have I done wrong now. I told Dusty his promotion of acting Commander and will be in charge of the Major crime unit and can have my office for the next month only. I told Crystal that I did need her back in her old job but running both offices, for the next month. She can choose whoever she would like to work under her I told

Crystal that she can break the news to Rachel Todd my office manager with Dusty beside her poor Rachel not having a clue of what had gone on upstairs today. Her gossip machine has blown a fuse today. I told Crystal a inspector Moore had been added to the team of integrity unit being the number two and since Chief Insp Jason in so longer with us Insp Ryan will be acting Chief Insp for the next month. I took him to one side and out of the ears ear reach of others. I explain what I wanted him to do and was he up for it. Bringing charges against the Ex-Police Commissioner and Assistant Police Commissioner Uncle Billy and the Stork. He said he loved the opportunity. He had no idea where his previous Boss Chief Insp Jason was, he did not show up for work from a few days, it was then I could see the change in his face when I told him that his previous boss had been at work in this building laying in the morgue with two holes in his head and a large hole in his neck. Due to a failed removal of myself with the help of Sgt Amy fuller at that they were a item. Nothing would surprise me about Amy anymore I thought to myself I had to inform Chief Insp Ryan that they are still together Amy is laying in the morgue with a couple of holes in her head also, next to Jason. The staff with were running the top two offices were given their marching orders from Crystal. They were given a transfer to another department. I followed Chief Insp Ryan downstairs and watched through the two-way window while he laid the charges against Uncle Bill and the Stork. After a leg tag was placed on each of them. They will be placed under house arrest. I did not want to have them sent out to a prison cell before their trial. In fact, it would be at least six months before Uncle Billy and the Stork would stand in front of a judge after today's charges were read out in front of a judge in a special sealed court the press could speculate on what was going on I left the office of Carol Kelly to simply make the statement you could say she simple blew the sinking boat out of the water before it sunk even more. The words of Carol Kelly were simple, the two accused plotted together to remove me from face of the earth, by the use of two Police officers, who made me dig my own grave, until I was rescued by an elite team of devoted police officers well you could not call Sgt Penny Maze a team with Dr Rebecca Mitcham who help save my life after I was shot. Their names were held back during the interview with Chief Insp Ryan both Billy and the Stork were played the confession of Chief Insp Jason Riley that he was adjusted by Billy and the Stork that was going to happen and I had to be removed.

Poor Chief Insp Ryan had no idea what his boss was up to with Amy Fuller, he just thought it was sex and more sex, the actual amount of time he was spending with her. I did comment that Chief Insp Jason was lucky that Amy did not fall pregnant!! I let him leave my office with that thought. Next to see me was Rachel Todd who had not even given me a hug on my return.

"He had better get his finger out old Dusty, "I gave Rachel another hug on her comment.

"It will be fine only for one month no more, with that Ducky walked in and simply said "Working with Aaron has never been happy in downstairs in the sex crimes and family Unit".

I had my phone ring and it was a voice from the past Sam Tickner once an Inspector who did work with Ducky, Alf Jackson and Peter Knight until he got busted for selling drugs to support his Family of six children. I cried out to Ducky who was talking to Crystal outside my office.

"Hey Ducky guess who isa back in town Sam Tickner of all people!!"

"Out of prison" asked Ducky

"Yes, two years now and he would like to meet me. how about you just show up to throw petrol on the fire in about one hour later Sgt Maze showed up now all the people had simply gone. I pointed to a desk next to Crystal's desk and Penny was pleased with that, "You never mention anything about what was going to happen today talk about the "Shit hitting the fan" Boss". I just laugh at her comment and simply said "feeling hungry well let us have a chilly egg bacon rolls and two thick coffee shakes and settle down a bit before my real job gets under way. Sam Tickner had lost weight in prison; he had been Adelaide to see if he could fund his ex-wife Edna and the six kids had not seen since he went to prison. The he asked if Kate was? I simply explain that his old work mate Alf Jackson ran her over in the Nightcliff shopping car park twice and she did almost four years now I could see on his face that he had no idea. He asked about my four boys all grown up ad the eldest is off to university in a few months, working at night stocking shelves in a supermarket. Three times he mentions Kate being dead. I told him Alf Jackson is dead I put six bullets in him and also John Knight also dead and both turned the wrong way and gone to drug dealing. Then in step Ducky who once worked with Sam Tickner back in the good old days.

"Acting assistant police commissioner now" Ducky told him and he did make t sarcastic comment how both of us have done well in the police force. After a while Ducky left after a quick adventure about the old days. Sam was always to the point. He wanted to know what did happen to his out of two million drug haul. He was owed half a million. Alf Jackson and John Knight, plus roll of his ex-wife Edna and her boyfriend Simon Fuller who was the one who was caught first and went to prison and was out in seven years. Alf and John and his wife Edna got away with it.

I have to admit each year I grow older and this world does get smaller. A Senna Fuller the sister to Edna was asking to talk to me I have to admit I had not lost that name in the hug list of people inside my head. She did remind me that she was the thin blonde at the wedding of Sam Tickner and Edna. I even danced with her which left my wife Kate a little surprised. I have to say I am no dancer. I do like to prop up the bar rather than dance. Finally, after a few laughs she told me that Sam Tickner is back in town and he tracked her down. Simon Fuller himself out of prison for two years now works in a mine a fly in and fly out. Two weeks on and one week off. She had taken the force of Sam Tickner throwing her against the wall and he did demand his cut of that drug deal. I told him to think back and Simon went to prison also he got no money, those bloody pricks Alf and John the two police officers took all the money, for themselves. Alf purchased the Royal Oak Pub it was a dump, his mother did not win lotto the money came from the drug deal, plus other money that Alf had been slowly putting away Senna also mention that Sam did have one hundred thousand under the floor boards that Edna took off and headed for Perth in western Australia. A new identity new phone she had never spoke to her since, but she does receive a birthday card from each year and on the letter a Perth postage stamp. I told Senna that I will take care of it. Her husband would be home in four days and he will hunt down Sam Tickner and most likely kill him. I thank her for her time and update and to finish off the conversation she also said "Regards to your wife Kate from me!!" I could tell that Senna also had not heard the sad news, about Kate. There was somebody banging on the naughty door inside my head and I did know that I must take care of Sam Tickner. When I received the call from Sofia and Tilda that Sam had been to the house and he said he was an old friend of mine, which still did not get him any entry to meet the boys, I knew Sam Tickner you have pushed my button a little too far now and it was time for me to act.

I did decide to hand ball Senna to Ducky. The woman's shelter in Parap would be a good place for her to hide, the shelter is run by the nun's a Lovley Bunch of ladies who will stand for no nonsense. I explain to Ducky that Senna's husband must not go after Sam Tickner or he will end up back in jail and his feet will not even touch the ground. Ducky gave me a salute just like in the damn military and made the comment, "Your wish is my Command General Brown sir!!"

I looked at the clock and being the top dog, um big boss now or even the ring master in this circus I can go home whenever I would like to just about to leave and the news that Uncle Billy has had a heart attack and almost in the ambulance on the way to the hospital. My heart did jump a beat, I felt so sad now. I have known him for a good twelve years never understood what he did in that traffic room all day, a boring job I always thought. I went in to tell Ducky who was about to meet Senna and fix her up with some temporary. accommodation with the nuns.

"I wonder how Violet Adam the Stork will take this now she is on her own and all fingers will be pointing at her. In more ways than one!!"

I arrived home to have some time with the boys, Jay would be off to work at the supermarket in a couple of hours. He was enjoying his job in his words "You could train a monkey to pack shelves". With the help of his music in his ears he was what I call a "Happy chappie". Tilda came down and told me that Sam Tickner had a real aggression in his attitude after being denied entry to my home so he could wait for me he went and sat on the garden wall for around one hour. I told her that he was once an Inspector in the drug unit and we worked together until he put his hand out for some drugs to sell himself, he is not long out of prison. I did think that was joined by Sofia in the last piece of my conversation. We had dinner and all eat the same a tandoor chicken and rice. The boys got stuck into the ice cream and toppings. A game of pool would be on after a ride on their electric scooters before it got dark. I sat down to watch television and Jay went to work. Dr Rebecca arrived home late due to a domestic incident where a wife stabbed her husband because of his violence to her she could not take it anymore. They had five children between them. I did expect a report from Dusty in the morning. I do not normally ask about work at home but Dr Rebecca just poured out the sad details. She had a swim in the pool and then found the last bowl of tandoor, chicken in the fridge. I did notice that she had drink one whole bottle of wine with her dinner. She slowly walked down the garden to her cottage on my mind was Sam Tickner, now at the doorstep of my house. Deep down I felt my boys could be in danger. I found a burner phone and used it to meet Sam Tickner in around one hour. I knew once I put down the phone that my voice could be traced back to me. a studio stupid idea I had. I left my police and personal phone at home; I left the television on in the lounge and the boys went to bed a little later than normal due to it being school holidays. The beach front at Nightcliff, only twenty minutes' walk was our meeting place. Inside my jacket a small thirty-eight with a silencer. I out that in the back of my trousers. Sam Tickner showed up in a car, I was to learn that he had stolen it from the bed and breakfast where he was staying. He would replace it, he tried to convince me we drove off to a side street dark and not the place you would want to walk late at night. We got out after he question me about the half million dollars. I told him that it is coming with Senna who also is bringing some extra cash. Sam was pleased that we had come to our senses but still called both of us "scum bags" and then went on to call me a liar. I just laugh it off and Sam did forget to keep his eye on the ball, something that our old dead friend ex police commissioner always said "Do not take your eye off the ball" he did mean a split second could cost you, your life.

I went to look around the corner to make out that Senna was a little late. She was just like her husband Simon Fuller he was late and that is how the drug squad caught them both with a bag of drugs. Alf Jackson and John Knight had bolted with the money. Myself at the time I was tucked up in bed with Kate I had no idea what members of my police team were up to.

Poor Sam was slowly like the kettle you are boiling for some tea or instant coffee. "Where is that bitch, that slut might have bolted with a million dollars that does belong to me, you are that stupid to trust her Aaron!!

It was that time to come clean and tell Sam there is no meeting with Senna and above all there is no wind fall heading your way. Tonight, or any other night much to my surprise, yet again I did expect Sam to wave a gun in my face. Being told that I was a "asshole" by Sam.

I had to reply "I have been told that by professional people asshole, lowlife I should set an example being a high-ranking office. I took off my jacket and looked at Sam still waving that gun.

"What you want to fight me, you are nuts I got a gun". I simply started to wave my arms like a boxer with my first folded, ready for the punch. Being told once again that "I was nuts" and he was not the first person to tell me this.

I simply watched Sam looking me and that moment he took his eye off laneway at huge speed. Might have burnt some rubber. This was the chance that I was watching for and shot Sam with the gun from the back of my trousers I put two bullets into his head. He fell he was dead before he hit the ground, but I still told him "Never take your eye off the ball Sam". With that I open his mouth a little wider after I bent down to blow two more bullets into his mouth to blow out his tonsils. I found in the boot of the car a petrol can. I did the old burn the car act so no trace of my DNA could be found.

I ran down the lane across a small park and was home before I knew it. When I arrived home, I found Dr Rebecca sitting in the lounge watching my television. Her television had finally reached the point of no return. I simply told her that I had been for a while along beach road to catch the night sea breeze. It was something that Kate and I used to do after the boys had gone to bed. Not good parenting some would say leaving four boys on their own at home late at night. I would say

"Stick your head up your ass matey and mind your own business!!" I went to go and grab a few beers, I did notice or was it my imagination, the bonding between Rebecca and myself was working out and one would say getting closer, the kiss on my cheeks, the tongue down my throat and I was now heading for the garden cottage to be taken full advantage of and I did hope to be sexually assaulted once the television was turned off. Rebecca did say that she had not had sex for a while, I had to admit that much water had past under the bridge, since I was with Kate. I did remember my work out with Penny and was I counting that in my private conversation in my head. "No, I was not". Rebecca gave me what I would call a in the morning Jay had arrived home and caught he coming out of the garden cottage after Rebecca kissed me in the door way. What could I say to my eldest son "I had been a naughty daddy?" Jay just gave me the thumbs up and a cheeky smile. I did imagine in some ways the he was happy for me, yet again it was now almost four years since his mother had died. I made the coffee and got some toast for us both. Jay sat opposite to me eating some muesli with some mango on the top and simply said 'I have no objections to Rebecca and you becoming involved. I will let you tell the other three boys. Your secret is fine with me my lips are sealed just like concrete.

"How could I tell him that it was our first date, sex on your first date Father" I did imagine Jay telling me.

The alarm bells were ringing and I had to admit to Dusty that I was supposed to meet Sam Tickner who had demanded money from me. I was going to the bank today to withdraw the money, a cool half a minute dollar. I had arranged with the bank earlier today over the phone. I knew that although I am the boss, Dusty would check out my story. I was home last night I told Dusty, I did walk to the park and looked at Nightcliff Jetty before I came home. I had been a very long day, I was then asked if I had an alibi, I had to reveal to Dusty that Dr. Rebecca was giving me a work out and taking advantage of my body at most of the night. Dusty was not none for a smile, yet I do imagine he does have one sitting on the toilet, when his cheeked explore. I did know Dusty had bowl problems and that is why he is always chewing on some bowl release gum. Dr. Rebecca drops by my office and thank me for last night in front of Sgt Penny that did not go down well by the look on Penny's face. I had a call from the prosecutor ion office to meet me at the bed side of Uncle bill with Carol Kelly. I arrived and I hope it was going to be a full confession from Uncle Bill so this case would not have to go to trail and the public would realize what a shambles the administration of the police is in fact a complete shambles in Darwin. Well, it had not gone on my way of my line of 'thought. In fact, Uncle Billy with tubes coming out of his arms had ''Done a Deal'' between the dick head prosecutor and her lady ship Carol Kelly he was going to resign from the position as Top Dog or should I say Circus master and so no house arrest no ankle bracelet but a reduced pension instead and a slap on his wrist. I of course did mention about him giving his blessing of me being shot and buried in the ground we only had the words of a tape confession of a dead and corrupt man. Carol Kelly had to stick her nose in and mention this is good politics and it will look like the Police administration will continue to shine in the eyes of the public' I did feel right at that moment to tell Carol Kelly to stick her job where the sun does not shine anymore. Uncle Bill told me he can play golf again without people asking about his ankle bracelet and hold his head up at the Masons Lodge. Uncle Billy let me know his wife has left him and moved down the road to live with her sister even the home help has quit after he did admit that he had been a very naughty boy. His wife told him that he should have stuck to Traffic Control now that did bring a smile to my face on leaving him.

Today was not a good all-round day for some. I had the call from Dusty that Violet Adams the Stork had hung herself. If only she could have waited just another twenty-four hours she might have ended up with Uncle Bill full time in her life A suicide note did state she could not live without Bill Skinner in her life, although he was married, but he did love both his wife and me. To face the music alone would be just too much for her to handle. Hanging yourself alone was no way to end your life. I always thought that there must have been just one person who that the Stork could have turned to. No Violet she did not have many friends in her work and private life. I did notice Ducky showed me earlier when I sat her down and told her. "It is the changing of the old guard of Uncle Bill and now the Stork now dead in the past twenty-four hours both of these people could not really handle pressure of life apart".

I had to agree with that Ducky told me that Senna had settled in well, she had phoned the woman's shelter earlier today. Ducky had also taken the job of watching over Ex Chief Insp "Dusty" with the watchful eye of the office manager Rachel Todd. I do not really agree with the "tactics" of spying on members of the team, but just sometimes you have to. I find that Dusty at times would fit into the placement of not knowing if it was "New year or New York" a quote from my late grandmother a person who was a very good judge of character Insp John Mitcham and Sgt Andy Moore had been busy with the investigation of a stabbing in Nightcliff about one hundred yards from the school. A first nations person was stabbed with a bone handle hunting knife. In fact, I was to learn he died from that knife that he owned. Stabbed six times Dr. Rebecca said the killer was in a rage the other most notable thing was that it was around the time of the death Sam Tickner only five minutes' drive away. I almost swallowed my egg and bacon chilly sandwich when I was told that finger prints that belong to Sam Tickner were found on the body of the first nation person who went by the name of Uncle Bill Rock face. Trying not only to digest my bacon, egg and chilly roll. I was also trying to understand all of these new facts that were being presented to me from Rachel Todd and Insp John Mitcham with Commander Dusty. In his new role from ex Chief Inspector to sitting in my chair and trying to look intelligent or even if he knew what he was doing. He made the point that all information should be going through him now. I am afraid that Dusty had lit the fuse for the bomb to go off with Dr Rebecca and Rachel Todd who both told him that he does not listen to advice and is most of the time he is "Bloody stone deaf" or even on another planet and not listening to their comments. I had to step in and call a truce between them all.

"So let me see, you are saying that Sam Tickner actually killed somebody Uncle Bill Rock face within an hour of being shot himself. There was a witness, a woman who was a neighbor saw Sam Tickner run to his car from the house that Uncle Billy had died in. this world is slowly becoming even smaller, I was to learn that the couple who owned the house that Uncle Bill Rock face or simple known as Uncle Bill was sleeping on their sofa since he was released from prison. Rachel Todd always full of information told me that Uncle Bill was in prison with Sam Tickner. I just sat there silent, drinking my cold coffee. All this time Ducky was sitting to the side of me, kind of riding shot gun over this meeting. I had to sit and listen to Dusty who went over the facts about the death of Sam Tickner. His theory and only his theory was that Sam and his passenger left the car, Sam chased the unknown passenger and for no reason so far known to Dusty, just simply turned and shot Sam Tickner, then set light to the car to hide his DNA. The woman who saw Sam Tickner jump into his car after the brutal killing of Uncle Bill was sure that there was a passenger in the car with Sam Tickner, it did look like a man but it was dark outside she told Insp John Mitcham and could not be one hundred percent sure!! At the back of my head, I had come to realize that I had once again got away with a clean-cut murder. They all left and Ducky stayed behind for a quite word was her explanation. What Ducky was going to tell me, I was not sure that she should had an eight thirty appointment in the Nightcliff shopping Centre car park with Sam Tickner, my heart jump a beat and I thought that Ducky was in the car with Sam Tickner. I was so wrong and really Ducky should have kept her mouth shut after ten years of having the burden of this tale on her conscience. I was on holiday with Kate and the kids camping. Ducky led the raid on the drug deal that caught out Sam Tickner and Simon Fuller who was the money man. Sam Tickner had the bag of cocaine worth around two million. The understudy of Ducky was the "Tornado" Eric Barnston, some called him Mad Eric, we called him the" Tornado," an acting inspector who just loved the sound of handcuffs. It was rumored that he slept with a set under his pillow but I do not listen to gossip most of the time.

Ducky told me that Alf Jackson also an inspector working under me, plus John Knight a crafty not to be trusted Chief Inspector who was my boss. I had to reach for a packet of mints listening to Ducky, tell me that Alf and John had offered her two hundred thousand in cash if she turned a blind eye to what they expected to happen at the drug deal. They would snatch the money Sam Tickner would be holding the drugs, that he had stolen over the past year from drug raids along with Simon Fuller would be placed in handcuffs with no problem of the loose cannon "The Tornado" Ducky stood back, the deal went down, Alf had the money from Simon Fuller and drove the car for John Knight she did imagine. After the visit to the watch house and Sam Tickner and Simon Fuller who only got a small bag of cocaine were charges. Ducky told Alf and John Knight to keep the money and stick it up their ass.

It was only two weeks later Ducky "Spat the dummy" and put in for a transfer. I had to say to her that I had no idea, she was showing a tear and now that Sam Tickner is dead and she did suspect that Sam knew that Alf and John Knight had pointed the finger in his direction and just let "the Tornado" Eric Branston take control for he just loved the glory and it was another step for him to get the approval of becoming a real inspector. In fact, he did and was to transfer down to Alice Springs. It was working out perfect for the Tornado who had a wife, who did not want to live in Alice Springs it was up in Darwin near her family on she was going to leave him and take two children first up did thank you Ducky for her honesty but deep down I told her I wished that she had not told me this information the story about meeting Sam Tickner at eight o'clock, I simply said do not mention that to acting Commander Dusty at any cost.

If only I could confess to all the crimes I had committed to Ducky. I went on instead telling her that Sam Tickner was going to meet me around nine o'clock near the night cliff pier in that far end of the car park but he never showed up so I went back home. I ran there in my night jogging routine. Ducky did laugh, I had to admit that I was between the bed sheets with Dr Rebecca later that night. I also told Dusty that private information that he went to check up with Dr Rebecca who simply told him to fuck off and mind his own bloody business. It was the night off for Dr. Rebecca and she had a Dr Ann Casey go out to see the body of Sam Tickner. Later at four o'clock in the morning the couple who owned the house that Uncle Bill was found dead when they arrived home from a BBQ in Acton Street, to discover Uncle Bill stabbed to death. It was strange to think all over the seafront and within five minutes' drive both murders of Uncle Billy and Sam Tickner had happened all within the same hour I told Ducky, who asked me what I am going to do about her past knowledge of the drug deal between Alf and John Knight and Sam Tickner and Simon Fuller. I simply replied the case closed and will remain dead and buried.

My lips are concrete, go on a like your life the past is the past and let it rest. I am tired of listening about the criminal life of Alf Jackson and John Knight they are dead and buried and both died at the hand of my gun, not proud of this fact but, I still get a nightmare about shooting them both. I had to let Ducky gave me a hug and a kiss saying thank you and I was a true friend.

"Anyway, so you and Dr Rebecca are at it, like rabbits I suspect anyway she always had a twinkle in her eye when talking to you" laugh Ducky.

On leaving being asked "How Rachel Todd will take this gossip of the two lovebirds?"

"Well, I do suspect that Rachel knew I was going to have sex with Rebecca even before I actually did know myself!!"

My ears were burning once Rachel Todd finally got hold on my new love life. In fact, I wanted to put a note on the notice board. All four of my sons were happy for me. They knew that Rebecca would never replace their Mother Kate and to my surprise. I must say that Rebecca did show a great interest in their lives. Playing pool, learning how to fish and making up for the four years they had missed a mother figure. Rebecca moved into the main house. Marriage was never on the agenda in my mind anyway; I was happy to have her as my partner the boys called her their new mom to their friends. The month-long top position did turn into another two weeks and finally two months. I did decide to retire on the wage of a Police Commissioner. I was going to belong a landscape artist and sell my paintings at Parap Market. In my dreams more like it if the truth was known I could not landscape paint to save my life.

I had a big farewell party and I was very surprised that Sgt Penny Maze did not come. She did not even say goodbye to me. I had nothing that Rebecca would often talk about the unsolved cases of the murders of not only drug dealers but a couple of Police Officers. They all had been killed in a special way and all left with a bullet in the mouth. I tried to show little interest my Police career was now done and dusted. I wanted to forget my past. Rebecca was endless in her constant pursuit she had come to the conclusion that the killer just had to be a police officer, I just sat and listen to how she come to this conclusion. When I thought, she was going to even point the finger in my direction at one point. I became a little upset and simply blew a gasket and told her to talk about something else. She then explains that the new Commander Dusty Gilmore found a pile of unsolved shootings and wanted to get even more promotion and another feather in his hat and another medal to pin on his chest.

In his mind he was being able to solve the mystery shooting where "you failed". She went on to say, that the forensic team have not been that busy so he handed me the collection of files, to read and come up with a conclusion. I had to say sorry to Rebecca, but I am no longer in the Police force and to be truthful I do not give a "F" anymore to be honest.

"What landscape painting, it was all a bloody pipe dream" I sat down after I grabbed a cold beer we started to talk about Derek "Hard" Steel shot near his brother's home in Humpty Doo. I told her that it did seem to be a robbery gone wrong, money was stolen from the wallet of Derek who had been simply flashing it around in his brother's wine bar. Rebecca had to admit she found no evidence to link anybody to the death of Derek "Hard" Steel. Sgt Billy Mayford shot on the seafront in Nightcliff!! We moved on to Max Wayne shot in a basement car park. I replied a gangland killing was the conclusion of the team. Then finally, Diana Watkins found shot upside down in her car. I did not understand why she had raised these crimes I had signed off on them but I also left them with what I called an open ending in other words to be continued at a later date

After hitting a root of a tree. I had to explain that she was driving straight at when Sgt Amy Fuller and myself. Went I moved towards the car, Diana was still alive and told me I was a useless prick on something to that meaning, she went for a gun and I shot her in the head. I did go on to say that ten minutes later I shot John Knight who was in a relationship with Diana who was given her marching orders after all she had done in making my life and my son's life a misery. John Knight did confess to a lot of crime over the past few years. Went it got to that moment of handling himself in John Knight had other ideas, a large bag full of money could not make me turn a blind eye. He took his eye off the ball, so I had the chance of the use of my spare gun, in the back of my trousers, John at the time had what we thought was the drop on me, and I was unarmed after dropping my gun on the ground. Rebecca did comment that Derek Hard Steel and Sgt Billi Mayfair, also Max Wayne were all shot in the same manor, also the weapon used was never traced I did try and when I put on my surprise face on, but it was hard to be a liar to the woman I am living with and by all accounts my wife; excepted a bit of scrap paper and a cheap wedding ring we went to bed and I felt that Rebecca was restless, I found her going over those damn files again. I tried to get her to come to bed but in her own words "Duty does call". I had no idea what she meant in that short statement the next day all was good, I was alone in the house, I went for a walk down to Nightcliff Jetty I got a coffee from the new mobile café there.

I walked and talked to a few fishermen who were having no luck today fishing off the Nightcliff Pier. I got home and looked at those paint brushes and now had finished painting a total of six pictures. The boys came home from school, Jay had slept most of the day before he went off to his night shift job at the local supermarket Rebecca did phone to say that she would be late tonight she got called out with a shooting incident once again.

The boys played pool after dinner, I sat and watched some final of a cricket match. I fell asleep when the doorbell rang. I went to answer the door, I opened it and nobody there, I turned to see a shadow in the front garden. I went to say can I help you when I felt a monster pain in my head. I felt my head had caved in; blood was pouring down my face. I was laying on the grass and I must have passed out. I do remember that siren in the ambulance, I do remember a torch light being shined into my eyes. I do remember or I do I remember now being wheeled into a surgery. People standing over me and I heard somebody say he is lucky to be alive, we will try and save him but we need to get that bullet out of his head. I could hear a lot going on but my eyes were covered voices talking and people poking me. Let us hope he will make some sought of recovery I kept hearing from the voice of a doctor. I was awake in what time of day I just had no idea ..

What had happened? I did try to understand the words "You were shot in the head" straight away I thought about my three boys at home. I found I could not speak with this tube in my mouth, I could not even remember how to put two words together anyway. A nurse would often hold my hand tight. I had no idea if I had visitors, time once again meant nothing to me. The blinds were down on the windows so I could not really tell if it was night or day. It was almost a week before I started my occupational physical lessons of how to walk again. I must say these nurses and doctors had a lot of patience with me. I was happy to see my four boys again, led by Jay then Jim and Joe and following up the rear was Jaz the youngest. Rebecca had been sitting with me while I was in recovery many times Jay told me. Rebecca was at work has stop her coming they explain the neighbor with that big black dog "Biggles" found me laying on the ground bleeding the front door was open so he sounded the alarm. There was Police everywhere for the next day I was shunted off to hospital with a hole in my head. I still of no memory of what happen on that fatal day, at this point in time I cannot even remember what I had for breakfast. A visit from my four boys daily, who did believe I would be home very soon and once again trying to beat them at pool. I could not remember what pool was I do remember that you can swim in a pool. A small heated pool was where once a day I would be taken to do physical lessons, I always could not help myself cocking my leg like a dog and peeing in the pool. A visit from "The top surgeon" who had saved my life. He did remind me that we had met before, five years ago at a crash site where his wife was killed when some criminals were being chased by members of my team. He found my attitude was very comforting and I even came to the funeral of his wife. I was pleased that I had done something worthwhile in my life apart from being the father to four teenage boys. I was told my wife had died four years ago by Jay my eldest son. Her name was Kate and that we all miss her daily. I had met a new Lady in my life Rachel who is a doctor who works for the Police just like I used to.

I seem to in my own way, slowly put a picture together of my life. It was not time to go home, daily visits from a physio Nurse to try and get me at least walking around without pushing this blood trolly in front of me. I was trying to walk with a stick and slowly that was becoming my way of getting around. My speech therapy session was now only seeing me now just twice a week. Having my four teenage sons around me would improve my speech. Yes, it was a long road but I could travel this road by walking and talking my past was coming back and the twins Tilda and Sofia were a great part of my recovery. I had visitors and to be honest I had no real idea who they were. It was in a strange way trying to fix the gaps in a giant puzzle of my life. A Rachel Todd and a Sgt Penny Maze would make a weekly visit time was passing slowly and I know that I was annoying asking them questions about our relationship in my slow drawn-out conversation. It only took three months before I felt I could play pool again swim in that pool daily in our garden and Jay would take me for a drive around the city and country now.

He had past his driving test and was now studying at university. I really enjoyed our trips for an hour or more. He in fact pushed me to my limits and even shouted at me to make me understand. This Rebecca who I now was treating like a second wife was often what I would call distant. She had a job with long hours and I was glad when she came home to keep me company much to my surprise Jay himself had taken over the Family Finances, he felt Rebecca although my partner was still not family in his eyes. I did feel that there was some little tension between them. I was sleeping downstairs in the lounge and then I started to get myself up those stairs it took a month before

I finally succeeded It was very important and kept getting a lecture from the twin housekeepers Tilda and Sofia who told me if I get up there how am I going to get down.? "On my ass" I told them and yes, I could climb the stairs up and down. So, I moved back upstairs to my old bedroom that I was now sharing with Rebecca a visit from Rachel and Sgt Penny.

Was in their words a very long time coming. Nobody had been seen and nobody was a suspect in my shooting that left me struggling with life for six months. I now could understand and slowly hold a conversation at my own pace. I often I simply forgot the words or could not explain myself and the person I was talking to would help me. In their very own pain taking way we could have a conversation. I had missed so much about how the Police complex had changed and they did reflect that in their eyes not for the best. Frank Tyler was now top dog Irene Moore and Dusty Gilmore was still leading major crime and head of all detectives. He was trying to play football without a ball Rachel that is how Rachel came to describe him. I did remember Dusty "He was a very annoying little prick "I told them and they both laughed. All new members of the team except Rachel and Sgt Penny who is no longer a driver and Dusty had decided to drive himself around she was now tied to a desk but an office mole according to her and right hand to Rachel gathering the information to help other members of the team.

Rachel came and sat next to me on the couch that I offer used as a bed. These headaches came and go and taking tablets is not always the way to go. Holding my hand and that look in her eyes of what I am about to tell you, I do not want you to be upset. I had to just look at

Rachel and I did remember those moments. "How or where can you even start?" they asked me.

So, I said "What about the beginning"

They took me on a painful trip to the night I was shot. They had proof and I would find it hard to swallow that Rebecca was not at work that night. In fact, was in the arena of my home and not at work. Some evidence that I must admit could not really understand with all of these figures and a chart to look at. They traced her phone; she was in the area of my house and then drove off and parked the other side of Rapid Creek when she was called, she remained stationary. The police and even two of my sons Jim and Joe had tried to contact her after I had been found shot in the head. I was found by a neighbor with Biggles the dog who found me and started to lick the blood off of my face. Gareth the neighbor thought that I was drunk but the front door was open and he phoned for an ambulance, then the Police and finally the ambulance well they did arrive after a second urgent call.

Rebecca did arrive and to quote Sgt Penny was what she could only describe "in a strange funny mood". Not struck down in grief like Sgt Penny would expect. All she was interested in was getting her team here to gather evidence her team found nothing over the next day. I was in hospital; the four boys were waiting outside my private room and Tilda and Sofia kept them under control. The thought of the loss of their Father would be devastating to them. I defied the critics and was wide eyed and legless was a way of putting in my own little way a few days later.

Sgt Penny would stake her job on the line that Rebecca was very well in a world of being "Cagey" with her attitude. Evidence was slow and to quote Rachel she would want to know who shot me. Was the killer still out there? Good old Dusty just treated my shooting like any other case, in fact to quote him Rachel told me "He said it was gang land related, some drug low life decided it was pay back even Rebecca herself joined in on the that chorus. I did think that they could be right. The only problem was of the phone tracking on the phone of Rebecca, there was no evidence that she pulled the trigger but I do remember the days leading up to me being shot I had with Rebecca. I slowly in my own time what cases that she decided to question me. In all fairness Rebecca had been pushed by Dusty who told her he wanted proof to get this so called "cold cases" over and done with.

Even Rachel did admit that at times Dusty was a little out of control and had a fixation about solving these cases that I had left on my desk, for him to sought out. He had two months to discuss them with me before I did retire and start my new "Police free life". Now he never mentions them to me or even got my opinion. I told my two friends Rachel went back to my comment about this discussion I had with Rebecca that did cause us to start shouting at each other. I was trying to be honest with Rebecca I was not hiding anything.

I sat looking at these two very trusted friends who had my backing always, now Rachel Todd it was not eight but more like nine years she had stood by me. Sgt Penny only together a few months, she had saved my life by shooting Sgt Amy Fuller my ex-driver in the end and saved my life. I was about to be placed in the grave that I just finished digging. Chief Insp Jason once my right hand was under her thumb. Amy Fuller turned out to be a "very wicked person" to quote my grandmother once again. I could see that Rachel and Sgt Penny had left the ball in my court about what to do with this information. Myself I was going to confront Rebecca without any delay. I went upstairs and removed the wooden panel, I found one last thirty-eight and a silence, two bullets and I placed them all behind a cushion on the sofa in the lounge. After dinner the boys played pool and I sat down with Rebecca, telling me that she was thinking about retirement. I was soon going to pop that question; it was not going to be about a marriage like Rebecca was expecting instead that question she did not want to hear.

"Why did you shoot me Rebecca?"

A rather mumble and a twisted reply before that punch line.

"I could not let you get away with all of these murders that you had committed Aaron, you cannot take the law into your own hands and just go around putting bullets into people heads like you have. I have found a direct pattern and in the long list of people I did suspect only you stood out. I am not sorry but I failed you. I was a bit confused was she going to go to old Dusty and give a statement or was she simply going to keep her mouth shut. I knew that I could not take a chance either way now. I was now like a wounded bull in a China shop ready to escape I waited for her to make the next move. She stood up and said "she was leaving and will be back tomorrow for her belongingness". She stood out on the garden path and told me exactly what she thought about me, I was hiding behind the disguise of being this father of four boys doing it tuff bringing them up alone wanting sympathy and getting people to feel sorry for me. She went on to tell me the real truth in her eyes, that if the truth was really known.

Nobody really like me; they only suck up to me to keep their jobs when I was the so called "Boss of detectives". I had one last word to say to Rebecca had she shared this information with anybody else especially Dusty her new best friend and I already had an update by Rachell Todd that old Dusty had been revitalizing and experimenting in the world of sex with Rebecca.

She said "nobody". With that I pointed the gun and put a bullet right between the eyes, the second bullet I open her mouth and pulled the trigger. It was a trade mark in my killing now. I went inside and made the call to the Police Complex not to admit that I had shot her but somebody ran the door bell, Rebecca went to answer it, and then thinking she had been gone a while. I got up and found her dead on the garden path. I told Dusty on his arrival who looked like death warmed up and was in a distressful state looking at the body of Rebecca that the Killer came back for round two, this time he or she shot Rebecca instead of me. "Bloody drug Gangs while trying to get some sought of revenge on me".

"Listen Aaron I will take all of this under my wing and I will leave no stone unturned". It was then that I did think to myself you are just talking out of your ass cheeks once again Dusty I had a light bulb moment I did wonder if Rebecca had confessed to Dusty during their sexual aerobics about shooting me. This was way out of my normal line of thought I even suspected that Rebecca had planned already to move into the home of Dusty I did try and imagine Dusty having sex with Rebecca it would be like trying to raise the titanic. I did comment to Dusty that it had been six months since I had been shot and all the talk have led to a road to nowhere so far not even a whiff or sniff of evidence. With the raised tone of my voice which sounded the alarm to my four boys who came running out to me after watching football in the pool room. and now I had to inform them about the sad death of Rebecca. They all bowed their heads in silence and I gave each of them a cuddle for strength and support from me then they just went back to the pool room after telling Dusty they saw and heard nothing. Until they heard my voice shouting. Old Dusty did his" I am in charge" act and got his team into action I then went to grab a cold beer and raised it in memory of Dr. Rebecca Mitcham and quietly said to myself. "I have no regrets of what I have done today, it just had to be done just like all the others I had shot over the past year or so. In my eyes I had made a difference to society with my actions. Now some would say I simply had lost control and should have got some help for my mental state of mind; and I would say I was simply that I was "Living on a Razors edge".

AUTHOR BIOGRAPHY I

Arfer Apple came to Australia just over forty years ago to take up a position of an executive Chief. He had traveled all over this timeless land to settle in Darwin around twenty years. He fell on hard times and was afflicted with Leukemia. He ended up living in a homeless shelter for a year until he got his life back together. He wrote a script for a radio show that he was involved in. "Life with a View" which was a story of twins of first nation people who built a female home on a deserted farm. His second book was "legless in the garden shed" a very black comedy about a three-legged dog, with only one eye and no tail after he was run over by the female of the home on her Harley Davidson. Book three was "Book a quickly dog take" the story of a group of dogs and their dysfunctional owners. Books four and five was the start of his black comedy crime books. "A Chain Reaction" and "A Place in time" book six was "The Strength That Lies Within" was the story about believing in yourself a Police Inspector does get demoted to the basement file room and slowly he does get his old job back. Then followed the "Dark Secret Trilogy".

AUTHOR BIOGRAPHY II

A heartwarming story of a Police Inspector with a broken marriage, suspension from work. She was diagnosed with breast cancer and had to have a double mastectomy on the day she left hospital she was handed her divorce papers. She would now after one year wanted to return to work but only her terms. This is the start of the story of her fight back with dignity. Now taking the position of Chief of Detectives in a man's world. I started to write the story during with my very own experience during my term during Chemo.

Books ten and eleven are twenty-eight short stories with individual crimes and characters simply called "Extraordinary Life of Crime" volume one and volume two.